THE SHADOW DANCERS

DIVISION SERIES #3

ANGUS MCLEAN

Published 2016 by Smoking Gun Publications

ISBN 978 0 473 56086 7

The story contained within this book is a work of fiction. Names and characters are the product of the author's imagination and any resemblance to actual persons, living or dead, is entirely coincidental.

ALSO BY ANGUS MCLEAN

Chase Investigations Series

Old Friends

Honey Trap

Sleeping Dogs

Tangled Webs

Dirty Deeds

Red Mist

Fallen Angel

Holy Orders

Deal Breaker

The Division Series

Smoke and Mirrors

Call to Arms

The Shadow Dancers

The Berlin Conspiracy

No Second Chance

Nicki Cooper Mystery Series

The Country Club Caper

Early Warning Series

Martial Law

Getting Home

Stand Fast

THE SHADOW DANCERS

BY ANGUS MCLEAN

1

London
May

The hotel room was small but adequate and smelt of sex in the mid afternoon. Moore rolled onto his side and propped his head up so he could see into the bathroom.

The woman in the shower was tall and curvy, with shoulder length blonde hair and heavy breasts. She had a pale birth mark shaped like a speech bubble on her inner left thigh. He watched as she turned the water off and stepped out, grabbing a towel from the rack. She dried herself quickly and caught him watching.

'Didn't you see enough before?' she enquired with a cheeky grin.

Moore pushed up and swung his legs over the side of the bed. His feet touched the worn carpet.

'I saw plenty,' he said. 'Doesn't mean it's enough.'

She finished drying herself and applied deodorant and perfume from her handbag. She stepped back into the room and found her knickers on the armchair by the window. They were flimsy pale blue satin.

The woman's name was Michelle McGregor, and she was thirty eight years old. She was also Alan McGregor's wife, which for Moore added a thrilling extra dimension to their affair. Any chance to get one over that brown-nosing prick was an opportunity that had to be taken. He knew the consequences of being caught would probably derail his career, but at the moment he really didn't care.

Moore watched her get dressed before standing himself, naked before her. He was an even six feet with a thick dark rug on his strong chest. He was greying at the temples, his dark hair cut short. His torso was lean and hard.

Michelle secured her gold necklace and tossed her hair. She straightened her red sundress before grabbing her handbag.

'Best I get a move on, lover,' she smiled, and kissed him hard on the lips.

Moore kissed her back, touching her hips and pulling her to him. She pulled back momentarily before he felt her relent. His tongue found hers and he pressed harder against her, hoping she would respond, eager for more. He started to ease backwards towards the rumpled bed, but she put a hand firmly on his chest and pushed away.

'No,' she said, 'I can't. I need to go.'

'Come on,' he said, trying his best boyish smile. 'You don't need to go just yet...'

'I do.' She was definite now, and he knew there would be no changing her mind.

He sat down on the edge of the bed anyway, watching as she checked she had everything. He wanted to say something but didn't know what. He wanted her to stay but knew she wouldn't, and couldn't.

'Happy birthday, big boy,' Michelle smiled, leaning down and giving him another quick kiss on the lips. 'Hope you're having a good day.'

Moore gave a small smile in return. 'So far, so great. Thank you.'

She tapped his nose with a painted nail and moved to the door.

'I'll be in touch,' she said as she opened the door. She checked the corridor outside before turning and blowing him a kiss. 'See ya.'

Moore nodded and watched the door close. The lock clicked into place and silence fell on the room.

He was alone again.

He hadn't seen her for three weeks, what with her own commitments and him in Singapore for half that time. Far from being an R&R trip, it had been an annual exercise with other operators from The Division. It had been wet and exhausting, and had ended with an Anzac Day dawn service and too much rum.

Now here he was in a budget London hotel, celebrating his birthday by screwing the wife of a colleague.

Moore shook off the gloom that threatened to descend. It didn't matter. She was someone else's wife; no point mooching around like a love struck school kid.

He checked the G-Shock on the bedside table. 11am. Time to get back to work.

He headed for the shower.

2

When Moore got back to Haymarket an hour later he parked the silver Mondeo in a public car parking building in a nearby street and walked the last distance to the office.

The office was at New Zealand House, the High Commission that was home to various diplomats and Government departments including Immigration and Defence, and a number of private businesses.

Tucked into a small office on the sixth floor of the tower was the resident Intelligence Officer, carrying the ostensible title of Staff Officer. In New Zealand House that role was held by Alan McGregor, an experienced Senior Intelligence Officer. He was also an eternal bore and an unabashed sycophant who was trying his best to work his way into the diplomatic ranks.

Practically every embassy around the world had at least one such position, and everybody knew the real reason for their presence. McGregor had been perturbed to hear he was being joined by a second officer, and a former SF operator at that, and had gone out of his way to isolate and minimise Moore's position as an Intelligence Officer.

Moore responded by building his own contacts and networks, and most recently by screwing McGregor's wife behind his back. A further point of resentment for McGregor was the fact that Moore was not just an IO and technically under his supervision, but he was also in the direct line of command of Division 5. The existence of this unit was ultra-secret, and McGregor only knew because he had to.

Known as The Division, the small hand-picked team were all ex-Special Forces or counter terrorism operators. They reported straight to the Director of the SIS, and their brief was the black operations that were required from time to time by the Government.

Moore took pleasure in the fact that he could blackball McGregor on any tasks he received from the Director. He just wished there was more demand for his special skills.

The intelligence services of the host nation and other embassies all tried to keep tabs on each other, and Moore was confident that he was widely known within the circles. He made no secret of it within the Five Eyes group and had always found that approach useful, although the South African Resident always grated on him, but was far more reserved with other services.

The Russian FSB had a strong presence in London-Moore was always careful not to meet contacts at a sushi bar after the Litvinenko assassination-and the Chinese and North Koreans always took an interest in the Kiwis.

Some of the embassy staff themselves resented the intelligence presence and others were excited about having a real spy working amongst them.

Shifting from being a Staff Sergeant in the SAS to a trainee intelligence officer in the Security Intelligence Service had been a huge jump, and he'd almost thrown it all in during his first year in Wellington. Crap pay, back at the bottom of the pole again, and he'd wondered what the hell he'd done. A phone call to his old Regimental Sergeant Major at Papakura had led to a conversation with the Deputy Director (Intelligence) of the SIS.

He wasn't like the other trainees, he explained. He wasn't a spotty computer nerd, he wasn't a razor-sharp lawyer and he was certainly no Walter Mitty. He'd been around. He'd been at the coalface using the intelligence supplied by the spooks; he knew the value of getting it right.

It transpired that the Deputy completely agreed and had moved him six months later to a posting in the Philippines, then to Singapore and ultimately to the plum job in London. His role was 95% standard intelligence officer, 5% fixer. It meant he got the occasional opportunity to utilise his old skills, so he didn't feel completely removed from that world.

Moore took the lift to the sixth floor with a foot long sub in his hand and best intentions of catching up on some work for the afternoon. Although he'd heard there was a new girl downstairs in Immigration who was both a gymnast and a stunner, so he may need to pop down there later on to say hello.

Moore sidled past McGregor's office, seeing he was on the phone with his head down, and ducked through the next doorway into his own broom cupboard office without being spotted.

He shut the door, opened his lunch and tucked in ravenously. Chicken teriyaki on wheat with sweet onion and everything but olives, washed down with water.

As he got older Moore was conscious of his sugar intake, so the water was his concession. He ate half the sub before quickly scanning the BBC news online then opening up his emails to catch up on new intel reports. He was still working through the list when his door opened and McGregor appeared. He paused in the doorway and looked down his nose at Moore.

'Hard at work, I see,' he said, sneering at the half eaten sub on Moore's desk. 'No surprise there.'

Moore ignored the jibe and took a sip of water.

'So where've you been swanning around all morning, Robert?' McGregor rocked on his heels and lifted his nose even further in the air. He knew it irritated Moore to be called by his full first name.

'I'm working on something for the Director,' Moore said easily, picking up his sub. It was a complete lie, of course, but McGregor could never prove it-he didn't have the balls to check with the Director himself.

Moore took a bite and chewed slowly as he looked steadily at the man before him. He could tell it annoyed McGregor, so as soon as he finished he took another bite. The sweet onion sauce really made it.

'Well?' McGregor prompted, rolling his hand as if to hurry him up.

Moore shrugged and pointed at his mouth while he took his time. He washed the mouthful down with a draft of water and licked his lips.

'Well what?' he said.

McGregor's lips pursed. 'Well what are you working on? "Something for the Director" tells me nothing.'

Moore shrugged and allowed himself a small smile. 'Well I guess that's what I'm telling you, then. It's a job that the Director has given me. I don't think I have authority to disclose the details to you at this stage.' He gave McGregor a smug look. 'Sorry, I guess you don't have the clearance.'

McGregor's face went paler than normal, and his eyes became pinpricks. 'Don't try and play bloody games with me, Robert. You can sit there as smug as you like, but let's not forget who pulls the strings around here.' He looked Moore up and down with disdain. 'And it's not some washed up grunt masquerading as James fucking Bond.'

With that he turned and stalked out.

Moore picked up his sub and lined up the next bite. 'Say hi to your wife for me,' he muttered. The sub was still good but somehow the interaction with McGregor had left a sour taste in his mouth. Everything about the man irritated him, but he couldn't pretend to himself it was just that.

In truth he was more irritated with himself than the man whose wife he was bedding. He'd tipped over into his forties and it didn't please him. He liked his job and he loved London, but in the last couple of months he'd slipped into a funk that he neither recognised or liked, or could see a way out of. With it had come a growing pattern of risky behaviour.

He was rarely home with deliberately working longer hours, he was pushing himself harder in his physical training, and he was drinking more. There'd been a fight outside a pub a few weeks back, something he never normally did-a lippy young lager lout had exchanged words with him and it ended up with blood on the footpath and Moore's semi-conscious opponent being dragged away by his mates.

Moore had gone before the Police arrived and nothing further had come of it, but he was acutely aware that he had been acting out of character.

The affair with Michelle was something else. It had started two months ago after a function at the High Commission, a drunken screw in an empty office that he had immediately regretted, but it had quickly became a regular occurrence with clandestine meetings in cheap motels and B&Bs.

Never the same place twice and always paid in cash under an assumed name.

He even used an untraceable burn phone to keep in contact with her, and never text her. But no matter how careful he was, the spectre of exposure loomed over him like an impending storm.

He was still brooding when his landline buzzed.

The voice at the other end was blunt and familiar. Jed Ingoe, the Operations Officer for The Division and a former Regimental Sergeant Major of the SAS. Widely known as Jedi, he had lost a leg in an IED explosion in Afghanistan and took medical retirement, immediately being recruited to help run The Division.

'I suppose it's lunchtime in London town,' Jedi said without preamble. 'I'm surprised you're not down the pub with a curry and a pint, networking.'

Moore chuckled. 'Things've changed since your heyday, Jedi,' he said, 'it's all lunchtime runs and motivational books now.'

Jedi made a scoffing sound. 'Sounds inspiring,' he said. 'I know you've got nothing major on at the moment Rob, which is good; I've got a job for you.'

Moore gripped the phone tighter and leaned forward in his chair.

Jedi usually tasked him via email, only ever ringing if it was a sensitive job. 'We're encrypted, then?'

'We are,' Jedi replied. 'Don't worry, this won't take long.'

Moore's heart sank; he'd been hoping for something juicy, something to get his teeth into and drag himself out of this funk.

'The Minister of Foreign Affairs is currently over there, as you know. He's doing some networking before heading over to Greece for the Battle of Crete commemorations in a week or so. His daughter Natalie lives in Surrey, and he's supposed to be catching up with her while he's there. It appears she has gone missing in Turkey while on a trip there.'

Moore raised an eyebrow to himself. Turkey was a hotbed right now, with the Russians bombing neighbouring Syria, the resulting refugee crisis and increased political and radical unrest in Turkey itself. Intelligence reports were coming in thick and fast and Kiwi travellers had been warned to steer clear for the time being. It surprised him that a Cabinet Minister's daughter had been silly enough to travel there.

'So it's a lost and found mission,' he said with more of an edge than he'd intended.

'More or less,' Jedi said. 'It's not your normal job, I grant you that, but he's a pretty influential figure and the request has come from the top, so that's what we'll do.'

By "from the top" Moore wasn't sure whether Jedi was referring to the Director of the Security Intelligence Service or the Prime Minister. Ultimately it didn't matter, given their respective positions, but he always liked to know who he was actually working for.

Jedi gave him an address, a country hotel in the Guildford borough down in Surrey. Moore noted it down and listened while Jedi gave him some brief instructions. Apparently the Minister would make time to see him tomorrow at 10am, which suited Moore. It amused him, though, that he was expected to be available at that time. The Minister wanted, so the Minister got. Paul Oldham was a mover and shaker in politics, with clear aspirations of getting the top job. As far as Moore could recall, he was about number three or four in Cabinet.

'No problem, Sarn't Major,' he said. 'I'll be there.'

Jedi chuckled down the line. 'Good man. I suppose you'll be ditching the company car and taking that little rocket of yours for a spin?'

Moore smiled to himself. He had taken Ingoe for a spin in his Jag last time the boss had been over, and the old warrior had vowed to never drive with him again.

'Of course,' he replied. 'I'll be sure to claim for my miles, don't worry.'

'Just be aware too, that our friends at Millbank are aware.'

He was referring to the Security Service, known as MI5.

'How?'

'We briefed them. The Minister's on their patch, and it could be relevant. They're keeping an ear out for us, and I've asked them for papers for you. You'll be going to Istanbul, and I'd rather you travelled as a Brit than a Kiwi.'

Moore raised an eyebrow to himself. 'Something I'm missing, Jedi?'

'Not at all. Just being cautious is all. Slowly slowly, catchy monkey. One of theirs will be in touch, I expect.'

Moore said nothing. It was unusual that they would ask for assistance from another service like that, when he had multiple identities himself under various nationalities. He trusted Jedi's judgement though, so said nothing.

'Haven't heard from Archer for a while,' he said, referring to one of the other members of The Division, 'is he on anything good at the moment?'

'He's still around town,' Jedi answered vaguely. 'Anyway, I don't have time to chat. Things to do.'

'Same,' Moore grinned, 'I'm flat out.'

Jedi snorted again, bade him farewell and rang off.

Moore sat back and made a steeple of his fingers as he considered the information he'd just been given. It wasn't the most exciting job, but at least it would get him out of the office. Any chance to travel was good.

He glanced out the window at the city beyond. It was constantly moving, a real living and breathing beast, and every time he looked out that window he still got a buzz. So much happening, so many opportunities.

He tore himself away and turned back to his computer. He decided he better do some background work on the Minister's daughter.

At least his lie to McGregor was now covered.

3

After work Moore had skipped a trip to the pub and instead walked to Leicester Square.

He jumped the Northern Line to Camden Town and walked from the tube station into the less developed area of Camden, to a small but busy gym in a back alley.

It was run by a bald headed guy called Wizzle who, in his youth, was a renowned East End leg breaker for hire. He eventually got sent down for a long lag and came out nearing forty and with a renewed view of life. That wasn't to say he had entirely left his former life behind him, but he now ran a very successful gym with an emphasis on boxing.

The members were a rough bunch, with tattoos and scars the normal uniform. There was not a speck of Lycra in sight, and even the women who attended were harder than most female squaddies Moore had known. Wizzle had three rules in his gym; no crime, no black music and no 'roids. Any breaches of these rules led to immediate expulsion and sometimes a beating, depending on the breach.

Moore changed quickly into shorts, T shirt and sneakers and left his bag in an open locker, knowing it would be safe. He warmed up on a bike, skipped for ten minutes then hit the speed bag for another five before moving to the heavy bag for twenty. Soaked in sweat, he did a short but intense set of free weights-there were no machines, of course-and finished up with a series of stretches to cool down.

He saw a girl walk past towards the office, her black leggings leaving nothing to the imagination. She was long and lean and tanned, with flowing brown hair and high cheekbones which belied her Scandinavian-Slovakian heritage. She caught his eye as she opened the office door and he gave her a short nod. Lana was Wizzle's girlfriend, and despite her beauty she was not somebody to be overly familiar with. She gave him a cool smile in return and closed the door behind her.

He was getting a drink when he saw the door open again and Wizzle approached. He was average height and average build, a few years older than Moore. There was not an ounce of fat on his body, which was heavily tattooed and straining at his T shirt.

'Alright Kiwi?'

Moore wiped his face on his towel and nodded, still getting his breath back. 'All good mate.' He ran an eye over the gym owner. 'Looking a bit tubby, Wizz. Slacked off a bit?'

Wizzle grinned. 'Yeah, but I'll never get as soft as you, pal.' He waited while Moore took another draught of water. 'How's your boozing?'

Moore swallowed and considered his answer. It wasn't like Wizzle to ask after his members' welfare. 'Fine, why?'

Wizzle shrugged his rock-like shoulders. 'Just askin'. I heard you had a run in down the Red Lion the other week.'

It was Moore's turn to shrug. 'Storm in a tea cup mate, just some pissed idiot who thought he was all that. I can't even remember what the guy looks like now.'

Wizzle nodded. 'Unfortunately, he remembers you.'

Moore looked at him warily. 'Mate of yours, is he?'

Wizzle gave a snort. 'Not 'alf.' His face was giving nothing away. 'They call him Romper, as in Romper Stomper. He's a crazy little fuck, but he's stupid. Does stupid shit like trying to step out guys bigger and better than him.'

Moore nodded silently. That much was true.

'But, if you turn your back or he gets you down, he'll fuckin' 'ave ya. I know of two guys he's knifed in the back, and at least a dozen he's kicked the shit out of on the deck.' Wizzle rubbed his jaw thoughtfully. 'Like I say, he's a crazy little shit. But 'is bruvver, he's a different story. He'll just stab ya in the face. Jimmy the Blade, they call him.'

'Because Mack the Knife was already taken?'

'Do I look like I'm laughin', Kiwi? Know what they call Jimmy's boys? The Cuttin' Crew.'

An 80's pop song by the band of the same name popped into Moore's head, but he kept it to himself. Now didn't seem like the time for jokes. Instead he nodded and tossed the towel over his shoulder.

'Thanks for the heads up,' he said. 'I appreciate it.'

'I know these boys, Kiwi,' Wizzle said, his voice low. 'If you want, I can fix it.'

Moore knew exactly how he would fix it, and he shook his head. 'No thanks,' he said. 'I'll play it as it comes.'

Wizzle considered him for a moment before nodding slowly. 'Your call, mate.' He leaned in closer, his voice low again. 'But remember what I said. The offer stands.'

Moore nodded his thanks and turned away, feeling a weight on his shoulders. The last thing he needed right now was this shit.

4

An hour later he unlocked the front door to his flat and shut the world behind him.

He had to admit to himself that despite his bravado to Wizzle, he'd been more cautious than normal on the way home, checking for a tail and feeling like a pussy for doing it. Still, it was better than getting a switchblade between the ribs.

He locked the door and kicked off his sneakers in the entrance vestibule. He had a momentary flashback to an incident a year or so ago when he had been confronted by Archer, waiting for him when he got home. His colleague had held a suppressed Sig on him, in the mistaken belief that Moore was a traitor. He had genuinely believed it was about to be lights out. It wasn't a pleasant memory.

He made his way up the carpeted stairs to his small flat, dropping his bag on the floor and taking his purchases into the kitchen. He'd stopped at an off licence and a curry house on the way home.

First things first though.

After a brisk shower he dressed, took the curry from the oven and the beer from the freezer and sat on the couch to watch the news. The chicken tikka masala was spicy and good, the naan was perfectly garlicky and the Kingfisher that washed it all down was ice cold and smooth. He wondered if he was turning into a Pom.

The news included coverage of the day's developments in Turkey and he saw protests with plenty of chanting and flag waving and anger. Russian jets bombed Syria and politicians talked rhetoric.

Moore flicked it off and stared out the window at the darkness beyond.

A number of thoughts tumbled through his head; the buzz of anticipation that came with a new task, the envy he felt for Vince and Nga, the need for action. He wondered what Archer was up to now-obviously something, given Ingoe's vague response.

Despite not knowing what Archer was involved in, Moore was even envious of that, regardless of how stupid the notion was. He felt like the last kid waiting to get selected for a team, when all the cool kids had already been picked.

Not the first time recently, he wondered what the hell he was doing.

5

The flat formed the top floor of a converted house, and Moore's landlady lived downstairs. She was a retired house wife and lived alone, her Special Branch husband having been killed by a terrorist bomb in County Armagh some years ago.

She was a sprightly old bird and kept the gardens picture perfect, and never missed a trick. Moore was convinced she was on the books for MI5, having been referred to the flat by a contact in that service.

It didn't bother him; she was a good landlady who often gave him baking or leftovers, and didn't mind his comings and goings at odd times. She also parked her little Toyota sewing machine on the street and let him use the single garage to house the Jag.

At six am Moore closed the garage door and rolled out onto the road. He wore his sharp Hugo Boss navy blue pinstripe with a crisp white shirt, the deep red silk tie knotted with a double Windsor.

The 4.2 litre six cylinder engine gave a throaty purr as he accelerated away and aimed for the A501.

He was soon heading south west, the sleek black Jag attracting the odd envious look as it moved easily through the traffic to the A219 and down to the southbound A3. The Jag was a 1970 E-Type Series 2 open two-seater and as far as Moore was concerned it was pure sex on wheels.

The Series 2 had wider bucket seats than the earlier models, which suited his frame, and the 4 speed gearbox-although not as economical as a 5 speed conversion-was as smooth as anything else he'd ever driven. He'd bought the car from a deceased estate not long after arriving in England, and had had some work done to restore it almost to its original glory.

He had his iPod shuffling through a '70's Brit rock play list, hits and misses from The Kinks, Status Quo, the Faces and other classics of that era.

He hit traffic near Putney and crawled for a while before turning off to a greasy spoon he'd been to before in New Malden.

He sat alone against the wall and took his time over a reasonable full English, mopping the sauce and juices up with his toast and washing it all down with a pot of strong tea. Feeling re-energised he got some fresh air outside before he hit the road again.

By the time he finally crossed over the M25 into the Guildford borough the iPod had moved on to an 80's glam rock collection and he could almost feel the hair spray and smell the bourbon emanating from the speakers as Cinderella, Bon Jovi, Night Ranger and Van Halen rocked out. The road was good now and the Jag took a left onto the A25 before dropping down towards the tiny picturesque village of Shere.

Moore had been here last year with Danni, enjoying a fantastic pub lunch when she visited for the four days her mother had allowed. He had been excited because a movie had been filmed there some years ago with Kate Winslet. He liked Kate Winslet. Danni thought she was "quite pretty for an older lady."

Following the directions on his GPS he bypassed the village itself and carried on to a narrow country lane flanked by high hedgerows, slowing down as he made his way half a mile further before a wide gap opened on his right to reveal a long driveway.

He turned in and saw a sprawling property before him, wide green fields with a three storey ivy-covered country house straight ahead and a large pond to the left. Horse stables could be seen past the house and a wooded area further on. It all seemed to be contained within one property-just the sort of place that he imagined an eccentric wealthy squire lived with some domestic staff and a trusty dog, shooting pheasants, riding and fishing for wild brown trout in the nearby Tillingbourne river.

Moore eased the Jag to a stop in the turning circle at the front of the house, the tyres crunching on the pebbles as he pulled up. A fountain statue dominated a circular garden in the eye of the turning circle. A silver Range Rover was parked off to the side. It looked like this year's model, maybe last year's. Beside it was a red Ferrari 458 Speciale. Moore couldn't pick the year, but it didn't matter-it was a goddamn Ferrari.

As he was getting out of the Jag he was met by a smiling young man in a brown moleskin jacket and casual chinos. His black hair was slicked down and his face was unblemished and soft.

'You must be the bloke from Haymarket,' he said, gripping Moore's hand and pumping it too hard. 'Tristan Stevens is the name.'

Moore squeezed back and the younger guy quickly let go. 'Rob,' he said. He didn't feel the need to explain that it was his name.

Tristan tossed a glance at the Jag. 'E-Type,' he said appreciatively. 'I prefer it in red myself.'

Moore glanced at the car and then back at Tristan, his head cocked inquisitively to the side. He didn't say anything.

'Come this way, the Minister's waiting to see you.' He rolled back his cuff, checking what looked to be a new Rolex. 'You're in good time, well done.'

Moore wondered if he was aware of how condescending he sounded. Tristan looked to be on the good side of thirty, with the smooth good looks of a city trader and the cocky attitude to go with it.

'What's your role here?' Moore asked as he was led into the ground floor entrance way and up a broad set of stairs. The wall beside them was dotted with oil paintings of country scenes and men with bad hair.

'I'm an adviser to the Minister,' Tristan said blandly. He paused at the top of the stairs and turned to Moore. 'Now, sorry to have to ask, but are you armed?'

Moore was faintly amused. 'No.'

Tristan started to reach towards him. 'I know what you secret squirrel types are like, and I don't mean to be offensive...'

'Then don't be.' Moore locked eyes with him. 'I said no.'

Tristan hesitated then withdrew his hand. A slight flush coloured his cheeks. 'It's just I have to take the Minister's security very seriously, that's all. I'm sure you understand.'

Moore gave a curt nod. 'I do.'

Without further discussion Tristan turned and led him into a spacious drawing room. Matching suits of armour flanked the mantelpiece, where a log fire flickered. More oil paintings adorned the walls, the drapes were heavy and rich and the furniture all appeared to be mahogany.

A middle aged man was approaching them, his hand extended and a politician's smile on his face. He was lean and healthy looking and had a full head of salt and pepper. He was in casual country attire that probably cost more than Moore's Ones.

'Thanks for coming,' he said, shaking Moore's hand briefly. 'Paul Oldham.'

'Rob.'

Oldham nodded and gestured towards a horse shoe of antique couches arranged around a coffee table near the fire. Moore removed his jacket and put it down beside him. Tristan disappeared and Oldham took the couch opposite Moore.

'Great house,' Moore commented, looking around.

'Thank you.' Oldham leaned forward with his elbows on his knees, his hands together. 'It's been in the family for years and one of my cousins looks after it. I get to use it when I'm over here, which is regrettably not as often as I would like.' He shrugged and gave a look of chagrin. 'Such is the life of a politician, I guess. Always working.'

Moore kept his thoughts to himself. 'It must be difficult,' he said politely.

Tristan arrived with a tray and laid out plunged coffee and oat biscuits.

'Thank you Tristan.' Oldham smiled and waited for him to leave before pouring the coffee. 'Milk?'

'A little, thanks.' Moore took his cup and a biscuit. He wondered if it would be uncouth to dunk his biscuit. The Minister wasn't, so he held fire and took a dry bite instead. The biscuit tasted fresh baked, and he wondered if baking was one of Tristan's duties as well. 'So, I understand you have some concerns about your daughter Natalie,' he said.

Oldham took a sip of his coffee and nodded. He put his cup down and looked at the floor, the weight of the world seemingly on his shoulders. Moore suppressed an eye roll and waited.

'Natalie is what you could call something of a free spirit, I guess,' Oldham said eventually. 'She's always had a very innocent view of life, naïve even. Always sees the best in people. She had a pretty normal upbringing, as normal as it can get with a career politician for a father anyway.' He gave a small smile. 'She had the best we could provide for her, and once her mother passed away I did the best I could for her, with the able assistance of a nanny. She had the best schools, overseas trips...pretty normal, really.'

Not quite the normal Moore had known growing up, but again he kept his thoughts to himself.

'When she left school she went to Auckland University and studied history, did well enough and then ended up on her OE.' He spread his hands. 'As far as I know everything was good over here, she seemed to be enjoying herself and doing all the normal things young people do on their OE. She's got good friends here, they're all very concerned-I've been in touch with them.'

Moore nodded and sipped his coffee. The biscuit was gone but he wasn't sure on the social etiquette of helping himself to another.

'When did you last hear from her?' he asked.

'She posted on Facebook while she was in Istanbul, I saw that. I spoke to her last before she left, but I have to confess I didn't actually know she was going over there.' He shook his head, frustration etched on his face. 'By Christ, if I'd known I would've said no. The place is in turmoil and the Russians of course have been bombing the blazes out of Syria next door. It's too bloody dangerous over there for a young girl.'

Moore was silent. The man seemed genuinely pained, and Moore wondered how he would have felt himself if it was he and Danni in their shoes. It was too horrible to contemplate.

'Who did she go with?' he asked instead.

Paul Oldham shook his head. 'I don't know. As far as I know she went on her own, I asked her friends and nobody seemed to know.'

'Do you have an itinerary or know where she was staying, what she was doing, anything like that?'

Oldham shook his head again. 'No.'

'Has she been formally reported missing to the Police?'

'No, good Lord no.' Oldham was emphatic. 'Can you imagine the media trolls with that?'

Moore said nothing. He finished his coffee and put the cup down.

'Do you have her address here? Any contact details for her friends?'

'Of course. I'll have Tristan email them to you. You'll need to go over there, of course, and start looking for her.' He slapped the back of one hand into the palm of his other, holding Moore's eyes for emphasis. 'We need to find my little girl, Rob. We need to get boots on the ground and start turning over rocks, get people talking to us. In my experience someone will know where she is, and they will talk to us...given the right approach. A robust approach.' He slapped his hands together again, in case Moore hadn't got the message that he was deadly serious. 'We need to find her, and we need to bring her home.'

Moore said nothing, just gave a slight nod. He'd noticed how common it was for white-collar workers, particularly politicians, to spout militaristic phrases in such situations. He blamed TV. Oldham sat back now, watching him.

'Did you hear what I said, Rob?' Oldham's tone was sharp. 'Or am I talking to myself?'

'I heard you perfectly clearly, sir,' Moore replied.

Oldham pursed his lips and took a slow breath. He seemed to be struggling. 'You don't say much, do you?' he said.

Moore considered his answer. 'I'm more about just doing it,' he said carefully.

'No need to talk about it,' Oldham said.

Moore gave a slight shrug. 'Not usually.'

Oldham was silent for a few moments, studying him. 'What are you?' he asked. 'I presume you're some kind of intelligence operator? A spy?'

'I am.'

Oldham nodded. 'Have you done this sort of thing before? Found people?'

'I have.'

'And you've been to these sorts of places before? Hot spots and the like? You've...operated...in places like this before?'

'Yes.'

Oldham nodded again, absorbing the information. He paused, as if debating his next question. 'Are you good?' he asked. His tone was softer now; this was the father speaking, not the politician.

Moore considered his answer. He knew the man wanted some kind of reassurance, an undertaking that he was going to go and find his daughter and everything would be just dandy and normal life-his kind of normal, anyway-would just resume. But he also needed to be honest.

He met the Minister's eyes. They were anxious, emotional.

'I am,' he said. Oldham's eyes took on a gleam, a hopeful glimmer. Moore deliberately crushed it with his next words. 'If she's there, I've got every chance of finding her. But you need to be prepared for the worst.' Oldham visibly flinched. 'She may be dead.'

Moore paused and let that sink in. He could see Oldham turning it all over in his head. His stomach would be churning, his heart slamming against his rib cage, his mind racing. Moore needed him to go through that storm of emotions and come out the other side. He didn't want the Minister holding out false hope and then being floored when it all went tits up.

'But if she's there, I can find her. And if she can be brought home, I'll bring her home.' Oldham raised his eyes to Moore. They were moist. 'That's all I can promise.'

The Minister slowly nodded, and Moore knew the message was starting to sink in. He stood and extended his hand. Oldham shook it and Moore gave him a plain business card with the High Commission's details on it and a nondescript email address.

He showed himself out.

Tristan met him down by the front door. He was texting when Moore came down the stairs and looked up, his thumb a blur as it whipped across the screen. As the assistant dropped the phone into his pocket Moore noticed it had a customised case, silver with some kind of wing design on the back. He felt his lip begin to curl and fought it down. A phone was a tool, not a damn fashion accessory.

Tristan held the door and followed Moore down the steps to the pebbled turning circle.

'He's very stressed,' he said, his hands tucked into his pockets and a serious expression on his smooth face. 'Very emotional.'

Moore gave him a sideways look. 'I managed to pick up on that.' He went round to the driver's door of the E-Type.

'Poor Natalie,' Tristan continued. If he was perturbed by Moore's reply he didn't show it. 'I just hope to God she's okay. She's a real angel, you know?' He shook his head and sucked his teeth, a picture of worry. 'A real angel,' he repeated.

Moore jangled his keys to give him the hint, and Tristan looked up.

'Thanks for coming out,' he said. 'Have a good drive back to wherever you've come from.' He grinned widely, all traces of worry gone now. 'I guess we don't need to know where, do we? Nudge nudge, wink wink.'

Moore bit his tongue. 'Not really,' he agreed.

Tristan smiled knowingly. He nudged the closest tyre with his polished shoe. 'See if the old beast's got it in her for a good run.'

Moore had opened the door and was starting to get in. He stopped and straightened up. He indicated the Ferrari with a toss of his chin. 'That yours?'

Tristan smiled smugly. 'Sure is.'

'Looks pretty. Slick.'

Tristan nodded, unsure if Moore was complimenting him or testing him.

'It's great to be all flash and gash,' Moore said. He tapped his fingers on the roof of the Jag. 'But the old dog's been there and done it, and still is.' He flashed a wry grin at the younger man. 'Catch ya later, Slick.'

With that he got in and fired up the engine with a throaty roar. He checked the rear view mirror as he shifted into second down the drive.

Tristan watched him leave.

6

The email from Tristan came through within ten minutes of Moore leaving the house. He was nothing if not efficient.

The address he gave was for a flat in Sutton.

It was a commuter town situated in Surrey, south of London proper, with a direct train connection into Victoria. Moore had never had cause to go there before, and he found it like many similar commuter towns.

The high street had the same shops, the same basic layout, and the same chavvy kids strutting round-the boys in shell suits to hide their lack of upper bodies, the girls in as little as possible, with tattoos, bling and push chairs all round.

Moore followed his electronic directions to a residential street just a short walk from the town centre, and drove by the address for a recce. It was a bland two storey block of concrete flats, and Natalie Oldham's flat was in the middle of the top floor.

He parked the Mondeo down the road and sat for a while, observing the surroundings. It was a quiet street, the houses close together and interspersed with blocks of flats. Not council housing by the looks of it-too well kept for that-but soulless regardless.

Cars came and went, the odd jogger, a couple of dog walkers. One peroxided girl with her guts hanging over the top of her track pants, a fag in one hand and a mobile in the other, a snot-nosed kid with a rat's tail running ahead of her while she talked at top volume into her phone.

'Dante! Dante! Wait there!' She waved her fag at the kid who was waiting patiently at the kerb. She turned her attention back to the phone as she waddled after him, past Moore's car. 'Fuck, little prick innit...got arseholes for ears, know what I mean?'

Moore watched the little kid watching his mother. He looked about four years old and was clearly taking in every word she said. Moore's left hand itched to snip the kid's rat's tail off. His right hand itched to smash the mother's phone on the footpath while he shook some sense into her. Somehow, he thought, that would be a pointless exercise.

Once they were out of sight he got out and walked back the way he had come. He first cut around the back of the flats, negotiating his way through a rickety side gate and past children's toys and rubbish bins to check for a back fire escape.

There was nothing.

He retraced his steps and took the stairs to the second storey, noting that although a couple of the down below occupants seemed to be home, there was no sign of life upstairs. He passed the first couple of doors and stopped at the middle flat, number 8.

The windows were closed and there was no sound from inside. There was no indication of an alarm. The longer Moore stood at the door without entering, the more likely he was to draw attention to himself. The door lock was a standard tumbler unit, nothing special. He withdrew a tool from his coat pocket and set to work quickly.

The tool he used was an electric lock pick, similar to a small hand drill, and he fitted what he assessed to be the right sized pick where a drill bit would normally go. Slipping the pick into the key lock Moore triggered it and listened to the pins slide free, allowing him to turn the lock and open the door.

Within seconds he was inside and shutting the door behind him. A quick scan revealed no alarm control pad or motion sensors. The door locked behind him. He put the lock pick away and took the measure of the flat. It was furnished by Ikea and thrift stores, with two medium sized bedrooms and an open plan lounge/dining area. The lounge had French doors out to a tiny balcony, barely big enough for a pair of deck chairs.

Moore slipped on a pair of thin leather gloves he'd brought with him and got to work. He checked the wardrobes-all female clothes. The only sign of a bloke was a birthday card to "N" from "Jules," signed off with multiple kisses.

He presumed the N was Natalie, but there'd been no previous mention of a Jules. Another mystery to be solved.

He carefully went through the bedside table, finding a partially used box of condoms in amongst the usual papers and junk people tended to hide away in their drawers. The papers were mostly general correspondence from the tax department, employment agencies, prospective employers and letting agents-all the usual things for a youngster on their OE. The important thing was that they identified the room as Natalie Oldham's.

Moore checked under the drawers but found nothing. The dresser held basic clothes, trinkets and a few photos. The photos were all either selfies of Natalie in various places, or group shots. There was no single recurring face to identify the mysterious Jules.

He moved back to the wardrobe and went through the pockets of the clothes there. Nothing. The boxes and bags on the floor and the top shelf gave the same result.

Moore stepped back from the wardrobe and took stock. Despite the fact that Natalie was travelling and therefore would have taken some of her belongings with her, he found the lack of personal belongings unusual. The biggest gap was electronic gear. No thumb drives, memory cards or accessories for devices. He guessed she would have taken her phone and camera with her, but he'd expected to find a laptop or tablet at home. The only thing he found was a power cable that appeared to be for a laptop, but no sign of the device it belonged to.

He pushed the thought aside for now and moved to the next

bedroom. It had twin single beds and an initial search revealed belongings for two other girls.

Judging by the clothes one was slim and sporty, the other bigger and frumpier. There was documentation for a Shelley Parker in a drawer. He photographed it on his phone for later reference.

He moved from there to the living area. A large comfortable couch and a couple of armchairs, all of which had seen better days. A TV and stereo in the entertainment unit which dominated one wall. He had just opened the cabinet on the entertainment unit when he caught a flicker of movement through the kitchen window as a figure passed by.

Moore straightened up and paused, hearing a key in the lock.

7

Moore darted to the French doors and let himself out, quietly shutting the door behind him.

There was a narrow lip of wall on either side between the frame of the French doors and the balcony railing, hopefully enough to hide him from the view of whoever had arrived. He pressed himself against the wall and held the door closed with his foot. With any luck whoever had arrived home would not notice the French doors were unlatched, nor would they come out onto the balcony.

Moore glanced around, checking the neighbouring properties for prying eyes. A nosy neighbour was all he needed right now. Being arrested for burglary would be kind of hard to explain.

He could hear movement inside the flat, and risked a peek around the edge. He saw a figure moving from the lounge into the hallway to the bedrooms. He pulled his head back again and waited. A few seconds later he heard a door bang shut.

Moore stayed where he was until he was satisfied the flat was empty. He ducked back inside, secured the French door behind him and hurried to the front door. He could hear footsteps descending the stairs that he himself had used a short time ago.

He waited and in a moment saw a young guy emerge onto the footpath, pause and check his phone, then turn right and disappear from sight. Moore shut the flat door behind him and hurried down the stairs to the roadside. The young guy was ahead of him, digging keys from his pocket. He headed towards a dusty red Peugeot hatchback that had seen better days and Moore went in the other direction towards the Mondeo, reaching it as the red Peugeot approached.

Moore threw a quick look at the driver as the car went past. He was tall and lanky, with long dark hair and a pale complexion. He had the look of a backpacker or a student, and appeared to be oblivious to Moore's presence.

Seconds later Moore was tagged in behind the Peugeot, heading northwest on the A217. He let a couple of cars get between them and sat back, curious to see where the target would take him. Instinct told him this was the mysterious Jules, the giver of birthday cards.

Within a few minutes the red Peugeot indicated left and turned off onto a side street, threading its way through a residential area before pulling into the driveway of a block of flats.

Moore cruised past and found himself a park further up. He doubled back and went up the driveway of the flats. It was smaller but uglier than the block where Natalie lived, just six flats in two storeys.

He saw the red Peugeot was the only car in the tight parking area at the back of the block. He turned his attention to the flats themselves. There were no open doors or windows, no signs of life in any of them.

He went to the back door of the first one and listened for a moment. Nothing. The second one was the same. He reached the third flat on the ground floor, shadowed by a tall hedge badly in need of a trim. A kettle was starting to boil inside.

Moore knocked at the door, a sharp authoritative rap. A second later the door opened and the lanky, long haired young man faced him. He looked sullen and suspicious at the same time.

'Jules?'

'Yeah?'

Moore smiled inwardly. He was on the right track. 'My name's Rick. I work for the New Zealand embassy. I need to speak to you about Natalie.'

Jules' eyes narrowed. 'Why? I already spoke to you people.'

'I know, but I have some further questions, okay? It won't take too long.'

He started to step forward and Jules moved to close the door.

'I'm busy,' the young guy said sullenly, 'now's not a good time, man. I've had enough of talking about Natalie. Just leave me alone.'

Moore put a hand on the door and spoke quietly but firmly. 'Sorry Jules, but I'm also busy. We're very concerned about Natalie, and I think you can help me.' He held the sullen gaze. 'Mate, this could be very serious. I think you'd like to do the right thing, wouldn't you.'

There was silence for a few seconds while Jules mulled this over. Finally he relented and stepped back.

'Whatever, man.' He gave a heavy sigh and let Moore in.

The flat was small and untidy, with no feminine touches to indicate a female occupant. Not that Jules himself was exactly the essence of masculinity. He seemed to fancy himself as some sort of Bohemian, with a large Che Guevera picture on the wall, a number of ethnic trinkets, and a tatty cane swing seat hanging in the corner decorated with colourful cushions.

As Moore took a seat on the sofa-covered, of course, by a multi coloured throw-he noticed an oil painting on the opposite wall. It was a frontal nude of a young woman, sitting cross legged in a tatty cane swing seat, her hands clasping her knee and an enticing smirk on her face. She was small breasted and had long wavy blonde hair.

There was no mistaking it was Natalie Oldham, and had clearly been done in this very flat. The colours were sharp but the artwork itself was somewhat amateurish.

He shifted his gaze to Jules, who was looking serious.

'I don't suppose she sent a copy to her parents,' Moore said, and Jules frowned.

'I don't think that would have been appropriate,' he said sourly, plonking down into the lone armchair. 'So what d'you want to know that I haven't already told your colleagues?' He narrowed his eyes. 'And if you don't mind me saying, you don't look like a foreign service type. You look more like...I dunno, a cop maybe.'

Moore shrugged non-committedly. 'Takes all sorts,' he said. 'How long have you been with Natalie for?'

'I already told your colleagues,' Jules said.

'So tell me again.'

Jules sighed. 'Six months or so.' He shrugged. 'I don't let myself be restricted by the confines of time. Time is irrelevant.'

'And how did you meet her?'

Jules sighed again. 'Really? Come on, this is all so passé.'

'How did you meet her?'

'I already told your colleagues. Next question.'

Moore eyed him coldly. 'How did you meet her?'

Jules gave an exaggerated sigh and stood. 'I'm tired of these ridiculous questions. Why don't you just go and do your job, Mr Foreign Policeman. Stop wasting my time.' He held an arm out in a weak gesture towards the door.

Moore stayed where he was. 'You're wasting time while your girl-friend is missing somewhere in Turkey. How about you sit down and stop being so precious.'

Jules stiffened and his lips pursed. 'I've asked you to leave, so you better leave.' He gestured towards the door again and tried for staunch. He didn't come close to pulling it off.

Moore stayed where he was and eyed the younger man coolly. 'Or what?'

'Or...' Jules faltered. 'Or I'll...' He failed and they both knew it. He dropped his arm but stayed standing, seemingly lost for a Plan B.

'Your girlfriend is missing overseas,' Moore told him. 'Seems like you're the last person to have had contact with her. Now you're seen breaking into her flat and removing property.' Jules' eyes widened. 'It has all the hallmarks of something untoward going on.' Moore paused, holding Jules' gaze. 'So I suggest you sit down, lose the fuckin' attitude and talk to me like a grown up. Understand, Jules?'

There was silence for a moment before Jules' shoulders dropped and he sat back down.

'You've been watching me,' he said. Moore nodded. 'I didn't break in; I have a key.'

'What did you take?'

'Just a charger.'

'For what?'

'Nat's laptop.'

Moore felt his pulse quicken. 'Where's the laptop?'

Jules fetched it from his bedroom and handed it over with the charger. Moore put it beside him.

'You can't take it,' Jules told him. 'It's Nat's.'

'That's why I need to take it. Now let's get back to the start. Where did you meet her?'

Jules ran a hand through his hair and visibly relaxed. 'At an art exhibition, a friend of mine ran it as a one-off last year in Tottenham. I had some of my work on show, just a few oils, and she came over.' He shrugged. 'We got chatting, swapped numbers. That was that.'

Moore nodded. 'Just a casual thing then?'

'It was. Started off like that, anyway. She's pretty intense. She seems all fun loving and carefree and that, but that's just a mask. It's just the surface. Underneath she's like a duck, paddling flat out.'

'What d'you mean, intense?'

Jules sniffed. 'She's very deep emotionally, y'know? She's been hurt before, carries a lot of pain inside. But she doesn't want the world to know it.' Jules looked away, his eyes dark. 'Not even me.'

Moore nodded again. 'Like she's had a bad relationship?'

Jules shook his head now. 'No, more than that. I don't know, she never said. But it was more than just having a shitty relationship. I don't know much about her family-I never met them or anything-but they sound a bit...you know...stuffy.'

Moore raised an eyebrow. 'I haven't met too many politicians who were a bundle of laughs,' he said, and Jules gave a wry smile.

'Too busy feathering their own nests and keeping the people in line,' he replied. 'I'd never vote for any of them, ever; their corruption is endemic, no matter what side you're on.'

Moore left that alone. Politics weren't his game and held little interest for him. He knew what he believed and had realised a long time ago that no politician would ever have the guts to implement the sort of policy he favoured.

'What about Nat?' he asked. 'Was she political at all?'

Jules snorted. 'With her old man?' He shook his head. 'No. Not at all. In fact, she hated politics.'

Moore sat back and tapped his chin thoughtfully. 'So why didn't you go to Turkey with her?'

Jules was silent for a bit, as if considering his response. 'We agreed she would go on her own,' he said.

'Agreed?' Moore said. 'Or you didn't want to go?'

Jules said nothing, just shifted his gaze away and chewed his lip.

'Why didn't you want to go, Jules?' Moore kept his body language relaxed, but his tone was softly insistent. 'Maybe if you'd been there she wouldn't be missing.'

Jules' eyes flashed as he turned back. 'Don't you think I know that? Fuck!' He stood abruptly and stalked to the kitchen. 'I know that, okay! It wasn't me...she didn't want me to go. Okay?'

Moore nodded his acceptance of that, satisfied that he was now getting somewhere. 'Why not? Why go to a place like that on your own, especially a blonde white girl?'

'I know.' Jules took a breath and ran his hand through his hair again. 'I said all that to her, but she was dead set on it. Said it was something she had to do herself.'

Moore mulled that over for a moment. 'What exactly was she going to do, then? Was it something other than just a sightseeing trip?'

'I dunno, man.' Jules shook his head ruefully. 'I really don't know.'

Moore stood now, sliding his hands into his pockets and keeping his demeanour calm. 'Things were okay between you then? Even with her keeping secrets from you?'

Jules was silent again, his head down with his hair falling over his face, and Moore waited. He thought he saw a tremor run through the younger man's shoulders then heard a choked sniff.

Moore grimaced. The last thing he wanted to deal with was a crying angst-ridden artist. He waited some more.

Jules raised his head, swept the hair from his face and wiped his nose on his sleeve. Moore grimaced to himself again.

'We broke up, okay?' Jules turned wet eyes to him, his lip still quivering. 'Happy now? We broke up and she buggered off to "find herself," okay?'

Moore said nothing. God, it wasn't like he'd been shot.

'I take it that it was her call then? No indication it was coming?'

Jules looked away, sniffing some more. 'Not a clue,' he choked.

It looked like the dam had broken. Moore figured he'd reached the end of the road for today. He tucked the laptop and charger under his arm, and made for the back door. Jules was still in the kitchen, leaning his hip against the bench and crying softly.

Moore paused, feeling like he should say something to console him. Nothing came to him, so he nodded instead and left.

He didn't have much to say to a crying man.

8

Ari Khanna was an IT specialist whose main duties involved keeping the High Commission's systems running as they should.

He was also a highly skilled digital forensic expert and Moore regularly used him when his own limited knowledge ran short. He found the slightly built, bespectacled young man hunched over his desk examining the disassembled pieces of a cell phone. Ari looked up sharply when a Twix bar landed beside him. He was addicted to three things-gadgets, sugar and Asian porn. Moore went with chocolate today.

'To what do I owe the honour?' Ari asked, sitting back and eyeing the chocolate warily.

His nose twitched and he pushed his glasses up onto the bridge.

'What're you up to?' Moore asked, slipping the laptop and charger onto the desk surface beside the Twix.

Ari glanced at the Nokia in front of him then back at Moore.

'I'm trying to sort out a phone,' he said, 'what the shit does it look like?'

Moore had learned long ago that the normally mild-mannered Ari swore when he was under pressure, but usually got his expletives wrong. He suppressed a smile and shrugged nonchalantly. Not everybody could be a world class swearer.

'Pretty much like that,' he said. He gestured at the laptop. 'Reckon you could crack into that for me, check for emails or downloads or whatever it is you do?'

Ari didn't even look at the HP.

'Of course,' he said. 'Does a bear fuck in the forest?'

Moore fought to keep a straight face.

'Probably,' he said. 'How soon could you have a look?'

Ari sighed and waved at the disassembled phone. Moore realised now that it was broken, rather than pulled apart. Pieces of the handset were scuffed and cracked.

'Today?' Ari said. 'This can wait. It's personal, anyway. Besides, your buddy McGregor's a wanker.'

'McGregor?' Moore cocked an eyebrow. 'What're you doing for him? That's not his phone.'

Like everyone, McGregor had the latest iPhone from the company.

Ari slid the HP and charger onto his lap and checked it for damage.

'No.' He shifted it onto the worktop at right angles to his desk, alongside a tablet and another laptop. He glanced around conspiratorially and lowered his voice to a whisper. 'It's his wife's.' Another look around and Moore felt his pulse quicken. 'He reckons she's having it off with someone on the side.'

Moore's gut dropped to his boots.

'Really?' he managed. 'How come?'

Ari shrugged.

'Dunno. He just brought this to me and asked me to check it out. Must be her booty phone.' He grinned and pushed his glasses up his nose again. 'I'm presuming he broke it when he found it. He was pretty wound up when he brought it to me.'

'When was that?' Moore's heart was pounding in his chest, but he tried to play it casual. 'I haven't really seen him today.'

'Just before.' Ari's eyes narrowed. 'How come you're so interested, anyways?'

Moore shrugged.

'Like you said, he's a wanker. Couldn't blame his missus for stepping out.'

'I know, yeah?' Ari's face lit up and he chuckled. 'And she's some hot arse, bro. I'd tap that I tell you!'

It all sounded wrong coming from Ari, who was neither street nor a lady killer of any sort, but Moore rolled with it. He laughed awkwardly and turned to go.

'Let me know how you get on,' he said over his shoulder, 'you know where to find me.'

'You got it, brother,' Ari called after him, watching him go.

Moore stopped to get a coffee from the machine before heading back to his office. It was late in the day and desks were beginning to empty out. He was deep in thought by the time he got back and closed his door. It wasn't good that McGregor suspected something, not good at all. Moore had no doubt that Ari would find what he was looking for and then a shit ton of pain would come down on all of them.

Despite McGregor's personality defects Moore didn't wish him any actual harm. For the hundredth time in the last few months he gave himself a mental uppercut for being so stupid. It wasn't the first time that thinking with his little head had got him in trouble, but he swore to himself it would be the last.

He was too old for this bullshit. There was a good chance that he would get the boot from the Service if it was proven he'd been screwing a colleague's wife-or at least shifted sideways from his plum role in London.

He imagined himself sitting in a crappy office somewhere in South East Asia or Africa or, God forbid, Canberra. He shuddered at the thought. He had to figure a way to prevent that data reaching McGregor, and that left only two options; either intercepting it without Ari's knowledge, or going direct to Ari himself.

He was weighing the two options up when there was a tap at his door and it opened. The Beautiful People entered Moore's office. Vince and Ngawai Masoe were married, both about Moore's age, and they worked down the corridor. Both were Intelligence Officers using the covers of working for Immigration.

They had taken him under their wing when he first arrived in town, showing him around and having him over for dinner. He had given them their nickname, which he suspected they secretly liked despite their outward protestations and eye rolling.

Vince was a stocky half Samoan with broad shoulders and a big chest. His jet black hair was laced with silver and clipped short. At one time he had been a provincial rugby player on the fringes of the mighty Auckland team of the early nineties, before he nearly had his head taken off in a club game and dislocated his neck. He still played in a so-called social team, although his dreams of making the big time were now long gone.

His sporto image belied a sharp intellect and he was a skilled agent runner. In a former life he had been a police officer, where his talents with informants had been recognised on a joint op, resulting in him switching agencies.

His wife Nga was the longer serving of the two officers, and liked to remind Vince of the fact that he was her "junior." She had long dark hair tied back in a ponytail and wore dark-rimmed glasses. Her demure office attire failed to disguise her toned legs and womanly curves, but anyone who took an unhealthy interest had a second think coming.

Nga Masoe regularly boxed with her husband and was no stranger to sorting out issues herself. She had initially been recruited direct from university, but had shown her force of character by declining the offer until she had completed her full immersion Maori studies.

Once inside the Service she had gone on to specialise in languages, and was now fluent in three further tongues.

'What time're you knocking off bruv?' Vince asked. 'We're going for a trot if you're keen.'

A trot to Vince was more like a ten k run followed by a pint at the nearest Wetherspoons. Tempting as it always was to see Nga in her active wear, Moore knew he had a fire to put out.

'Better pass, bruv,' he replied, using the mock English term they had picked up for each other. 'Got a job on. Besides, you ran me ragged last time. I can't keep up with you anymore, mate.'

'Jeez, don't tell him that,' Nga said, pulling a face, 'he's got a big enough head already.' She gave her husband a cheeky grin. 'Looks like you'll just have to raise a sweat with me, dear.'

Vince cocked an eyebrow. 'Gimme half a chance, girl.'

Nga blushed and slapped his arm before backing out the door. 'Whatever, Junior.'

Vince shrugged expressively as if he was hard-done by and followed her, shooting Moore with a finger gun before closing the door behind them.

Moore stared at the door once they had gone, looking but not seeing. He envied them what they had. It seemed that a solid marriage these days was a rare beast.

His own had failed before the ink was barely dry on the certificate, and the only good thing to come out of it had been Danni. He'd come close since but never sealed the deal. There was always something else going on, some other priority pulling him in another direction. And now here he was, the wrong side of forty and banging the wife of a colleague, putting his career at risk in the process.

Moore wondered if he could sink any lower, and the thought seemed to darken his mood even further. He stood and turned to the window behind his desk, his hands in his pockets. The office wasn't so large that he had to actually walk to it, more just step aside from the chair and turn. At least he had a view of sorts though. He wondered if the pleasure he took from having a view was just another sign that he was getting soft.

Below the High Commission, people and vehicles bustled about. Worker bees, tourists, shoppers, flotsam and jetsam bobbing busily on the tide of life in the big smoke.

Moore found the view therapeutic, helping his mind switch off and meander where it wanted, following random paths with seemingly no meaning at all, until eventually a destination was reached and whatever problem he had been mulling over had some kind of an answer. Sometimes right, sometimes wrong, but always a place to start unravelling the knot.

His mind turned from the McGregor problem back to the job at hand. He disliked politicians on principle, simply because the majority of them seemed to have bugger-all life experience outside university and the Beehive. No life experience that qualified them to make the heavy decisions they made.

The fact that Oldham's daughter had gone off the radar would be no big deal if she wasn't a minister's kid. Had Oldham been a dairy farmer from the Waikato or a teacher from Timaru, nobody would give a shit. Problem was, he was a senior politician, and politicians pulled the strings of the civil service. Moore was just another puppet to him, a marionette made to dance by the puppet masters, the faceless drones in the background who made things happen.

'Screw it,' he muttered to himself, turning away from the window.

Brooding wasn't getting the job done. He turned his mind to the day's events, systematically working through what he had learned and who he had met. More than anything else, Moore focussed on the people. He had always believed that what was said was often less valuable than how it was put across. The unsaid word spoke volumes. He liked to dissect mannerisms and characteristics of the people he met.

Paul Oldham himself seemed genuine enough, for a career politician. He was obviously seriously worried about his daughter-probably as much for her as the potential embarrassment for his career, Moore thought cynically.

His assistant, Tristan, was a slimy little toad. A typical sycophant, a parasite feeding off the main man, buzzing round like a protector of some sort. He had the sort of arrogance that such people always carried, as if they themselves were someone because they were with somebody who was. Moore had taken an instant dislike to him, not helped by the snooty assistant's jibe about the E-Type.

Jules was very much playing the part of the tortured artist, wracked by angst and shackled by the constraints of a society that neither understood nor appreciated his individuality, but he also seemed pretty genuine beneath the pretentiousness.

He was distracted by the buzz of an incoming text on his cell. It was his contact at MI5, wanting to meet. Jedi had been on the money. He crooked a grin to himself.

He was always happy to meet her.

9

It was 3pm by the time Moore stepped off Regent Street into Liberty.

He made his way through the department store to the café, where he found his contact already waiting at a table for two.

He smiled as he approached and she stood to give him a quick peck on the cheek before sitting again.

Sarah O'Loughlin looked like what she was; a mid-forties mother of two teenage boys, constantly harassed and running late, and always wearing last year's outfits.

She was also a long serving Intelligence Officer with the Security Service, and was very good at it. She had been one of the first contacts Moore made when he took the London posting, and fortunately she remembered meeting him several years prior when he was on an attachment to Hereford. In her motherly way she had provided a steady guiding hand as he found his feet-as much as an officer from another service could, and probably a bit more besides.

Moore had nothing but admiration for her.

'Good to see you, Locky,' he said, draping his jacket over the back of his chair before sitting.

Sarah smiled. 'You know you're the one person who calls me that?'

'You know you're the one person I ever have high tea with?' he returned with a grin.

She shrugged. 'Being married for twenty years, it's the only time I ever get taken out,' she said, 'so I'll take what I can get, even if the firm's paying for it.'

Moore didn't bother checking the menu. 'I take it you've already ordered for us?'

'Of course.' She glanced around the café, which was about half full. 'How're things at Haymarket?'

'Same old.' Moore gave a shrug. 'You know what it's like. I had a refresher which was hard, good catch up though.'

'Boys and their toys.' Sarah smiled at him across the narrow table. Her eyes were hazel, but the right one had a tiny brown spot in it, some kind of an irregularity that he had never asked about. Her hair was short and tidy, dark brown with warm streaks to help camouflage the greys coming through.

'Aside from that just the normal stuff you already know about,' he said with a shrewd look, knowing full well that the Firm were very well informed about anything going on in their patch. Sarah flicked an eyebrow but said nothing. 'I'm glad this job's come up, at least it'll get me out of the office for a while.'

'Hmm.' Sarah paused and waited while a waitress delivered their afternoon tea-a pot of English Breakfast and a 3-tier plate of food. Beautiful sweets, delicate sandwiches and perfect scones with strawberry jam and cream.

Moore waited until she had selected a red velvet cupcake with frosting, before helping himself to a ham sandwich. They ate in silence for a minute while the tea steeped. Moore had never heard of "steeping" before his first high tea with Sarah.

'So,' Sarah said, delicately slicing off a piece of cupcake. 'How's the love life?'

Moore pulled a face and chewed. 'What love life?' he said. 'So much time, so few opportunities.' He gave her a cheeky grin. 'Why, are you putting yourself back on the market?'

'Fat chance.' She popped the piece of red velvet into her mouth. 'I heard a whisper that someone's wife is being fairly indiscreet.'

'Really?' Moore raised an enquiring eyebrow, wondering how the hell she had heard that. Haymarket was obviously leaking like a broken sieve. 'Who's that then?'

She studied him for a long moment across the table. 'Mrs McGregor, I hear.'

Moore said nothing. He picked up the pot and began to pour her tea. 'Wow. You do have good sources. Better than me I'm afraid, Locky.'

Sarah's eyes were amused. 'Really, Rob?'

He moved on to his own cup, being careful not spill the tea and mess up the linen. Sarah finished her cupcake and selected a fruit pastry.

'Apparently the lady herself is quite careless with who she mentions her activities too,' she said, a hint of seriousness entering her voice. 'I'd suggest that whoever was playing in that sandpit would do well to be very careful.'

Moore glanced at her as he put the pot down. Her face gave nothing away but her meaning was clear. He took the small milk jug and added a dash to each of their cups.

'I see,' he said finally, putting the jug down and looking at her. 'Is this an official message?'

'It's an official message between friends,' Sarah said quietly. She took a sip of her tea.

Moore did likewise. It was hot and strong. 'Common knowledge?' he asked.

Sarah gave a slight head shake. 'Reasonably,' she said. 'But I've connected dots that others probably wouldn't.'

Moore nodded. 'Point taken.'

There was silence between them while Moore chewed that over. He didn't want to ask the crucial question, and Sarah sensed it.

'As far as I'm aware he doesn't know the full details,' she said. 'I think it's just her boasting to a girlfriend, but the conversation was overheard by someone else. No names were mentioned.'

Moore selected a scone and spread it with jam and cream. 'Thanks for the info,' he said, and took a bite. 'I'll make sure that fire is put out.'

Sarah nodded and sipped her tea. She took a bite of the pastry and gestured at him with it. 'I do like these,' she said. 'Second only to The Ritz.'

Moore smiled, grateful that part of the meeting was over. They made small talk about her kids for a bit and she brought him up to date on their activities and sporting endeavours. She finished the pastry and watched him while he devoured another sandwich.

'Have you heard from Danni?' Sarah asked. Danni was his daughter, and lived with his ex-wife in Brisbane. At best Moore saw her a couple of times a year; as often as The Dragon would allow it. It was a constant sore point with him. Not that Danni seemed terribly bothered.

Moore nodded. 'Got a phone call a couple of days ago and a card for my birthday.'

'That's nice. Oh, and sorry I forgot as usual.'

Moore chuckled. 'You mean it's not on your calendar? I'm hurt.'

She gave a wry smile. 'Callum doesn't even know you exist. I don't think that would go down too well.' She reached down to her handbag and took out a white envelope. She handed it across the table to him. 'Compliments of HM,' she said as he tucked it into his jacket pocket. 'I expect it to be returned afterwards, of course.' She crooked a smile at him. 'No jetting off to Rio with your fancy woman or some other bint.'

Moore had the grace to blush and helped himself to a second scone to cover his embarrassment. 'Thanks,' he murmured.

'Any update then?' Sarah asked, draining her cup and taking the pot to pour another.

'Na.' Moore wiped cream from his lip. 'I'm just going to have to go over and see what I find. Bit of a needle in a haystack, I suspect.'

'What's your gut feeling on it?' Sarah watched him over the rim of her cup. 'Anything to be concerned about?'

'Aside from a naïve young chick travelling on her own in a country where people are blowing themselves up? Nothing to say it's anything but that.' He wiped his hands on a linen napkin. 'But who knows. At the end of the day it's a politician's daughter and the big boss wants me to look into it.'

Sarah nodded and finished her cup. 'Just be careful. I take it you're going on your own?'

He nodded. 'Yes Mum.'

'Don't "yes mum" me,' she scolded, pushing her chair back. 'Just do it.'

Moore grinned to himself and also stood, putting his jacket on. They made their way out to Regent Street again and paused on the footpath.

'Thanks for the cuppa,' Moore said.

Sarah leaned in and he kissed her cheek. She smelled like fresh vanilla and something else he couldn't put his finger on.

'Be safe,' she murmured in his ear.

Moore squeezed her arm and gave her a smile. 'Of course,' he said. 'We'll catch up when I get back. My shout.'

He turned away and headed for Haymarket.

10

Not only did the Brits not like foreign agents running round carrying guns, it was also bad practice.

A diplomatic passport wouldn't stop an officer from getting a bullet in the head if things went awry, which was a good reason for weapons to be kept under lock and key.

Moore kept a secure cabinet in his own office for some of his gear, but the rest was stored in the SCIF-a Sensitive Compartmented Information Facility-down the hall from his office.

This was an ultra-secure room, known as the "skiff room," where a handful of select personnel would retreat should the world ever implode and necessitate using the stand-alone comms facility.

He swiped his card and punched in two PINs before the door unlocked. He closed it behind him and went to the heavy steel gun locker in one corner, unlocking it with another PIN. A small number of firearms were kept there for defensive purposes, available to all trained embassy staff should the need arise. Of course, being a bureaucracy, not all those actually had access to the safe.

On the top shelf was a long narrow lock box, which Moore removed and placed on one of the worktops, being careful not to bump any of the sensitive comms gear there. He unlocked the box with his own small key and removed one of two Kevlar pouches, zipped closed and secured with a PIN-locked padlock. No need to check it-both pouches were identical. He locked the box again, secured the cabinet and let himself out.

As he turned away he noticed McGregor standing outside his own office, watching him. His expression gave nothing away. Moore ignored him and took the stairs two flights up to the High Commissioner's level.

The wide reception area was bright and cheery, with the original wall coverings from various Kiwi artists lending it a unique flavour. Moore liked the current High Commissioner-far from being a stuffy politico, he was a former surf lifesaver with a passion for skydiving. Whenever Moore was required to provide personal protection services for the boss, as he was known, they had got on well.

The High Commissioner's Executive Assistant was equally affable, but with the steely edge required in her position.

'Afternoon Gabby,' Moore smiled, crossing the foyer towards her desk.

Gabrielle Stone looked up, her brow furrowed. She was in her late thirties with stylish shoulder length blonde hair and light green eyes behind her glasses. Moore knew she was a lawyer by trade, and suspected she had quietly been placed in her position by the Service.

'Oh, it's you,' she said.

Moore casually leaned a hip against the corner of her desk. 'Sorry to disappoint,' he said, hoping his smile was engaging.

Gabby remained remarkably unaffected. A sign of a good EA, he decided. She wore a dark skirt suit with a sharp white blouse, unbuttoned just low enough to show the barest hint of cleavage. Moore appreciated the effort-the hint was more enticing than a blatant display.

'Bet I'm not the first girl you've ever said that to,' she returned crisply, and Moore recoiled with a grimace.

'Ouch,' he said, 'cutting. Wake up on the side of the wrong bed this morning, Gabs?'

She gave him stern. He gave her cheeky schoolboy, and she relented.

'No, but the boss is in a bit of a tizz, that's all. We do actually do a lot of work up here, you know.'

'I never doubted it,' Moore said. He passed the Kevlar pouch to her. 'Any chance you could flick this over to Ankara for me?'

She took it and weighed it in her hand.

'Is this what I think it is?' she asked.

'Probably.'

'When d'you need it there?'

'I'm going tomorrow.'

'No probs.' Gabby put it aside. 'It'll be there. I'll let them know. You going to pick it up?'

'Yeah, I'll be in touch with JJ once I'm over there.'

Gabby nodded efficiently. They still used a diplomatic bag facility, allowing them to send freight across borders purportedly without interference from the host nation's intelligence service. She turned back and looked at him, still leaning casually against her desk.

'Was there something else?' she asked pointedly. 'Or are you just lounging around now?'

Moore pushed up and straightened his pants. 'You old flirt,' he said with an easy grin and a wink, 'I haven't got time for your shenanigans.'

Gabby stifled a smile but her eyes twinkled. 'I haven't shenanigised since the eighties, Rob,' she said. 'In fact, I don't think anyone has but you.'

He backed towards the door to the stairs. 'Play your cards right, Gabby...'

'Bugger off,' she said, 'I'm busy.'

She watched him disappear through the door, and shook her head, a smile playing on her lips.

11

Istanbul was one of the many continental cities Rob Moore had never been to. The closest he'd got was fighting insurgents over the border in Iraq, but that was a lifetime ago.

He caught a cab to Heathrow for an early departure, ate a bland and expensive breakfast in the departure lounge and ended up sitting beside an overweight young woman in a Greenpeace T shirt who was in need of a good waxing. He ignored her and buried his nose alternately in a guide book and a well-thumbed paperback copy of Alistair MacLean's *Where Eagles Dare*, finishing with a solid hour's sleep before lunch. The flight landed at Ataturk Airport at 1245pm and by 2pm Moore was hunting for a cab.

The current tensions were evident in the faces of the people hurrying by without making eye contact, and in the numbers of armed soldiers and Police at the airport and on patrol. There was a definite edge in the air, something almost palpable, as if everyone was just waiting for something to kick off.

The taxi driver who delivered him to his hotel drove a battered grey Mercedes 280 like it was a dodgem at a fairground, heavy on the pedals and horn and jerky on the wheel, ear-rupturing Turkish pop music blasting all the while from the cassette deck.

Moore settled into the back seat and silently willed the ride to end. They pulled into a cobbled lane in the centre of the city, manoeuvring around other taxis and tourist buses until the driver pulled up outside the Altan Hotel and jabbered something at Moore.

He got out and grabbed Moore's bags from the boot, dropping them at the feet of his passenger with one hand and holding the other out for his fee.

Moore shoved cash into his paw and grabbed his bags, making his way to the front door of the hotel. He stood outside while a gaggle of young tourist girls-Scandinavian, by the looks, with their blonde hair and universal beauty-came through, chattering excitedly over each other as one of them read aloud from a Lonely Planet. He ran an eye over them as they headed off to explore. If they were typical clientele of the hotel, then he was certainly going to stand out, regardless of his cover.

Moore crossed the foyer to the desk and presented his passport with a smile to the young clerk.

The clerk booked him in without fuss and with minimal conversation, taking payment off Moore's credit card and copying his passport before handing him a key and a brochure.

'Upstairs to the second floor,' he said in flawless English, indicating the stairs off the foyer. 'Room 212. Okay?'

'Sweet as mate, cheers.' Moore gave him another grin and grabbed his bags. As he reached the stairs a girl came down and he automatically moved aside, glancing up as she came abreast of him. She was young, maybe mid-twenties, with long black hair tied back in a ponytail. She wore the standard tourist uniform of hiking shoes, cargo pants and a polar fleece, with a daypack over one shoulder. She was slim and slightly taller than average.

She cast a quick look at him as she went past, and he immediately noticed two things about her eyes. Firstly they were bright blue, the sharpest, clearest blue he had ever seen. Secondly, they were watchful. Not the normal watchfulness of a tourist in a foreign city, of a girl alone assessing a bloke approaching her. No, these eyes were wary, calculating.

In a second she was past him without a second look and making for the front doors. Moore paused to watch her go, unable to shake the tiny alarm bell going off in his subconscious, before continuing up to his room. Years in the game had ingrained strong instincts in him, and he had learned to trust these instincts implicitly, to literally trust them with his life. There was nothing he could do with that right now, so he filed it away and got on with the task at hand.

His room was half way along a corridor and faced out over the lane at the front of the hotel. The Altan clearly had a low budget for furnishings, which explained the backpacker rates. The room was basic but serviceable, with a double bed and a tiny kitchenette, and a separate bathroom.

Moore locked the door behind him and tossed his bags on the bed. He crossed to the front windows and pulled back the net curtains, opening the windows to let in some fresh air. On the road below a new tourist bus arrived and disgorged passengers. A small restaurant was across the road and, according to the guide book he'd read on the flight over, it offered mid-priced good local cuisine.

He had already decided to eat there tonight before getting his head down and aiming for an early start in the morning.

He turned back to the bed and began to unpack the Berghaus backpack. The late notice of the mission had meant a quick trip to a camping store to kit himself out for the trip. Most of the gear he kept in his small Camden flat was either ex-military or bought in New Zealand, neither of which was suitable for the task.

He had bought a new pack, hiking gear and travel kit. He paused as he uncovered the small electronic device buried in with his tablet and iPhone. No need to check for listening devices just yet, so he put it aside. In theory, nobody from the Turkish National Intelligence Service should know he was there, having travelled on a clean passport and having never operated in the country before.

Unless they'd been given a heads-up from somewhere.

Moore double-checked the door and wedged a door stopper under it before stripping out of his jeans and shirt and stepping into the shower. The water pressure was low and he had to crank it up to get some decent heat, but it washed away the stickiness of travel and in five minutes he was washed and dried.

He flopped onto the bed with the intention of getting his head down for an hour. He could still feel the knots and aches from the training exercise, and it was another reminder that he was getting older. Two decades of soldiering had brought with it plenty of aches and injuries, some of which still lingered.

Within a minute he was out for the count and when he woke it was to the sound of the evening prayer call. Speakers in the minarets of a mosque nearby-probably the big Blue Mosque, he guessed-called the faithful to prayer as the sun dropped in the sky and the temperature cooled.

He rolled off onto the floor and did a short series of stretches to loosen up before downing half a bottle of water. The thin carpet smelt funky and obviously hadn't seen a cleaner in some time.

Feeling rejuvenated he dressed in clean khaki cargo pants, an old black Rolling Stones T-shirt, and comfortable Merrell walking shoes. He checked his G-Shock; 5.30pm.

Moore tucked his passport and wallet into his pockets with his iPhone, secured the windows and locked the door behind him. He stepped out of the hotel into the cobbled street and paused beside a potted tree for a minute, absorbing his surroundings and letting his mental antenna scan the environment.

There were plenty of people around, movement and noise, but no alarm bells went off. He scouted the neighbourhood, doing a full circle around the block and sussing out what was there-shops, hotels, apartments, eateries, parking areas. He had no reason to suspect any trouble, but if things went belly up he needed to have some familiarity with his surroundings and possible escape routes in mind.

That done, he widened his circle and threw in a couple of counter surveillance measures without detecting any watchers. Satisfied, he stopped to buy bottled water then made his way back to the restaurant across from the hotel.

It was only moderately busy at 6.30pm and he took a table in a corner of the outdoor eating area with a good view of the comings and goings. He ordered a Efes Pilsen and supped it while he mulled over the menu and unobtrusively observed his fellow diners; mostly small groups of excited tourists.

The waitress returned for his order and within minutes he was enjoying a mezze of fried mussels on a skewer. That was quickly followed by grilled chicken kebabs with rice and salad, and he got the distinct impression that as the tables filled up so the waitress' desire to get him moving also increased.

He took his time finishing the kebabs and ordered a second beer, feeling himself unwinding nicely as the food settled and the evening livened up. Coloured lights were strung along the adobe style walls of the restaurant and background music came from somewhere inside.

Moore was almost ready to go when he spied a new arrival taking a seat at a long table nearby. The rest of the table was occupied by what appeared to be a tour party of twenty-somethings who were settling in for a long night with flowing beer and loud chatter. The same grumpy waitress who had served Moore found a space at the end of the table and brought a chair over for her.

Moore recognised the newcomer as the girl he had spotted earlier at the hotel, the one with the clear blue eyes and watchful look. She was clearly not part of the tour group and seemed anxious, unsmiling and keeping her head down as she quickly scanned the menu.

Moore sat back and watched as she waved the waitress back over and gave her order. While the waitress hurried off and the tour party raised a loud toast to something of importance only to them, the girl checked her surroundings and Moore felt her eyes flick over him as he took a sip from his bottle.

He put the bottle down and caught her give him a second glance. She casually looked away when she realised she'd been seen, and struck up a conversation with the nearest diner.

Moore nodded subconsciously to himself. Just as she had clocked him, she was also no tourist. What exactly she was remained to be seen.

He finished his beer and put the bottle down. The girl started to look as he made his way towards the door, but caught herself and pretended she hadn't noticed. He walked past her and paid his bill at the bar.

When he left a minute later the girl was starting her meal.

Thirty minutes later the girl exited the restaurant alone, her hands tucked into the pockets of her puffer. She turned left and moved away from the Altan hotel.

Moore stepped out from a doorway and dropped in behind her, hanging thirty metres back as she went to the end of the cobbled road and left again, heading up a hill and left into the next street. Foot traffic had thinned out and Moore paused at the corner, watching as the girl headed back parallel to the Altan.

When she disappeared through the front doors of a building half way down, Moore moved forward. He walked straight past, giving just a quick side glance to register the name of the hotel before continuing on. He turned off into a narrow alley he had seen earlier and dug out his phone to do a quick web search. The Grand Central Hotel was a standard tourist hotel, definitely a grade or two better than the Altan, but still suitable for the budget-conscious traveller.

He put the phone away again and made his way back towards the Altan. Pausing at the front entrance of the hotel, he realised that the back of the Grand Central faced him. Presumably the girl-whoever she was-was staying at the Grand Central, so why had she been at the Altan earlier? Visiting perhaps? Doing a recce?

He had more questions than answers and no immediate plan to fix that, so he headed up to his room to get his head down.

Tomorrow was another day and there was work to do.

12

When Moore entered the lobby at 4am the only noise he could hear was someone snoring for Africa.

He tracked the noise to the back office behind Reception, where he saw an open door accessing the back office. The night shift clerk was asleep there with his feet on the desk and his head back, out for the count.

The office was small, with a small kitchen bench and a couple of shelves of files.

The rest of the hotel was silent, the street outside empty. A white board on an easel by the Reception desk listed a couple of tour departures for the morning, the first at 6am. He was confident that, all going well, he had time to get what he wanted and get out unseen. He couldn't see any CCTV cameras, but even if there was one it shouldn't matter.

His sock-covered feet were silent as he padded across the lobby and stepped over the low swing gate at the end of the Reception desk. He didn't want to open the gate and risk a squeaky hinge waking the clerk.

A high counter top provided cover for him from any passers-by on the street.

As he had hoped, the computer was on. He tapped the mouse and the screen came alive. He glanced over his shoulder at the human chainsaw barely two metres away; still no sign of stirring.

Moore ran his eye over the screen and took a minute to figure out what was what. The writing was all in Turkish but it was a standard layout. He found a search field and typed in the name Oldham, then hit Enter. The clack of the keys was as loud as snapping bones in the silence between snores.

The clerk stirred and stopped breathing for a few moments. Moore froze, ready to move if the man woke. The clerk inhaled sharply and gave a nasal rattle, then settled back into sleep again.

Moore checked the search results and found Natalie Oldham's name with her booking record. It showed she had paid with a credit card and booked Room 332 for four days.

Moore took out his iPhone and snapped a photo of the booking record before returning to the main screen. He took a minute to navigate his way through the system before he found current bookings.

Room 332 was unoccupied, but had new guests arriving that day. His mind started ticking over a plan as his fingers were closing the screen down again.

He edged back towards the end of the counter, painfully aware now of the slightest rustle of clothing.

Suddenly the chainsaw stopped and he heard the clerk's chair creak. There was a snort and a sigh. Moore stepped back over the swing gate and quickly ducked behind a tall potted plant against the wall. Adrenaline had kicked in and he waited, poised to see how things unfolded. He had a cover story prepared, but there were never any guarantees. If the clerk was at all suspicious, it could all go very bad very fast.

He heard the shuffle of feet followed by a yawn and the sound of a stretch. A fart split the air followed by a chuckle. Moore silently rolled his eyes to himself and waited.

The clerk shuffled round for a minute then there was the sound of a zip being undone followed by a sigh and the tinkle of running water on tin.

Moore remembered the sink in the back office and realised the clerk was having a piss into it. He ducked down and moved quickly around the front of the desk, making it safely to the stairs before the clerk finished his business.

13

Room 332 was right by the lift on the third of five floors. As rooms to break went into went, it wasn't a great choice.

Moore had been awake since the dawn call to prayer- not long after he'd got back to bed- but waited until the hotel's morning was in full swing at 7am, with the second wave of guests moving down to Reception for their tour.

He knew the clerk would be fully occupied and the cleaners wouldn't be into the rooms yet. If he'd had his kit and several minutes he could have easily picked the lock, but in the absence of either he went old school. The door was typical of a budget hotel-flimsy and with a cheap basic lock that did little more than hold the door closed.

Moore gripped the door handle with a hand towel as he applied maximum pressure to it and leaned his shoulder and knee against the door itself. The door flexed and he gave it a short hard palm strike just above the handle.

The door popped open with only a slight crack of the frame, and he was in. He shut the door behind him and paused in the small narrow entranceway, waiting and listening. It wouldn't be the first time a covert recce had been ruined by unexpected hotel guests, with the clerk taking a quick cashy that didn't go through the books.

Satisfied he was alone, he took five seconds to visually check the room. It was a studio, small and basic, with the same level of cleanliness of his own room. It was unlikely that Natalie Oldham had left anything behind in the room, but it had to be checked anyway.

Moore worked the room methodically, looking in, under, behind and on top of everything. Nothing. He did the bed last, lifting the mattress on its side and clearing one side before repeating the process for the other side. The only things he found were a dirty sock and a used rubber.

He dropped the mattress back down and straightened the covers, satisfied that he'd checked every nook and cranny available but frustrated that he'd come up empty.

He waited until the hall was clear before exiting and making his way to the stairs. As he started down he heard someone coming up, and the top of a head with long dark hair in a ponytail two flights below him. Instinct told him it was the girl from last night, and he hurried back up to the next floor.

Watching furtively over the railing, he saw her enter the third floor, glancing cautiously over her shoulder as she did so. She was wearing a black shell jacket and blue jeans. Moore descended again and watched through the safety glass window in the door. She went to the end of the hallway and stopped at the door to Room 332. She checked her surroundings again before slipping a key in the lock and entering.

Moore waited a few minutes, mulling this development over. He still had no idea who the girl was, but her actions told him several things about her. She was obviously connected to Natalie Oldham somehow, but wasn't acting in an overtly official capacity. She wasn't from The Service, and presumably not from the Brits either; American maybe?

Choosing the same time as he had to toss the room showed she was smart. And he hadn't seen a shadow or companion yet, so presumably she was working alone.

Deciding that time was not on his side, he made up his mind to approach her front on. If nothing else, at least it would tell him what her motive was. He was opening the door when the lift suddenly dinged further down the hall and two men stepped out. Moore ducked back into cover and watched as they moved to Room 332.

The older of the two, a pudgy man in an ill-fitting brown suit, used a key to unlock the door. The younger man, taller and stronger looking, put his hand into his jacket before following the other man into the room.

Whoever they were, Moore knew they weren't good news for the girl. He stayed where he was for another minute to see how things developed. He had no desire to tangle with the Turkish intelligence services, considering he was operating there without their knowledge; it would just make things messy, and probably completely blow the job.

It wasn't long before the door to Room 332 opened and all three of them emerged. The pudgy man had the girl by the arm and was hustling her along. The younger guy, who Moore decided was the muscle, had his hand still concealed in his jacket.

They stood by the lift and the pudgy man jabbed the button. The girl tried to pull her arm free and the pudgy man snapped something at her. She responded and the pudgy man belted her across the face with a back hand.

Enough was enough and time was running out.

Moore had too many questions and he figured she could answer at least some of them. He couldn't afford to let her disappear into the bowels of a faceless interrogation centre.

He opened the stairwell door and headed towards them, his head down while he played with his phone, moving steadily but with an affected limp. He could sense the three strangers all looking at him as he got closer and he glanced up, tucking his phone into his pocket and giving a polite smile as he reached them.

The girl's right cheek was pink and her face was defiantly scared. She made eye contact with him and he knew instantly that she recognised him. The pudgy man was in his fifties, with a standard Turkish moustache and slicked wavy hair. He was shoulder height on Moore. The younger guy was Moore's own height and in good shape, in his late twenties maybe, with a tidy beard and a tailored grey suit.

The younger guy kept his right hand concealed in his jacket and eyed Moore with suspicion as he stopped beside them and waited for the lift. The pudgy man gave Moore a surly look and grunted something to the muscle.

The young guy stepped forward and blocked Moore from the lift.

'Is ours,' he said as the lift car arrived with a ding behind him. 'Take the stairs.'

'Sore leg, mate,' Moore said, slapping his thigh for emphasis. 'Can't walk too far, gotta take the lift.'

The muscle was not amused. 'Go away,' he said, gesturing down the hallway with his head. 'Take a walk.'

The lift doors opened and the pudgy guy moved forward with the girl, still holding her arm.

'I'm getting old, mate,' Moore said with a friendly grin. 'Be a sport and let me share your lift, eh?'

'I tell you before,' the young guy said, taking a step forward and reaching for Moore with his left hand.

It was a rookie mistake.

Moore snatched the hand in his own right and pulled it down and out, jerking the young guy immediately off balance. His left hand flashed out in a bent knuckle strike to the young guy's throat, driving his knuckles into the Adam's apple. The young guy automatically reached for his throat and Moore stepped in, slamming his knee up into the guy's gut.

The pudgy man was turning when Moore pushed past the young guy and kicked him straight in the side of the thigh, brutally hard. The pudgy man shrieked and started to go down, releasing his grip on the girl as he did so.

Moore turned to the young guy again, seeing him leaning against the hallway wall and regathering himself. His right hand was snaking into his jacket for whatever weapon he had concealed there; Moore had to assume it was a gun.

Moore shoulder charged him, slamming him back against the wall and pinning him there sideways, his gun hand trapped between them. He raked the edge of his foot down the guy's shin, ripping his trouser leg and bringing a sharp burst of pain to his opponent. The guy got his left hand free and reached round, scrabbling for Moore's face.

The girl was struggling with the pudgy man, blocking the lift doors open now, and Moore saw her land a good jab to his face.

The young guy's hand was searching for Moore's eyes. Moore seized the hand and ripped it away from his face, bending the fingers back and pulling away, opening the guy up again for another strike. The guy was strong though, and faster than Moore had anticipated. His right came up in a hook to Moore's ribs that took the wind out of his sails.

As Moore absorbed that the guy snapped a foot into his ankle and a right jab to the side of Moore's head. Black spots burst in his skull and he staggered back into the wall. The young guy pulled his jacket open and went for a pistol in his waistband.

Moore lashed out wildly with his foot and connected with the guy's knee, distracting him long enough for Moore to push off the wall and regather himself. He snapped a double left jab to the guy's face and followed through with a solid right hook, knocking the young guy sideways. Moore stepped into him, slamming a knee into his thigh and going for an elbow strike to the temple that should put him down.

As he moved into the strike the pudgy man crashed into him from behind and slammed him into the wall. The young guy staggered clear and went for his gun again.

Moore pushed away from the pudgy man, grabbing him by the collar and jerking him aside, knowing he didn't have time to get to the young guy before he drew the gun.

The pudgy man was flailing at him, but the girl was free of him now. Moore saw the young guy get his hand on the pistol and start to clear it.

The girl pounced forward, landing a decent kick to the guy's hip as he twisted away from her. She was on him then, fists flashing at his face then grabbing at his gun arm. They struggled together like a couple of drunks on a dance floor.

The pudgy guy started yelling now and grabbing for Moore's face. Moore turned and threw him against the wall. As the guy bounced off he took an elbow strike to the nose that dropped him like a sack of spuds.

The other two were still wrestling when Moore came in, and he could see that although the girl was obviously strong, the guy was going to win the battle. The young guy saw him coming and twisted the girl in between them as a shield.

Moore grabbed the back of the girl's jacket and held her steady while reaching past her and raking the guy's face with clawed fingers. The guy shrieked and closed his eyes, momentarily distracted. It was long enough.

The girl had the guy's gun arm still gripped tightly, and Moore pushed her to the side, exposing the young guy's back to him. He slammed a brutal jab to the guy's kidneys, then another, feeling him start to slump. The girl pulled the gun arm out and locked onto the hand, which was gripping an old Tokarev automatic.

Moore drove his foot into the back of the guy's knee, buckling the leg and sending him to a half kneel, following up with a vicious rabbit punch to the side of his neck.

He could hear loud voices and running feet from the direction of the stairwell. It was time to get the hell out of Dodge.

The girl had the pistol free and the young guy was effectively out of the game for now, moaning and gasping on the floor. The pudgy guy was starting to get up, his face bloodied.

'Gimme that.' Moore snatched the Tokarev from the girl and dropped the magazine from it. As he racked the slide and cleared the chamber the girl moved towards the pudgy man and booted him hard between the legs.

He let out a strangled cry and clutched himself as he fell forwards.

'Arsehole,' she snarled at him, and Moore looked at her with surprise. She had a distinctly Kiwi accent.

He tossed the pistol aside as the door from the stairs burst open and a man charged through, a club of some sort in his hand. There were at least two other heads behind him, and they were moving fast.

'Let's go!'

Moore grabbed the girl's arm and pulled her with him towards Room 332. The door crashed open with a single kick, the lock exploding this time, and they raced in.

A shot sounded behind them, removing any doubt about the intentions of the Turks.

Moore dragged the cheap dresser into the doorway and moved to the bed, knowing they only had seconds before the guys were on them. The girl clicked on and helped him flip the mattress up and ram it into the tight doorway as well. It wouldn't keep them for long, but it was better than nothing.

He hurried to the windows and swung one open, looking down. They were three floors up but there was a canopy over the footpath below. No balconies and no trucks conveniently parked. He glanced at the girl. Maybe sixty five kilos, he reckoned; fifty percent lighter than him.

She joined him at the window, looking down first and then at him.

'Are you fucking kidding?'

'You wanna get shot instead?'

The door was getting pounded now, bodies crashing against it. They had about five seconds if they were lucky.

'Get up there.' Moore helped her climb onto the window ledge and edge out. 'Aim for the canopy,' he said.

'No shit.' She took a breath and jumped.

Moore quickly climbed up behind her, seeing her hit the canopy on her side and bounce, one side of the canopy's frame bending under her weight. She was moving for the edge when he dropped, his gut leaping into his throat as the wind rushed past him.

He went down sideways and hit the canopy like a spastic starfish, trying to spread the impact and avoid plunging straight through the canvas. It ripped immediately and the frame broke, dumping him in a tangle on the ground in front of a group of shocked tourists. Phone cameras flashed as he hauled himself to his feet and looked up.

Two of the guys were glaring down from the open window at them.

14

'This way.' The girl was gesturing for him to hurry up, and he did as he was told.

They legged it down the cobbled street, ducking into the first side street and into the first alley off that. The girl was fast and Moore worked hard to keep up.

The city was still waking up and Moore felt horribly exposed as they ran down the nearly empty roads.

After another turn he called her to a stop.

'Take your jacket off,' he told her, stripping off his own shell. He crammed it into a rubbish bin and untucked his shirt. The girl followed suit but held onto her jacket.

'Can't I just carry it?' she said, 'I don't want to dump it.'

'They'll be looking for us and they'll remember our clothing,' he said. 'Ditch it, we need to keep moving.'

She reluctantly binned it, immediately looking different in her grey cargoes and blue long sleeved top.

'Catch your breath and get your head together,' Moore told her. 'If those guys find us we're fucked. Stick with me and do what I say, okay?'

He could see her natural instinct was to question him, and he bit his tongue. Generation fucking Y were supposed to be smart and strong; he hoped that was true.

He led her at a brisk walk to the end of the road, scanning constantly for threats. They found a taxi parked up, and woke the slumbering driver.

'The President Hotel please mate.' Moore climbed in the back with the girl and kept an eye out as they drove to the large hotel.

Alighting there, Moore quickly found another taxi and told the driver to take them to the Spice Market.

'Market not open yet,' the driver said in a thick accent.

'No problem,' Moore smiled genially, and waggled his fingers like legs, 'walkie walkie.'

The driver grunted and accepted the fare, dropping them outside the market. He grunted again when Moore paid him, but said nothing else.

They got out and found an ATM. Moore took a large lump of cash out and pocketed it, then did the same with a second card. Whatever he'd just got himself involved in, somebody would be looking for them. They had to keep moving and leave no sign. Cash was king.

He saw the girl watching him as he did his transactions, and he wondered for the hundredth time exactly who she was and what she was up to.

The next stop was a shop just opening that sold all the usual overpriced junk aimed at tourists. Moore found the hat rack and grabbed a couple of tacky caps, adding a pair of touristy T-shirts. The girl waited silently while he paid in cash. Moore went outside and took his shirt off, pulled the T-shirt on then added the hat. He looked to the girl.

'I'm not taking my top off,' she said.

'Put it over the top then,' he replied tersely, 'I'm not looking for a perv.'

She did so, adjusted the cap and waited while he binned his shirt.

'Right,' Moore said, putting his hand out. 'I'm Rob.'

'Katie.' She shook hands firmly and seemed to thaw slightly.

'Let's go for a walk first then get a coffee and get acquainted.'

. . .

TWENTY MINUTES later they were at a table with a makeshift breakfast.

'I'm looking for my friend,' Katie said. 'She's gone missing over here somewhere.'

'Natalie Oldham?'

She nodded. 'You obviously know who she is, and who her dad is.'

'Uh-huh.'

'I saw you lurking round the hotel,' she said. 'You're obviously looking for her too.'

Moore nodded. 'How do you know her?'

'I used to flat with Nat at Otago Uni,' Katie explained, 'she came to the UK before me. I only came over a few months ago and crashed at her place.'

'In Sutton?' Moore took a sip of his coffee. It was thick and strong and welcome. The café was on the outer of the Grand Bazaar, which didn't open for another half hour.

Katie nodded. 'I'm sharing a room with another mate of hers-we're both all over the place with shifts and stuff, so it works okay.'

Moore nodded, thinking back to the second room he'd searched in the flat.

'You're not Shelley Parker then?' he said.

'No. Katie Simpson. Shelley's the other chick, she's an Aussie. Her and Nat temped together for a bit.' She looked at him suspiciously as she sipped her coffee. 'How d'you know about her?'

Moore shrugged non-committedly. He wasn't prepared to play all his cards just yet. 'Who do you work for?' he asked instead.

'I'm with an agency at the moment, temping. Office work. I'm supposed to be starting an investigation job next week, in the NHS.'

Moore cocked an eyebrow. 'You're a cop?'

She nodded. 'Back home, yeah. I took unpaid leave for two years for an OE.' She smiled wryly. 'It was going great.'

'Where are you based back home?'

'Porirua, Hutt Valley. I'm a Detective,' she said with obvious pride.

Moore nodded. Things were starting to fall into place. The Hutt

Valley and Kapiti-Mana were neighbours to the capital city, but they were different beasts. Wellington was home to politicians, commerce and plenty of white collars. Porirua and the Hutt were home to meth heads, gangsters and all other categories of degenerates. It made sense then that she was no stranger to fights and aggression.

'So how did you end up in Istanbul, snooping around?' he asked.

Katie smirked and put her cup down. 'Hold on a second,' she said, 'what about you? Who are you? What're you doing here?'

She waited him out as he carefully considered his response. She was clearly used to being the one asking the questions, not answering them.

'My name is Rob. I work for the New Zealand embassy in London.' He gave a self-deprecating grin. 'Just a pen-pushing civil servant, but I'm trying to find Natalie.'

'Because of who her old man is, or just because she's a Kiwi who's gone missing?'

Moore shrugged. 'Both, I guess. Her father being a Cabinet Minister adds an edge to it I suppose, but I'd probably be here anyway if he wasn't.'

She raised a doubtful eyebrow but said nothing. 'Who were those guys at the hotel?'

'No idea.' He drained his cup and reached for the pastry it had come with. 'They didn't like you though.'

'True that,' she agreed. She took a bite of her own pastry. 'They didn't really say much, just grabbed me and pulled me out. Then you came along. Did they shoot at us?'

'Yep.'

She nodded and absorbed that. Moore figured she'd probably never been shot at before. She brushed a crumb from her lip and narrowed her gaze. 'You were pretty handy back there.'

'Well I don't normally jump out of windows when I first meet someone,' he smiled, 'but it seemed like a good idea at the time.' He touched his right side gingerly. 'Kinda hurt a bit though.'

She looked like she was going to say something but changed her mind and held back. That was okay; he didn't really want to answer too many questions just yet.

'So what do we do now?' she asked instead.

'I need to make a call,' he said. 'I don't think talking to the cops here will do much good.'

'Already did,' she replied. 'Got nowhere.'

'Did you give them your details? Name, where you were staying?'

'Yeah.'

He considered that. Possibly the guys at the hotel had been cops then. Or maybe intelligence officers. Either way it didn't matter. She was now known to the Turkish police, and it wouldn't take a genius to link her to the hotel incident.

It put them in a very precarious position.

'Right,' Moore said, 'as of now we need to keep our heads down. You can't go back to your hotel, and we definitely can't go back to the Altan.'

'What about my stuff? I've got my camera, my tablet...'

He shook his head firmly. 'No. No way. Those guys that tried to lift you were probably either cops or intelligence. If not, then they were bad guys. None of those are good options.'

She frowned, clearly unhappy about losing all her gear. 'So what do we do then? I've got my wallet and phone and that's it.'

'Passport?'

'In my bag.'

Moore pursed his lips thoughtfully. 'Never mind, we can sort that out later. Right now we need to get to Ankara. I'll make a phone call.'

'What's in Ankara?'

He looked at her as he dug out his phone. 'The embassy.'

15

Since the last resident left after an untidy drug scandal almost a year ago, the High Commission in Ankara did not have an intelligence officer on the staff.

Instead they relied on their military attaché for such services, and Moore had dealt with him before. Jeff Jenkins was an experienced RNZAF Squadron Leader, winding down the military term of his working life with a view to moving into another chapter. He was a fanatical marathon runner and amateur photographer, both habits which were of use in his role.

He answered the phone immediately when Moore rang. The conversation lasted two minutes and Moore and Katie were soon on the move again.

Another taxi took them to a car rental agency, where Moore hired a silver Audi A3 for three days with full insurance cover and a card for the toll gates on the expressways. The guy behind the desk did his best to sell an upgrade and extension of the term, all done with the biggest smile and most sincere advice for his best customer, but he was fighting a losing battle. Moore compromised and took a GPS unit to shut him up, and minutes later they were on the road.

Moore stopped at a service station to fuel up on gas and supplies, including snacks, bottled water and toothbrushes and paste. He grabbed them each a pair of cheap sunglasses and found a paper map on a rack-GPS wasn't always the best option. He also snaffled a car charger for his iPhone, having left his back at the Altan Hotel.

He needed to get his hands on at least a couple of pay-as-you-go phones, but that would have to wait until later.

Katie proved to be a good navigator and got them out of the city and heading west. He got her to use the map system on his phone instead of the rental agency's GPS unit; even though they were easily enough traced through the car's own computer and the toll road cameras, the less sign they left behind the better.

'Four hundred and fifty k's,' Katie said, settling back into her seat with the iPhone in her lap. She pointed ahead. 'Go that way for ages.'

He cocked an eyebrow at her as he accelerated and joined the flow. 'Really? That's your advice?'

She shrugged and tucked her hands between her thighs. He noticed they were firm and slim in her cargoes. 'It's what the map lady says.'

Moore focussed on his driving, finding the traffic a challenge. Indicators seemed to be optional and there were clearly an excess of driver's licenses in the Weetbix packets here. He had a million thoughts jumbling in his head right now, but he needed to stay focussed on the task at hand.

Thinking three steps ahead but taking one at a time was the key to staying in the game. He didn't know exactly what they were dealing with, but it was clearly more than just some rich kid running away to "find" herself. The fact that there were others involved-either cops, the intelligence service or organised crime-was not good. In this part of the world he considered them all to be enemies until proven otherwise.

Organised crime could mean human traffickers or ransom-demanding kidnappers. Spooks meant big trouble-politicians, spies and big business all went hand in hand. Cops in Third World countries were always bad news. Corruption was rife and it was easy for people to disappear.

His mind turned to Paul Oldham and his sidekick, Tristan. There was no doubt that Oldham could pay a ransom if one was demanded, but it hadn't been. He wondered if the politico was involved in something else, maybe something shady, something that wasn't being disclosed just yet. Definitely possible, if not probable.

One of his most pressing needs right now was to get rid of the girl. Even though she was a cop and seemed to be doing okay so far, this was a whole different ball game. Cops weren't trained for this sort of gig and she would just be a liability. He needed to debrief her then hand her over to JJ at the embassy and move on with the hunt.

As he glanced at her sideways he found her staring straight back at him. Although her eyes were shielded by her sunnies, the set of her jaw told him she knew what he was thinking. There was a stubbornness there and he knew she would not take kindly to his plan.

Moore looked away and concentrated on the road ahead.

Too fucking bad, he thought to himself. This was no game of tiddly-winks.

16

JJ called them five minutes before their scheduled meet and gave them directions to a café on the outskirts of Goksu Park in the heart of the city.

As a meeting place it was ideal-being a major tourist attraction the park was large and busy, providing plenty of cover in open sight. It also made sense to change the meeting place at the last minute, allowing JJ to hopefully spot any tail they may have picked up along the way.

Moore followed Katie's directions and kept a subtle eye out while he did so, but by the time they alighted from the Audi he had not seen his colleague or any other watchers.

They walked the last block to the café, taking their time and switching back twice before Moore was confident he'd spotted the watchers. He stopped outside a restaurant and called JJ.

'The girl in the grey jacket,' Moore said without preamble, 'she one of yours?'

JJ chuckled down the line. 'Yep.'

Moore watched the woman walk past on the opposite side of the road, seemingly oblivious to their presence. She looked like a local. Late twenties, shoulder length dark hair, stockyish build.

'What about the guy in the brown long sleeved shirt with the daypack?'

Moore could still see him from the corner of his eye, standing around aimlessly near the corner of the street, looking everywhere but at them. If he was one of JJ's contractors, he was clearly new at the game.

'Not mine,' JJ replied, an edge to his voice now. 'I've only got the one. I have you outside the restaurant with the green door. Where's he?'

'Fifty metres from us on the corner, east side. Local, mid-twenties, stubble.'

There was a momentary pause. 'Don't know him. You sure?'

'A hundy. He took us from our car to here.'

'Could be MIT,' JJ said, referring to the Millî İstihbarat Teşkilâtı, or National Intelligence Organisation. 'Unlikely though.'

'Either way, we're blown. I'm ditching this phone and I'll call you in exactly'-Moore checked his watch-'twenty one minutes. Find another RV.'

He abruptly disconnected and turned to Katie, who had been listening silently. 'Let's go.'

As they walked away from the watcher he quickly deleted his call log. He had no contacts or messages saved. That done, he powered off the iPhone. If they were being tracked via its GPS, he needed to make it as hard as possible.

He turned left into the first alley they came to and they sprinted down it together. Moore hurled the handset onto the roof of the building as they reached the end and turned right.

'Nice and easy now,' Moore said, slowing to a walk and catching his breath.

Katie fell into step beside him. 'What the hell is going on?' she said.

'Don't know, but somehow we got burned,' Moore replied. 'We can't meet with JJ because we don't know if he's been burned too or not, so we need to get space and reassess.'

They cut left into a side street, moving among ambling

pedestrians.

'Right now he'll be on the move too, and at least he knows the area and has someone watching his back.'

Katie shot him a look as they reached the end of the street and paused. 'So you're not a pen-pusher from the Embassy then?' she said sarcastically.

Moore eyed her seriously. 'Not really,' he said. He gripped her arms. 'You need to trust me and do what I say, when I say it. I don't know who's rumbled us, but whoever it is is probably electronically tracking us somehow.'

'Even I ID'd that guy though,' she replied, 'they're not that good.'

'He's probably just a diversion,' Moore said tersely, 'to see what we're going to do.' He checked his watch again. 'We've gotta move.'

They headed off again and waved down the first taxi they saw.

Moore suddenly realised he had no idea of where to go and felt his cheeks redden as the grease-haired young driver stared at him in the rearview mirror.

'Tarman Hotel please,' Katie said.

The driver scowled. 'Two minutes,' he said thickly, 'you walk.'

'No no no, you drive,' she told him. She leaned forward and patted Moore's knee as she gave the driver an apologetic look. 'He is not very well, you see.' She whispered conspiratorially, 'He's old.'

She gave the driver an impish grin and he finally relented, shaking his head to himself. Moore sat back and looked at her, saying nothing.

The driver dropped them outside the small hotel and Moore handed him enough cash to make up for the short ride. They waited until the cab drove off before walking away. Moore checked his watch again.

'Fourteen minutes,' he said. 'We need to change our clothes and get new phones. Nice work on the directions, by the way. How'd you know about this place?'

Katie shrugged. 'I just remember the name from the map, that's all. It flagged up and I remembered it because it sounded like "tarmac."'

'And "old"?' he said. 'You couldn't think of something better than that?'

She shrugged again, grinning this time. 'It worked, didn't it?'

They found a small shop nearby that sold cheap phones amongst a plethora of other cheap crap, and Moore paid cash for two phones and SIM cards. It cost extra for charged batteries but he didn't care; he didn't have time to shag around waiting.

He flagged another cab and asked to be taken to the nearest department store. After some translation issues and the passing of cash they arrived eight minutes before he was due to call JJ back.

'Full change of clothes, two or three sets,' he said, 'and something to carry it in.'

'In eight minutes?' Katie said. 'I'm a girl. Are you fuckin' serious?'

'Ten minutes,' he replied. 'Meet me back here. Go.'

Katie shook her head and headed straight for the women's department. Moore made his way to the men's area and in five minutes he had selected three full sets of clothes including socks and underwear. He deliberately chose plain, unremarkable gear that would help him blend into the background. He grabbed a small suitcase from the luggage section and shoved everything into it, before firing up one of the burn phones and dialling JJ.

'Ormani Hotel,' JJ said quickly, 'room 512. See you there in one hour.'

He cut off and Moore stripped the phone down, dropping the pieces in his pocket as he headed back to RV with Katie. To his surprise she was waiting, her arms full of clothes and a suitcase at her feet.

'I hate shopping,' she said as soon as she saw him. 'And none of this will probably fit anyway.'

Moore gave a small smile and led the way to the payment desk.

His credit card took another hit. He knew it would leave an electronic trail, but the bad guys knew they were there anyway. Five minutes later they entered another department store, making straight for the public toilets.

Moore was pleased to find the toilets were new rather than the old hole in the floor, unoccupied and smelling of disinfectant. He smashed the pieces of the used burn phone and flushed them down the drain first.

There was no disabled access so he locked himself in a cubicle with his suitcase balanced on the commode and stripped off completely. After removing the tags from his new clothes he dressed again quickly, the clothes fitting well enough for what he needed.

He crammed all his old gear into one of the plastic shopping bags and wrestled his way out of the cubicle again. Katie emerged from the women's toilets ten minutes later, also carrying a shopping bag full of her old gear. She was right about the new clothes-not the best fit and she looked more like a 40 year old housewife than a 20-something traveller in comfortable jeans, a chambray shirt over a T-shirt and a pair of flat shoes.

She looked irritated and Moore was too slow suppressing a grin.

'Don't say a goddamn word,' she warned him as they headed for the exit. 'If this wasn't a serious situation I'd hate you right now.'

They walked to a side alley and found a Dumpster to dispose of their old gear, before Moore called a stop to regroup.

He was running low on cash and they also needed to get their bearings. Spotting an ATM further down, he sent Katie to it with his card while he checked the map and got his head together. By the time she got back with a wad of cash he had a plan to brief her on. After running through it and having her repeat it back to him, he did the same with a contingency plan.

He noted that she didn't question the need for a back-up plan, and was pleased that the gravity of their situation had sunk in.

That done, he checked his watch again.

'Forty five minutes,' he said,' let's go.'

YET ANOTHER TAXI ride took them to a café a block south from the Ormani and Moore sent the driver on his way with a hefty tip. As per their plan, Katie found a table inside the café and slid the two suitcases in beside her. Moore got coffees for them both and took his with him when he left, also leaving her the second burn phone. He found another kiosk and bought himself a replacement phone, paying twice as much as last time for a charged battery. He gave Katie a hang up call so she had his number and carried on, conscious of time.

Given the events of the last few hours, Moore was trusting nothing and it was important to get eyes on the hotel before the meet. There was no way he wanted to blindly stumble into something, and he also didn't want to compromise JJ; diplomatic status didn't always count for much.

Moore sipped his coffee and acted as nonchalant as he could while he did a walk past of the hotel's front entrance. He boxed around and did a complete circuit of the hotel before finding a doorway to watch from across the road and several buildings down. The hotel was eight stories high, all white and glass, with a ground floor restaurant and bar.

The front entrance was busy with cars and pedestrians coming and going. It was a good place for a meet; busy enough that it was easy to blend in. It was a concern that there was also rear and side entrances, but there was nothing he could do about that.

With eight minutes to go Moore spotted JJ's female assistant doing a walk by, and two minutes later she entered the front of the building. She carried herself confidently, and when she looked over her shoulder as she entered the lobby, he got a quick look at her face. She wasn't unattractive.

Moore wondered idly if JJ was tapping her. If he was, who cared? Moore knew he was in no position to make moral judgements. JJ was a minute behind her, walking purposefully with a briefcase in one hand and a coffee in the other. He was a lean man in his late forties with thinning brown hair and the easy gait of a runner.

Moore gave him another two minutes then followed, ditching his coffee cup before cutting round the side of the hotel and taking the less-used side entrance. He wasn't challenged as he took the lift to the fifth floor, the doors opening softly into an empty corridor.

17

Room 512 was to the left and he knocked twice then once more before standing back from the door.

JJ opened it and ushered him inside, securing the door behind him. Moore took in the studio room at a glance. There was no sign of JJ's assistant. JJ himself was keyed up.

'I don't know who that watcher was,' he said. 'As far as I know I wasn't followed and the MIT don't know you're here.'

'What about your sidekick?' Moore queried, going to the side of the window for a glance out.

'Evin? No. She's a pro.' JJ shook his head firmly.

'Well we've completely changed outfits,' Moore said, 'so hopefully that's shaken whoever it is.'

'Good. Here.' JJ opened the briefcase on the bed and showed Moore the contents. Inside was the holstered Sig P229R pistol he had sent from London with two spare magazines and a box of ammo, a new iPhone, an envelope of cash and his legend package-passport, driver license and two credit cards, all unused. There was also a new passport in Katie's name, backdated and carrying sufficient stamps and marks to appear genuine.

He checked the pistol, chambered a round and secured the

holster to his belt.

'You sure about this?' JJ asked, a trace of nervousness in his voice. 'You get caught with that here and you're fucked, mate. We won't be able to help you.'

Moore glanced at him as he distributed the other items around his pockets. 'I get caught without it and I'm fucked,' he replied tersely. 'Somebody already took a pop at us this morning.'

'Yes, us; what's the story with this girl? Obviously she's a friendly?'

Moore succinctly filled him in and JJ listened intently. When the briefing was over the former airman nodded once.

'Right,' he said. 'I'll leave it to you to update Mr Ingoe and be in touch. Where will you be?'

'Around,' Moore said vaguely. He trusted JJ but the less anyone knew, the better. 'I'll give you a ring once I know whether today's events change anything for the Director. Either way, I need to get rid of this girl. If I'm sticking around, she can hop a plane back home. If not, I guess I can take her back.'

JJ cocked an eyebrow and smirked. 'Tasty is she, Rob? You dirty dog, you know what they say about dipping the wick...'

'Huh.' Moore snorted. 'I'm old enough to be her father, man. And she knows it.'

'Many a fine tune...'

Moore ignored the ribbing, but was pleased to see the other man had relaxed somewhat. The wrong kind of tension led to mistakes, and mistakes could be fatal. 'Let's go,' he said. 'You leading the way?'

'Visitors first, mate,' JJ replied, sticking out his hand. They shook firmly and JJ ushered him to the door. 'I'll hear from you, hotshot.'

Moore opened the door and gave him a wolfish grin. 'Watch your back, flyboy.'

With that he was gone, taking the stairs at the opposite end of the floor to the lift. As he descended, his mind was buzzing as he planned the next moves. He hit the third floor landing at the same time as he heard a door open somewhere above him. He paused and looked up, just in time to see a flicker of movement as if someone had stepped back from the railing.

Moore froze, all his senses pinging. He heard a door open again and close softly, maybe three floors up. Or was it on the fifth? He wasn't sure, and was torn between competing needs. His operational head told him to keep moving, get distance from the meeting point, but his heart was shouting at him to go and check on JJ.

'Bollocks,' he muttered to himself, shaking the paranoia off and continuing downstairs; JJ was a big boy and could handle himself. Moore's priority right now was to get the hell out of Ankara and find out where he stood.

He hit the ground floor and took the rear entrance, boxing north around another block before doubling back on himself abruptly and scanning for watchers. Despite not seeing anything obvious his antenna was going nuts and he couldn't shake the feeling he was being watched. He tried another couple of blocks, throwing in plenty of angles, but still saw nothing.

With his hackles on edge he made his way west and gradually south for another twenty minutes, before deciding it was time to just get the hell out of there.

Katie was waiting patiently and saw him coming. She passed him his suitcase and together they exited the café, leaving a tip on the table for the chubby waitress.

They walked south and took a couple of turns before Moore finally spoke, guiding Katie into a shopping centre. They stopped just inside the floor to ceiling glass frontage and he scanned their backs. Satisfied that they were at least temporarily safe, he rapidly brought her up to speed as much as he needed to.

'We're going to leave the car here and head back to Istanbul by train,' he said. 'By then I should know the state of play with finding Natalie, and I'll get you to the airport.' He saw her jaw set and a determined look come into her eyes. He held up a placatory hand. 'I know that's not what you want to hear Katie, but that's how it needs to be okay? It's bloody dangerous here and you're going to be much safer either back in London or Wellington.'

'Fuck that,' Katie retorted, 'I didn't come all this way to be treated like a bloody kid. She's my friend and I promised to find her, so you can either tag along with me or do your own thing, but I'm staying here.'

Moore opened his mouth to argue but she stopped him with a warning finger. He could see the fire in her eyes and felt his own anger rising.

'No,' she said, 'you can play the bloody hero all you like but you don't call the shots for me, alright? I'm here and I'm doing it, whether you like it or not.'

'And how do you plan on doing that with no support, no money, no passport, no plan and no fucking idea what you're doing?' he demanded. 'This ain't tiddlywinks here, this is a Third World country full of bad bastards who don't like nosey palefaces poking around asking questions. Or did you forget that little incident at the hotel?'

At the same time as Katie opened her mouth to reply, Moore saw a familiar figure over her shoulder. Crossing the pavement towards the entranceway was the guy in the long sleeved brown shirt. His eyes had locked onto them and gone was the vaguely confused look. He was oblivious to everyone else around them, zeroing in like a homing beacon.

Moore saw now that he was only in his early twenties and his stubble was patchy. His body still had the slightly gawky, uncertain look of youngsters his age, but his face was set and focussed. 100% concentration.

The second thing Moore noticed was that his torso was bulkier than his frame suggested, with a distinct spread around his chest and stomach above spindly legs in cheap jeans.

His right hand was clutched tight around something, with a wire running from his hand to the folds of his shirt.

His eyes met Moore's as he got closer and his lips tightened, his whole face pinching as he began to move faster, his hands coming out from his sides as if he was welcoming them to his home.

Moore knew instinctively that the only thing the young guy was inviting them to was his own version of paradise. He grabbed Katie's arm and began to run into the mall, dragging her almost off her feet as he shouted, 'Bomb! Get down! Get down!'

18

People turned to look at the two crazy tourists as the young guy stepped across the threshold of the entranceway several metres away and raised his hands, shouting something unintelligible.

Moore threw Katie forward, knocking over another shopper as he dived to the floor and slid, skittling a middle-aged couple like pins and covering his head, his mouth half open. Katie was beside him and shouting something he couldn't hear.

With a thunderous explosion the young martyr detonated, filling the entranceway with a blinding orange and yellow flash. Glass burst out of shop windows.

The entranceway itself and nearby shoppers were thrown like rag dolls as the intense pressure wave burst forth. Wet flesh and shards of bone burst out as the bomber's body was obliterated.

Smoke and dust filled the air and Moore kept his eyes clamped shut tight as he was lifted off the floor and tumbled across the hard polished floor.

When he came to a stop he immediately scanned, seeing Katie a few metres away with her arms over her head.

The bloodied body of a man was twitching beside her and Moore realised he had shielded her from the blast. Everywhere he looked were people screaming and running. An alarm of some sort was sounding. Debris and body parts and blood covered the floor near the site of the detonation. A fallen pot plant was in flames.

His ears were ringing and his mouth was filled with dust. He spat and snorted snot and spat again, trying to get to his feet but getting bowled by a panicked shopper who knocked him flat and stomped on his back.

Moore pushed up and fended off another runner, scrambling towards Katie who was also starting to rise. Her eyes were wide and she was covered in grime. He saw her mouth moving but couldn't hear a word.

He got to her and grabbed her arm, helping her up and shouting at her to move. His voice sounded detached and far away, as if it was someone else speaking.

Her legs went from under her and she dropped to the floor, pulling him off balance. As he started to go down too, he sensed movement to his left, from the direction of the entranceway. Controlled movement rather than the panicked scrambling of the shoppers.

He swivelled, instinctively reaching for the Sig under his jacket, fingers closing on the grip as he spotted the two men. Both were in casual gear with neatly trimmed beards and daypacks. They were focussed on the pair of dazed Kiwis and both had their right hands tucked under the front of their shirts.

Moore knew that if these guys were more suicide bombers then they were fucked. He ripped the Sig free and dropped over Katie, pushing her flat as he took a knee and brought the Sig up, sweeping the safety off.

Sprinklers began to shower everything, adding to the confusion.

If he was lucky he may be able to drop one of them before they took themselves and everyone else to a paradise full of virgins. They were about fifteen metres away now and moving.

It was almost a relief when he saw the guy on the right produce a pistol, shouting something at his mate who was a shade slower.

Screaming people were immediately behind them, and a teenage girl staggered across their path, holding her bloodied hands in front of her as her mouth moved soundlessly.

Moore triggered his first shot into the right hand guy's chest, sweeping left and punching out further, nailing the left hand guy with a double tap in the gut, then moving right again as the first guy started to drop. The first guy involuntarily fired a round into the floor and it whined off into the distance.

Moore snapped a fast shot into his chest, let the guy drop to his knees then rose up and pumped another double tap into his face. Brains and blood splattered the dirty floor behind the body as it slumped down.

The guy on the left was on his side, clutching his gut as blood rapidly leaked out. His pistol was still in his right hand and he tried feebly to raise it. Moore squeezed two rounds into his chest and put him flat on his back. He moved forward and kicked the pistol aside. Lifeless eyes stared up at him. The first guy was leaking fluids in a wide pool.

Moore scanned for more threats, saw nothing, and turned back to Katie. She had got up and was watching in silent horror.

Moore grabbed her hand and hustled her away, further into the shopping centre, keeping the Sig in his hand as they ran from the scene. They reached a back exit and joined the throng of people pushing their way out, getting into the fresh air and hurrying away. Moore holstered his weapon and kept Katie at his side as they got free of the crowd and pushed their way through the onlookers who were flocking to the scene.

Sirens were sounding and already Police cars were arriving.

They made it to the next side street and he slowed the pace, deliberately sucking in air and getting himself back in control.

'Stop,' Katie panted, 'stop stop.'

He pulled up and stood aside as she bent at the waist and emptied her guts on the footpath. She heaved and gasped and spat for a good minute before slowly easing upright and putting her hands on her hips, breathing deeply.

‘What...what the fuck,’ Katie gasped. She spat and wiped a string of saliva from her chin. She unconsciously wiped her hand on the leg of her pants. ‘What the fuck was that?’

Moore rubbed a hand over his face. ‘I think we pissed somebody off.’

19

The Turks were experienced at dealing with terrorist assaults, particularly after the ISIS attack on the Ankara Central Train Station not so many months ago, and in a short space of time the city was locked down.

The bombing had everyone on edge, adding to the tension from the current air strikes over the border, and they barely made it out of the immediate vicinity before roadblocks were in place and armed Police and soldiers were swarming everywhere.

Moore and Katie paused at a shop to buy bottled water and hand sanitiser which they used to wash the dirt and crap off themselves before each draining a bottle to rehydrate. Having lost their suitcases in the chaos back at the shopping centre they were once again in need of supplies, but didn't have time to stop yet.

They ditched their upper layers instead and bought replacement lightweight jackets at a street market before hopping a bus to the train station.

Moore paid cash for tickets for the next train to Istanbul and while they waited they used the toilets to freshen up as best they could. He kept an eye on Katie when they regrouped and bought coffees. She loaded hers with sugar and downed it in silence, avoiding his gaze. He passed her the replacement passport JJ had supplied and a fold of cash in case they got separated.

Once they were settled in their Economy Plus seats Moore ensured there was nobody within earshot before he leaned over and spoke quietly.

'It's okay to be a bit freaked out by it,' he told her. 'It's a horrible experience to be in a situation like that.'

Katie said nothing, just stared out the window as they rolled out of the station.

'I don't know who those guys were, but they were specifically targeting us,' he said. 'Somehow they knew we were there and picked us up. The two guys who came in after the bomber were the clean-up crew, there to make sure the job was done.' He paused, choosing his words carefully. 'The only way to deal with them was to meet force with force. It was them or us.'

'What about the other people?' Katie said quietly, her gaze still fixed out the window. 'What about them? All those people? They did nothing.' She gave a slight shake of her head. Her arms were folded tightly across her body. 'They didn't deserve that.'

Moore nodded silently. 'No,' he said, 'they didn't. They were just innocent victims, in the wrong place at the wrong time. They did nothing to bring that hatred into their world.' He touched her arm gently, and she jumped. He withdrew his hand. 'And neither did you, so it's okay to find that hard to get your head around.'

Katie half turned now, looking at him sideways. Her arms were still wrapped across her belly, holding tight. 'And you?' she asked, an undercurrent of anger in her voice now. 'What about you? Did you bring that hatred into our world?'

Moore said nothing as he considered his answer. It was a curly question.

'Who exactly are you?' she persisted. 'You just blew two dudes away and didn't even blink an eye. I'm puking my fuckin' guts out and you're planning your next move.' She took a breath and stared at him for a long moment. Her pulse was visibly throbbing in her neck. 'That's not normal, man. What's up with that shit?'

Moore gave a mental shrug. She needed to get her head around this and fast. If she didn't, she'd be more of a liability than he already thought.

'I do jobs like this for the Government,' he said softly. 'I used to be in the SAS.'

Katie frowned at him quizzically, not comprehending.

'Army Special Forces,' he explained. 'The Special Air Service.'

She nodded. 'Right. So this is all your buzz then? This is what you do.'

He gave a short nod. 'This is what I do.'

Katie let out a slow breath and unfolded her arms, clasping her hands in her lap instead. 'What the fuck has Natalie got herself into?' she wondered aloud.

Moore sat back and dug out his new iPhone. 'That's what we need to find out,' he said.

They fell into silence while Moore logged into a private chat room. He knew that at the other end there would be some overly intelligent geek monitoring all traffic who could get a message to Ingoe.

DAWN LIGHT WAS CREEPING through the slats of the blind when Archer's mobile buzzed on the bedside table.

It was in his hand before the third ring sounded. The figure next to him stirred.

'Yep.' His throat felt dry and croaky. He hadn't been asleep long.

He listened, his eyes gradually easing open. They were gritty and sore. He nodded to himself as the caller came to the end of the message.

'Right,' Archer rasped, 'I'm on the way.'

He disconnected and slid the phone back onto the bedside table. He checked his watch and hit the back light. Time enough.

He rolled over and slipped an arm around the slumbering form, inhaling her scent and burying his face in the nape of her neck. He felt her begin to respond.

There was definitely time.

20

Adapazari

The Adapazari Railway Station was right in the city centre, so Moore and Katie disembarked and quickly lost themselves in the crowd. Police and soldiers were patrolling the area on foot and the tension in the air was palpable. A TV on the wall in the station was showing footage of the bombing scene and witnesses babbled excitedly to the camera, some in tears.

The last thing they wanted was to be stopped for a shakedown or to stand out from the crowd, so they stayed among other pedestrians, all the while moving with purpose. As the crowds thinned out Moore took Katie's hand and walked decisively to the street, never looking back as they lost themselves in the city centre. She didn't protest at the sudden intimacy.

It didn't take long to find a quieter side street where they could regroup and get their bearings on the iPhone.

'We need to either keep moving or stay put,' Moore said. 'The more we move, the more likely we are to run into a Police checkpoint or something. I'm banking on the cops not knowing who we are though, and our new passports should be enough to get us through.'

'Someone knows who we are though,' Katie interjected, 'and where we were.' Her brow furrowed. 'Someone knows an awful lot.'

'Too true,' he agreed. He could see the stress in her face and her rigid shoulders, and knew she was feeling the immense pressure. 'We could probably do with parking ourselves for a bit, getting a decent feed and hopefully hearing back from the powers that be.' He gave her an encouraging look. 'Don't you think?'

'I won't argue that,' Katie replied. 'I'd kill for a good meal and a stiff drink.'

'Done. But first,' he gave a grin, 'we need to do some more shopping.'

'Fuck that, I hate shopping!'

'Never had a woman argue against shopping before,' he said, 'but you can't book into a decent hotel with no luggage.'

Katie rolled her eyes. 'I know, I know...it just sucks.' She rolled her neck and shoulders as if warming up for a fight. Her joints popped as she moved. 'Come on, let's do it.'

They took a cab to the impressive ADA Shopping Centre, which had exactly what they were looking for. Moore sensed that Katie needed company so stuck with her, patiently waiting while she ducked in and out of shops to make her purchases.

He joined her in a pharmacy to purchase toiletries, otherwise he stayed out of the way. Forty five minutes in he handed her a cup of coffee and took her bags.

'Better?' he asked, as she took a hit of caffeine.

'Mmm, better.' She glanced around them at the usual hustle and bustle of the mall. Despite the signage it could've been a suburban mall in Anytown. 'Certainly a better shopping experience than last time.'

He watched her for signs of overt emotion, but all he saw was sadness. She wrapped her hands around her cup as if she was cold.

'Good,' he said. 'Well if you're finished, you can help me get some gear.'

'God, that's more painful than shopping for myself,' she groaned.

'I'll need some comfortable Y-fronts,' he said, ticking off his fingers, 'some flannelette PJs, Velcro shoes, and a nice pair of slacks. And maybe some adult nappies.'

She pulled a face. 'Okay, sorry about the old man joke. I can't believe you're still sore about that.'

Moore cracked a smile. 'Let's go. It's about time I had some new jeans anyway.'

Ten minutes later he was done and everything was loaded into two suitcases. As Katie observed while waiting for a cab, it was deja vu.

IT WAS late afternoon by the time they checked into a hotel on the outer edge of the central business district.

Moore reluctantly paid with a credit card, knowing that an electronic trail could easily be tracked. At least the card would have a record of use, having been used for regular subscriptions and random bookings like all the cards used to support legends.

He had spent some time trawling the internet before deliberately selecting a standard 4-star hotel regularly used by tourists, knowing that they would melt into the background easily.

A man his age with a much younger woman would stand out using a backpackers' lodge, and he wanted to avoid arousing any suspicion. At least at this place he would just look like any other middle manager away for a dirty city break with his young secretary.

Ideally they would keep moving, get some distance while they waited to hear back from HQ, but he sensed that the recent events had shaken Katie up more than she was letting on. If he was going to be stuck with her for any length of time he needed her to be in one piece.

They took a room on the fourth floor and a porter carried their bags up. Closing the door behind the porter, who was happily tucking a cash tip into his pocket, Moore surveyed the room.

The separate bedroom to the left had an inviting queen size bed that he was confident he would never get to use. The bathroom featured a spa bath which looked equally as inviting-again, he didn't fancy his chances. He had a sudden mental image of Katie slipping naked into it and felt a kick in his chest.

He glanced self-consciously at her, but she was too busy checking the mini bar to notice. He pushed the thought aside and tried the sofa in the living area. That would be his for the night.

He dropped his bag on the luggage rack and took Katie's into the bedroom. She appeared in the doorway behind him, a small bottle of gin in her hand. She fiddled idly with the cap as if unsure whether to open it or not.

'Fill your boots,' he told her. 'I'm just doing a once-over before I get myself sorted.'

'I wasn't sure...are we actually going to stay here?' She looked concerned. 'Or is this another diversion?'

'Unless we have to move for some reason, we're getting our heads down here tonight,' he said. 'Tomorrow's another day.' He gave a smile. 'That couch looks really comfy, so the bed's all yours.'

She gave a wry smile in return. 'What a gentleman.' She cracked the bottle open. 'In that case I'm having a drink and a bath. I think I stink.'

Moore took the bottle from her and stepped past, heading for the kitchenette. 'I make a good gin and tonic,' he said. 'You get your bath ready.'

He busied himself at the bench, half filling a glass with ice before adding a good measure of gin and topping it with a slug of tonic. He was pleased to find a lemon in a glass dish at the mini bar and took a knife to it, adding a healthy slice to the drink before carrying it into the bathroom.

The bath was filling and Katie was watching it absently, her mind clearly elsewhere. Moore handed her the drink and she nodded her thanks. Her earlier confidence had gone and she had withdrawn into herself. She looked like a lost little girl as she took her first apprecia-tive sip.

'Wow,' she said, 'that's got a kick.'

Moore nodded. 'I'll be out there,' he said.

He closed the bathroom door behind him and finished his recce of the room. He wiped clean the small vegetable knife he'd used to cut the lemon, and put it aside as a potential weapon. He located a larger sharp knife and added that to the collection.

The door seemed sturdy enough but the lock was flimsy like on most hotel doors. The screws securing the chain though were bedded properly into a solid frame, and he slipped the chain across. He shifted a chair from the table to just inside the entrance, ensuring the entry of any unwanted visitors would be temporarily obstructed.

The windows didn't open, but he could see a drainpipe within reach if the window were broken.

Recce complete, he checked over his belongings and made sure he was ready to move quickly. He plugged the phone in to charge and checked the chat room messages.

Nothing yet.

Satisfied that, for now, everything that could be done had been done, he settled himself on the couch with the room service menu and a bottle of water. He heard the odd splash from the bathroom and some traffic noise outside but aside from that the room was silent.

He reflected on the day and wondered again exactly how the bad guys-whoever they were-had tracked them. It was a problem that he knew sooner or later would have major consequences-although, of course, a bombing and shootout in a shopping mall was hardly minor. With that in mind he flicked on the TV, finding a local news channel that had current updates on the incident.

It was all in Turkish with no subtitles, but it didn't appear that there was anything new to report. Lots of serious looking people were talking sombrely and there were clips of the carnage.

He knew how lucky they had been to escape with their lives today, and wondered just how long their luck would hold out.

The more he thought about the mission the more he realised he didn't know. But someone did, that much was clear. Someone was behind the scenes, pulling the strings. A puppet master, playing with lives, jerking the strings of the helpless marionettes like Moore and Katie in some macabre game.

There was a name for them in intelligence circles, these people that lived in the shadows, blending with the night like cold blooded chameleons. People that made decisions and took actions that had terrible consequences for others, bringing death and mayhem and upheaval to innocent lives, bringing down governments, dictatorships and democracies alike.

Known as shadow dancers, they were as much a part of the spy world as faceless bureaucrats, financially motivated allegiances and dead letter drops.

Who the shadow dancers were who were at play here, Moore didn't know. But he promised himself, before this mission came to a close, he would.

And revenge would be sweet.

21

When Katie finally emerged from the bathroom she was dressed in jeans and a plain white T-shirt. Her hair was wet and her feet were bare.

The strong gin had helped but her gut was sore from vomiting, and she was sure her eyes were still puffy. She wasn't sure how she should feel-sad? Angry? Thankful she'd survived? She had no idea. She'd dealt with deaths and trauma before, but this was different. There weren't too many suicide bombings in the Hutt Valley.

She found Moore standing at the window, staring out at the twilight sky and the lights beyond the hotel. His back was to her and she watched for a moment, studying him. His broad shoulders tapered to a trim waist. His arms were muscular and hard. His legs were thick and strong.

She wondered his age-he had the physique of someone probably ten years younger than she guessed he was. SAS, he had said. She knew a little about them, having grown up with a brother who had been an armchair warrior.

Tough, ruthless soldiers. Highly trained killers.

He had certainly shown that today, the way he'd first reacted to the bomber and then taken out the two gunmen, barely batting an eyelid. Fast and efficient, all over before she even knew what was happening. She'd seen the Armed Offenders Squad in action back home, the Black Pyjama Boys as they were known, armed up and all in black, crashing into the lairs of bad men to take them down without a shot fired.

She'd always been secretly in awe of them, as many cops secretly were.

But this guy, this Rob Moore-if that was even his real name anyway-was in a different league altogether. He scared her and made her feel safe at the same time.

As he turned to her the ambient light caught the silver at his temples. His face was shadowed as he smiled at her. He had a nice smile, she thought. Genuine.

Katie realised he was speaking and she snapped back into the now. 'Sorry?'

'I said we should get something to eat. You must be hungry.'

She wondered if he had heard her throwing up in the bathroom. She felt embarrassed.

'I know I'm starving,' he continued. 'Room service okay?'

Katie shrugged. 'Yep. I'm not that hungry, but that'll be fine.'

She took the menu he passed her and quickly scanned it. 'Lamb mussaka,' she said.

Moore rang down, adding a chicken pilich kebab for himself plus a feta and olive salad to share. He poured her a glass of water and they sat on the couch. A news reel was showing details of the bombing. Katie took control of the remote and flicked through until she found a movie. They watched in silence and it took her a minute to recognise the movie.

'Is this Austin Powers?' she asked.

'Uh-huh.'

She glanced sideways at Moore. He was fully engaged with the movie, a constant half smile on his face. He chuckled as the bad-toothed swinging lead character danced to an old Divinyls song, the chuckle graduating to a full laugh by the time the fembots began to explode.

Katie grinned to herself. 'Based on reality then?' she said.

'Yep.' He nodded earnestly. 'I always defeat the baddies by dancing provocatively.'

'And they always wear next to nothing?'

'Totally. And have machine gun jubblies.'

'Jubblies?' She cocked an eyebrow and laughed. 'Really, is there no better name?'

'Would you prefer dirty pillows?'

'What?'

'You need to watch the whole movie.'

The room service order arrived and Moore took it from the waiter at the door. Katie watched, guessing that he was deliberately not allowing an unknown into the room. While he secured the door again she uncovered the food and took a seat. She dug a fork in for the first taste, and looked up as Moore joined her.

'Sorry,' she said through a mouthful, 'I couldn't wait. This is so good.' She covered her mouth self-consciously. 'How rude.'

'Get into it,' Moore said, sitting opposite her. 'It smells great.'

She tucked in and subtly observed as he made short work of his kebab and cleaned up most of the salad as well. He was a systematic eater, leaning over his plate and taking big bites, seeming to relish every mouthful.

As Katie ate she felt herself begin to relax. Her pace slowed down and she felt the colour returned to her cheeks. Finally she sat back with a satisfied sigh and wiped her mouth on a napkin.

'That was great.' She popped a stray olive into her mouth and chewed. 'I needed that.'

Moore nodded and stood, going to the phone again. He called Room Service to order Turkish apple tea for two. When he sat again he used the last piece of bread to wipe his plate clean.

Katie sipped her water and studied him across the table.

'Penny for your thoughts,' he said, wiping his hands and sitting back.

She shrugged. 'Nothing.'

'Feeling a bit better?'

She nodded. 'Yep. Sleepy though. I'm knackered.' Just saying it made her yawn.

Moore smiled, automatically yawning too. 'It's the post-adrenaline rush. Your body dumps this huge amount of adrenaline in your body when it feels under threat. When you don't need it anymore you drop from a hundred to zero.'

Katie nodded, saying nothing.

'Sometimes you get the shakes, the jitters. Sometimes you throw up or get the shits. Usually you get tired.'

Katie wondered if it was normal to have all the symptoms in one hit. She felt him watching her and avoided his gaze. She didn't want to discuss it right now. He probably knew anyway.

The waiter arrived and they drank hot sweet apple tea, served in glasses, on the couch. The curtains blocked the world outside and created a safe cocoon where Katie could relax. She felt her eyelids getting heavy and took their glasses out.

'See you in the morning,' she said, heading for the bathroom. She paused at the door and looked back. Moore craned his head, looking at her expectantly. 'Thanks,' she said. 'You saved my life today.'

Moore gave a small nod, a twinkle in his eye. 'Yeah, baby.'

Katie gave a short laugh and shook her head. 'I mean it. Thank you.'

Moore gave an appreciative nod. 'All good,' he said. 'Sleep well.'

Katie hesitated, wondering if she should invite him into her bed. He was a good looking man, she thought. She wondered what it would be like to be held in those strong arms, for him to make love to her. She felt a stirring, hesitated again, and mentally shook her head.

'Goodnight,' she said.

22

Moore was woken suddenly.

Both eyes snapped open and he lay perfectly still, all senses alert. Something had disturbed him, something intangible. The room was silent and dark. He pushed the blanket aside and rolled off the couch, halfway to his feet when he heard the key in the lock.

Dressed only in his briefs he snatched up the Sig from the floor beside him, the door crashing against the safety chain. There was a muttered oath then a louder crash as a body impacted against the door.

Moore sprang over the couch towards Katie's door, the door smashing open behind him.

'Katie!'

Men burst in and torch beams swept the room, accompanied by at least two red laser sights.

He heard Katie's feet hit the floor at the same time as the beams found him. In that split second he had to decide how to react. He had no doubt he could hold his own in a shootout, but if these guys had pro gear then they were probably pros, and legit. He couldn't afford to shoot a cop or an intelligence officer.

A red dot centred on his chest and a thick accent shouted, 'Drop it!'

Moore slowly put the Sig down, raising his hands. A dark figure recovered the weapon. Torch beams blinded him. Katie came to his side, dressed only in the white T-shirt and pale blue cotton knickers. She pressed against his side, her nails digging into his arm.

There were at least three torch beams covering them and Katie also had a red laser dot on her chest now. Any false moves and they would be mowed down.

'On the floor! Face down!'

'Do as they say,' Moore said quietly.

'No talking!'

They started to get down on the floor but before they were down one of the men lunged forward and grabbed Katie by the arm, yanking her forward and tossing her to the floor away from Moore.

He resisted the urge to react, spread eagling himself instead. Two men moved forward and dropped on him, knees in the back holding him down, a hand pressing his face into the carpet. His arms were jerked behind his back and bound with flexi-cuffs.

A hand on his face wrenched his head back and a hood was pulled over it, plunging him into total blackness.

The hood was claustrophobic and smelled like onions. It felt like sacking. His eyes began to water with the stench and he forced himself to breathe as best he could with two men kneeling on him.

Panic was a killer.

He was kept down that way for another minute or so before being hustled to his feet. Nothing further was said as he was manhandled from the room, his captors making sure they bounced him off the doorframe as he went through.

Moore sucked it up, knowing the drill.

They led him down the hall to the stairs, hurrying him down with strong hands under his arms, barely needing his own feet to move him. When they reached what he judged to be the basement a door opened and he felt a rush of cold air on his exposed skin.

He could smell exhaust fumes and heard a car running. He could also hear movement behind him somewhere, hopefully Katie; it would be better if they weren't separated.

A sliding door was cranked back and he was bustled into what he guessed was a people mover, shoved into the back seat with a captor squeezing in beside him. A gun barrel was jabbed in his ribs.

He heard more movement and the vehicle shifted as more bodies took the seat in front of him.

Maybe they weren't as pro as he'd first thought; it was more effective to separate the prisoners, isolate them, leave them wondering. At least if Katie knew he was near she may take some strength from that. He cleared his throat to let her know he was there and the gun barrel jabbed in painfully.

'Shut up,' a guttural voice growled.

He heard a cough in return and knew she'd switched on. Good girl.

The door slid shut and the vehicle moved off.

Moore tracked their movements in his head for about the first minute before he lost it. They were in a strange foreign city, captured at gunpoint by an unknown enemy, caught with a gun and literally their pants down.

Whatever was going on, Moore thought, they were fucked.

23

After what Moore estimated to be half an hour the vehicle pulled off the road into an alley or driveway, the tyres crunching on gravel or litter before pulling up sharply. The door slid open and the people in front of him were moved out.

Hands grabbed him and dragged him out, banging his head on the doorframe as he stumbled out. One of the men chuckled.

No, he thought, not as pro as he'd thought.

The air was fresh and cool, and he could smell garbage. He took another sniff. Animals and pasture. A farm, maybe.

He was hustled across stony ground then onto what felt like dirt and loose straw. The smell of animals was stronger. It felt like they were inside now.

The unseen men manhandled him across the floor, a door opened and he was shoved into another room. The floor was cold bare concrete. He stopped himself and straightened up, hearing Katie cough again. He turned in that direction, just in time to take an unexpected fist to the gut. He moved with it, bending over but sensing the knee coming up towards his face and twisting away enough to take it on the shoulder instead.

A kick buckled his knee from behind and he started to go down, a body slam knocking him flat.

Moore braced himself, curling his knees up, knowing what was coming.

Lights came on and it felt like they were all involved, boots slamming into his torso and legs, no holding back. Just when he thought they were leaving his head alone a boot took him straight in the back of the skull and stars exploded in his head.

He rolled away, his skull a solid block of pain, another boot stamping on his leg and another slamming into his back. The wind was knocked from him and he gasped for air, the fetid onion stench filling his nostrils and mouth.

He was dimly aware of more movement somewhere nearby, accompanied by grunts and cries of pain.

He figured Katie was getting the same treatment. Obviously these guys were equal opportunities kidnappers.

Moore got his breathing under control, sucking down slow breaths and oxygenating his blood. The flexi-cuffs were digging into his wrists and his body ached. He knew this was just the beginning.

Sure enough, hands roughly dragged him up to a kneeling position and his head was pushed down to face the floor. His ankles were crossed. The hard floor dug into his knees and the position strained his whole body.

He knew what to expect from interrogation training in the Group, and knew what to expect, but he'd never been captured before. This was the real deal and he knew they were in the shit.

Somebody was standing over him and every time he moved at all to relieve the pressure a hand slapped him back into position.

It was important to get a mental grasp on the situation. He couldn't control anything physically-that was just something he had to endure. Stress positions, intimidation and isolation were used to break you down. Beatings were amateurish and largely ineffective on properly trained operators, aside from inflicting pain.

Mental strength was the key here, and he prayed that Katie had it.

You had to take yourself out of your pain and focus on something else.

Moore's go-to place was the rugby teams of his younger years. He'd grown up playing rugby, watching it, dreaming it. Although he was a handy enough loose forward, and aggressive, he'd never quite had the talent to go anywhere with it.

When he'd run through the names of all his teammates in high school, he started on the Waikato team of 1992-93. They'd been a great team, winning the National Provincial Championship in '92 then beating the touring British and Irish Lions the next year. Moore had been at Rugby Park to see it, on leave with a bunch of other young infantrymen. He'd been a Lance-Corporal then and supposedly looking after the rest of the lads. As he recalled, they'd got drunk after the game, had a fight with some students outside a pub and hightailed it before the cops got there.

After what seemed like an eternity he was manhandled to his feet and backed against the wall. One of the men moved him into a squat position and stepped back. Moore settled into the position. He did squats in the gym and knew he could normally hold it for at least four minutes. That was before a beating though. He knew that Wizz could squat for close to ten minutes.

The burn of the lactic acid made his legs shake and eventually, after what he calculated was roughly five minutes, he tried to push up. A hand on each shoulder held him in position, and two men chuckled. They sounded Turkish.

His legs were shaking and he felt like he was doing a spastic dance, his teeth gritted and eyes clenched shut, before they lifted him up and turned him round. They moved him backwards then down onto his front on the concrete. He heard a slosh then a bucket of ice cold water was tipped over him. He gasped and lay there, the concrete quickly getting colder, seeping up into his body. His briefs were soaked and clinging. He noticed that they had avoided wetting the hood-no waterboarding yet then.

Moore lay there, trying to decipher the muffled noises he could hear. He was certain he heard Katie say something, followed by an animalistic grunt. A muffled shout from her, sudden movement, laughter and a loud slap. A thudding impact and a snarl, a heavy whack then the sound of someone hitting the deck. He heard Katie screech something then a dull thump followed by gasping.

She was nearby. He wasn't sure what had just happened, but he could take an educated guess.

'Yeah baby!' Moore shouted in his best Austin Powers impression, hoping to give her a boost by showing defiance.

He didn't know if she heard but their captors didn't appreciate it. Someone stepped in and booted him in the left thigh, giving him a dead leg. He took it with a grunt, rolling that way, and someone else came in with another swinging boot.

This one collected him in the face and he instantly tasted warm salty blood in the back of his throat. He could feel it running down his lips and chin.

Moore coughed and snorted, trying to clear the blood and snot from his nostrils so he could breathe properly. He spat out a sticky gob, dribbling it out into the hood. It smeared on his chin and stayed there.

Someone kicked him in the side and muttered something. He took the hint and stayed silent.

24

The floor was freezing. Before long he could feel his core temperature lowering, and he began to tremble.

He pressed his face against the concrete as best he could, using the cold to help staunch the blood flowing from his nose and hopefully reduce the swelling a bit.

He went back to the annals of rugby history, working through the Otago team-another favourite of the early '90s era-before he was hauled to his knees again.

The cycle continued, the same pattern being used interspersed with a few kicks and knees, and by the time Moore had got through the Auckland and North Harbour teams of 1994, he was on the third round.

As he was being pushed to the cold wet floor again he heard Katie being lifted and moved away. A door opened and shut. Silence fell, aside from the shuffling feet of the man standing over him and the sound of his own breathing.

The hood had become his world. He assessed his captors again. Some knowledge and experience, yes. Professional, no. Dangerous, absolutely. He wondered what they were doing with or to Katie. He guessed they had picked her as the weaker of the two, and being a female she was certainly more vulnerable to a bunch of male thugs.

Kneeling in the stress position for the fourth time, his body locked up in painful knots, Moore came to some conclusions about their captors. They were not Police, nor were they intelligence services. These guys were either organised crime thugs, terrorists, or private contractors of some sort.

If they were terrorists, it was only a matter of time before the orange jumpsuits came out. If they were any of the other options, there must be an interrogation coming at some stage.

If that was ever their intention, his captors were taking their time. He lost count of how many cycles of stress positions he went through, finally giving up at fourteen. He decided to just go with it. There was nothing he could do to stop it, so it seemed like a better idea to just roll with it, compartmentalise each cycle into a box and work through until the cycle began again.

Thoughts of Danni forced their way into his head and he angrily banished them. No point thinking about her right now, unless she was bursting in the door with an Armalite in her hand.

Moore fell asleep at some stage, a fitful, painful slumber of sorts. Just enough to relax slightly without feeling rested. He was woken for another round of stress positions, man-handling, a few kicks and punches and unintelligible shouting in his ear.

He had no idea how long it all went on for but guessed it had to be close to a day. Time had lost all meaning to him. All that existed was the hood, his physical pain and the captors. His mouth tasted like a sun-baked gravel pit and his tongue felt thick and heavy. His stomach was achingly empty, and for some reason all he could think of was Turkish Delight. He didn't even like Turkish fucking Delight.

'Water,' he croaked to the man he knew was behind him, not needing to put it on much at all.

He had been kneeling with his head hung forward for what he figured was close to twenty minutes. His knees were beyond pain and his back muscles were so tight and stiff they barely seemed capable of moving.

'Silence.'

Moore took a slow breath through his nose, mentally flicking a switch. He'd had enough.

'Water,' he repeated.

'I say silent.' The man's tone was more forceful now.

'I say water,' Moore retorted thickly.

He heard the man's feet shift, coming round in front of him now. He heard the rustle of clothing and knew what was coming.

Warm piss splashed over his hood, dribbling down his face and chin. He screwed his eyes shut and clamped his lips tight. He wasn't quite desperate enough yet to drink the guy's piss.

The man chuckled to himself.

'Water,' he said with a thick accent.

His clothing rustled again as he tucked himself in and moved away.

Moore kept his eyes shut and refocussed himself. Obviously this guy was just a sadist, so there was no point playing the sympathy card.

He knew that best practice in hostage situations was to try and glean intel while delaying the kidnappers' action as long as possible, and hoping the rescuers would hurry up and get there while planning your own escape. But this was different. There was no rescue team standing by, and escape options seemed limited at best just now.

Fuck them, he decided. It was time to take the offensive.

'I want to talk to your boss,' he said.

'Shut up.'

'Get me the boss.'

'I say shut up.'

The guy shoved him flat on his face with a heel between the shoulder blades.

Moore fought to breathe.

'Get me the boss, arsehole.'

He could smell the man leaning in close over him.

'I am boss,' he snarled.

'You're just the monkey,' Moore told him, 'get me the zookeeper.'

'You fuck you!'

The guy landed a decent punch to the side of Moore's head.

The door opened and a second voice sounded. The man over Moore replied and the other voice said something short and sharp. The door closed again and Moore sensed the man stepping back.

'The boss,' Moore insisted. 'Go get him, dickhead.'

The man's cigarette breath wafted into Moore's face.

'Boss come soon. Then you know.' He chuckled. 'You know.'

'I know you hit like a fuckin' limp-wristed cock sucker,' Moore replied.

'Fuck you!'

The guy was angry now, snorting like a bull as he launched into a frenzied assault, his fists raining down on Moore's head and torso.

The door opened again and there was a shout then running feet. The punches stopped when the newcomer got to them and there was an angry exchange of Turkish between the two men.

Moore lay there, catching his breath and trying to clear his head. The boy had some weight behind those hits and he was hurting, but it had been worth it. He now knew more about these guys, and information was power. With information he could plan.

He heard angry feet stomping off and the door closed. Another voice sounded, this one older and obviously better educated.

'You are still alive, yes?'

'Barely,' Moore said. 'Thanks, you're a good man. He's an animal.'

'You shouldn't provoke him,' the man said. 'He does not like you being rude to him.'

'I want to speak to your boss, when can I do that?'

The man was silent for a moment as if weighing his answer. 'Soon,' he said. 'It will be soon.'

'Could I please have a drink? I think he broke my nose.'

'No, no drink.'

'I need some water please, he really hurt me.'

'I said no.'

'Will this look good for your boss, us all beaten to shit? It won't look good on the cameras.'

'You don't worry about that. There is no need.'

Moore digested that. It wasn't good. He tried again. 'When is he coming here, your big chief wallah-wallah?'

'Big what?'

'Your boss. When can I speak to him?'

'Soon, I say soon.' The man gave a small chuckle. 'He is very keen to talk to you too.'

'I bet he is. We have a lot to talk about. He needs to know what we have to say, and I don't think he'll like it.'

The man was silent for a moment. 'Why you say that? He won't like it?'

'I'll tell him when he gets here. I'm sick of talking to the bottom feeders.'

'Now you are rude. Maybe I get my friend back in here.'

Moore managed a snort. 'He said you need him to do the dirty work for you.'

'I think it time for you to shut up for a minute.'

'What's your big chief's name then? If I'm going to get killed here I should at least know his name.'

'You are scared. You should be scared.' The man crouched down beside him. 'You talk to him, it is the last conversation you have in your life.'

'So tell me his name then. Or are you too scared I'm going to escape and tell everyone?'

The man snorted. 'I am scared of nothing. I believe in Allah, the one true prophet. He is leading us to glory against the infidels of the west.'

Moore gave another snort of derision, but his mind was racing. 'Can you stop breathing on me please, your breath smells like an old man's cock.'

There was a flurry of movement as the man stood and booted him in the side. 'Your juvenile insults mean nothing to me, spy. You will soon be leaving this world.'

'So will you, you fuckin' retard. Is your mother still alive?'

There was a pause. 'Why? Why you ask this of my mother? It is not your concern.'

'Is she in Allah's Paradise or not? It's not a difficult question; yes or no?'

No pause now, and the unseen man's tone was proud when he spoke. 'She is indeed in Paradise, awaiting me to come join her.'

'Good. She must be missing you fucking her in the mouth. Now go get the boss, you dirty goat fucker. I'm sick of talking to you.'

'Infidel! You will suffer for your sins!'

The man moved away, pausing only to stamp twice on Moore's back, good and hard, before moving away.

The door opened and banged closed again. Moore took a slow breath and wondered how he managed to make friends so easily.

25

He began to scrape the side of his face against the wet concrete.

The rough surface gained traction on the cotton at the same time as it began to graze his skin. He ignored the pain and focussed on wriggling, shaking his head to loosen up the hood. It wasn't secured under his chin, and after what felt like a lifetime he had it halfway up his face. He could see ambient light now.

He worked harder, dragging the hood against the floor and shaking his head. He pushed up to his knees and bent over, feeling the hood beginning to flap a bit now as he shook his head as vigorously as his aching neck allowed.

He rolled onto his back, awkwardly moving his bound hands to the side, and bent forward, bringing his knees up together in a crunch. He got the loose end of the hood between his knees and pulled it off in one go.

He rolled to the side and then up, breathing hard with the exertion. His face stung but he could see now and breathe properly. He was in a concrete block room, maybe fifteen square metres, with a steel door on the far wall and a small barred window above it.

He was alone and couldn't hear any sounds beyond the walls.

He took a quick assessment of his body, which was easy-everything hurt, nothing broken.

He snorted and spat snot, then moved to the wall, searching the surface for any kind of irregularity, any edge that he could use on the plastic flexi-cuffs. He knew guys who could manoeuvre their bound hands over their legs to the front, but they were all skinny little racing sardines, not members of the Hundred Club with hips almost as wide as their shoulders.

Finally he found a small ridge of unevenness where the bricklayer had failed to clean up a dribble of excess cement between two bricks at about knee height.

Moore knelt down and backed up to it, feeling around until he had the right spot then setting to work. The kidnappers had put a cuff round each wrist then linked them with a third in the middle, giving some flexibility. They were wide cuffs though and it would take some doing to get free.

Rubbing the linking cuff steadily up and down, Moore tried to avoid losing any more skin but it was impossible. He focussed on blocking out the pain and just getting the job done. The sooner he got his hands free the sooner he could have a crack at getting out of here. There was no way he was lying down for these bastards.

Their intentions were clear.

His shoulders and arms ached with the effort and he had to keep stopping to rest and let the circulation return to his muscles. Mentally counting the minutes, Moore had got to eight when he heard footsteps approaching outside the door.

More than one set, maybe two, and some kind of stumbling, dragging sound. Muted conversation between the men.

Moore went for it on the ridge, scraping at it like a man possessed, knowing he had only seconds. He could feel the cuff coming apart but he knew in his heart it wouldn't be soon enough.

He had the sudden, horrible thought that he'd blown it for them both, signed their death warrants by trying to escape.

But no, he knew they were dead anyway, so he carried on, scraping like crazy, straining his arms apart to try and break the plastic bonding. His hands and wrists were grazed and blood was running freely. Sweat ran down his brow and neck. Every drop that got within reach of his tongue was lapped up and recycled.

He was nearly there.

The footsteps halted and there was the sound of the door handle being turned.

Moore pushed up to his feet, giving up on the flexi-cuffs and bounding over to the door, his bare feet soundless on the concrete floor. He stood to the side, still straining at the cuffs behind his back, knowing they were nearly there. His fingertips could feel the big rip, only a few millimetres to go until he was free.

The door started to open.

These fuckers were going to interrogate them and kill them. They'd be two more Western infidels in orange jumpsuits, beheaded on an internet video for all to see, all for the glory of a bunch of religious zealots who couldn't play nicely with others.

Fuck them, he wasn't going down easy.

26

The door opened wider and a shaft of light fell in. Katie was pushed across the threshold, coming from Moore's right.

Moore's arms quivered with the effort behind his back.

A hand on Katie's arm, an arm covered by a cheap shirt, a foot. Barely half a metre away from him now.

The cuff was tearing, as slow as a glacier melting, and the man was right there. There was no time now.

The man took a step into the room and his mate was right behind him. Moore launched forward.

His right foot smashed into the side of the first guy's left knee, ripping it apart as he drove through with full force. The guy cried out and started to go down, clutching at his knee. Katie jerked and turned her hooded head in his direction as if sensing him there. He could see her white T-shirt was rumpled and bloodied.

The second guy was still moving forward, as his brain processed what was happening. As he came across Moore's vision he started to turn. He was bigger than the first guy and had a folding stock AK slung casually over his right shoulder, away from Moore. He was also dressed in cheap casual wear.

Moore went for a knee strike on him too but the guy saw it

coming and pulled away, bending down to try and block the kick. Moore went for Plan B instead, feigning with another low kick. The guy tried to grab it while fumbling for his weapon, and Moore planted his foot solidly, snapping his upper body forward.

His forehead smashed into the guy's temple and knocked him sideways. As the guy stumbled Moore came in again, landing a solid side kick now to the inside of his right knee, buckling it and helping send him to the floor.

The first guy was wailing and rolling on the floor. He didn't have a visible weapon, so Moore focussed on the second guy, who was struggling to his feet. The AK was off his shoulder now but he had it by the sling-a piece of clothesline by the looks of it.

Moore slammed his right foot into the guy's face, his heel landing square on the chin and snapping his head back. He crashed into the doorframe and let out a choking gasp. Moore was on him now, stamping down with all his weight, landing strikes to his balls, his guts, his chest and up to the face again.

The guy was wheezing and seemed to have forgotten all about his AK. Moore didn't let up. If this guy got up they were in serious shit.

He stomped again, smashing his heel into the guy's face, a second time, a third, each blow causing the guy to slump lower to the floor. Blood was flowing from a broken nose and split lips and his eyes were unfocussed.

Moore was breathing hard and totally zoned in on the guy. He heard something behind him and threw a quick glance around. The first guy was still clutching his knee with one hand but was trying to draw a pistol from under his shirt with the other.

Moore diverted momentarily, kicking him fair in the balls and making him squeal. He let go of the pistol and grabbed for his jewels instead. Moore hammered a foot into his face and heard a dull crack as his head impacted the ground, before turning back to the second guy. He could see he was out of the game now, but as long as he was alive he was still a threat.

With total focus and cold blooded ruthlessness, Moore lined him up and stomped straight on his windpipe. There was a gargling sound and the guy's tongue hung out, his eyes bugging as he weakly tried to grab at his throat.

Moore stepped back, knowing the guy only had seconds to live before his oxygen ran out and he choked to death.

He breathed hard, sucking in lungful's of air.

The first guy was out cold or dead-either way, he wasn't moving. The second one was twitching and gurgling. Moore waited a few more seconds then the second man went limp. His hands flopped to the floor. He had a sheathed knife on his belt, a dagger of some sort.

Moore got down on his knees and twisted around, getting his fingers on the knife and tugging it free. He fumbled with it, his shaking hands managing to drop it twice before he got a good grip at the right angle and slipped it into the tear he'd already made in the flexi-cuffs.

He sawed steadily and in a few seconds the bond broke. He shifted his arms, rolling his shoulders to get the blood flowing again.

He turned to Katie, seeing she had moved off to the side and was standing rock steady, obviously listening intently.

'Katie,' he hissed. 'It's me.'

'Rob? What the fuck just happened? Are you okay?'

'Yep, turn round and I'll get you free.'

She jumped when he touched her but she complied, awkwardly lifting her arms to give him room to move. He cut through her flexi-cuffs and lifted her hood off. He could see blood and grazes on her face.

'You okay?' he asked, getting the tip of the blade under the plastic round her wrist and sawing off first one cuff then the other.

She nodded while she rubbed at her wrists. 'Here, give me that.' She took the knife and set to work on his cuffs. 'Those dirty fuckers.'

'Did they…' he fumbled, unsure how to ask. 'Are you okay, really?'

She nodded again, removing the second cuff. 'Yeah. I thought they were going to rape me. That one,' she jabbed a finger at the second man Moore had killed, 'he had a crack in here, tried to finger me and grabbed my tits.'

She looked harder at his still form.

'Is he dead?'

'Yes.'

'Good. Fuckin' rapist.'

Moore rubbed his own wrists and swung his arms in slow circles-it was too painful yet to move very fast. He moved to the second man and took the AK he'd dropped. A quick frisk found a spare banana magazine in the guy's pocket.

He undid the guy's boots and pants and yanked them off. The pants were close enough to his own size but the boots were too small. He did the same with the first guy, stripping off his boots and pants and handing them to Katie. The guy had a cheap cell phone in his pocket, which Moore seized.

He also took the guy's pistol-a Yavuz 16 version of the Beretta 92F, the standard sidearm of the Turkish military. He checked the weapon's condition and handed it to Katie.

'One up the spout and there's the safety,' he said, showing her. 'You've got fifteen rounds.'

They dressed themselves and Katie laced up the boots. She straightened up and nodded to him that she was ready.

Moore bent to check the pulse on the first guy, and realised he hadn't quite made it to Paradise yet. He flipped the guy over and stripped the laces from the second guy's boots, using them to tie the first man's hands behind his back. He hauled the guy to his feet and tore the cheap shirt off him, wadding a large piece of material and shoving it into the captive's mouth then knotting a sleeve around his head to hold it in place. The captive was completely naked and bleeding, and when Moore hauled him to his feet, the guy's shattered left knee buckled under him and he jerked into consciousness with a muffled screech of agony.

'Let's go,' Moore hissed to Katie. 'Stay close and we'll try and get outta here quietly. If we get sprung though, shoot first. Okay?'

She nodded. He could see she was flapping.

'We'll be okay,' he told her firmly. 'Deep breaths, clear heads. Speed, aggression, surprise. Yep?'

Katie nodded again.

'Let's go.'

He locked the captive under his left arm and moved to the door, checking the way was clear before moving out. They were in a hallway, bare dirt floor and damp wooden walls. A single light bulb hung further along. They stayed close to the wall and moved down, weapons at the ready.

At the end was a doorway with no door, and a lighted barn beyond. Moore hung back in the shadows until he was satisfied that the room was clear. He edged up to the doorway and scanned.

It was being used as a store room of some sort, with a rack of empty shelves and a few discarded cardboard boxes on the floor. On one of the shelves he saw their bags, obviously looted from their hotel room.

A rickety table was in the centre of the barn with two mismatched chairs and a wooden crate pulled up to it. A set of cards was on the table, an ashtray overflowing with cigarette butts, a plastic jug of water with a cup. A walkie-talkie sat there, silent. A bare bulb dangled above it.

A pedestrian door was ajar at the far end of the left hand wall, and Moore could feel a breeze coming through, carrying with it the smell of farm animals. The main barn doors were closed straight ahead of him.

He began to move forward again, the captive under his arm protesting through the gag as he was hustled awkwardly. Moore tightened his grip round the guy's neck.

They were scarcely two steps into the room when they heard movement then the pedestrian door was pushed inwards. A head appeared followed by an arm and leg, then a third man was in there, looking at the door handle as he reached for it.

He was dressed similarly to the other two but was younger, and had a folding stock AK slung over his shoulder by a piece of rope.

Moore and Katie froze as the guy pushed the door closed behind him then began to turn as he stepped forward, still oblivious to their presence.

Time stood still for a second as he took a step and raised his head.

The captive under Moore's arm grunted and began to struggle. The third guy's head snapped up sharply and he locked eyes on them. He grabbed for the AK swinging at his hip, and it all went noisy very suddenly.

Moore had his own AK braced in his right fist and he swept the safety off as he brought it on target, at the same time as the captive wrenched violently and half broke free.

Katie's pistol cracked loudly at his shoulder and he felt a spray of wetness across the side of his face and neck. He saw the third guy had the AK coming round, then a splash of red appeared on the guy's chest and he stumbled backwards.

Moore squeezed off two rounds single handed, dropped the dead weight of his captive, and got a proper grip on the AK. He snapped two more shots and saw the third guy going down, the rifle in his hands but his brain unable to send the message to operate it now. Another red splash appeared on the guy's shoulder as he hit the deck on his knees then Katie's Beretta fired again and his head jerked back, blood and brain spraying the wall behind him.

Silence fell.

27

Moore's ears were ringing like Notre Dame's bells.

He glanced to Katie, who still had her pistol up in a Weaver stance. He gently waved his hand at her, knowing she would be as deaf as he was. He indicated his intentions and moved forward, checking the room properly then closing the door. The third guy was rocking backwards on his knees, leaking fluids onto the floor from multiple wounds.

Moore toppled him over with a foot and grabbed the AK he'd dropped. The room stank of burned cordite, spicy food and the metallic stench of blood.

He waved Katie in and pointed at their bags. While she busied herself he checked on their captive. The guy was as dead as a doornail, half the back of his head missing. He'd obviously moved across Katie's arc when he tried to break free, and took an unintentional round in the skull.

Moore left him and re-joined Katie. She had pulled a bag onto the floor but was now bent at the waist, breathing hard.

'We need to go,' Moore said. He grabbed his own bag off the shelf and put it by the door.

He went back to the table and filled the cup with water from the plastic jug. He handed it to Katie and told her take it slowly. She downed half of it in one go and let out a sigh of satisfaction. Moore waited until she'd finished it before filling the cup again and drinking from the jug himself. The water was warm and had an unpleasant tang to it, but it was better than a terrorist's piss and Moore drank.

He wiped his mouth and put the jug down before crossing the room again. He cracked the door open and peered out. Darkness everywhere, not a light to be seen. He edged out and took in his surroundings.

They were definitely on farmland. He couldn't hear a thing aside from the occasional animal noise, although his ears were still ringing from the shooting. No sign of anyone else.

He moved further out from the building and had a quick scout around. There was another building of some sort thirty metres or so away, maybe stables, all in darkness.

No sign of a vehicle.

As his eyes adjusted to the darkness Moore spotted a water trough nearby and crossed to it, the stony ground hard beneath his feet. He scooped handfuls of water and washed as much blood and crap off him as he could.

Katie appeared in the doorway behind him, perfectly silhouetted by the back lighting, and he ushered her back inside.

'Get dressed,' he said. 'We're going to leg it from here.'

She put the Beretta on the table and opened her bag on the floor. Moore stood ready with the AK by the door, keeping guard while she stripped out of her bloodied T-shirt.

She was bare breasted beneath it and Moore turned away self-consciously while she found a bra and put a fresh blue T-shirt on over the top. She dropped the cheap pants and pulled on a pair of her own jeans, socks and trainers.

As soon as she was done it was Moore's turn. He tossed the stolen pants and sodden briefs aside and pulled on cargo pants, socks and boots, and a grey T-shirt. He zipped up his bag and grabbed the walkie-talkie off the table.

He searched the room for anything useful, finding a large torch in working order and another burn phone. He recovered a spare magazine from the third guy and handed it with the second AK to Katie. He took the Beretta back and tucked it into his waistband, gave her a ten second lesson on the AK and they were good to go.

Moore killed the light and they waited in the darkness for a couple of minutes, getting their night vision sorted before venturing out. He felt better now, properly dressed and with a weapon in his hands.

Even after the beating he knew he could tab for hours if he needed to, and his mind set was good. He was also feeling more confident in Katie after the contact inside. She had acted fast and efficiently, and dealt with the threat in front of them.

The death of the captive was unfortunate, not least because Moore wanted someone to interrogate, but in the circumstances he couldn't blame Katie for that.

They moved in the darkness, crossing a yard towards a driveway. Beyond it they could make out a road.

Moore was about to speak when he saw a shifting shadow on the road. Through the ringing in his ears he faintly heard an engine. It was a vehicle without lights, approaching from the right.

'Car!' Katie hissed, grabbing his arm.

Brake lights flared red in the darkness as the vehicle slowed then they heard the first crunch of tyres on gravel.

This had to be the boss, whoever the hell he was.

'Move!'

Moore hurried to the left, reaching a stone wall and hunkering down beside his bag. The vehicle was coming up the drive. He could make out the shape of a people mover.

'Get over!' he hissed, covering her while Katie clambered over the wall and dropped out of sight. He quickly followed with his bag, just as the vehicle came into the yard and pulled up near the main barn doors.

This could be an ideal opportunity to take a prisoner who could shed some light for them on what exactly the hell was going on. Either that or it could all go tits up in a big way.

28

The headlights flicked on, lighting up the yard for moment, before the engine was cut and the driver's door opened.

A Turk in jeans and a shirt stepped out, lit up by the interior light. He had a full beard and a slim build. The rear door slid open on the far side and Moore craned his neck to see.

A second man climbed out of the back, this one more solidly built, in casual gear and carrying an AK47 in his right hand with the stock folded. He said something and a moment later a third man emerged from the back of the people mover. In the cone of the interior light Moore could just make out a suit and a balding head.

The second and third men moved to the front of the vehicle and the first man shut his door, killing the light. The engine ticked in the stillness.

One of the men muttered something and they began to move towards the barn doors. Moore tracked them silently, his night vision near perfect now.

They were nearly there when the second guy-Moore presumed he was the bodyguard-hesitated and held out a hand to the suit. The barn light was off and it obviously tripped his alarm.

The driver immediately turned and scanned behind them, his hand going under his shirt for a weapon.

Moore pushed up from behind the stone wall eight metres away with his AK up on line. He triggered his first shot before they even knew he was there, dropping the driver with a gut shot.

He moved the barrel to the right, squeezing off a double tap at the BG, who was turning towards him and starting to step protectively in front of the suit.

The first round missed but the second took the BG in the arm, causing him to grunt loudly. Moore gave him two more, both through the chest, and saw his form drop in the darkness.

The suit was moving now, feet scraping at the stony ground as he began to run. Moore hurdled the stone wall and punched out a double tap at his fleeing figure, the beige of his suit easy enough to see in the darkness.

The suit stumbled and went down, scrabbling in the dirt.

Moore paused over the driver, who was in spasms on the ground and trying to stem the flow of blood from his gut. Moore put a round in his head and moved past to the BG. The bigger man was on his side, hands covered in blood and the front of his shirt reddened with his life force. He wasn't moving but Moore made sure anyway, another round to the head.

By the time he got to the suit and flicked the torch on, the balding man had blood bubbling over his lips and down his chin, indicating some kind of internal bleeding. The man managed a smirk as he stared up at his killer.

'Who are you?' Moore said, although something was tugging at the back of his memory, some vague kind of recognition. 'What's your name?'

The man smirked again and muttered something Moore didn't understand. Moore had the impression he was an educated man, so he almost inevitably spoke English. The look on the man's face indicated he understood perfectly well. He repeated the questions in Arabic anyway, and got an immediate reaction of surprise.

'So you do understand,' he said, watching the man carefully.

'I will tell you nothing,' the man responded. Blood bubbled over his lips. 'I will die first.'

The memory tugged harder at Moore's brain, there but just out of reach. He knew he knew who this clown was, or had at least seen his picture somewhere.

'There's no question of you dying, shitkicker,' Moore told him. 'The question is how?' He poked the barrel of the AK down into the guy's right thigh, jabbing it in painfully. The man grimaced but said nothing.

'You won't shoot me,' the man coughed, 'you have rules.'

'Not out here mate.' Moore gestured at the empty blackness around them. 'There's no one here. No witnesses.' He ground the rifle barrel into the thigh again, bringing another grimace of pain. 'No rules.'

He heard Katie arrive behind him, and in that moment he snatched the memory from the clouds in his mind.

They called him The Doctor. He was Jordanian and had been a dentist in a previous life, but since the War on Terror had begun he'd been deeply involved in the insurgency. There was solid intel linking him to the torture of many informers over the years, as well as training other terrorists in the dark arts of torture. He was highly placed in ISIS and as such he was a high value target for the Allied forces.

Moore stood over him, studying his face and committing it to memory. He dug out the seized cell phone and found the camera function.

The Doctor helped him by leering at the phone and weakly snarling a curse as Moore snapped several images in the torchlight. They were probably going to be crap quality, but short of beheading the man it was the best he could do.

'Why us?' he asked The Doctor.

The man sneered dismissively. 'You will never know,' he said. He coughed wetly and a large pinky-red bubble expanded at his lips before popping and dribbling down his chin.

Moore handed off the AK to Katie and roughly flipped The

Doctor over on his side. The man tried to struggle but the fight had gone from him and Moore easily pinned his arms behind his back before tying them with The Doctor's own belt.

He ripped the front from The Doctor's bloodied shirt and blindfolded him, then grabbed him by an ankle and dragged him across the stony ground to the water trough he'd found earlier. The terrorist squealed with pain as his flesh was ripped by the rough ground.

'Go inside and get one of those hoods and the water jug,' Moore told Katie, passing her the torch. She looked uncertainly at him. 'Go!'

A minute later he pulled the hood over The Doctor's head and tied it off with a shoelace from the dead bodyguard. He tied the man's ankles together with the bodyguard's belt. He hefted the man under his arm and stood as if carrying a heavy roll of carpet. The Doctor's feet were higher than his head and he was securely bound.

The Doctor began to struggle, knowing what was coming. The world was aware of waterboarding as an enhanced interrogation technique-commonly accepted as torture-and a number of Islamic terrorists had been subjected to it by Western forces.

Nobody could resist the stress it put them under, with most subjects surrendering within seconds.

29

Moore balanced The Doctor's head above the water trough.

'Why did you kidnap us?' he rasped.

A muffled curse was the only answer. Dropping his grip he dunked the terrorist's head into the water, holding him steady as the man struggled. Mentally ticking off ten seconds, he lifted again and brought the head up.

The Doctor gasped, shaking his head in the wet hood.

'Try again,' Moore said. 'Why did you kidnap us?'

The Doctor used English now. 'Fuck you, you pig.'

'Wrong answer.' Moore dunked him again, giving him a fifteen count this time.

'He's gunna drown,' Katie said, sounding panicked.

Moore glanced sideways at her. 'Maybe,' he grunted. 'It's his choice.'

The Doctor came up again, his chest heaving and his body shuddering. Moore knew that with internal injuries his prisoner was not going to last long.

'Last chance,' he said, hefting The Doctor for a better grip.

'Just tell him,' Katie urged the terrorist, and he turned his head towards her as if only now becoming aware of her.

'You're...the...one,' The Doctor wheezed.

'What? What d'you mean?' Moore's arms were trembling with the strain of holding him up.

The Doctor took another heaving breath. 'The...one.'

'What does that mean?' Moore said. 'How do you know her?'

'You...die...dog.'

Moore braced his feet and dunked him for the third time, his whole body tensing up as he held the pose and contained the prisoner's thrashing for fifteen long seconds. Finally stepping back, he pulled The Doctor free and dumped him on the ground. The prisoner heaved and strained for air, and Moore knew the end was near. Either the guy was going to go toes up or he'd talk.

He freed the tie on the hood and lifted it far enough to uncover The Doctor's mouth, allowing him to breathe. Blood streaked vomit dripped from the inside of the hood. The Doctor gaped like a fish, struggling to fill his lungs with oxygen. He coughed and spewed, gasping some more.

'What do you mean she's the one?' Moore asked, crouching over him.

'The white girl,' The Doctor wheezed, 'she will die.' His chest heaved and shuddered as he finally got his lungs open properly.

Moore mentally counted off-one full breath.

'This girl?' he said. 'Or another one?'

'The white girl.' A second full breath. 'New Zealand...girl.'

Third full breath.

Moore tugged the hood down over his mouth and The Doctor twisted, trying to break free. Moore rose half way, holding The Doctor's legs under his right arm, the man's shoulders and heads at an awkward angle on the ground. He took the water jug from Katie.

The Doctor thrashed hard now but Moore held firm.

'Which white girl are you talking about?' he demanded. 'This girl or Natalie Oldham?'

'Paradise waits for...'

Moore cut him off with a torrent of water over his face. The wet hood clung to the terrorist's mouth and nose, bringing on an instant sensation of drowning, and he thrashed hard, whipping from side to side. Moore maintained a steady pour until the jug emptied. He passed it to Katie. In the torchlight her face was pale and drawn, her eyes wide. This was so far from her world it wasn't funny.

The Doctor let out a keening wail as he sucked in air. Moore kept him in the same position, knowing the pressure on his upper body would cause The Doctor immense pain and fear breaking his neck.

'Tell me about Natalie Oldham,' he demanded. 'You start talking, Doctor, and I'll stop this.'

'You know him?' Katie said with surprise.

Moore gave a grim nod. 'Yeah, I know who he is.'

'You know...nothing!' The Doctor screeched from beneath the wet hood. He kicked out to no avail.

Moore gave him a shake. 'Tell me about Natalie Oldham. Where is she?'

The Doctor switched back to Arabic. 'May Allah be praised...'

Katie stepped forward now and began the pour, a steady stream of dirty trough water cascading down onto the terrorist's face. He spluttered and coughed and writhed, weaker now. The Doctor let out an animal-like screech and bucked hard, Moore hanging on desperately to contain him.

He mentally counted off the seconds, reaching fifteen before giving Katie the nod to stop. He dropped The Doctor down again and lifted the hood to help him breathe. Blood covered the chin and flowed down onto the throat.

Alarmed, he jerked the hood up further. The Doctor was spasming now, thin gasping sounds emitting from his bloodied mouth.

'Fuck!' Moore ripped the hood away and grabbed the torch from Katie, shining it on the terrorist's face. It was waxy looking and twitching, the mouth wide open. He checked the carotid pulse-nothing.

'Is he dead?' Katie asked, a distinct quaver in her voice.

'The fucker bit his tongue,' Moore muttered, peering into the blood-filled mouth.

'Did I kill him?'

'No.' Moore stood, pushing away from the body. 'He refused to talk; better to be a martyr than surrender to us.'

'He bit his own tongue off?' Katie sounded incredulous.

Moore looked at her. 'This ain't fuckin' tiddlywinks, Katie. These pricks are fanatics. He would rather choke on his own blood than give in.'

'Jesus Christ.' Katie stepped back, a hand to her forehead as it all sunk in. 'Jesus fucking Christ...'

'They may be jihadists, but there's nothing holy about these bastards,' Moore said grimly.

He took his AK back from her then checked the pockets of The Doctor's suit. He found a small amount of cash, a smart phone and a small, wicked looking dagger with a blade barely ten centimetres long. He stuffed them all into his own pocket, then dug into the inside pocket of the jacket.

He produced a tall, slim black leather wallet. He put it down and held the light on it while he unfolded the wallet to inspect the contents. What he found made his blood run cold.

'What the hell is that?' Katie asked, leaning over his shoulder.

Moore slid out one of the tools. It was a scalpel with a long handle. Katie let out a gasp of horror. Alongside the scalpel was a pair of needle nosed pliers, a vicious looking dental hook, and various other implements.

Moore looked up at Katie. 'Tools of torture,' he said simply.

He stood and pocketed the torture kit. He checked the car and found the keys in the ignition. He went back to the bodies of the driver and bodyguard and snapped photos of them on the burn phone. He turned to Katie.

'Let's go.'

30

Twenty minutes later they arrived on the outskirts of Adapazari.

Moore pulled the people mover into the car park of a truck stop and parked up in a dark corner. A couple of big rigs were parked up and the diner/gas station was open.

He checked the smart phone he'd taken from The Doctor and saw it was almost fully charged. Rather than mess around with it and risk tripping a self-destruct trigger in the hard drive, he used the burn phone instead.

Punching in the Ops Room number from memory, he waited for several seconds before the connection opened with a bland male voice.

'Hello.'

'Hotel California,' Moore said, 'five-two-eight-six-three-nine.'

Silence for a moment.

'Heat?'

'De Niro and Pacino.' Moore glanced at Katie who was watching him with a quizzical look. He rolled his eyes at her.

'Location?'

'Adapazari. Track this phone. I've been burned and need an urgent exfil. I have a passenger.'

More silence. He had no idea who he was talking to but he had to trust that what he needed would be done.

'Stand by.'

The phone went dead. He looked at Katie.

'Hurry up and wait,' he said.

She said nothing, and he knew she was still processing what they'd just been through.

Four minutes later the phone rang. He hit the go button but said nothing.

'Piccadilly Circus at lunchtime,' came Jedi's voice down the line. 'The man wears a yellow raincoat.'

'I prefer orange myself,' Moore replied, 'especially on a Tuesday.'

Whoever came up with these security codes was obviously retarded, he thought.

Jedi got straight to business and Moore listened intently. Two minutes later he disconnected and spent another two minutes messaging the photos to the Ops Room. He pocketed the phone and turned to Katie.

'What's going on?' she asked. She had her arms folded across her chest and looked pale.

'We need to get moving. We've got a pick up coming in about an hour and a half. We're going to stop here for ten minutes for a clean-up then head to an RV.'

Katie nodded again. He could see the exhaustion and strain in her face. He reached over and touched her knee.

'This is all good,' he said. 'We just need to get ourselves sorted and get moving, then we'll be outta here, okay?'

'Uh-huh.' Katie nodded and unbuckled her seatbelt. 'Let's do it then.'

Moore had recovered his Sig from the car, where someone had obviously stashed it as a trophy for later, and he checked the weapon's state before slipping it back into the front of his waistband. He followed his companion across the darkened car park to the toilet at the side of the gas station. It was unlocked and he waited outside while Katie used the facilities. He found a tap around the back and cupped his hands to wash his face, neck and hands.

A quick visit to the gas station shop restocked their supplies and a few minutes later they were on the move again. Moore's hands and face smelt of the fragranced handy wipes and antiseptic he'd bought, he was steadily rehydrating and he'd cleaned up half a block of chocolate.

Katie was quiet, munching her way through chocolate and crackers as the road hummed beneath them. Moore left her alone, figuring that she needed to work through the night's events in her head in her own time.

He knew what it was like. No matter how skilled he was, the darker arts had never been as easy for him as for other operators. The first man he'd killed had been a sniper shot at 350 metres in Kabul, dropping a guy who was spotting for insurgents waiting to ambush a Kiwi patrol. It was over in a second and he'd barely thought of it since.

There had been others since then, and he was not immune to the demons who came creeping, sometimes at night when he was vulnerable, sometimes in the broad light of day when the battlefield was the furthest thing from his mind.

There had been one occasion when he was mountain biking in the Waitakere's and an hour into it he came round a curve in the track and nearly ran down an insurgent standing to the side with half his face blown off.

The bastard had followed him, appearing at every turn in the track for the next hour, just standing and staring at him with a single cold, dead eye, and congealed blood bordering the gaping wound in his head.He hadn't been seen for over a year now but Moore was conscious that he would probably never fully leave.

They'd been driving for nearly an hour when Katie finally spoke.

'It's pretty fucked up, isn't it?' she said.

She paused as if compiling her next sentence. Moore waited.

'I mean...that was pretty fucking intense wasn't it?'

'Yep.' Moore nodded, his eyes on the road. 'It was.'

'They were going to kill us weren't they?'

'No doubt.'

'And that guy...the one at the end. In the suit. He was a bad guy, wasn't he?'

He could feel her looking at him now. He kept his eyes ahead.

'He was. They all were.'

'But he was someone wasn't he? You knew him.'

Moore nodded again.

'He was someone alright.'

'Who was he?'

Her stare was penetrating his skull now and he fought hard to resist. He knew what she wanted, what she needed. Confirmation that her perception of the situation was accurate. Affirmation that they'd done the right thing. Fair do's, but she was not in the circle of trust yet.

'He was a senior member of ISIS. He was an interrogator and torturer.' Moore glanced at her now. 'The world's a better place without him in it.'

Katie gave a small nod. Her eyes were still wide. Moore hoped she didn't have any more questions on The Doctor. She didn't let him down.

'I don't how I should be feeling about what happened,' she said quietly. 'I know it's wrong but I feel...I dunno...relieved, or like...kind of glad?' She shook her head as she struggled with the emotions. 'Not glad...but like, more than relieved I guess.'

Moore nodded.

'Fair enough,' he said, 'you should. I know what you mean, and it's okay to feel like that.'

'But glad that someone's dead?' Katie's tone was confused.

'It's not about being glad,' he said. 'Not glad. Relieved is good, it's normal.' He felt like he was talking to a raw recruit, and in some ways he guessed he was. 'You should be relieved that you survived; like you said, it was pretty fuckin' intense. But you made it through in one piece, and nobody can ask for more than that.'

Katie was still silent, but he knew he had her ear now. She was listening to the voice of experience, seeking solace and comfort. It was important to get this right, for her sake. It was a one-shot deal. If he screwed this up, she would struggle to get her head round it, if she ever did.

'Those guys brought the fight, remember. They kidnapped us. They planned to kill us. This was all their game.' He looked at her again, meeting her gaze firmly. 'But we played it better, Katie. We beat them at their own game and we walked away from it. Your training, your instincts, your guts-that's what got you through. And you should be proud of that.'

She went silent again, jamming her hands between her thighs and staring out the window at the darkness beyond. Moore alternated between watching the road and checking on her. He saw the glisten of a tear rolling down the side of her nose and she turned further away, subtly wiping it away and giving a sniff.

'I was shitting myself,' Katie said suddenly, 'but when we came out of that room, it was like there was hope. I knew that we at least had a chance of getting out of there.' She turned to him now, crossing her legs under her and leaning half against the door. 'You probably don't get that though, do you? You must live and breathe this shit.'

Moore pulled a face.

'Fear is a healthy emotion as long as you can control it. If it paralyses you from acting then you're dead. But if you can get a grip on it it makes you more aware of what you're doing, less likely to do something stupid.' He glanced at her. 'I still get nervous. I'm glad I do. If I didn't I'd be a psychopath.'

'Have you ever been wounded?' Katie asked.

He gave a short nod.

'Couple of times.'

Katie fell silent again and Moore didn't elaborate. She didn't need to know he still carried shrapnel, and she didn't need to know about the months of rehab he'd gone through to get back to active duty again.

31

They drove in silence for another half hour, until the phone on Katie's lap told them to turn left in fifty metres.

Moore followed the instructions and they took a narrow side road off the highway for another half a klick before pulling up. They were at a deserted gas station in the middle of nowhere. Paint peeled off the sides and the pumps were long gone.

They got out and stretched their legs, the night air chilly but refreshing. Moore rolled his shoulders and arched his back, popping a stiff joint in his neck. He shook himself like a dog and took some deep breaths, clearing the fug from his brain. As he drained his water bottle he saw a set of headlights approaching from the other direction.

At the same time his iPhone rang. An American accent started talking as soon as he answered.

'Move that vehicle around the back, man. We're thirty seconds out.'

The connection was gone just as quickly as it appeared and Moore followed the instructions, guessing their exfil crew had them under obs via night vision gear-or possibly from an unseen aircraft.

The other vehicle pulled in as he alighted from the people mover again. The high beams blinded both of them as the doors flew open on the other vehicle and dark figures fanned out.

'Hands on the side of the car,' barked a voice from behind the lights. 'Feet apart.'

Moore and Katie did as they were told and were quickly frisked and disarmed. Their watches and phones were taken from them. Their papers were checked and the people mover was cleared. Moore kept his head down until hands turned him and a torch was shone in his face.

Behind the light a bearded white guy checked his face against his passport before cutting the light and walking him to the other vehicle-a van with tinted windows and bench seats in the back.

He was guided into the middle row and Katie was placed beside him. She looked at him in the darkness but said nothing.

The driver had stayed put with the engine running. Two guys got in behind them, both carrying compact Colt Commando rifles. Their bags were loaded in and the last guy took the seat in front of them, turning to address them as the van began to move off.

He was a thickset man somewhere in his thirties with a ginger-tinged beard. Like the others he was dressed in a loose fitting shirt of neutral colours and jeans. He had a baseball cap down low over dark eyes.

'Welcome aboard the Exfil Express,' he said. 'My name's Todd and I'll be your tour guide tonight.'

His accent was from somewhere in the Mid-West, Moore guessed.

'Don't worry about the rest of these dudes here,' Todd continued, 'they're just along for the ride. Just sit back and relax, we'll wake you when we get there, okay?'

'Where's there?' Katie asked.

Todd grinned somewhere within the forest of a beard.

'Well there is there, missy,' he replied. 'It's not here, and that's a good thing right?'

Todd held up their pistols. The van was picking up speed.

'I'll hang onto these for now. I understand you also have some phones to share with us?'

'Got 'em here, Top,' one of the guys behind them said. His accent was pure Southern California-laid back surfer dude.

Moore turned to look at him and the guy grinned back, pearly whites in a deeply tanned face topped with a blonde mop.

'Hey buddy,' the guy grinned.

Moore tilted his chin, saying nothing.

'Good talk man, we should do it again sometime.'

Moore gave a smile and turned back to the front.

'Thanks for coming to get us,' he said to Todd, who was clearly the leader. 'Appreciate it.'

'Anything for our Kiwi pals,' Todd replied. 'Get some shut-eye if you like, we got a drive ahead of us.' He kicked a bag at his feet. 'Got some scoff here if you haven't eaten.'

Moore nodded his thanks and settled into his seat. He didn't need to eat and there wasn't much else to say. He guessed these guys were either Delta Force or Green Berets-or the 1st Special Forces Operational Detachment (Delta) and the US Army Special Forces, as they were officially known-or maybe from the Special Activities Division of the CIA.

Whoever they were, they were good and he felt safe in their hands. Within minutes he was asleep.

He was awoken some time later by the van slowing down. Moore felt Katie's weight against him when he woke. It wasn't unwelcome. It was still dark outside and he could hear propellers turning.

Katie woke when the van came to a stop and the side door was thrown open. Todd alighted and spoke to someone out of sight if the passengers. Katie stirred and lifted herself off Moore, wiping her mouth self-consciously.

'Where are we?' she croaked.

'No idea,' Moore said honestly. 'And I'm guessing we probably don't need to know?'

His last comment was directed at the guys behind them.

'You got it, dude,' the surfer grinned.

Katie turned and looked at him and the grin got wider.

'How y'doin' pumpkin? Good sleep?'

'Pumpkin?' Katie gave him quizzical. 'What am I, five? You wanna twirl my pigtails too?'

The other guy snorted. He was a lean Hispanic with a pock-marked face and a piece of his left ear missing.

'I mean no offence, ma'am,' the surfer said quickly. 'Just tryin' to be friendly.'

Todd poked his head back into the van and gestured for them to get out. They joined him on a darkened field of some sort. A Blackhawk helicopter awaited them, rotors turning.

'Follow me,' Todd said.

He led the way and stood aside as they climbed in the rear of the chopper. One of the two crew helped them into their seats and got Katie buckled in while Moore sorted himself out. Moore noticed that both of the crew wore flight suits with no insignia.

Todd and his team joined them, the doors were shut and within seconds they lifted off.

Katie's hand grasped for Moore's in the darkness and he gave it a reassuring squeeze. He sat back and let the tiredness wash over him. There was nothing to do and no point trying to figure out where they were going, so he followed the age-old soldier's practice of grabbing sleep where he could.

32

The sun was up when they came in to land in a military camp surrounded by fences and wire.

Moore had no idea how far they had come but he estimated the Blackhawk was probably somewhere near its maximum range, which most likely put them in Iraq or Saudi Arabia.

The pilot put them down gently and the side door was thrown open, letting in a swirl of dust. Todd's boys jumped out and led their passengers to a waiting Humvee. Within a minute the vehicle pulled into a compound, large steel gates clanging shut behind them as the Humvee motored through.

He saw a pair of armed-up Humvees parked side by side, a mechanic working underneath one, a trio of soldiers standing nearby.

No, he thought, not soldiers-operators. They had the beards and weather beaten appearance of warriors, the casual clothes over desert boots, the front slung carbines.

He heard another door rolling open then they were entering a hangar of some sort, the door sliding across behind them again. The Humvee pulled up and Todd turned to them.

'Standby here, folks,' he said, before getting out and disappearing.

Moore and Katie sat in an uncomfortable silence with the operators until Todd arrived back, waving them out of the wagon.

The hangar was huge and sectioned off into private areas. It looked to Moore like any of the dozens of such bases he'd been in around the world. He could smell hot food and diesel fumes.

A non-descript man in desert fatigues with no insignia stood off to the side, watching them. He was in his forties, six foot and muscular. He gave a slight nod when Moore made eye contact. Moore nodded back.

Another man appeared, this one much younger, barely five and a half feet tall and with curly black hair and a tidy beard. He looked like a young Billy Crystal. He wore faded jeans and a U2 T-shirt, with a John Deere cap. He stood with the older man, neither of them speaking.

'Follow me, folks, and bring your bags,' Todd said. 'We'll get you bunked down so you can have a shower and some chow.'

He led them through a door into one of the sectioned off areas, past a bunch of Army cots and gear strewn about. A guy lounged on one of the cots reading a Batman comic. He ignored them as they walked past.

Todd took them through another door, down a short corridor and showed them into a smaller room. Two cots were set up with sleeping bags unrolled. Sets of clothes were stacked at the foot of each bed.

'Sorry,' he said, 'we thought it was two guys. We can move you somewhere else if you like, miss.'

Katie shook her head, putting her bag down.

'All good,' she said.

Todd pointed to the other door opposite.

'Bathroom's through there,' he said. 'It's pretty good-this is supposed to be an officer's quarters, but he ain't here yet, so it's all yours.' He grinned. 'Make yourselves comfortable.'

'How long're we here for?' Moore asked.

Todd shrugged nonchalantly.

'You got me, pal. I'm just the messenger.'

'Can we make a call?'

Todd smiled apologetically.

'My understanding is not yet,' he said. 'But should be no problem later. Some guys wanna talk t'ya first, I think.'

Moore nodded resignedly.

'So shower, eat, and hurry up and wait,' he said. 'Same old.'

Todd's deep eyes studied him for a moment.

'You got it. Just come back through that way when you're ready to eat and we'll take you to the chow hall, 'kay?'

With that he left them to it.

Katie lifted her bag onto one of the cots and unzipped it.

'I dunno about you, but I'm screaming for a shower,' she said.

Moore took the other bed and dug out his toiletries with a change of clothes. He checked the bathroom and saw there was a single shower cubicle and a tiny sink.

'You go first,' he said.

Katie closed the door behind her and Moore sat on his cot. Despite the proficiency of their hosts-and he'd always admired the American operators-he disliked being at the mercy of somebody else. He stretched out on the cot with his hands behind his head and thought while he waited. By the time Katie emerged with damp hair, dressed in fresh black jeans and a long sleeved white shirt, Moore had come to some conclusions. He kept them to himself for now.

'Better?' he asked.

Katie nodded as she brushed out her long dark hair. He noticed she had a St Christopher's medal on a thin silver chain around her smooth neck.

'It's nice to get all the dirt and sweat off,' she said. 'I'm knackered though.'

Moore grabbed his gear and headed for the bathroom. Ten minutes later he was showered and shaved. He dressed in clean khaki chinos and a black T-shirt.

Katie was waiting by the door and led the way through to the other dorm room. The Batman fan was asleep now, snoring beneath the comic over his face.

Todd was in the hangar talking to the short U2 fan when they came out. He broke off and came to them.

'Time for some breakfast?' he said. 'Or lunch or dinner-doesn't make much difference.'

'Lead the way,' Moore invited him. 'I could chew the arse out of a low-flying duck right now.'

Todd cocked his head quizzically.

'That sure is descriptive, pal, but I don't think we've got duck on the menu today. Maybe some chicken though.'

He took them out a side door into the bright sunshine and across a dusty compound to another building. Moore scanned around and saw huts dotted about. Razor wire topped the high walls and he saw a guard tower on one corner.

A small group of operators were at a corner table in the dining hall, mugs of coffee in front of them and carbines near at hand. They looked up and nodded to Todd, and looked curiously at the newcomers.

The scullery was manned by a tattooed cook with a Fu Manchu moustache.

They each grabbed a plate and piled them high with beans, over easy eggs, hash browns, and toast. Todd fetched coffee and took them to the opposite side of the room from the group of operators. For five minutes they ate in silence, Todd watching them with amusement while he supped his coffee.

Finally Moore pushed his plate away and sat back, munching on a slice of whole wheat toast. He swallowed, washed it down with a swig of coffee and eyed Todd across the table. The American watched him carefully, an amused half-smile on his face.

'What's on your mind, pal?'

Moore put his mug down.

'Bragg?' he said.

Todd's moustache twitched.

'Papakura?' he countered.

Moore took the first step.

'Yep.' He shrugged. 'Used to be, anyway.'

Todd tilted his chin.

'And now?'

Moore met his gaze.

'The Service,' he said.

Todd nodded slowly, as if his suspicions had been confirmed. He tapped a thick finger against the side of his mug. He nodded again; decision made.

'Delta,' he said.

It was Moore's turn to nod.

'Thought so,' he said. 'Still, or used to?'

Todd smirked.

'Still,' he said.

'Not Langley then?'

Todd shook his head.

'No, not Langley. Maybe one day.' He stroked his beard and turned to Katie, who had watched the dance in silence. 'And you, Miss Katie?'

She looked at him.

'Me what?'

'You're SIS as well?'

She shook her head.

'Na, I'm a cop.'

Todd shot a quick look to Moore, who nodded.

'Seriously? What the hell?'

'Long story,' Moore said.

Todd cocked an eyebrow.

'Kinda changes things a bit,' he said.

Moore set his jaw stubbornly.

'No need to,' he said.

Todd frowned.

'I think that's maybe not your decision, pal,' he said. 'It changes things for us, being what we are; we got op-sec considerations.'

'No reason it should,' Moore insisted. He leaned forward too, elbows on the table in a mirror of Todd's position. 'Op-sec is fine; I'm vouching.'

The tension between the two men was palpable. Katie wiped her mouth on a paper napkin.

Moore knew it was a turning point, but despite the food in his belly he was exhausted and didn't give a shit anymore. He knew what Katie had been through and he realised he believed in her. No longer was she an outsider. She had his vote and that was all that mattered to him.

He held Todd's level gaze. Finally the other man gave a short nod.

'I hear you,' he said.

Moore drained his mug and set it down with a clunk.

'So,' he said. 'Some people want to speak to us.'

He glanced up as the surfer dude and his Hispanic mate entered the room. They joined the team at the other table. He turned back to Todd.

'They do,' the American said. He leaned forward further, lowering his voice. 'Langley.'

Moore glanced first at Katie then back to Todd.

'Sweet as,' he said. 'Give us five minutes to let the food settle and I'll call base, then we'll talk to them.'

Todd nodded, stood, and walked away.

Moore leaned in close to Katie, lowering his voice as he spoke urgently.

'Just answer their questions,' he said, 'they want intel, not evidence okay? Tell it how it was. Remember I interrogated the guy in the suit while you were inside checking for any intel we could find; you had no part in that, right?'

She nodded quietly.

'What're you going to say about that?' she asked.

'I'll be honest about how I interrogated him and he answered some questions.' His face was serious and he hoped she got the message. 'This is war, remember, not some back street of provincial New Zealand. Different rules apply.'

Katie nodded firmly.

'Got it, no worries.'

'Good. Let's do it.'

33

The Billy Crystal lookalike took Katie first and told Moore not go too far.

He wandered out into the hangar and spoken to Jedi via phone-which he had no doubt was listened to anyway-and received brief instructions. The Director was happy to cooperate fully with the Americans and gave them the green light. Jedi also confirmed that the Police were aware of Katie travelling overseas but not the reason behind it.

Moore asked for an update on Natalie Oldham.

'Nothing so far,' Jedi told him. 'The techos got us some stuff to work with from her computer, but so far we don't have anything we can work up. Her father's on our case about it-well, his little sidekick is anyway-calling the boss every day wanting to know where we're at with it.'

The Ops Officer's tone was one of frustration.

'He's a funny wee fella,' Moore commented.

Jedi grunted down the line but refrained from voicing his own thoughts.

'The Minister is very keen to get traction on finding his daughter,' he said instead, 'and that means the Director is too. Do what you need to do, Rob.'

'I don't even know what bloody country I'm in at the moment, mate,' Moore replied. 'Has JJ come up with anything back in Turkey?'

There was a pause and for a moment Moore thought he'd lost the connection.

'JJ's dead,' Jedi said bluntly.

Moore felt a kick in his chest and physically recoiled. He pulled the phone away from his ear and stared at it, hearing Jedi's voice from far away.

'What? What d'you mean he's dead?'

'Not a hundy on that yet. It appears that he fell down the stairs at the hotel where he met you, broke his neck.'

Moore's mind immediately flashed back to the impression he'd had on exiting the hotel himself, the movement he'd detected above him in the stairwell. Could it have been an assassin? A killer who eluded him and dealt to JJ by throwing him down the stairs? The way things were going so far, he certainly couldn't rule it out. He kept it to himself for now though, knowing he had nothing factual to base his suspicions on.

'What about the woman he was working with?' he said. 'Evin, I think her name was?'

'No idea mate,' Jedi said. 'Never heard of her. I'll follow it up.'

'Once we're clear from here we can head back to Ankara and chase her up,' Moore offered. 'She was with him on the day; she has to have seen something.'

'I'll keep you posted. In the meantime, play nicely with your new friends.'

Moore grinned to himself and disconnected. He turned and looked around him at the inside of the hangar. Sure enough, one of Todd's crew was not far away, keeping a not so subtle eye on him.

Moore put the phone away and headed back to the chow hall.

He got himself another coffee to fight off the fatigue, and when he resumed his seat he was joined by the surfer dude and his team-mates. Todd was nowhere to be seen.

'Jerry,' said the surfer dude, extending his hand. 'This is Joel, Chuck, Marko, Knees and Bobby.'

Moore shook their hands in turn.

'Rob,' he said.

'So you were with The Group?' Jerry asked, sitting opposite him.

'Yep. Fifteen years.'

Jerry let out a low whistle, and so began the informal interview that always took place when operators from different units came across each other-did you know so-and-so, where you on such-and-such an operation, what troop were you in?

Moore relaxed in the easy chatter, feeling comfortable in their company, although he wasn't fooling himself that he was still at their level. These were battle-hardened warriors, at the peak of their powers, constantly training and fighting.

While one of the guys-the short muscle-headed guy, Bobby-regaled them with a story about a British SAS trooper they'd had on attachment, Moore had a sudden flash of self-doubt.

He was a few years out of this game, despite the regular operations and training he did, plus he realised he was at least five years older than any of them. His life was certainly softer now than it had been. Gone was the hardnosed Special Forces NCO, the expert at unconventional warfare, replaced by a spook who, although still highly skilled, played a different game. A string-puller; a shadow dancer.

No, he told himself, that's bullshit. He knew that he'd acquitted himself well in the last few days, and his words to Katie came back to him.

Your training, your instincts, your guts-that's what got you through. And you should be proud of that.

Looking at the operators around him, he realised he was being unfair to himself. It was like comparing a former top athlete with the current star of the team. He forced the negativity from his head and tuned back into the conversation, hearing his name being called.

He looked up. Billy Crystal was at the door, waving for him to come.

Moore pushed himself away from the table.

'Thanks for the chat, fellas,' he smiled to his companions, 'we must do it again some time.'

THE BILLY CRYSTAL lookalike had introduced himself as Pat and sat with Moore in a Portakabin decked out as a lounge of sorts.

The debrief was audio recorded. They sat in plastic lawn chairs.

Pat had run through the preliminaries then got straight into it.

'We've been to the farm. The phones you recovered gave us some valuable intel,' he said. 'You know who the suit was, I guess?'

'The Doctor,' Moore confirmed.

'Got it. We have solid intel linking him to ISIS and particularly to eight murders-civilian informers mostly plus a couple of aid workers. Ten to one he's had a hand in many more than that.'

Moore nodded. None of this was news.

'One of the other guys there was a known player, often acted as The Doctor's bodyguard. Iraqi, ex-Republican Guard-one of Saddam's boys. He's been on a watch list for a long time.' Pat adjusted his lapel mic. 'The others were unknowns, appears they were all Turks. We're doing some more work on them.'

Moore listened intently, disinterested in the individuals but eager to know where they had come from and how he had come to cross their path.

'So how about we start at the beginning and you run me through your interactions with these guys.'

Pat sat back, his body language open and relaxed. It was like talking to a shrink, Moore thought.

He did as he was asked, taking the spook through each step of the previous hours, from the time he had landed in Turkey to the exfiltration by the Delta Force team. He spoke succinctly, not wasting words, and offering no opinions. He explained how he had sent Katie back inside the building after the contact at the farm, and how he had interrogated The Doctor using pain compliance.

He thought he saw a flicker in Pat's otherwise impassive face at that point, but nothing was said. He hoped that Katie had kept to the brief-too bad right now if she hadn't, he had to stick to his story.

When he was finished, Moore sat back.

'And here we are,' he said, gesturing around them. 'Somewhere in Northern Iraq, I'm guessing.'

Pat gave a small smile but didn't bite.

'So just to clarify,' he said, 'you managed to free yourself except for your hands, and you attacked the two guards when they entered the cell with your colleague? You disarmed and incapacitated them both with your hands bound behind your back?'

'That's right,' Moore said.

'Are you serious? You had your hands tied behind your back, and you took out two guys armed with AK47s and pistols?'

'Yep.' Moore looked him in the eye. 'That's what happened.'

Pat shook his head, either in disbelief or amazement-he was too professional to give much away. Either way, it annoyed Moore, but he bit his tongue.

'Then as you attempt to escape from the cell you are surprised by a guy in the outer room, and you both shoot him.'

'Correct.'

'And during this your prisoner is shot in the back of the head.'

Pat met Moore's gaze. He had expressionless brown eyes.

'Correct.'

There was silence for a long moment. Moore knew that Pat was using the silence, wanting him to fill it with a further explanation. He stayed silent.

'It could almost sound...I don't know...a bit like an execution,' Pat said.

His tone was neutral. Moore shrugged.

'It could. But it wasn't. He moved the wrong way in a dynamic situation and was accidentally shot.' He shrugged again. 'Regrettable perhaps, but it happens.'

Pat nodded.

'Uh-huh. Then outside you're about to leave on foot when the vehicle arrives and you engage the three occupants, killing all three.'

'They got spooked by something and we had our hand forced,' Moore said. 'The plan was to stay out of sight and try and take their vehicle. It didn't work out and things went noisy.'

Pat gave another slight nod.

'So you shot all of them?'

'I did.'

'All three of them, without either of you being wounded, even though they were armed?'

'That's right.'

'That's some pretty serious shooting,' Pat commented.

Moore nodded, said nothing. It wasn't his place to praise his own work.

'So the driver and the bodyguard die instantly and The Doctor survives a short time.' Pat made eye contact again. 'Correct?'

'Yes.'

'You send your colleague inside to check for any intel, and you interrogate him using, aghh...pain compliance techniques?'

Here it comes, Moore thought. She's dropped me in it.

'Yep,' he said confidently.

Pat nodded thoughtfully.

'Where did you learn pain compliance techniques, Rob? It's not something you can study at university.'

Moore held his gaze.

'I was in the Special Air Service for a long time.'

He left it at that, letting Pat draw his own conclusions.

'I see.' Pat leaned forward and picked up a remote off the floor. He used it to stop the recorder, and unclipped his mic.

Moore did likewise, passing the device over.

'Thanks for that Rob,' the spook said.

They stood and shook hands. Pat guided him to the door, not speaking further until they stepped outside into the bright sunshine.

'Just FYI, buddy,' he said, slipping on a pair of Oakley blades, 'it seemed pretty obvious that some, agghh, non-pain-compliance techniques were also utilised back there. Nothing documented, of course,' he added hastily, seeing Moore's expression, 'it was just an observation from one of the guys who went to the farm.'

He smiled, his eyes hidden behind the coloured lenses.

'I got no issues myself, okay...just be careful is what I'm saying.' He glanced over his shoulder at the Portakabin they had just left. 'And that's why I'm saying it out here, okay?'

Moore nodded, getting the message-the official recording device was off but the room was wired up nonetheless. He heard a volley of shots somewhere over the other side of the hangar, a pause then another volley. Pat didn't bat an eyelid.

'Kudos to you guys, buddy,' Pat said, extending his hand again. 'You did just great back there.'

Moore shook his hand firmly.

'Thanks,' he said. 'You got a range here?'

'Sure, over yonder. The boys're probably putting down some rounds.'

Moore smiled inwardly at the spooks terminology-spoken like a true non-combatant.

'And your colleague?' Pat let out a low whistle and crooked a grin. 'She's a real pistol, ain't she?'

Moore shrugged.

'She's pretty typical for how we breed 'em down under,' he said with a poker face.

34

He left Pat and followed his nose round the far side of the hangar, realising the camp was much bigger than he had originally thought.

The sound of pistol shots led him to a steel pedestrian gate in the boundary wall, manned by a guy in shades, body armour and a helmet over his civvies. A HK G3 was in his hands.

He opened the gate for Moore without being asked and called him 'Sir' when Moore thanked him. He stopped short of wishing him a nice day.

A firing range had been set up beyond the boundary with a large earth berm as its backstop. Alleys were marked out with targets at the end.

Todd, Jerry and a couple of the others were there, all wearing protective glasses and ear defenders. Katie was the only shooter, also decked out in protective gear, with a sidearm holstered on her hip.

As Moore approached he saw Todd hit a switch on a remote control he held. A target at the end of Katie's alley flicked around, thirty metres or so away, presenting her with the upper half of a paper soldier carrying a rifle.

She reacted quickly, snatching the pistol from her hip and bringing it up smoothly as she took a step offline to the right.

Moore stuck his fingers in his ears as she pumped a double tap into the target, stepped back left and gave it another two. It sounded like a .45.

Even from this distance Moore could see she was hitting the target in the centre mass with all her shots. He joined the operators at the table they had set up as she covered down the target. Jerry gave him a thumbs up as a welcome.

'Threat!' Todd barked.

Katie reacted instantly, bringing the pistol back up and putting another round through the target's chest. She stepped offline and moved, squeezing off shots as she moved tactically forward.

Suddenly the target in the alley to her left flicked around, presenting a woman holding a baby. Katie swung to face it, her gun coming up, then the target in the alley on her right snapped around.

Katie swung back to face another soldier and squeezed of a fast shot, going wide. Her second shot took him in the chest and her slide locked open.

'Stoppage!' she shouted, stepping away and dropping to a knee as she ejected the magazine, jerked a spare from the magazine pouch on her belt and slammed it into place, sweeping off the slide release with her thumb and pumping a double tap into the second target's gut.

'Stop!' Todd called, switching the targets back side on.

Katie holstered her weapon and turned around, removing her ear defenders. She had a satisfied grin on her face.

'Nice shooting,' Todd said, also removing his protective gear.

Jerry moved forward with her and went to check the targets.

Moore looked questioningly at Todd.

'She asked about our weapons,' the Delta operator explained. 'Thought it might be good to get her back in the saddle.'

Down range Jerry said something and gave Katie a loud high-five. They both laughed. Moore felt a stab of annoyance and wondered exactly what saddle they planned to get her into.

'You've been there,' Todd continued, 'sometimes guys get gun-shy after an incident. Me and my guys make a habit of getting straight back on the range after an op, get back in the game.' He chucked his chin approvingly towards the targets as they were swapped over for fresh ones. 'She's pretty damn good too, pal.'

Moore had to agree. Aside from a couple of wide shots she had consistently hit centre mass. More importantly, she had held her fire when confronted by the innocent civilian.

'That's a pretty sweet gun,' Katie grinned as she and Jerry rejoined the group at the table. 'I've never fired a forty five before-it definitely kicks more than our Glocks.'

'You did real well,' Jerry drawled, 'we'll have to get you on the team, huh?'

She grinned girlishly and Moore felt his irritation kick up a notch. He noticed one of the other guys roll his eyes in the background as Jerry kidded with Katie.

'That the HK?' Moore asked, wanting to break the moment.

'Sure is,' Jerry replied, turning away from Katie to look at him. 'Want a try, show us how the Papakura boys do it?'

Moore sensed more than a hint of a challenge in his words and gritted his teeth. He was starting to dislike the surfer dude and his attitude, which seemed more cocky than laid back.

'Sure,' he said, knowing he had no real choice.

He accepted the ear defenders and glasses he was offered, then the holstered pistol and magazine holder from Katie. He threaded the pouch onto his left front side and the low profile tactical holster onto his right hip.

Todd passed him two fresh magazines and he loaded the pistol, racking a round into the chamber. It was the Special Operations Command version of a standard civilian Heckler and Koch Mark 23, with a 12-round magazine. He knew it was a favourite of the American SF guys, and had used it before-albeit a long time ago, he thought.

'Listen to my commands,' Todd told him, 'reload if you have to, shoot it as you see it. Range is live,' he called out, indicating for everyone to don their protective gear.

Moore moved up to the forty metre mark, flexing his fingers and mentally engaging the gears. He knew this was a test from the Delta boys, soldiers always being keen to see what their compadres from other units could do, but he felt it was more so from the cocky Jerry. The guy obviously had designs on Katie and saw him as some kind of threat. Embarrassing Moore on the range would only serve to help his cause.

Moore set his stance and waited, eyeing the target down range.

There was no command from Todd, just an electronic whir and the target flicked around, presenting him with an armed soldier.

The HK came out smoothly, the safety swiping off as it came up, and Moore drilled an instinctive double tap into the soldier's chest, stepping off and scanning for threats.

The target switched back and the one in the right hand lane swung round. Moore turned and gave the soldier two in the chest, heard the left hand target switch back behind him and spun, seeing another soldier and pumping a shot into his face then two more into the chest.

Both targets snapped back and the original figure in front of him turned again.

Moore squeezed a shot off, nailing him through the nose, and began to move forward, the pistol at the high ready. By now it was just an extension of his arm.

With a whir both the neighbouring targets flicked back around, confronting him with a dual threat.

Moore dropped to a half crouch and put a single round into the chest of the left hand target, swivelled with the pistol still up, squeezed a double tap into the right hand chest and swung left again, putting his last round into the left eye of the left hand target before the slide locked open.

He dropped the mag and slammed the replacement home, the three targets switching back side on, his thumb releasing the slide and chambering a fresh round as a new target spun to face him. This was in the next lane over on the right, the distance giving a sharper angle.

He stepped that way, crabbing a couple of steps sideways, recognising the figure of a woman with a baby. He held his fire, scanned left behind him, and saw the target in the corresponding lane to his left spin around. He was at a narrow angle now and maybe thirty five metres away.

The HK came round fluidly and Moore took an aimed shot, his index finger squeezing through to trip the trigger. The round drilled through the face of the target and suddenly all four of the targets he'd already engaged flicked around.

Moore shifted his aim to the next target along, drilling a double tap into the chest, moving to the one directly in front of him and giving it two in the face, two more in the face for the next one then ignored the woman with the baby in the last frame.

He moved backwards, the HK barking as it spat a final round into each of the four threats. All four targets took a bullet in the forehead.

He swung back to the target directly in front of him and gave it a last bullet to the head.

The slide locked back and Moore stopped, lowering his weapon. Blue smoke curled from the barrel and ejection port.

He popped out the empty mag, released the slide and holstered the weapon.

He sensed the others joining him.

'Pretty good,' Todd observed, stripping off his shades as he approached.

One of the others checked all the targets and gave them a thumbs up.

'Nailed it,' Todd said with a grin. 'Nice work, pal.'

Moore shrugged.

'Bit rusty,' he said, 'it's been a while.'

Jerry squinted at the target straight ahead then turned to Moore.

'Two in the mouth,' he commented.

Moore looked at him, cocking an eyebrow.

'Must've had a big mouth,' he said drily.

35

He and Katie ate lunch with Todd's team, and near the end they were joined by the older man who had been with Pat the spook when they had first arrived that morning.

He was still in unmarked desert fatigues. His skin was deeply tanned, which only enhanced the blue of his eyes. He was in his mid-forties, Moore estimated.

'Boss,' Todd greeted him as the man arrived. 'This is Rob and Katie. Guys, this is the boss, Major- '

'Mike,' the newcomer said, extending his hand. 'Call me Mike.'

They both stood to shake hands before he sat, one of the boys giving up his chair and fetching him a coffee unbidden. It was obvious that the boss was held in high regard by the men. Mike nodded his thanks and took a sip.

'You were always the best barista on this team, Joel,' he said. He turned his attention to the two Kiwis across from him. 'I hear you did okay out there on the range.'

Moore hiked his shoulders.

'We appreciate the opportunity to have a run,' he said, 'your guys know their stuff.'

'I've just been speaking to your boss, Jed,' Mike told him. 'He's a good man. I've met him a few times over the years. Shame what happened to him.'

'It was,' Moore agreed. 'Best RSM we had in my time.'

'I understand he's given you the authority to saddle up with us,' Mike said. 'Pat's got an update for us, so I need you all' -he glanced around the team- 'in the briefing room at 1315 hours.'

There was a flurry of nods and checking of watches.

'In the meantime Toddy, get these guys decked out will ya? We should have enough kit to spare.'

Enough kit to spare was an understatement.

One thing Moore had always admired about the American military was their supplies. Unlike what he'd been used to, there was plenty of everything.

The store room was in the hangar, rows of gear of every description stashed behind a counter manned by a soldier in his late twenties. He had a vicious-looking scar running through his crewcut from the top of his left eyebrow back to the crown of his head. His left eye was glass. He didn't say much as he sized up the two guests.

'Morning Streak,' Todd said to the younger man. 'I need you to kit these folk out for me. Same as I got this morning, pal.'

Streak nodded wordlessly and headed back into one of the aisles of shelving.

Katie looked at Moore questioningly but said nothing. A few moments later Streak reappeared with an armful of neatly folded desert fatigues. He plonked them on the counter in front of Katie and leaned over the top to peer at her feet.

'Eight,' he said quietly and headed to another rack for a pair of desert boots.

He passed them over and repeated the process for Moore, then added a kit bag to each pile and looked to Todd again.

'Weapons, Top?' he asked.

The Delta team leader shook his head while Moore and Katie crammed their new gear into the bags.

'Not just yet,' he replied. 'Thanks Streak.'

He winked at the storeman and led his guests back towards their quarters.

'Training accident,' he explained before they asked, 'he got hurt during Selection and Assessment. We kept him on in a support role rather than throw him on the scrap heap. He's a good kid.'

'Good call,' Moore said.

It was typical of a Special Forces unit to look after their own if they could, even those who hadn't been badged. He hefted the bag in his hand.

'What's with all this? Something you're not telling us, mate?'

Todd crooked a grin and paused outside the dorms.

'I guess we'll find out in about,' -he checked his watch- 'twelve minutes. I'll come get you in ten. Just come as you are for now.'

With that he left them. Katie looked at Moore again. He waved her inside and they dumped their gear in their quarters before sitting on the cots to face each other.

'What the fuck is all this about?' she said with a perplexed expression. 'I mean, it's great that they helped us out and everything, and I like getting free stuff, even if it is camouflage gear, but...I'm supposed to be searching for my missing friend in Turkey, not running round the desert playing soldiers. I get the impression there's something going on here that we're not being told. Unless' -she gave him a suspicious squint- 'you're full of shit and are just keeping me in the dark.'

Moore sighed and spread his hands.

'Look, I know as much as you do at the moment. If I knew more I would tell you.' He caught her look. 'Honestly, I would. My goal for you is to get you the hell outta here. Whether that means back to Turkey to look for Natalie is a different question altogether.'

She gave him that suspicious squint again.

'Well it's pretty bloody dangerous, isn't it?' he said, and began to tick off points on his fingers. 'Since you've come to Turkey you've been assaulted by a couple of heavies who tried to snatch you, you've been shot at, you've gone on the run, you've had a suicide bomber try to blow you up, you've been kidnapped by ISIS terrorists, you've had to kill a guy to escape, and now you're somewhere in Iraq with Delta Force.'

He spread his hands again and looked her in the eye.

'It's hardly the standard fuckin' Contiki is it?'

'Iraq?' she said, 'really?'

'I think so, yeah.'

'And who the hell are Delta Force anyway. Wasn't there a movie about them?'

'Basically a Yank version of the SAS. They're extremely good. And yes, there have been many movies-most of them shit.'

'What's our next move?' Katie asked. 'Do we have to stay with these guys? I mean, are we under some kind of obligation or what?'

'For now, we stick with them,' Moore said. 'At least until we hear what they have to say at this briefing. It's supposedly some new intel, so hopefully it's something of use to us. At the end of the day you and I are trying to do the same job, which is find Natalie Oldham. Somehow that's tied up with whatever these guys are currently tasked with; I don't know how, but it is, otherwise those pricks wouldn't bother snatching us.'

He paused, carefully weighing up his next move.

'The only thing I haven't told you,' he said, and she cocked an expectant eyebrow at him, 'I spoke to my boss this morning. My contact in Ankara was killed after our meeting.'

Katie sat up straighter, all ears now. Shock registered on her face.

'He was found at the bottom of some stairs with a broken neck. It's been treated as an accident, but I doubt it was that.'

He explained what he had seen and heard as he left the stairwell, and Katie nodded, accepting his suspicions.

'So what do we do about that then?' she asked. 'I'm guessing the Turkish cops probably won't work too hard on it.'

'We'll see what these guys have got to tell us today and we'll go from there,' he replied. 'JJ was a good man, if he was taken out then somebody needs to be held to account.'

Moore felt his blood pressure go up as he said it, and he looked away, his cheeks flushing with anger.

'Well lucky you've got a detective on the team then, eh,' Katie said brightly after a moment. 'Come on, we better go meet your pal.'

36

Todd escorted them to a secure briefing room, where they found the major and Pat, along with Todd's team assembled on folding chairs facing an AV screen.

Pat killed the lights and took centre stage, Mike standing off to the side. Moore and Katie took the empty front row with Todd.

'Okay folks,' Pat began, 'we've analysed the electronic data from the guys our New Zealand friends encountered. As we know, the main man was Mohammed al-Rishawi, known as The Doctor. He was a relative of the female terrorist executed in Jordan last year for burning a pilot alive in a cage.'

Moore had seen the video the terrorists had broadcast of that execution, and an unwelcome image of it flashed back through his mind. It had sickened him at the time and was no better in retrospect.

Pat addressed them directly as he continued.

'We identified Obasi Karim and Kassim Karim as the guards you overpowered. They were brothers, and were known ISIS sympathisers. The bodyguard was another Jordanian, Rashad Yildiray, well known to us for a number of years. We're not sure on the other two yet, but they both appear to be Iraqi.'

The spook flicked up photos of all the players from the farm. The ones they had identified featured in surveillance shots, whereas the two unknowns-the driver and the guy they had shot inside-were shown in situ in all the goriness of their violent deaths.

'Needless to say, nobody's mourning the loss of these guys. Now, taking it back a step,' Pat said, flicking up a new surveillance photo.

The image resonated with Moore but he couldn't quite put his finger on it. It looked like a still image taken from CCTV.

'Our Kiwi friends were also on-site when the suicide bomber blew himself up at a shopping mall in Ankara the other day. This here is the bomber entering the mall itself, moments before the detonation.'

Moore nodded to himself, recognising the guy now.

'Ali al-Jamil was an Iraqi, previously unknown to us. ISIS have released the usual rhetoric about the bombing, but given the bomber was seen following these guys it seems reasonable to deduce that they were specifically targeted.' Pat flicked up a series of images from the mall bombing. 'Last count is twenty two dead, not including the bomber himself and the two shooters who followed him in.'

The screen changed to another CCTV still, this one showing the clean-up crew entering the mall.

'We haven't ID'd these guys yet, I'm picking they're Iraqi also, probably came over the border with al-Jamil. We're currently trying to retrace their steps.' He gave a wry smile. 'Not getting much assistance from our Turkish friends, however. As an aside though, as far as we're aware they haven't identified the two shooters or our friends here either.'

He brought up a headshot of a bearded, middle aged Iraqi. Moore recognised him immediately, and the murmurs among the Delta operators told him they knew the face too.

'Nassim al-Hussein, as you know. He's Top Twenty for us, presently sitting at number nineteen, and has been on the run since the 2006 Sadr City bombings. Our intel identifies him as a principal organiser of suicide bombers.' He glanced down to Moore and Katie. 'I don't know what you guys know about them, but suicide bombings are usually extremely well organised and planned. We believe he was one of the organisers behind Sadr City, which killed two hundred and fifty seven.'

Katie stiffened noticeably.

'How solid is your intel on that?' Moore asked.

Pat eyed him coolly.

'Solid enough for the FBI to request we actively hunt him down and kill him,' he said. He turned back to the screen, clicking through to an aerial map. 'This is Qahira, a village about forty klicks this side of the Syrian border and close enough to Turkey. It's been taken and retaken numerous times by various factions over the years-Kurds, the Coalition, ISIS. Traditionally an area frequented by Bedouin and of little economic value to anyone, it's a lot of sandy dirt and scrub and not a lot else. Last known population in the area is roughly fifty people, if that.'

He flipped up a series of shots depicting a basic village of adobe huts and cooking pits, shepherds herding goats and villagers staring unsmilingly at the camera.

'A pretty standard village as far as we are aware,' Pat continued, 'however it is linked to al-Hussein through his father, who was born there. There's been some scuttlebutt over time that al-Hussein has sought refuge there while on the run.'

'How recent?' Jerry interrupted.

'The last piece was from a prisoner around six months ago. He said al-Hussein had spent a night or two there before moving on. We hit the vill within hours but came up empty, not even a sign that he'd been there and nobody was talking of course.'

Pat flicked back to the photo of The Doctor, and now he smiled.

'Jumping forward to today, this is where our electronic analysis comes into play. Our good dentist friend's phone had made a call shortly before his arrival at the farm to another phone which we have triangulated to Qahira.'

'How close?' Todd asked, stroking his beard with one hand.

'Right in the heart of it,' Pat responded, still smiling. 'Naturally we don't know who the user of the other phone is, with it being a standard burn phone and all, but that phone has itself made a call to young Master Ali al-Jamil, just half an hour before he blew himself up in the mall.'

Moore felt his pulse pick up. Now they were getting somewhere. He listened intently.

'Where was that call from?' Todd asked.

Pat cut back to the aerial shot of Qahira.

'Right here,' he said.

Now Mike stepped forward and took the lead, his hands clasped behind his back.

'This intel was put together around 0800 hours today,' he rasped. 'We inserted a small team on foot around 1100 hours. They have established an OP on Qahira and are giving us live intel. From what they can see there is definitely some activity in the village, however they have not eyeballed any persons of interest.'

He had everybody's full attention.

'If they sight al-Hussein, they have instructions to take the shot.' The major looked around the assembled troops. 'He is to be taken out and the team are to withdraw immediately.'

He took a few paces to his left and stopped again, before turning back to Pat.

'Give it to them,' he said.

Pat stepped forward again, and addressed Moore and Katie specifically.

'The twist in all this is that we've been trying to figure out why these guys are so interested in you two. It just doesn't make any sense, unless there is some kind of link between what you are doing and these guys' business, which you would think would be extremely unlikely. However…' He clicked through to a passport-style facial shot of Natalie Oldham.

Moore sensed a shuffling among the operators behind them as they took in the photo. Pat turned his attention to the group of men.

'This is Natalie Oldham, daughter of a New Zealand politician, who is currently believed to be missing somewhere in Turkey. She is a friend of Miss Katie Simpson here, who has travelled over from

London to look for her in an unofficial capacity. Rob is here as a representative of the NZ High Commission, also looking for her.'

The screen changed to a typed paragraph of dialogue.

'This is an excerpt of a conversation snatched yesterday between The Doctor's phone and another as yet unidentified user. You can read it for yourselves.'

He stayed silent while they all read the passage.

They do not have the same value as the other one. She will be a wonderful tool for our leader.

You are right my brother. She is certainly a tremendous coup for us. I cannot imagine the surprise when they see her.

May Allah be praised, my friend. Every blow we strike to the hearts of the infidels brings us closer to our own Paradise. God is great.

'The first speaker is The Doctor, al-Rishawi. As I say we don't know who the second guy is, can't get a match on the voice recognition, but it's a fair bet it's someone pretty close to the action, since they were clearly talking about our two Kiwis and Miss Oldham.'

'What time was this?' Moore asked.

'Nearly an hour after the bombing,' Pat said, 'while you two were on the train.'

Moore nodded slowly, thinking.

'What we are taking from this is that these guys have Miss Oldham and see her as some kind of an ace card to play. The expectation is that either a ransom demand will be made or -' he avoided eye contact with Katie now -'she will appear online in an execution video.'

Moore unconsciously reached out and touched Katie's hand. It was trembling. She clenched hard, her nails digging into his palm.

'Neither of these things have happened yet,' Pat said uncomfortably. 'And of course we need to keep an open mind...

'So what's with us?' Moore said. 'I've been told to ride along with you, you've issued us some gear...why are we here?'

Mike stepped up again.

'We suspect that Miss Oldham may be being held in Qahira. It makes sense to keep her out of the way somewhere quiet, handy to a couple of different borders, easy to move.' He rocked on his heels. 'Our plan is to get in there and see for sure. We know something's going on there, and all signs point to it being her.'

Katie released Moore's hand and spoke for the first time.

'And what if you're wrong? What if she's not there? Isn't there a chance that your intel will be blown and they just move her and become more careful?'

Mike considered his answer carefully before responding.

'That's true Miss Simpson, and it's a good point. But right now, we got nothin' else. The intel looks good and we've got the capability to act on it.' He hiked his shoulders. 'These guys are always damn careful; it's not every day we get enough to go kicking doors. If we don't act on it, we could miss a golden opportunity to rescue a hostage.'

He fixed her with a firm but almost fatherly look.

'This is what we do, Miss Simpson, and we are damn good at it.'

She nodded and sat back in her chair. Moore interjected before the major could continue.

'So you're babysitting us then,' he said, with more than a hint of accusation in his tone.

Mike turned his gaze to him. The fatherly tinge disappeared in an instant.

'We don't do babysitting, friend,' he rasped. 'You are here, standing by for us to bring Miss Oldham back. When we do, the three of you are straight on a plane back to NZ. Once you leave here she's your responsibility.'

Moore held his gaze and bit his tongue. Mike broke the stare and looked to Todd.

'Break off,' he said, 'and get a plan together.'

The Delta operators stood and filed out in silence. The door banged shut behind the last man. Pat lingered in the background behind the major. The tension in the air was unmistakable.

Moore stood and Mike picked up the eyeball again.

'I want to go on the op,' Moore said bluntly.

Mike lifted his chin a fraction, staring at him.

'Why? We don't need you out there.'

'Why not?' Moore countered. 'What can it hurt? You know my background; your guys saw my skills today. I've been given clearance by my head shed to co-operate, and that's all I want to do.'

'We don't take civilians along on operations,' Mike said. 'Sorry, but it's not gonna happen.'

'Bullshit,' Moore snapped back, his hackles rising. 'I've worked with you guys before, I know how you operate. I spent a goddamn week in a hide in the mountains of Afghanistan with two of my guys and a spook from the agency. If it's good enough for us it's good enough for you.'

He felt Katie's hand on his arm and pulled away angrily.

'Look, we've got an interest in this situation here, Major. This isn't some kinda fuckin' jolly I'm asking for. All I'm asking for is a professional courtesy, in the interests of our special relationship.'

They were almost toe to toe now, and neither man was backing down. Moore could feel the anger coming off Mike in waves.

He heard the door open behind them but didn't break his stare.

Todd's voice broke the moment.

'Ahh, boss...may I have a minute of your time?'

Mike's eyes flickered but he didn't move. Moore knew he was pushing his luck, and that banging heads with the Delta commander was the wrong move, but after the actions of the last few days his frustration levels were dangerously high. He had the scent of the hunt and no interest in being a spectator.

'Not now, Top,' Mike grated, 'I'm kinda busy.'

''ppreciate that, boss,' Todd said easily, 'but this is kinda important.'

A vein throbbed in Mike's temple. His eyes were boring into Moore's skull with an intensity only managed by school principals and commissioned officers.

'What is it?' he growled.

'Well boss, I know it's not a good time, but...me and the boys have had a Chinese Parliament, and I'm asking a favour.'

The major finally broke his stare from Moore's face and turned to his NCO. His face and neck were flushed as he stalked over and took him aside. They spoke in hushed tones, their backs to the others.

Moore glanced to Katie and Pat while they waited. Both looked wide-eyed and tense, and he gave himself a mental uppercut for his bullheadedness. He knew he'd just made a major fuck up he couldn't come back from.

After several tense moments the two soldiers turned and came back to where Moore waited. The angry red had crept down Mike's face to his neck, but his lips were still pursed. Todd stood at his shoulder, looking apprehensive.

'Seems this is your lucky day, Mr Moore,' Mike growled. 'It may be one of my failings, but I tend to listen to my men. They can be a bunch of bandits at times, but they tend to talk sense. They've asked for you and Miss Simpson to accompany them on their mission to Qahira.'

Moore threw a momentary glance over the major's shoulder to Todd and got a tiny flick of the eyebrows in acknowledgement.

'But understand this, son,' the major continued, waving a finger of warning for emphasis, 'you follow the directions of the team and don't make me regret my decision. And if, by God, you ever front me like that again...I will kick you so hard you'll be growin' ass hairs outta your ears, you understand?'

Moore gave a nod and let his breath out through his nose. He swallowed his pride and did his best to look contrite.

'My apologies, Major,' he said and extended his hand. 'I was out of line.'

Mike gave a brief nod and shook his hand. He was smaller than Moore but his grip was crushing.

'Done,' the major said. He turned to Katie. 'Ma'am.'

With that he marched out, Pat falling in behind him.

'Jesus fuckin' Christ, pal,' Todd breathed, as soon as the door had closed. 'You are one lucky son of a bitch, you know that?' He glanced over his shoulder and jerked a thumb at the door. 'You don't know who he is, do ya?'

'He's Major Mike,' Moore replied blithely, and Todd shook his head in amazement.

'He ain't just some chucklehead officer, pal. He rose up from an enlisted man. He's been passed over for further promotion twice-shoulda been running the unit by now, but the brass say he's too "operationally oriented," whatever the fuck that means. Remember the Mog in ninety-three?'

Everybody knew of that conflict, immortalised on celluloid as Blackhawk Down. Rangers and Special Forces troops had fought a pitched battle in the Somalian capital of Mogadishu for hours, blasting their way out of the city after a snatch and grab mission went wrong.

'The major was a young Ranger back then, and he won the Silver Star that day.' Todd met Moore's gaze. 'That's a big deal. He won another in Iraq, plus a chest full of other shiny shit. Nobody, I mean nobody, fronts up to the major and walks away from it.' He stroked his moustache and shook his head again. 'You're either dumb as a brick, or you got some serious cajones, pal.'

Moore wasn't sure how to respond, so he thanked the other man instead.

'I certainly didn't expect to get invited along,' he said.

'Is it both of us?' Katie asked, her eyes glistening with excitement.

'Sure is,' Todd told her sombrely. He checked his watch. 'Better get moving. We want to get the both of you back down the range for some trigger time before we load up. Let's hustle.'

37

The Americans were as generous with their weaponry as they were with uniform.

Moore and Katie were issued weapons and left at the range under the watchful eyes of one of the unit's instructors, a wiry Texan named Duke. He ran them through skills and drills on the Armalite M4 carbines, which both of them were comfortable with-Moore had used the M4 and variants for years, and the Bushmaster version was the standard issue Police rifle.

After an hour Duke told them they would move onto basic patrol tactics. Katie was up front about her lack of tactical training, which amounted to almost nothing, so the Texan dismissed Moore and sent him back to the base.

'No point tryin' to teach y'all this, sport,' he drawled. He settled his ball cap on his head a little snugger and turned to Katie, who was loading rifle magazines at the table. 'I'll give you some one to one, ma'am, and see whatcha got.'

Moore was happy to get back into the hangar and find Pat.

'I need some info,' he said without ceremony, locating the spook coming out of the chow hall with a steaming mug in his hand.

'That so?' Pat glanced at the mug, and Moore peered at it.

'What the hell is that?' he asked, wrinkling his nose at the floral scent.

'Chamomile tea,' Pat muttered, avoiding eye contact.

'Seriously?'

'What is it you're wanting, Kiwi?'

'What the fuck is chamomile good for?' Moore persisted, 'don't old ladies drink that shit?'

Pat sighed heavily.

'Look, the guys don't know okay? I only drink it when I know they're not around.' His cheeks flushed. 'My wife doesn't want me drinking too much coffee, okay?'

Moore shrugged.

'Whatever. Anyway, I need some info.' He paused until Pat looked up. 'On one of our staff in Turkey.'

IT WAS NEARLY dinner time when Katie appeared in the doorway to the chow hall.

She spotted Moore at a table with Todd and Knees, gave a quick wave and paused at the serving counter to grab herself a bottle of water before heading over.

Moore ran an appraising eye over her as she took the chair beside him. Her boots were dusty and her grey T-shirt was stained with sweat. He couldn't help but notice that the T-shirt was tight across her breasts. She had sunglasses pushed up on her head and a smudge of gun oil on her cheek. She was grinning and seemed on a high.

'Have fun out there?' he asked as she popped the cap on her bottle.

'That was awesome,' she enthused, 'the Police need to get some of this training going back home.'

Moore and Todd exchanged knowing looks, both recognising the intoxicating buzz of weapons training.

Duke and Jerry came in and headed over, both also dusty and

sweat stained. Jerry took the seat beside Todd so that he was directly opposite Katie, leaving Duke to take the end of the table.

'Go alright, pal?' Todd asked.

The Texan nodded his approval and removed his ball cap to run a hand through his curly hair. It was damp with sweat.

'Pretty decent,' he drawled. 'We just did some basic room clearing and tactical approaches and movement. Got ol' Jer to partner up for the team parts.'

'She did real good,' Jerry agreed, giving Katie a bright white grin across the table. 'Real good. Gave me a run for my money, that's for sure.'

Katie reddened slightly and took a draught of water. She shifted her body round to face Moore, tucking a foot up and resting her knee on his leg. He wondered what the other operators thought of the show of intimacy, but he didn't protest.

'Thanks heaps for doing that,' she said to Duke, 'it was really good. I haven't had a shoot up for ages.'

'M' pleasure,' he drawled, glancing to Jerry.

There was a pregnant pause and Moore glanced at him too, noticing him staring at Katie's knee on Moore's leg. The other man became aware and looked away self-consciously.

'We got a briefing at nineteen hundred,' Todd said, breaking the moment. 'We'll go the briefing room straight from here, okay?'

Moore gave him a tilt of the chin in acknowledgement, and Katie drained her bottle, setting it down on the table.

'Right,' Todd said, pushing up from his seat and looking to his two men. 'Let's go get some shit sorted out before then.'

Katie also moved as the three operators walked out, standing up and grabbing her empty bottle.

'Come on,' she said with a cheeky grin, 'come with me.'

Moore watched her walk to the bin and drop the empty bottle in. The fatigue pants she wore were firm across her buttocks. Fatigues were notoriously unflattering for women, but somehow she managed to make then look good.

He shook his head and stood, following her out of the chow hall, through the unoccupied operators' room to their own quarters.

The door banged shut behind them and Katie turned, grabbing Moore by the front of his T-shirt and leaned up, kissing him hard on the mouth and he responded, their tongues seeking each other out as they pulled hard against each other.

He was surprised at the sudden turn of events, but not enough to stop. She was a desirable girl, no doubt about that. The hell with it.

Moore grabbed her sculpted buttocks with both hands and lifted her onto her tip-toes as they wrestled in a passionate embrace.

Katie broke the lock and ran her hand down his chest to the waistband of his pants, tugging at the button there.

'This better be good,' she panted as she won the battle with the button and started to pull his pants off his hips.

Moore grabbed her T-shirt and yanked it up over her arms, tossing it aside. He cupped his hands over her plain black bra and squeezed her breasts, feeling her nipples hard against his palms through the fabric.

Katie let out a moan as he tweaked her peaks between his thumbs and forefingers.

'I want it hard,' she gasped, 'and fast.'

Moore didn't reply; words were superfluous. He knew what she wanted and he was going to give it to her, no mistake about that. He reached behind her and unclipped the bra, letting it fall away as he moved to her fatigue pants. Her hands were doing likewise, skinning off his pants and briefs and freeing him to her hands. He gave a guttural groan as she went to work, and he jerked her pants down.

He realised they both still had their boots on, and broke the moment to bend down, his head at her thighs.

Katie ran her hands across his head. 'Easy, tiger,' she breathed, 'I don't know you well enough for that just yet.'

'Boots,' he grunted, tugging them off her feet.

'Oh,' she chuckled, still running her hands through his hair.

He quickly did the same to his boots and kicked them aside then straightened up again, dropping his hands to her hips as he kissed her passionately. Her black cotton knickers were still there and he hooked his thumbs into the waistband, yanking them down then using his foot to push them clear of her feet.

He pressed her back against the wall and lifted her right leg, locking his mouth against hers again as he found her wetness. Their tongues lashed at each other and Katie let out a sudden gasp as he entered her, easing his way in at first then thrusting hard, holding her weight as he did so. Her nails raked at his shoulders and back and his legs trembled, their breathing laboured, their sweaty bodies rubbing against each other as they ground together.

Moore found Katie's neck with his free hand and laced his fingers into her hair, breathing the air from her lungs as he drove into her, the friction building rapidly until she began to quiver and clung to him helplessly, clenching tightly and tipping him over the edge seconds later.

When the last waves subsided they eased apart slightly, catching their breath and feeling the sweat running down their bodies.

Katie looked up at him with those vivid blue eyes, damp hair framing her face, her cheeks flushed.

'Good to see you can follow instructions,' she panted with a smile.

Moore grinned and kissed her lips, softer now, tenderly. He straightened up, letting her leg down as they separated.

'I do what I can,' he said modestly.

He ran a finger down her nose, her chin and throat, and down her chest between her pert breasts. He rested his hand there, feeling her heart thumping against his palm. She leaned against the wall, unabashedly naked, watching him. She reached out and twirled her fingers in his thick chest hair.

'I bags first shower,' she said, pushing away from the wall.

Moore held her slim hips, pulling her against him. He bent and kissed her again. She reached up and put her arms around his neck, kissing him back. She hooked an ankle behind his leg, pressing against him. He could feel her willingness and his own body responded in kind.

'Be a shame to waste water,' he murmured as she guided him towards the bathroom.

38

A pair of giant Chinooks dropped them ten klicks from Qahira just before dawn.

The unit rolled out of the aircraft in their vehicles, establishing an all-round defence while the big birds lifted off again. Dust and crap blew everywhere, limiting their vision even further.

The unit was saddled up in four Desert Patrol Vehicles and a Polaris MV850 All Terrain Vehicle, packing an awesome amount of firepower between them.

The DPVs could each take a driver, a vehicle commander and a gunner. Each of them had a classic Browning M2 .50 calibre machine gun mounted to the roof's, manned by the gunner who was encased in the roll cage, and two of them bore dash-mounted Mark 19 40mm automatic grenade launchers. The other two each had a venerable M60 7.62mm machine gun affixed to the dash.

Each DPV also had an AT-4 84mm light anti-tank weapon strapped to each side of the roof. Two of the DPVs were a man short, enabling them to uplift the two-man sniper team on the way in to the village.

Moore and Katie were on the ATV. Like the others they wore light helmets and goggles, with gloves and body armour over their fatigues. The quad bike had a 7.62mm M240 light machine gun mounted to the front rack in front of Moore, with a box of ammo attached to the side of the receiver.

Along with the rest of the unit each of them was armed with a 5.56mm M4, Moore's with an M203 40mm grenade launcher clipped beneath the barrel for extra versatility. He carried several bombs for it in his webbing, and like Katie he had an HK .45 strapped to his thigh in a low slung holster.

They carried a small amount of water, rations and emergency kit in grab bags attached to the rear of the ATV by bungees. The plan was to be back at base for lunch, so there shouldn't be any need for more gear.

Moore had to admit that despite his change in career from the frontline of combat to the world of espionage, it felt good to be back in camo's, tooled up and heading out on a mission with a team of warriors.

Once they could see, one of the DPVs led them out, Moore dropping the ATV into the middle of the group. They got clear of the drop zone and headed towards their RV with the sniper team, who had left their OP under the cover of darkness. Within minutes the column of vehicles pulled up short of a wadi and two figures emerged from the lip of the gully. They joined the unit, speaking briefly to Todd in the second DPV before climbing aboard two of the vehicles.

They moved off again, one of the DPVs up front as a scout. Dawn's grey light was up now and the sun was starting to rise. The night time desert chill was easing and Moore felt more comfortable now, settled into the vehicle and their role in the unit.

Within minutes the scout vehicle called a halt through the earpieces they all wore. Moore braked, feeling Katie press into him from behind. She was perched on the back of the Polaris, her legs either side of his hips, hanging onto the rear rack for dear life as they bounced across the rough country.

Just as Pat had described it at the briefing earlier in the day, it was sandy, scrubby desert country, full of holes and dips that the drivers couldn't see until they were practically on top of them. Moore made sure that he mimicked the movements of the DPV in front of them, and before he knew it they pulled up short again, going into an all-round defensive position.

Once the dust had settled and all they could hear was the ticking of the cooling engines, Todd gave the last briefing over the net, just a few words to make sure everyone was focussed and knew what they were doing.

With that they headed out again, the last leg of the short journey taking them past another wadi and across an expanse of open ground straight to the village. Not until they were nearly on top of the village could Moore actually make it out, it was so small. Just a handful of basic mud and stone huts, a fire pit smouldering in the centre of the assembly, with an animal enclosure of some sort on the far side.

Two of the DPVs skirted round the village to cover the other side and the other two broke away to cover each flank on the near side. Moore brought the ATV to a stop and waited, watching as Todd and Jerry dismounted and moved quickly to the closest hut, the biggest of the handful, which they had identified as the head man's hooch.

People were emerging from the huts in the grey dawn, curious to see the soldiers who had disturbed them. Curious, but not afraid. Moore watched carefully, eyes flitting everywhere, assessing each new face as they appeared, checking for weapons or signs of hostility.

Nothing.

Todd and his sidekick spoke to the head man, a stooped old boy with skin like a worn boot and maybe a couple of teeth. A younger man stood with him, maybe a son or nephew, somewhere in his forties and fully bearded. To Moore he had the tough, watchful look of a fighter. Then again, most males in this part of the world did.

A third guy hung in the background, young enough to be a grandson by the looks of him.

The two soldiers spoke to them for a few minutes, firmly but not aggressively.

By now it seemed that the whole village had risen, gathering around the centre while someone stoked up the fire pit. Goats bleated in the background and a skinny dog wandered about aimlessly. It wandered over to the ATV and stared at Moore for a moment before it came closer and paused to piss on the closest wheel.

The skinny young man was hanging round the fringes of the head group, not part of the conversation but close enough to listen. Every time somebody looked at him he looked away or nodded and smiled a big toothy smile, as if he didn't understand what was being said.

The longer that Moore watched him, slipping glances across without trying to be too obvious about it, the more obvious it seemed that the guy was paying full attention. Given his age and related lack of standing in the tribal hierarchy, it made Moore wonder why.

Knees was moving around between the unit's positions, having a quiet word and checking arcs as he did so. When he got to Moore he stood beside him, looking out at the open ground around the tiny village.

'Tough country,' he commented. 'Hard people, homes.'

'You got that right.' Moore lowered his voice. 'Who's the young fella hanging round the head honcho?'

'Mustafa, the old boy's grandson. The other guy's the son.' Knees glanced at him curiously. 'Why's that? You recognise him?'

'No. Just curious.'

Todd's voice came over the net.

'We're gettin' nothin' from these guys,' he said. 'Says they don't know what we're talkin' about. Start on the east corner and check the huts. Kiwi and Katie, cover us from the flanks.'

There were clicks of acknowledgement and the team dismounted, moving quickly to their pre-designated positions.

Moore readied his M4 and took a post that gave him a good visual on one side of the village, glancing over to make sure Katie was in position. She was, weapon in hand and looking alert.

He turned to check his arcs, and saw that the two Delta men had stepped away from the head honcho's group and had their heads together. Likewise, the old boy and his son were conversing in low voices. The young guy Mustafa was shuffling about, kicking at the dust beneath his feet as if he was just killing time.

Moore wasn't buying it. The guy seemed off, too alert and too eager to play dumb. He pushed his talk button.

'Todd, keep an eye on that young guy,' he said. 'I think he's listening to you guys.'

He got a double click in acknowledgement.

Casting an eye back over his arcs and shifting the M4 in his grasp, Moore couldn't shake the bad feeling in his gut. Maybe he'd been out of the field for too long, but this whole situation was giving him the shits. He spied movement from the corner of his eye, and looked just in time to see Mustafa disappear behind a hut near the head honcho.

'Todd, the young guy,' he radioed over the net. 'He's gone behind that hut, he's up to something.'

'Find him,' Todd came back immediately. 'We'll distract the head man.'

Moore waited a moment before moving in that direction, keeping his eyes outwards to cover the flank, moving as if he was patrolling his patch. In his peripheral vision he spied the two Delta men showing a map to the two Iraqis and getting their full attention.

He got past the closest hut, out of their sight, and dropped any pretence of patrolling. He moved fast and silent, his M4 at the ready. He reached the hut where he'd last seen the young man and tucked up close to the side as he moved.

He could rushed Arabic in a low tone, urgent sounding. He ducked round the side of the hut and Mustafa appeared from his left, head down as he spoke quietly into a cell phone.

Moore wasted no time, ramming the barrel of his rifle into the young man's gut and causing him to double over with a whoof of air. He snatched the cell phone from the man's hand and put it to his own ear, but the connection had been cut already.

He shoved the phone in his pocket and grabbed Mustafa by the scruff of his neck, dragging him back around the hut into the communal area and throwing him to the ground. Mustafa curled into a ball, groaning, clearly expecting to be filled in.

Todd trotted over with Jerry at his side, both with questioning expressions. Moore produced the cell phone, waggling it in the air for all to see.

'Caught him making a sneaky call behind the hut,' Moore explained.

Todd pressed the talk switch on his radio, alerting the team. 'Heads up, got a spotter here. Eyes on.'

While the team immediately stood to and watched for threats, the three men stood over the fallen Mustafa.

'Who did you call?' Todd demanded.

The village headman scurried over, reaching out to the fallen man who was now clutching at his gut and milking it for all it was worth.

'No English,' the headman jabbered, 'no English.'

'Bullshit,' Moore snapped, 'he was listening to everything you said before. He knows damn well.'

'No English!'

Mustafa groaned loudly and tried to sit up before collapsing back pathetically. His eyes were screwed shut and his face was a mask of pain. The head man looked up at them, distinctly aggrieved, and in the background a woman began to wail.

'Get up,' Todd said, reaching out a hand to help Mustafa to his feet.

The wailing got louder and there was a crackle over the net.

'Incoming, Top, half a klick out from the west,' came the voice of one of the operators, 'two technicals, both loaded up.'

Moore looked that way and could see a faint trail of dust being kicked up by vehicles. The next instant came another transmission from a different soldier.

'Got the same from the north, Top. Got fifty cal's on the back.'

'Fuck it,' Jerry drawled, 'better get ready huh?'

Todd pressed his talk button.

'Remember the rules, boys,' he said calmly. 'Show the flag and let's find out if these guys are friendly or not.' He released the button and slapped Jerry on the shoulder. 'Go mount up.'

39

Jerry hustled off and Todd met Moore's gaze. 'Gimme a hand to...'

He was cut off by the sound of firing from the north, followed by a heavy burst from one of the DPVs. Villagers started scrambling for cover.

'Contact contact,' came the transmission. 'Two vehicles engaging us from the north.'

'Incoming from the east,' came Katie's voice, high and excited over the net. 'Got two utes...fuck!'

More shooting sounded, a heavy machine gun mixed with the light pop of an M4. Katie was obviously returning fire.

'What the fuck is a "ute"?' Todd asked as they both began to move.

'Pick-up truck,' Moore shouted over the din, 'I'll go check on her.'

He sprinted to the nearest hut, hunkering down behind it, peering round to get a visual on the threat from the north. All he could see was a lot of dust and a utility vehicle of some sort racing towards them, a heavy machine gun hammering out rounds from the back of it. All around was the sound of shooting, the deep slamming of the unit's fifty calibre machine guns, the thumping of a Mk19 as it belted out 40mm grenades, and the light cracking of an M4.

He realised Katie was probably the only one firing her rifle, the others either utilising the heavier weapons on their vehicles or realising the enemy were still out of effective range for small arms.

The villagers had all disappeared, he had no idea where to, but the centre of the tiny village was deserted. He wondered if they realised that the enemy fire wasn't selective-anyone in the way would get torn apart, whether they were Iraqi or American.

He ran in a crouch over to where Katie lay prone, and dropped down beside her. She squeezed off another shot before looking up.

'What're you shooting at?' he said.

'Baddies.' She pointed vaguely in front of her. 'At least one ute with a machine gun, could've been two, it was kinda hard to tell.' She looked almost indignant. 'They shot at me.'

'Yeah.' Moore settled himself, scanning for targets. 'They do that.'

Katie fired another shot beside him and he laid a hand on the receiver of her M4.

'Stop firing until you see a clear target. You're just wasting ammo.'

He scanned again, not seeing anything in the open ground in front of them. Shots still sounded from the unit's other positions, and he heard a burst of chatter over the net.

'Watch your nine, Knees...Roger, got 'im...It's getting' hot over here Top, we got three technicals at the west, guys everywhere... Roger, comin' to ya.'

Moore scanned again then rose to a knee, about to speak when he caught a flicker of movement in the ground before them, a hundred yards out. A scrubby bush twitched and grew bigger, then an insurgent with an AK appeared, running in a crouch from behind the bush to Moore's left. Moore brought the M4 up and sent a double tap his way without success, another guy popping up from behind the bush.

'That must be a big fuckin' bush,' he muttered to himself as he sighted at the second guy and fired on him, missing again.

Both men had dropped down and were returning fire now, forcing Moore to drop flat again. Yet another man darted from behind the bush, this one coming forward before going prone, a fourth racing up past him. Moore took a bead on the fourth guy and put a round through his torso.

'Where the fuck are they coming from?' Katie shouted.

'Must be a spider hole or a tunnel,' Moore replied, hitting his talk button and sending a quick update to Todd.

He sniped single shots at the first guy who had appeared, seeing little puffs of dust kick up around the man as his rounds went wide. The sixth shot caused the guy to jump and lift before slumping to the ground again, his gun going silent. Rounds came overhead, whining off the rough ground and buzzing through the air. The shooting wasn't particularly accurate-yet-but the volume was increasing.

'Concentrate on the guy on your right,' he told Katie. 'Single shots, aim and squeeze. Anybody gets up, drop 'im. Yeah?'

'Yep.' She gave a nod without looking at him, tucked in over her rifle.

Moore crabbed sideways to reduce the target for the insurgents, taking a new position a few metres away. As he got down he saw another two guys emerge from the bush and split off in different directions, both firing from the hip as they doubled forward.

He sent a couple of rounds their way to keep them on their toes, then settled his sights on the slower of the two and clipped him as he went down. The man thrashed on the ground and fired his AK wildly in all directions. Moore left him to it-a wounded man occupied the enemy more than a dead one.

He shifted his attention to the bush itself, which he guessed had a hidey hole of some sort behind it. He loaded a HE grenade into the M203 launcher attached to his rifle, sighted and squeezed it off. The grenade arced through the air and overshot by a few metres, sending up a plume of sand and grit as it detonated.

The insurgents around it shouted between themselves and their firing intensified, a couple of them leaping up and charging forward as their mates covered them. Moore triggered several short bursts at them, seeing one of them go down but he wasn't sure if he'd hit him or not.

He reloaded the grenade launcher and adjusted his aim before popping it away. This one exploded in the bush itself and blasted pieces of foliage everywhere, exposing the mouth of a tunnel that had previously been concealed.

As Moore swapped out the mag on his rifle he saw another insurgent scramble out of the hole with an AK, followed by two more. They were like cockroaches, scampering quickly to cover, with more following behind.

The next thing to appear was a RPK light machine gun.

Moore chambered a round and sighted, pumping off a double tap at the machine gunner and winging him with the second round. Another insurgent grabbed the gun and darted off to the side to set it up. Moore focussed on him, getting off a few more shots before the incoming rounds forced his head down.

He hit the talk button.

'We've got an RPK over here Todd,' he said urgently, 'and about eight or ten enemy.'

The RPK opened up then and bullets flew overhead. Moore tucked down tighter, hoping Katie was doing the same.

'We're going to bug out,' Todd came back, his voice almost drowned out by the roar of a .50 in the background. 'The helo's are picking us up from the RV as soon as.'

Moore fired a burst at an insurgent moving positions before ducking down again and crabbing away to his left.

‘Each position drop smoke on the count of four,’ Todd instructed over the net. ‘As soon as it’s gone, move out fast but cover your ass.’

There were clicks of acknowledgement and Moore quickly rammed a smoke grenade into the breech of the M203. As the countdown in his ear finished, he fired it off and red smoke began to billow out as soon as it hit the deck.

‘Come on!’ he shouted to Katie, leaping up and letting rip several bursts at the enemy’s positions.

She raced back towards the Polaris and he emptied his magazine, automatically dropping it out and slapping a new one in, the movements fast and fluid and without conscious thought. He fired off another ten rounds then legged it after her.

40

Moore leaped into the saddle and fired it up as Katie perched on the back and grabbed the rack for support.

He kicked up a dust cloud as he threw a tight turn and raced away from the village. The pounding of heavy machine guns and grenade launchers was deafening and lead filled the air all around them. He subconsciously tucked his body lower as he opened the throttle and made ground.

After a hundred metres he braked sharply and skidded to a halt at the base of a low rise, turning side on to check behind them. Two of the Delta vehicles were peeling away while the remaining two gave cover. Moore recognised the nearest DPV as Todd's. Jerry was driving, with one of the snipers up top as the gunner.

Moore could see the commander gesturing at him and pointing to his right.

He turned and looked behind them.

A group of three technicals were approaching, loaded down with men and rear-mounted machine guns, maybe half a klick away.

'Bollocks!' He revved the engine and took them over the rise, slapping Katie's leg and pointing so she was aware.

As they accelerated he saw a shift in the angle the technicals were taking. Instead of continuing to come across to take them from behind they now saw the fleeing ATV and two of them broke off at an angle to intercept it.

With the RV only a few miles away they had no option but to just go for it. With the number of enemy on the ground, standing still to fight would mean certain death.

Moore throttled up and went for it.

It looked like the technicals had GPMGs of some description rather than fifties, which meant less range but probably more control-although handling anything on the back of a moving vehicle was a nightmare. Both guns opened up and tracer started arcing around them, well wide.

He risked a quick glimpse over his shoulder and saw Todd's and the other DPV had stopped to give cover to the other pair, who were now haring towards them.

Another glance to his right saw the two technicals closing the gap, both machine guns still hammering at them. Some of the gunners in the back were also firing wild shots, completely ineffective at this range.

Moore realised that they were either going to intersect the enemy or be cut off by them, and the closer they got the more danger they were in from the machine guns. He scanned, spied a small dip up ahead to the right, and steered towards it, throttling back as they got closer.

He eased the ATV in and came to a stop, the dip less than a metre deep but hopefully enough to throw off the aim of the machine gunners.

'What're you doing?' Katie shouted, deafened by the gunfire and engine noise.

Moore pulled himself up to the M240 on the front rack, checked the action and steadied himself.

'We can't outrun them,' he replied, settling the stock into his shoulder.

The two technicals were slowing and starting to turn already, preparing to approach.

He wasted no more time, squeezing off a couple of short bursts to get his range in. After a small adjustment he sighted on the left hand vehicle, a red Toyota with about half a dozen gunners in the back.

Another was hanging out the front passenger's window firing an AK wildly with one hand. They were maybe three hundred metres away now, well within range for him.

Moore squeezed a short burst and saw dust kick up beside the vehicle. He adjusted slightly and put the next burst through the side of the technical. He gave it another burst then a third, the Toyota slowing more and the machine gunner in the back ripping off a long burst that stitched the sky.

Moore focussed on the guys in the back and pumped three rounds into them, seeing one guy fall back into his comrades.

The next burst took the machine gunner and threw him over the side. The technical swerved but didn't stop. Moore gave it a longer burst into the cab, shattering the windscreen and thinking he saw a spray of blood as he nailed the driver or passenger.

The technical swerved properly now, crashing into the side of the other Toyota, this one coloured a dirty white. The second driver steered away as his passengers cut loose, and rounds flew high over the ATV.

Moore raked the side of the first technical with two bursts as it turned almost completely side on, hitting at least one more gunner in the back before the technical hit a rut and dropped its front wheels, coming to a stop.

The second technical turned a full circle, kicking up dust, before accelerating hard at them head on.

Moore brought the M240 on line and put a short burst of 7.62mm rounds into the engine block. Steam burst forth and he hammered it again, seeing it starting to slow before he raised the barrel slightly and put five rounds through the windscreen.

He saw the driver slump but the technical kept coming, only two hundred metres away now. The machine gun in the back was hammering at them and he could feel the rounds cracking through the air, indicating the shooter was getting more accurate.

Moore snugged the stock into his shoulder and sighted at the silhouetted figures in the back of the technical. He stroked the trigger, the big gun jumping in his grasp.

The first burst went through the cab and took out the machine gunner. The second blew apart more of the cab and the technical started to curve around, exposing the left side. Moore put a third burst into the back of the vehicle, seeing another body drop, before raking it with a longer burst and dropping back down into the saddle.

'Hold on!' he bellowed, completely deafened now.

Katie slapped his shoulder and he rode the Polaris up out of the dip.

The second technical was still cruising along of its own accord, but he couldn't see anyone in it. He pointed the nose of the ATV in the general direction they had originally been going and opened it up, racing across the hard top with the wind and sand whipping at his face.

After a minute he slowed up to a stop and checked behind them. He could see the four DPVs chasing them, a dust cloud behind them. He could see a vehicle on fire somewhere in the background, black smoke billowing skywards. Rounds were still whizzing overhead and he realised that although he couldn't see the pursuing technicals due to the dust and sand, that hadn't stopped them from firing anyway.

Katie shook his shoulder and held out the GPS unit, showing him they were heading in the right direction and only a couple of klicks away now. He nodded, gave a thumbs-up and revved the engine again.

They led the way towards the RV and could see two Chinooks approaching. In theory they should be up and away within two minutes, but there was no chance of that happening with a gang of angry insurgents on their tail.

He pulled up short of the RV and turned the ATV to face the oncoming Delta operators. Katie unslung her M4 and dismounted, standing beside the ATV with the weapon at the ready. Moore put the

M240 into the shoulder and waited, letting the DPVs get closer. He could see the pursuing technicals now, machine guns spitting wild fire.

An RPG flashed through the cloud and sailed off overhead. Katie ducked instinctively and looked at Moore with wide eyes.

'What the fuck was that?' she shouted. 'A rocket?'

Moore nodded. 'They love 'em.'

A second rocket propelled grenade came their way, this one narrowly missing one of the DPVs and slamming into the desert floor, exploding in a burst of gravel and dust. The DPVs all took evasive action, cutting in different directions to throw off the shooter. The RPGs weren't heat-seeking and it took a pretty good shot to hit a moving target, especially from an unstable platform.

Moore watched as the four DPVs roared towards them, ignoring Todd's gesture to get moving. He could see the enemy better now, with the DPVs only a couple of hundred metres away, and he realised that the insurgents were catching up. Past them he could see more vehicles heading their way, a second wave of insurgents giving chase.

Wherever these bastards were coming from, they were spawning like goddamn rabbits.

Two of the first group looked to have parked up as a fire base, with the others continuing forward on the flanks but slowing down, leaving a clear field of fire down the middle for the fire base to hammer the escaping Americans.

It was a pretty basic tactic but Moore had always been a believer in simple things-the less complicated a plan, the less chance of fucking it up with a blue on blue.

Unfortunately, it left him and Katie in a direct line with the enemy fire base. He tucked the M240 into the shoulder and sighted on the two parked up technicals. Both had big 12.7's in the back and there was at least one guy with an RPG kneeling off to the side, making sure he didn't wipe out his own guys with the back blast. The RPG had an effective range of about two hundred metres but he knew the grenades could travel nearly a klick before self-detonating. A lucky shot was just as deadly as an accurate one.

The 12.7's started hammering and he could see bullets plowing into the ground behind the racing DPVs. The Chinook rotors behind him were getting louder.

One of the DPVs cut to its right and blocked Moore's line of fire just as he was about to trigger a burst. A second later an RPG cut the air where the DPV had been and continued through at head height, flying past the ATV and disappearing into the wild blue yonder.

Moore heard Katie swearing again and blocked it out. He had a bead on the rocket man now and squeezed off a short burst. The guy looked up in surprise from his reload and Moore fired again, sending him scurrying for cover.

The two technicals now focussed on him and bullets started to fill the air, buzzing like angry hornets. He knew he only had a matter of seconds before someone got lucky. He took aim at the left hand vehicle and sent his regards, seeing a window explode and someone jump off the back. He shifted his aim slightly and went for the machine gunner.

The first of the DPVs reached them and spun in a tight turn, bringing its guns to bear on the enemy. The second one was there now, moving past the position.

Moore instinctively knew that his time on the gun was up and dropped back into the saddle. As he reached for the handlebars a burst of machine gun fire cracked past his head and the M240 was hit.

The barrel took the impact of at least one 12.7mm round and spun, whipping overhead as Moore ducked down. He threw himself sideways off the Polaris, deafened by the thumping of the Mk19 on the nearby DPV, sending 40mm grenades back towards the enemy.

A third DPV screamed to a stop off to his left and he could vaguely hear Todd bellowing at him.

Katie dragged him to his feet and shouted at him too, before she realised he couldn't hear a thing. She pointed first at him then at the ATV, and he got the message. A quick look showed him the first Chinook was coming in to land, a huge shit storm of sand and crap being blown up. Two of the DPVs were heading for it.

Moore threw his leg back over the saddle and revved the engine. Katie leaped on behind him, the M4 slung again, and wrapped her arms around his waist. Despite the situation, it wasn't an unpleasant experience.

He spun the ATV around and headed for the Chinook. The rear ramp was down and one of the DPVs was already boarding. The second Chinook was hovering overhead and he could see its guns flashing as it gave covering fire to the ground unit.

He wasn't sure whether they would get all five vehicles on board the first chopper or whether it meant the second one would have to land too. A second later, the problem was solved anyway.

He felt Katie grip him harder and heard an explosion behind them. He instinctively slowed and looked back. One of the DPVs was on its side and in flames, the fourth vehicle turning back for it.

Moore spun hard and motored back to help.

The enemy technicals were still three or four hundred yards away, but he knew that gave them only seconds.

The commander and driver of the fourth DPV were already out and going for their buddies when the Polaris pulled up. The gunner kept up suppressing fire with his Mk19 while they tried to pull the crew free.

Moore joined them, recognising Todd's bloodied face as he was pulled free from the flaming vehicle. He didn't seem to be hit but he was definitely out of the game. The gunner, Marko, had been thrown free when the vehicle went over and one of the D-boys rushed to him. He was clutching his leg and writhing in pain.

Moore and Katie joined the third operator-Moore couldn't recall his name immediately- who was trying to pull the driver clear. It was Jerry. He was out cold and limp. The flames were at the back of the DPV but working their way steadily forward. The D-boy produced a knife and slashed the driver's harness, but it was obvious his legs were trapped in the mangled front of the DPV.

'Stoppage,' called the gunner on the other DPV, 'I could do with a hand, guys. These assholes are persistent.'

Katie didn't hesitate. She unslung her M4 and ran to the rear of the wreckage, taking a knee and starting to squeeze off shots.

'That's some girl,' the operator beside Moore commented as they both pulled at the steering wheel.

Moore grunted and pulled harder. He could see they were making headway. The Mk19 started up again. The other Delta operator-Moore thought it was Joel-hustled past with the sniper/gunner over his shoulder. Even from a fleeting glance Moore could tell the guy's leg was badly busted.

'Need your bike,' the guy who might have been Joel called as he went past.

Moore nodded; it made sense. He put his weight into the steering wheel, hearing the gunner call out again.

'We got two of the technicals down, boys. Still got three comin' at us though.' He fired off a burst of grenades. 'It's getting' pretty hot up here.'

With a final grunt Moore and the other operator-Bobby, he remembered now-twisted the steering wheel aside far enough to clear the tops of Jerry's legs. They each grabbed an arm and hauled at him, sliding him free and clear of the vehicle.

Moore left Bobby to it and joined Katie, who was swapping magazines. She flashed him a grin as she slammed a new one home and worked the bolt. Three spent magazines were in the dust at her feet.

'All good?' she asked.

'Wait for the call,' he said, unslinging his own weapon. 'Looks like you're having fun.'

'Fuck yeah!' She triggered a burst for emphasis.

'Take a breath,' he said. 'Breathe and focus.'

He could see she was high on adrenaline and feeling bulletproof. He'd been there before; the thrill of battle was intoxicating. It was also dangerous, and the last thing he needed was for her to do something stupid and get herself killed.

He could see the last three technicals less than two hundred yards away now, guns blazing and dust clouds billowing behind them. The two others from the fire base were also close behind now. He saw an RPG streak through the air, then another, and another.

He realised the insurgents had turned their attention to the giant Chinooks and were trying to scare them off. They probably figured that if the big birds disappeared the ground troops left behind would be easy pickings. They were probably right, but there was no way Moore was going down easy.

He triggered a burst towards the enemy and turned as he felt a slap on the back. It was Bobby, the operator he'd been working with.

'I'm taking Top and Jer in the DPV,' he shouted over the din of the Mk19 and Katie's M4. 'The ATV's gone already. You guys gotta leg it, okay?'

Moore nodded.

'We'll try and get one of the vehicles back for ya, but move your asses now!'

Moore nodded again and slapped Katie's shoulder. He jerked his thumb towards the waiting chopper. 'Let's go!'

Together they turned and ran for it, the Chinook a couple of hundred yards away. Rounds were flying overhead from the Delta boys and the guns on the choppers. As they came clear of the wrecked DPV more rounds came overhead in the other direction as the insurgents tried desperately to bring them down before they reached safety.

A hundred yards out now and his lungs and legs were feeling it. His mouth was dry and gritty.

An RPG streaked past, wide of the Chinook, and more bullets punched through the air. The first Chinook lifted off and the rotor wash from the closest machine was blowing a massive shitstorm all around them.

'Keep going!' Moore rasped to Katie, giving her a push ahead. He turned and brought the M4 up, triggering off half a dozen short bursts at their pursuers. He moved his grip down to the 203 beneath the barrel and squeezed off a 40mm bomb for good measure, unable to see much but hoping for the best, before turning and running again.

He could see the loadie at the tail gate shouting and waving at him, and at least a couple of the D-boys unleashing covering fire over his head.

He reached the tail gate of the big bird as it started to lift off and he threw himself up, scrabbling for a hold and feeling hands jerking him to safety. The tail gate began to close and he staggered to a seat against the wall, Katie flopping down beside him. He looked at her as the Chinook thundered into the sky, unable to hear a damn thing over the rotors.

Her hair had come loose and was framing her face, which was streaked with sweat and dust. Her fatigues were filthy. She held the M4 nose-up between her feet. She was grinning.

She held a hand out for a low five, but Moore ignored the gesture, looking past her to where the team medics were tending to their wounded.

Todd seemed dazed but okay, sitting up and having a dressing taped to his forehead. His sniper/gunner was on his back with one of the boys stabilising his broken leg. The medic and another operator were occupied with Jerry, who seemed to be semi-conscious and in pain. The medic had ripped his pants legs open and was tending to his legs. Moore pushed up and made his way over, standing out of the way. Katie joined him, and they watched for a minute, the soldier known as Knees watching from the other side.

Knees leaned over and the medic spoke into his ear. The Hispanic soldier's face was solemn as he nodded and straightened up. He saw the two Kiwis and came over, leaning in close to be heard.

'Can't feel his legs,' he explained. 'Could be nerve damage. Hopefully it's only temporary.'

Moore nodded. He could feel the concern in the man's voice.

'Won't find out til we get him down and into the base hospital.' The Delta operator looked at each of them in turn. 'I hope it was worth it, huh?'

Moore nodded again and straightened up. He knew words were no use right now. Warriors hurt like anyone else. He gripped the man's shoulder and pulled him in.

'Thanks,' he said simply.

Knees gave a short nod and went back to his team. Moore guided Katie back to a seat. She wasn't grinning now, and he knew that the reality of combat had just hit home for her. It wasn't all Hollywood action where everyone went home afterwards, joking and laughing. Soldiers bled and broke and died.

They sat in silence for the rest of the flight.

41

'The sniper team had no idea about that tunnel,' Pat explained at the debrief. 'We got no idea where it goes, it may have gone off into a wadi or even to the mountains, who knows. Maybe they got a bunker down there. Whatever it was, it's gone now.' He gave a grim smile. 'Soon as you all got the hell outta there we sent some gunships in and they blew the shit outta it.'

He saw the concerned look on Katie's face.

'The villagers were all gone, scarpered for the hills after your battle.' He stroked his short beard. 'Who knows how many of them were sympathisers and how many were just your average villager? My money's on all o' them bein' sympathisers, otherwise why would they have a tunnel?'

'What's the sit-rep on the boys, boss?' Knees asked from behind the two Kiwis.

'AJ's got a badly broken femur,' Mike replied, speaking for the first time. His tone was sombre. 'Jerry's got a broken tibia and sounds like some nerve damage, hopefully it's only temporary but we have to wait and see.'

Moore felt his gut tighten.

'Todd's concussed, he'll be fine just needs a rest up.'

Katie gave a heavy sigh and reached for her water bottle. Moore sat back, his thick arms crossed across his chest. He held the major's gaze.

'Any concerns about the intel you got?' he asked.

Mike paused before passing the baton to Pat with a nod.

'Pat?'

The intelligence officer stepped slowly forward.

'We are revisiting what we have,' he said cautiously. He put up a hand to hold Moore at bay. 'I know where you're coming from buddy, believe me I do. But what we had was solid. We had to act on it, okay?'

'I'm not questioning what it appeared to be,' Moore replied evenly. 'I'm asking if you've looked a bit deeper now.'

'What exactly are you saying, Mr Moore?' Mike asked, rocking back on his heels and looking pensive.

'I think we were set up.' He looked from the major to the spook. 'Someone has jerked our chain.'

42

As soon as the US Air Force Hercules rolled to a stop on the runway Moore and Katie were up and moving.

The crew quickly had the tailgate down and were already ready to unload the anonymous pallets of cargo they had brought with them. RAF Northolt was dark and unwelcoming, just as it had been every other time Moore had been there-maybe arriving in the middle of the night didn't allow the base to put its best foot forward.

He waved his thanks to the crew and led the way down the ramp, seeing headlights sweep across the tarmac as he reached terra firma. He stepped aside and waited with his bag at his feet, Katie joining him and dropping her own bag.

A non-descript dark Renault pulled up and the boot popped open. Nobody got out and in the dark he could only dimly see two occupants. Moore tossed their bags in the boot and slammed it shut. He took the seat behind the driver.

Vince watched him in the rear view mirror, his dark eyes cool and expressionless.

'Home is it?' he asked, then glanced pointedly at Katie in the mirror. 'Or a hotel?'

Moore got the distinct impression he was in the dog box with his mate, the feeling confirmed a second later when Nga half turned in her seat and also looked at him. She looked as pissed off as her husband, but said nothing-yet. He knew it would come.

'My place thanks mate,' Moore said, hoping to break the ice but failing miserably. 'Thanks for coming out.'

'Nothin' better to do,' Vince grunted and gunned it towards the gate.

Nga looked over her shoulder at him again. Even in the darkness he could see real anger in her eyes. 'Been talking to Ari,' she said bluntly, and Moore felt his stomach drop. 'Yeah,' she said, 'that's right.'

'Am I missing something?' Katie asked pointedly.

'No,' Moore replied awkwardly, 'just something at work.' He knew she knew he was lying, but there was nothing he could do about it right now.

He sat back, feeling Katie's eyes on him across the back seat. He stayed silent, staring out at the darkness instead as they were waved through by an MOD guard at the gate and headed back towards London.

The buzz from the contact in Iraq was now gone, replaced with the weight of depression he thought he'd put behind him. He bunched his fist and pressed hard against his thigh. He could feel the waves of anger coming from the front seats.

He knew they were disappointed in him and he felt like a fool-a stupid, immature fool. Moore rarely let his guard down properly, and as a consequence he had few close friends. Vince and Nga were in that select group, and he knew he had let them down.

The Renault pulled up at the kerb outside Moore's flat. Vince popped the boot and stayed in his seat. Nga passed over a Jiffy bag containing Moore's personal effects without a word.

Moore got out, deliberately walking to the door without his bags. He unlocked and shut off the alarm before turning to Katie, who had arrived behind him with her bag and a quizzical look.

'Go and make yourself at home,' he said as coolly as he could manage, 'I've just gotta talk to these guys. I'll be up in a minute.'

She nodded and went in. Moore went back to the car and got in the backseat, bracing himself for it.

Vince gave him a frosty look in the rear view mirror. 'Been busy bruv?'

'Look…' Moore began, but Nga turned in her seat and cut him off.

'What the fuck, Rob?' she snapped. 'You been rooting McGregor's missus? Seriously?'

Moore looked resigned. 'Ari found something?' he asked. 'Does McGregor know?'

'Ari came to me,' Vince replied. 'He found texts and after your little visit to him, asking questions, he put two and two together.'

Moore groaned. 'Why'd he come to you?'

'Well,' Vince said, giving him a pointed look, 'we're supposed to be mates, eh? He thought he'd better make sure of his facts before he said anything to old Gingernuts.'

'So he's told him?'

'No,' Vince said, 'not exactly.'

'Don't worry,' Nga said, giving him the full force of her glare, 'your mate here saved your arse for you. Ari's fobbed it off with McGregor, said he couldn't find anything.'

'And McGregor bought it?' Moore frowned. 'Doesn't explain her having the phone though.'

'Don't worry about that either,' Vince cut in, jerking a thumb at his wife. 'Your little bit of fluff had a visit from Mrs Masoe, who laid out a few home truths to her.'

'She's told him she's unhappy in the marriage and had been on a dating site. She was going to use the phone for arranging to meet someone, but never followed through with it.'

Moore wondered if McGregor would really swallow that one. It was the modern equivalent of the oldest lie in the book. Nga caught his look.

'She knows better than to deviate from that story,' she said firmly. 'She's got too much to lose if she fucks this up.'

Moore raised an eyebrow but said nothing, waiting.

'But don't worry, you weren't the only one,' Nga told him, and he felt a slight kick inside. 'Looks like she's been a busy girl.'

He kept his mouth shut and hoped his face gave nothing away. He couldn't say he was surprised, but it didn't mean there wasn't a sting in the tail.

'And he's bought it?' he managed.

'He believes it because he wants to believe it,' Vince told him. He twisted in his seat now to look back at his friend. 'I don't know how it's going to iron out, but for now things are heading in the right direction.' He jabbed a finger at Moore, his eyes hard. 'But don't ever fuckin' put me in that position again bruv, yeah?'

Moore nodded, full of embarrassment and relief. 'Sorry mate. Both of you. Thanks for what you've done.' He shrugged. 'I screwed up big style, and I'm just lucky to have mates like you guys.'

Vince tossed his chin towards the flat. A light was on upstairs now.

'Better go attend to your contact,' he said.

Moore opened the door and started to get out, pausing when Nga called to him.

'Oi,' she said. He poked his head back into the car.

'Go get yourself checked out,' she told him, poker faced. 'Before your teeny-weeny falls off.'

Fair call, Moore decided, closing the door with a wry smile.

43

The day was shaping up to be fine and clear when they arrived at New Zealand House later the next morning.

Anyone who believed England didn't get good summers was clearly retarded, Moore decided as he led Katie in the side entrance. It felt like they had barely slept and although they had stopped for coffees on the way from the Tube, he was lacking energy.

They had been woken by a text from Jed Ingoe at 6am, telling them to be in the office by nine for a briefing. Sure enough he was waiting in the conference room when they arrived. Moore had paused just long enough to raid the stash of protein bars in his office before they made it to the briefing. Ingoe looked a million bucks in a fitted black suit with a subtle pinstripe and a discreet navy blue tie against a grey shirt.

He watched the two of them closely as they entered the conference room, standing to shake hands first with Katie as he welcomed her before gripping Moore's hand and nearly cracking a bone. He was much smaller and several years older than Moore but there was not an ounce of fat on him and, having seen him in action, Moore knew him to be hardest man he had ever met.

They sat across the table from him and he folded his hands in front of him. There was a glass of water and an iPhone to one side with two pieces of paper and a pen in front of him. Jedi slid these across to Katie.

'Before we go any further, these are two things I need you to read and sign. One reminds you that it is an offence to disclose the identity of any member of the New Zealand Security Intelligence Service, under the NZSIS Act 1969. That includes both myself and Rob here. The second stipulates that everything you have learned or participated in since becoming involved in the investigation to find Natalie Oldham is subject to the Official Information Act 1983. Okay?'

His expression left no room for argument. Katie signed both forms and slid them back across to him. He put them aside.

'I'm Jed,' he told Katie, 'I'm a senior officer in the Service. You already know Rob.'

Katie nodded, seeming a little overawed.

'Firstly,' Jedi continued, 'thank you for everything you've done so far. I understand you have acquitted yourself very well.'

She nodded mutely again. Moore took a sip of his cappuccino. It was nearly gone, and he wondered how long it would be before they got a refill. Ingoe wasn't a man for resting.

He wasn't disappointed. Without further ado Jedi directed them to debrief him on their activities in Turkey and Iraq. He listened to their accounts without speaking before recapping at the end and drilling down on points of interest.

Once they were finished he took over and brought them up to speed on developments they had been unaware of. Displaying a remarkable memory, he used no notes but simply spoke without pause.

'Our friends at Langley have done some further work on the intel they had been working off,' he explained, 'and it certainly appears to have been a false trail designed to bring you into a kill zone they felt comfortable with.'

'Who's they?' Katie asked. 'Are we still talking about ISIS?'

'We are,' Ingoe confirmed. 'But we are talking now about a faction of ISIS proper, maybe even a splinter group, we're not sure yet. Whatever they are, they are operating in traditional fashion by using small cells linking to the main network, each unit operating independently of each other but under the control of the larger organisation. The classic Active Service Unit.'

'The big question for us, I guess,' said Moore, 'is how the hell this actually relates to Natalie Oldham? Is she just a bog standard kidnap victim in the wrong place at the wrong time, or was she a specific target for some reason?' He spread his hands. 'Or is she even a kidnap victim at all?'

'Well what else would she be?' Katie asked bluntly. 'Are you saying she's a terrorist of some kind? A member of ISIS?' She shook her head emphatically. 'Doubt it.'

'We have to consider all possibilities,' Jedi said carefully. 'I'm not saying she is at all, but we need to assess whether she may be a willing participant due to her own beliefs, or a willing participant for other reasons.' He eyed Katie across the table. 'Have you heard of the Stockholm Syndrome?'

She shook her head.

'It's basically where a hostage or kidnap victim begins to sympathise with their captor and actually sides with them. It's reasonably common among victims, and can lead to them doing some crazy things they wouldn't otherwise do.'

Katie was silent now. The friend part of her brain was switching off and the analytical detective was coming to the fore.

'She is quite naïve,' she admitted, 'easily led. Lovely chick, but a real free spirit.'

'That's what her old man says too,' Moore said, and she gave a snort of derision.

'As if he'd know, he basically cut her loose when she was still a teenager and had bugger all to do with raising her during her formative years.'

Moore nodded quietly.

'That guy Tristan was more of a father to her than he was. She even used to refer to her dad as Paul, that's how much respect she had for him.'

Something twigged in Moore's head and he looked sharply at Jedi. The older man stared back.

'Sorry,' Jedi said, 'are you saying the Minister's assistant Tristan effectively raised Natalie?'

'Pretty much, from what I understand.' Katie shrugged. 'Her old man wasn't around much, and her mum died when she was young. She always had nannies and stuff like that. I think he came on board as a tutor or something originally and just stayed. I guess he eventually took a more official type position when the dad moved up the ranks and Natalie was grown up and moved out.'

'He barely looks much older than her,' Moore interjected dubiously.

'It's amazing what plastic surgery can do these days,' she replied, 'if he stood too close to a heater he'd melt. I think he's, like, close to forty or something.'

'What kind of tutor was he?' Jedi asked.

'Not sure really, I don't think she actually said.' Katie looked from Jedi to Moore. 'Why, you think there's something to that?'

'It certainly seems odd.' Jedi made a steeple of his fingers and turned to Moore. 'In the meantime, you've got the forensic results back from the IT guy?'

Moore had had an uncomfortable interaction with Ari just before the briefing. The IT specialist had studiously avoided any mention of McGregor and Michelle, and had simply handed Moore a wad of paper with a covering report.

He tabled the documents now.

'In summary, there was all the normal stuff on there-emailing, Viber, Facebook, online shopping etc. Of interest he found a deleted link to a chatroom, which remained in the memory of the hard drive. It only appears to have been accessed the once, and according to Natalie's itinerary, it was the night before she flew out to Istanbul.'

Katie and Jedi were all ears now.

'The chatroom itself is just a generic dating site, nothing of interest normally, but Ari was able to identify the login used which was…' he checked the report, 'White Lamb.'

'White Lamb?' Katie queried with a frown. 'That's a bit weird.'

'You've never heard her refer to that before?' Jedi asked, and she gave a shake of her head.

'Symbolic, perhaps,' Moore suggested. 'She's a white girl…a bit lost, a lost sheep?'

'So we don't know who she was communicating with on this site?' Jedi said, moving on.

'No. And if she's gone into a private chat room there's no way of knowing.'

This was a common tactic for terrorists and criminals, using the cover of a chat room for illegal communications, knowing they couldn't be tracked by the authorities.

'And the same with Viber,' Katie said, 'you can't track that either, there's no recording of the communications you have.'

That was another common method, and had been used by terrorists leading up to a several attacks. Technology was playing a huge part in the international terror game now, and it was a constant game of cat and mouse to try and catch up, let alone get a step ahead.

'So your IT guy can't take that any further?' Jedi wanted to know.

'Not without something more to work with.' Moore checked the report. 'That's the only lead he's ID'd from the hard drive. There's a bunch of stuff there, photos, various documents-travel stuff, CV, job applications, some poetry. I'll have a look through it and see if there's anything of interest.'

'I can help,' Katie volunteered. 'Got nothing else to do.'

Jedi considered her across the table.

'That would be very helpful,' he said, giving her a nod of approval.

The Ops Officer glanced to Moore.

'One last thing,' he said, his tone more sombre than usual. 'That girl that Jeff was using in Ankara, Evin? We've ID'd her, she's a local who he initially recruited as a source. Seems like he used her in a more official capacity, but strictly off the books-we have no record of her, so he must have covered her through his informer payments.'

'Makes sense,' Moore said.

'Problem is,' Jedi continued, 'she's dropped off the radar.'

'When?'

'Straight after he was killed.'

Moore noted the terminology-killed, not died. 'How do we know that?'

'I had someone go to her home; packed up and gone. Hasn't been seen since.'

Moore considered that for a minute. 'Playing the devil's advocate,' he said, 'she was his source, not an employee. It's not like she needs to check in with the embassy. But then, the timing...why would she disappear immediately after he dies? Presumably she was aware he'd died, there must've been some commotion around that. And she would've wanted to get paid.'

'From here in, she is a suspect in JJ's death,' Jedi stated. 'If you come across her, we want her.'

'For sure.' Moore felt his gut squirm. It seemed like they were chasing ghosts at the moment.

Jedi checked his watch. 'I'm flying to Crete later today,' he said, 'I'll be there until Sunday-the big ceremony is Saturday. If you need me, the phone'll be on. Although I'll probably be talking again to the Minister's people, so you'll have to leave a message.' He pushed out from the table and stood. 'In the meantime, I'll go see the man upstairs and you two crack on with analysing the stuff you've got there.' He gave a short nod. 'Good work, guys.'

Moore nodded and they watched him go, shutting the door behind him. He still moved like a cat despite the prosthetic leg.

Katie turned to Moore. 'So, before we get down to work, are you going to shout a girl a coffee?'

44

The analysis of the data Ari had recovered took them through to lunchtime, at which point Moore called time out and stood up.

'Gotta feed the machine,' he explained.

He locked the conference room behind them and taped a handwritten sign on the door-DO NOT ENTER.

He took her to a nearby sushi joint where they managed to slip in at the end of the lunchtime rush and grab bar stools at the window. They ate and watched the constant buzz of people shifting by, each lost in their own thoughts. The food was always fresh and fast and Moore was a regular there.

As he ate he wondered what would happen once this job was over. Last night in bed, as he held Katie close, she had talked about her family and her childhood. She spoke of them fondly and it had made him wonder if Danni would speak so highly of him. He doubted it, no matter how much he wished it were true.

After all he had been through with Katie over the last few days, he felt a connection, something real and strong. It wasn't just sex, it was something more than that. He wondered what she thought of it all-was he just a casual thing, an adventure of her youth?

He knew she had several months left on her career break from the Police, but did that mean she was going to stick around England, or even London? He didn't know. He didn't know, and it was twisting his gut, gnawing at him from the inside. With so many things he didn't know, one thing was sure-he wanted to be with her.

Beside him Katie put her chopsticks down and wiped her mouth on a napkin. She turned sideways on her stool, her knee pressing against his thigh. Her eyes were as blue as a summer sky as she watched him drain his orange juice and put the bottle down. She reached over and put her hands on his.

'Thanks,' she said quietly.

'It's on the company,' he replied with a wolfish grin, 'thank the taxpayers.'

'No,' she said, 'not for lunch. For everything else.'

Moore squeezed her slender hand, dwarfing it in his. 'No problem,' he said.

They were silent for a moment, holding the eye contact. It had been a long time since Moore had gazed into a girl's eyes with such feeling.

'You happy?' he asked softly, and she nodded, a small smile playing at her lips.

'Yes,' she breathed. 'I'm happy.'

Moore nodded, conscious only of the blood slamming through his veins, flooding his body with the feel-good drugs that such moments produced, the blueness of her eyes and the unspoken messages they transmitted, the press of her body against his.

Nothing else needed to be said.

When they got back to the office McGregor met them in the hall outside the conference room. He waved a hand at the sign on the door.

'What's all this about?' he demanded. 'I need to use the room.' He ran an eye over Katie from head to toe. 'And who's this? Where's her ID?'

Katie produced her Visitor Pass from her pocket, slipping the lanyard over her head.

'You'll have to find another room,' Moore told him, unlocking and opening the door. 'We're busy.' He couldn't help himself. 'Sorry Alan, but you don't have clearance.'

He ushered Katie in and followed her, leaving McGregor to glare impotently at the door as it closed in his face.

They had split the work up, Katie taking the photos as she was more likely to recognise people and places that may be relevant, while Moore painstakingly pored over the documents. Something was tugging at his brain, tantalisingly just out of reach, slipping in to give him a jab every now and then but dancing away again as he tried to grab it. Something somebody had said, or he'd read? No matter how hard he tried he couldn't get a hand to it. He pushed it aside, letting it float until it was ready to come back.

Once they had each finished their part they swapped over and double checked what they had. It was early evening when they finished and Moore's back was aching from leaning over the table for so long. Empty cups dotted the table around them, adding more water rings to the existing collection.

He collected all the paperwork into a bundle and locked it in his safe while Katie waited.

'So this is the office of a real life spook,' she observed wryly, looking round at the clear surfaces. 'So much personality.'

Moore closed the safe door and checked it before straightening up again. 'That's how we roll; nothin' to see here.'

Katie's eye fell to the frame on his desk. It was a white wooden frame with love hearts and a banner across the top that read Daddy's Little Girl. The photo showed Danni sitting beside Moore on a wharf, both of them dangling their feet over and holding fishing rods. She had her sandy hair in pigtails and wore a pink Barbie T-shirt. He was bearded and wearing a faded Ripcurl singlet. Danni was looking down at the water and Moore was watching her.

'She was four,' he said. 'That's one of my favourite photos.'

It had been a happy time with his daughter, an oasis in a storm of anger and hurt between him and her mother. His moments with Danni were diamonds in his life.

Katie put the photo back gently and they left the office, Moore carrying her bag in one hand. Ingoe had given him the message that Katie was to be held at a professional distance, and as such, had been booked into a central city hotel. Considering his current situation, Moore hadn't argued the toss.

As they walked past the SCIF room the door opened and they almost bumped into the Masoes.

'Oops, sorry,' Vince said, stepping aside to let Nga out. They both nodded and smiled to Katie.

Moore looked down at the locked pistol cases they both carried.

'Going somewhere?' he asked.

Vince glanced at Katie before answering.

'Your man wants us to go with the boss,' he said vaguely, and Moore got the message. 'He's coming too apparently.'

For some reason Ingoe had bumped up the security for the High Commissioner, and Vince and Nga had been assigned to his personal protection detail. It was typical of Ingoe that he would want to be on deck as well.

'Good luck then,' he said, 'enjoy.'

They went toward the stairs and Moore took Katie down to ground level in the lift. Instead of taking the Mondeo he flagged a cab and directed the driver to the Forsythe Hotel near Covent Garden.

It was a small efficiently comfortable mid-level establishment, meeting business needs without too many frills. The check-in process went smoothly and Katie was soon settled into her modest surrounds. Moore lingered, feeling awkward about leaving her, until she told him to just hurry up and go.

'I'm a big girl,' she said with a smile. 'Besides, I could really do with a bath and an early night, I'm shattered.'

Moore kissed her firmly on the lips before closing the door behind him and heading for the main exit out to Bedford St.

The summer evening was still light and warm enough, and he needed to stretch his legs. He crossed over outside the hotel and took the first left into Henrietta Street, following his stomach and heading towards Covent Garden itself. Despite the sushi for lunch he had a hankering for Wagamama's teriyaki beef donburi.

If he hadn't been so tired and pre-occupied, perhaps he would have noticed the ring closing in on him earlier. As it was, he was almost at the end of the street, a narrow service alley just coming up on his left when he registered that he was being followed.

45

His sixth sense kicked in when he realised there were two sets of feet keeping pace behind him.

He didn't break stride, but drew down a few short breaths through his nose, oxygenating his blood and getting it pumping.

He mentally readied himself for the next step, tossing up whether to make a move or see what his followers intended. The decision was made for him when a third man stepped out from the service lane as Moore reached it.

This one had a knife in his hand, held tight against his hip with the stubby blade pointing forwards. He was a scruffily dressed chav, maybe twenty-two if he was lucky, in a blue tracksuit. A trace of bum fluff clung precariously to his spotty chin.

He was speaking as Moore made eye contact, but his slang and street accent were so bad it was indecipherable. Moore gathered it was some kind of order, but it may as well have been in Polish.

The two guys behind him moved up, running now, and Moore judged he had about three seconds before they reached him.

Instead of surrendering or running, as he was clearly expected to do, he stepped forward fast towards the knife man, side stepping at the last second. The knife thrust forward and Moore caught the hand that held it in his left. He locked it tight and twisted the wrist, at the same time bringing his right up in an open hand strike to the guy's jaw, throwing his head sideways and back.

He twisted harder, causing the knife to drop, and kicked the guy hard in the side of his knee. There was a squeal of pain as the guy went down on his other knee.

Moore stepped again, turning to meet the two behind him. The first was nearly on him already, a glass bottle raised above his shoulder, ready to club down on Moore's head. He was stocky and wore a black hoody with some kind of white emblem on the front.

He got to start the swing but never finished it, Moore's right hand slapping the bottle away and his left jab slamming into the guy's side ribs. His right knee smashed up into the guy's solar plexus as he continued forward, and the guy dropped to the deck, the wind knocked out of him.

Something skimmed off Moore's right shoulder and thumped the side of his head as it went past, and he stumbled forward, leaping over the winded thug and turning. His head was ringing and he was glad it was only a glancing blow.

The third thug was bigger than the other two, blonde haired and with matching bling in both ears. His hair was plastered down with product. He wore a white shell suit. He had a blackjack of some sort in his right hand, and a knife in his left. He danced from side to side, a nasty grin on his face as he watched Moore.

'Tagged you, old man,' he jeered, obviously pleased with himself for succeeding where neither of his mates had. 'I fuckin' tagged you good you ol' cunt! I'll fuckin' teach you a lesson, you fuckin' whoofff.'

The last sound exploded from his mouth when Vince Masoe's boot flew up between his legs from behind and smashed into his scrotum, lifting him half a foot off the ground. He dropped both his weapons and collapsed in a heap, grabbing at his balls and gasping. A string of drool hung from his bottom lip.

'Not so fuckin' smart now eh, shit head,' Vince muttered, standing over him, his hands still tucked into the pockets of his jacket.

Moore glanced to his right, where the first guy started rising unsteadily to his feet. He was scanning round for a weapon when Nga stepped out from between the cars parked at the kerb. With one fast move she swept his feet from under him.

As he turned towards her and started scrambling back up, she delivered a perfectly timed strike to the side of his jaw with the heel of her palm. He went lights out and slumped down on his side.

The three officers looked at each other.

'Better move,' Moore said, 'thanks.'

'Thank your boss,' Nga replied, 'he wanted us to keep an eye on the girl, but we saw these dudes follow you instead. Didn't have a chance to call you.'

Moore nodded, glancing around. A few people were watching from across the road, but in true civilian style, nobody intervened. He was acutely aware though that London was literally dripping in CCTV, and they were probably on camera right now.

'Gotcha back, bruv.' Vince winked and fell into step with his wife as they walked away up the service lane.

Moore put his head down and walked the other way, his heart racing with the sudden adrenaline dump he'd had only seconds before. More than that, he wanted to know who the hell these clowns really were. Maybe it was just a mugging, some random street violence, but his instincts said no. It was rare that shit just happened, particularly when you were donkey deep in a job.

He spotted a walkway across the road to a swanky bar, and ducked over to it. The bar would definitely have cameras outside, but sure enough, there was a small alcove to the side just off the footpath, accessing other businesses.

A slick-looking couple were huddled in there, puffing on a sly joint before they hit the bar. They both jumped when Moore appeared and the guy quickly tucked the cigarette behind him, obviously thinking the newcomer was the Old Bill. The alcove reeked of dope smoke.

'A'ight mate,' the guy said, sussing him out. The platinum blonde with him adjusted the strapless red number that was struggling to keep her puppies in check.

Moore ignored them both and dug his phone out, rapidly dialling the Forsythe Hotel. Katie took forever to answer the phone and sounded both wary and weary when she did.

'Get dressed fast,' Moore said abruptly. 'Come out the front and up Henrietta Street, I'll find you.'

'Yup.'

With that she was gone and he put the phone away, stripping off his jacket and glancing at the couple again. The guy was sparking up the joint again, and tentatively offered it to Moore. The girl ran her eyes down him and back up again.

Moore ignored them and turned away, starting to move.

'Wanker,' the guy said to his back.

Moore turned his jacket inside out, changing it from a grey windcheater to a black one. He removed a khaki cap from the inside pocket and put it on, waiting in a doorway and watching the three hoods as they regathered themselves.

The one in the white shell suit was moving very gingerly, and the guy Nga had KO'd was unsteady on his feet. The one in the black hoody had his hood pulled up now and was rallying the other two, jostling them up towards Covent Garden while he fiddled with his phone.

Katie appeared across the road, hands tucked into the pockets of her black puffer jacket as she strode up the footpath, long dark hair flowing behind her. Moore crossed over and dropped into step with her, cutting her off before she could speak.

'Keep moving,' he said. 'Those three chavs jumped me and I want to see who they are.'

She ran a surreptitious eye over him as they eased back and maintained a steady pace.

'You look okay.'

He grunted. 'I had some help.'

His phone buzzed and he saw Vince's name appear on the screen. He connected.

'Going somewhere bruv?'

'Just on these clowns. Stay and watch the hotel would ya? I'll shout if I need you.'

'All good.'

Vince cut off and they followed as the three hoods entered Covent Garden and went straight ahead, past the Jubilee Market towards the London Transport Museum. There still hadn't been any sign of Police, which Moore took as a good sign. He wanted to track these guys and any cops would just spook them. As they walked he filled Katie in quickly.

'Lucky you caught me,' she said, 'I was about to hit the sack.'

'Done much surveillance before?' he asked.

'Nope, not really. We have a specialist team for that.'

'We'll keep it simple then, and stick together. May not last long anyway-I'm guessing they're going to a car or tube.'

Up ahead the three were still together, moving slower than normal due to the blonde in the white shell suit's tender condition. They were talking among themselves with lots of angry hand gestures from the black hoody, and were oblivious to their surroundings. People swerved around them and avoided eye contact.

Moore took the lead, tucking Katie's arm under his as if they were just another couple out on the town. They stayed offline to the hoods, in case any of them looked back, and kept a regular pace, slowing to look in windows as they passed still keeping a careful eye on their quarry. Moore also kept an eye for any other tails, either plain clothed cops alerted to the earlier fight, or other members of the group who were watching their buddies' backs. Nobody jumped out at him.

The hoods turned left at the museum and right into Russell Street, moving through the night owls who were out for drinks, dinner and shows. They hit a cross street and went left. The two shadows crossed over and followed them from the far side, changing positions so that Katie was closest to them while Moore was partially concealed. As they moved Katie pulled her hair back and tied it with a green scrunchy from her pocket.

'Bow Street,' she murmured, spotting a street sign. 'The Bow

Street Runners.'

'Who?'

'The first detective force in the old times. Hand-picked thief catchers.' She glanced at him, her eyes twinkling with amusement. 'Finally, something you don't know. Legendary.'

Moore kept the hoods in his peripheral vision. He spotted a car waiting at the next left, half on the kerb with the engine running.

'Heads up,' he said softly.

The three hoods made a beeline for it and piled in, the black hoody pausing to shout some abuse at a motorist who was trying to move past the parked black BMW. He kicked at the car as it went past and gave the driver the fingers.

'Nice,' Katie observed drily.

Moore tucked the plate number into his memory bank and watched as the BMW squealed away and took a fast left, disappearing from sight.

'I couldn't see the driver,' Katie said, looking up at him. 'Was this connected to Natalie, do you think?'

Moore shook his head briefly, his jaw setting.

'No,' he said. 'Something else. Nothing for you to worry about.' He gave her a smile and squeezed her arm into him. 'I'll follow it up tomorrow.'

Katie looked as if she was going to press it for a moment, but thankfully changed her mind. She leaned into him instead.

'I hope you're going to walk me home,' she pouted. 'I was just about to go to bed.' Her eyes twinkled mischievously. 'And you know what that means.'

Moore knew she slept naked. He felt a rising in his loins, not helped by the press of her lithe young body against him.

'Well,' he said, 'it is quite late and you are a girl...'

'I'm not usually out so late,' Katie said innocently, as they began to move again, huddled closer together now. 'It's a bit naughty, isn't it?'

Moore cocked an eyebrow at her.

'It is very naughty,' he agreed. 'I think you're in need of some rigid discipline.'

46

Moore was woken by the buzz of his phone and fumbled in the dark for it.

He was disoriented, torn from a deep sleep.

His first thought was that it was Danni, and he felt an instant kick of worry in his chest. Katie stirred beside him.

As soon as he answered he heard a woman's voice screaming down the line at him. He jerked the phone away from his ear and snapped the bedside light on, squinting at the phone's screen. Wizzle's name showed. It took him a few seconds to recognise Lana's voice, a curious mix of European-Scandinavian-East End accents. He waited for her screaming to pause before he could interrupt.

'What is it Lana? What's going on?'

'They stab Wizz and now he's bleeding everywhere and I can't stop it! He try to help you and now he's fucking dying you bastard!'

Moore felt his skin go cold. 'Where are you?'

'In the gym! They fucking come for you and he try to help you!' She broke off into sobbing and wailing and Moore rolled out of bed, tucking the phone into his shoulder as he grabbed clothes from the chair by the window.

'I'm coming to you now Lana. Hang up and call nine-nine-nine, understand? Get an ambulance there.' He yanked his jeans on. 'I'll be there in two minutes.'

With that he disconnected and shoved the phone into his pocket.

Katie pushed up onto an elbow, hair falling over her face. 'What is it?' she croaked. 'Who was that?'

'Shhh.' Moore leaned over and kissed her on the head. 'Go back to sleep. I'll be back soon.'

Thirty seconds later he was in a black cab, urging the driver to get a move on. It seemed an age before the cabbie pulled up outside the gym. Moore threw him a twenty and jumped out, seeing an ambulance already there with its red lights washing the otherwise empty street. Lana must've called them before she called him.

Wizzle was already on a stretcher and being rolled out the front door. He was bare-chested and his torso was streaked with red. Moore ran to him and saw a Police car approaching, blues and twos going, adding to the sensation overload. Lana was standing to the side, her white puffer jacket covered in blood and her hand to her mouth, crying hard.

The two paramedics ignored him as they loaded the stretcher into the back of the ambulance. Wizzle looked vaguely in his direction but was so out of it he probably didn't recognise him. Moore could see he had a large dressing covering his right cheek. He went to Lana and touched her arm. She cried harder.

'Who was it, Lana? Did you see it?'

'That fucking crazy little shit,' she cried, 'that Romper guy and his brother, and their friends. They stab him in the back and laugh and leave him there.' She met his eyes now, her face lined with running mascara. 'They didn't even care I saw them, Kiwi. They didn't give a shit I saw them. They just laugh and left him there.'

The Police car pulled up and Moore knew he only had seconds.

'Who did the stabbing?'

'What does it fucking matter who did the stabbing? He could be dead!'

'It matters,' he told her urgently. 'Who did it?'

'Both of them,' she said, quieter now. She glanced over his shoulder and he knew the cops were almost on them. 'Both of them.'

'Where would they go?' he pressed her, and she shook her head, her hair falling over her face.

'I don't know.' She pushed her hair back and wiped her nose on her sleeve. 'Probably their pub.'

'I'll be in touch,' he said softly. 'I'm sorry.'

He turned and almost bumped into one of the cops.

'Wait up there, sir,' the bobby said, his tone firm and authoritative.

'Sorry officer, I just stopped to see if everything was okay,' Moore replied. He glanced at Lana. 'The young lady was crying, as you can see.'

'Is that right madam?' the bobby asked Lana, doubt all over his face.

She met Moore's eyes and gave a nod. She knew the score. 'I don't know this man,' she said. 'He just stopped, like he said. It was me that called the ambulance.'

The ambulance moved off, lights and siren going, and Moore turned on his heel. He walked away quickly and as soon as he got round the corner he broke into a jog. He needed to get home and get his car.

He had no doubt that the bobby or his partner would be noting down his description, but he couldn't do anything about that right now. Even if they established his name, it wasn't linked to his home address and by the time anyone got through the layers to him he would have his story in place.

The patch on Wizzle's face indicated a facial stab-it had to be Jimmy the Blade. Stab wounds to the back meant Romper Stomper.

He made it to the flat and got into the Jag, taking a moment to catch his breath and compose himself before firing it up.

He drove away, with one thing on his mind.

THE RED LION was a shabby pub in a shabby part of Barnsbury and Moore parked down the road from it. Light leaked around the blinds in the front windows.

God only knew what had possessed him to drink there in the first place two weeks ago, and he regretted it to his very core right now. If he hadn't crossed that threshold then, he wouldn't be having to do it again now.

And there was no doubt in his mind that he had to. The cops would not get any joy out from Wizz and Lana, and if Wizz took matters into his own hands-as he undoubtedly would-he would be back behind bars before he knew it. Moore couldn't have that on his conscience, not when he had set the chain of events in motion.

The street was empty aside from parked cars at this time of night. A jet black Hummer took pride of place by the door, blocking a fire hydrant. Moore was confident that no parking warden would dare give it a ticket. He paused beside it and held a hand over the bonnet-warm.

He took a side alley to the rear of the pub and let himself in the rickety gate. The small courtyard was littered with boxes and rubbish. He opened the back door and let himself into a darkened kitchen. Voices sounded from the public area beyond another door. He took a few seconds to compose himself before pushing his way through the door into the bar area.

A man stood behind the bar, his sleeves rolled up and a black apron around his waist. He was bald headed and had a goatee. Tattoos lined his arms. Beyond him Moore saw five more men in a booth to his right, pints before them, laughing and talking. They had obviously retired for a nightcap after their outing to the gym.

The talking and laughter stopped as they clocked his presence. Moore recognised one of them as the thug he had dropped-Romper-and another as one of his buddies that night.

The barman turned and saw him. He took a step forward, his hand out to push Moore's chest.

'Who the fuck...' He never finished his sentence.

Moore slapped the hand down with his left and threw a hard

right jab into the barman's nose. As the barman clutched at his bleeding face Moore kicked him in the balls and grabbed his bald head as he bent forward. He drove the man down on his face and kicked him hard in the guts for good measure.

He stepped left around the bar into the public area, leaving the barman gasping and grunting behind him. The five men were rising, Romper and a guy who had to be his older brother on each flank. Romper squinted at him across the gap between them.

'That's him,' he said. 'He's the guy.'

Moore studied him. He was shorter than Moore and just as wide, but not in great shape. The one Moore had pegged as Jimmy the Blade was about Moore's height, leaner than his brother, with a proper hardness about him. He had a tear drop tat by his left eye and a goatee. In fact two of the others also had goatees-must've been the flavour around here. Like the brothers the other three thugs were all in their twenties. One was tall and skinny with neck tats, a shaved head and a goatee. The second was short, only five and a half feet, with sandy hair and a goatee. The third was wide in the shoulders and fat, with curly dark hair and a mono-brow over stubbly jowls.

Diamante studs were all round and they were all in track suits apart from the fat one, who had jeans on. He obviously didn't know that trackies had more give.

'You must be Jimmy,' Moore said to the leader of the gang.

'And you must be the Kiwi fucker who blind shot my little bruvver.'

Moore gave a sneer. 'If he didn't hit like a fuckin' pansy he might've won that, considering he had his two boyfriends with him.' Moore gestured at the tall guy and the Mono-Brow. 'I didn't catch their names-Woodcock and Splinter Lips, was it?'

The tall one bristled and glanced at Romper, who reddened. Moore smirked. 'Hit a nerve there, ladies?' He turned his attention back to Jimmy the Blade. 'I see you pricks aren't man enough to front up to your problem, so the problem came to you.'

Jimmy didn't flicker, just eyeballed him with his head cocked back and his thumbs hooked into the front of his trackies.

'You put a good man in hospital. Maybe even killed him.'

Jimmy gave a dismissive shrug and sniffed. 'Whatever, arsehole.'

Romper butted in. 'You come for some?'

Moore looked at him flatly. 'You called it,' he said quietly. 'This is on you.' He took a moment to look each of them in the face. 'Just remember that. This ends here and now.' He pointed deliberately at Romper. 'And it's on him.'

The group shuffled before him, readying themselves. Moore locked eyes with the tall skinny one. 'I'm gunna break your jaw,' he told him. 'You'll be eating slop for a month.' He saw the guy visibly flinch as the mental jab landed.

'Get 'im,' Jimmy ordered and tossed his head.

The short one and the fat Mono-Brow were the first ones forward, the short one charging in with his fists jabbing. It was clear he'd done some boxing at some stage. He should've spent more time on his footwork.

Moore stepped aside and easily dodged the jabs, getting outside the short guy's range and landing a solid left hook to his ear that sent him reeling. Mono-Brow was slow but his hands were like Christmas hams and if he landed one Moore was sure he'd know about it. He blocked a swinging right that jarred him to the shoulder, caught the left that followed up and twisted the arm outwards, throwing the fat guy off balance.

Moore threw a right kick into the fat guy's ribs and stepped in with a good left cross to the jaw, dropped the hand and broke his nose with a right hook. Mono-Brow staggered and put his hands to his face.

The short guy was coming back in and the tall guy was up now, a beer bottle in his hand. He smashed the bottle on the edge of the closest table as the short guy went for a side kick that he must've seen in a movie. He was too slow and too far away for it to be effective. Moore easily caught the guy's right foot in both hands and twisted, turning him away. He snapped a fast kick to the guy's balls and ducked the swinging broken bottle as it swept at his face.

He released the foot and snatched the hand with the bottle,

twisting the thumb out and breaking the grip. He caught the bottle by the neck as it started to fall and drove it down into the triceps of the arm he held. The broken shards stabbed into the skin and muscle and the tall guy shrieked.

Moore pushed him away and turned back to the short guy, who was cupping his balls with one hand and trying to catch his breath. Moore hooked him to the head again and dropped him.

Romper came at him, a blade jabbing forward in his right hand with short thrusts.

Moore stepped back and steadied himself, knowing that the real danger was just starting now. Jimmy was still hanging back, and Mono-Brow seemed to be trying to recover. The tall guy was still shrieking and clutching at his bleeding arm.

Romper gained confidence as Moore stepped back again, still jabbing forward with his knife. He didn't realise he was now isolated from his back up. Moore let him get close, less than two metres away now, and could see the excitement in the young thug's face.

'I thought you only stabbed people in the back,' Moore said, egging him on.

Romper gave a sick grin, still jabbing. 'I'll make an exception for you.'

Moore sensed the big jab before it came and side stepped at the same time as Romper stabbed for his gut. He stepped outside the strike and slammed the broken bottle down into Romper's shoulder, through the shell jacket straight into the shoulder socket itself.

When the downward momentum stopped he wrenched the bottle around, dragging the shards through the tendons and sinews there. Romper screamed like a stuck pig and dropped his knife, falling to his knees with his arm locked out straight.

Moore released the broken bottle, leaving it in the wound, and grabbed Romper's right hand in his. With the wounded arm locked out straight the elbow was an easy target and Moore smashed the heel of his left hand into it without mercy, blowing the joint apart in one savage strike. Romper's face went white and he dropped to the floor, unconscious.

Moore snatched up the fallen knife and stepped over Romper's limp form. Jimmy now had his own blade out and was shoulder to shoulder with the short guy, who was looking woozy and still holding his bollocks. Mono-Brow was leaning against a table, blood flowing down his face and his stance unsteady.

The tall guy was bleeding profusely from his arm wound but had stopped shrieking and seemed to be regaining some composure.

Jimmy weaved on the balls of his feet, tossing the knife from one hand to the other. 'You're pretty good,' he said with a cocky sneer. 'But I'm better.'

'Huh,' Moore grunted. 'I doubt it.'

The tall guy pounced forward now, thinking Moore was distracted. He went for a big left hook, his right arm hanging uselessly at his side, and Moore easily ducked under it. He dropped the knife into his left hand and drove up with a sledge hammer of a right uppercut, blasting up under the tall guy's jaw and causing an audible crack.

The lights went out and the tall guy fell backwards into the fat guy, who feebly tried to catch him but mostly missed. As Mono-Brow was distracted by his mate, Moore stepped in and slammed a side kick into his left knee, folding it backwards. The fat guy screamed and dropped awkwardly, clutching at his shattered knee.

The short guy saw a gap and took it, landing a couple of decent jabs to Moore's back before he could dodge them, and following up with an elbow to the back of the head that caused Moore to stumble forward and catch himself on a table.

Jimmy saw another gap and came in with his blade, swiping at Moore's face as he started to turn. Moore pulled his head back just in time and the knife sliced across his collar instead of his cheek.

He snatched the knife hand with his right and slammed it down flat onto the table. He held it there and stabbed Romper's blade through it, biting into the wood beneath. Jimmy gasped and reared back but was pinned to the table top.

Moore smashed a solid right hook to his temple and pushed him aside, going for the short man behind him.

As Moore came past Jimmy the Blade, the short guy stepped back and scrabbled for a weapon. He found an ashtray on a table and hurled it. Moore swatted the light plastic away like a fly and closed in. He grabbed the short guy by the front of his shell jacket and jerked him onto the tips of his toes.

'I'm sorry bruv,' the short guy panted, 'it's over, innit?'

'Almost.' Moore cracked him across the cheekbone with an elbow strike, let him slump slightly, then picked him up bodily by the front of his jacket and his waistband. He took two steps forward and hurled him across the bar into the display of bottles behind it. Glass exploded everywhere as the short guy fell to the floor.

Moore turned back to the other four. Jimmy the Blade was still conscious, breathing in painful gasps as he watched. Romper was awake again, struggling to sit up. The fat guy was conscious but completely out of the game. The tall guy was out cold.

Moore looked at Jimmy the Blade. The thug glared back at him, but Moore could see the fear there now too. He knew they had been bettered.

He stepped over to Romper and bent to look him in the face.

'Remember what I told you,' he said. 'This is all on you, tough guy.'

Romper let out a moan and gingerly held his broken arm. Moore moved over to the table now and picked up Jimmy's discarded knife. Like his brother's it was a switchblade with a long thin blade.

'You come near me again,' Moore told Jimmy, waving the knife before his face, 'or my friends…' He gestured at the carnage around them. 'And you'll wish it was just this. Understand?'

Jimmy said nothing, but his cheeks moved. He spat a gob at Moore. The saliva ran down his front. Moore glanced down at it then at the other man.

He grabbed Jimmy's right hand and yanked it down to the table.

Jimmy struggled but Moore was much stronger. He got the hand to the table but Jimmy bunched it into a fist, knowing what was going to happen.

'Suit yourself,' Moore said.

He rammed the knife into the back of Jimmy's hand and put his weight behind it, grunting as he drove it through until the tip hit the fingers on the other side. Moore gave one last shove and hit wood. Jimmy let out a wild screech now and locked eyes with Moore, tears running down his cheeks.

Moore held his gaze and with one swift move he snapped the blade off, tossing the handle aside.

'Good luck with that,' he muttered.

He stepped back now, breathing through his nose to get his heart rate back under control. 'Remember what I said.'

With that he turned and retraced his steps to the bar. The barman was on his knees underneath the countertop, fumbling with a revolver. It looked like an old Second World War-era Webley, with a big .455 cartridge.

The barman started to bring it up as Moore came around the bar. His nose was a mushy lump of red sausage meat and there was fear in his eyes.

Moore swept the barrel aside with his left, smashed him in the eye with his right, and wrenched the pistol from his grasp.

The barman tried to grab for it and Moore spun the Webley in his grip. He triggered a single shot, blasting a hole in the barman's wrist. The barman yelped and Moore straightened up.

He opened the cylinder and dropped the remaining rounds on the floor. He wiped the pistol on his jacket to remove his own prints and tossed it aside. The barman held his wounded hand and looked up at him like a scared animal.

Moore stepped over him and went out the back door.

47

The iPhone had vibrated its way across the bedside table and was tipping over the edge before Moore caught it.

He brought it to his ear and croaked a hello, his eyes still half closed in the darkness of the hotel room.

'Wake up, chucklehead,' came Jedi's voice. 'It's daytime.'

Moore squinted at the screen.

'It's three thirty a.m.,' he rasped, pushing up into a sitting position.

'Like I said, it's day time. Get your broken arse outta bed and in to work. I need you over here for a CP job.'

'What...'

'You'll find out when you log on,' Jedi interrupted. 'Get moving.'

He disconnected and Moore stared dumbly at the phone, his brain struggling to wake up. Katie stirred beside him, her bare leg nudging him.

'Whafubout?' she mumbled.

Moore clicked the bedside light on and squinted, turning away from the glare. It wasn't long since he'd slipped back under the covers.

'Come on,' he said, pushing the duvet back. She lay on her side with her back to him. He paused to gaze longingly at her lean form, then slapped her butt. 'Up and at 'em. Duty calls.'

She made a growling noise and rolled out of bed, shuffling to the bathroom. The light clicked on and she turned to scowl at him. Her hair was tousled and she was naked as a jaybird.

'Your job sucks,' she muttered.

She had only briefly questioned him about his excursion last night, and he'd brushed it off as a work thing. There had been no update on Wizz from Lana, and the hospital wouldn't tell him anything because he wasn't next of kin.

Forty minutes later Moore was at his desk, opening his dropbox. Sitting there was an intel report which hadn't been there last night. He checked the time it had arrived-only an hour ago, sent by Ingoe himself.

Moore scanned through it, his pulse picking up as he read. Katie came and put a mug of coffee in front of him before plopping down in the visitor's chair, her hands wrapped around a second mug.

He read it a second time before sitting back and staring at the screen with pursed lips.

'What is it?' Katie sat up now, picking up on his mood. 'Is it about Natalie?'

'No,' he replied, 'but it's not good. The Yanks have picked up SIGINT referring to an outfit called the White Lambs.'

Katie sat forward, all ears now. 'What's "sigint"?'

'Signals intelligence-electronic intel. They don't know anything about them, but there's been a couple of references to it lately-as in, the last month or so-amongst known players. The nature of the references is such that they believe they are referring to kidnap victims.'

'Victims? As in more than one?'

'Yeah.' He nodded, thinking as he spoke. 'There have been at least two instances that I know of in the last year where the child of a high profile person has gone missing overseas.' He paused to take a draught of the coffee. It was bland and lacked guts, but he needed a hit of something. 'There was the Aussie kid about six months ago, the son of that shipping magnate-Parker? He went missing from a backpacker's in Indonesia, turned up dead a few weeks later.'

Katie frowned and cocked her head. 'It happens though, it's not like Indonesia's the safest place in the world. He was probably stoned off his face.'

'Before that there was the American girl, Leanne Sinclair I think it was, she went missing from somewhere in Pakistan from memory. She died in a car accident trying to escape her kidnappers, something like that.'

'Who was she? It kinda rings a bell.'

'Daughter of a Congressman.' Moore took another hit of crap coffee. 'I need to make some calls before we go anywhere.'

'You think there's a pattern there?' Katie queried. She stood now, and he could see she was getting the same jazz that he felt.

'Definitely. Bit too coincidental, don't you think? The kids of powerful people from the Allied nations go missing while overseas, then turn up dead? Yeah it happens, but so often?'

'What can I do then?'

'Book us a flight to Crete.' He pulled his wallet out then changed his mind and opened his bottom desk drawer. He removed a cash tin and unlocked it.

Inside were three sealed plastic Ziploc bags. Each one contained a legend package in a different name-a passport, matching driver license, and a couple of credit cards. He opened the one with an Australian passport and handed her one of the credit cards.

'Use this one.' He took a sheet of notepaper from his drawer with a list of names and numbers. 'These are the airlines I use. Got your passport on you?'

'Of course.'

'Book me under this one.' He gave her the Aussie travel document.

'First class?' Katie asked cheekily.

Moore didn't smile. 'Whatever you can get, just get us there. Got a suit?'

'Back at the flat, why?'

'It's time to join the Secret Service. We'll have to swing by your place on the way.'

While she used the landline on his desk to start calling he drifted out to the hallway and used his mobile to call his American counterpart.

Michael was a CIA officer stationed at Grosvenor Square, the US embassy in London. Moore knew he would be almost up-the American was a healthy living Bible-basher from Iowa, who was always up before dawn.

Like most American spooks that Moore had met he was smart and a solid patriot, but very guarded in what he would give away. The conversation took less than two minutes and Moore moved on to his Aussie contact.

Stevo was an officer in the Australian Security Intelligence Organisation-ASIO-based in Canberra. They had staff in London too, but Moore knew Stevo from years back. It was about 2pm in Canberra and Stevo stepped out of a meeting to take the call. He listened to Moore's request and promised to call him back shortly.

He stepped back into the office just as Katie hung up and waved his credit card at him.

'Business class from Gatwick at 7am on BA,' she said. She hiked her shoulders. 'No economy seats available, sorry.'

Moore checked his watch. 'Half past four,' he said. 'We need to move.'

He grabbed keys from his drawer, locked up and led her across the road to where the Mondeo was parked.

It took fifteen minutes to race back to the Forsythe and grab Katie's bag, and another twenty to get back to Camden and into Moore's flat. He grabbed a suitcase and packed enough gear for four days, including a plain black lightweight suit with a couple of shirts and ties. He couldn't take any weapons with him, and just hoped that Jedi would have something for them at the other end.

He considered taking the Jag but the Mondeo was a company car, so less risk to him. They had crossed the bridge and were on the A3 passing Wimbledon Common when Stevo called back, his broad

Aussie twang filling the car over the hands-free set. So far they hadn't seen a single traffic cop or other Womble.

'Total DL, Robbo,' he said, 'Paul Parker was kidnapped in Jakarta in October, turned up dead in the city about ten days later. Official version is he drowned and it probably happened when he wandered off drunk and fell in a stream. Great tragedy for the family, rah-de-rah-rah, y'know the drill. There was some speculation in the media that he'd been snatched but we quashed that pretty quick.'

Moore nodded silently, his hands locked on the wheel as he flew down the A3220.

'And the real version?' he asked.

'Went there alone after some kind of fallout with the old man, supposedly to find himself or some gay shit. No question he was there for a good time-we got int that he'd been buying ganja and what-have-you off locals, behaving like your average naïve dickhead twenty-two year old backpacker.'

'What kind of fallout?'

'He was a bit of a dropkick, getting into drugs and hookers, not really the sort of scene the family approve of too much. The old man threatened to cut him off from the family tit unless he sorted his shit out-he didn't, so he got cut off. Pretty pissed off apparently, threatened the old man and basically buggered off.'

'Never to be seen again.'

A traffic camera flashed as they raced by and Moore was pleased he was in the company car-things like tickets could be dealt with.

'You got it, mate.'

'So why d'you say he was snatched?'

'One of the boys on the ground got word from a source that he'd been grabbed by ISIS.' There was a pause. 'And when I say snatched, we weren't entirely convinced on that, which ties in to the cause of death.'

'Not drowning then?'

'Na mate-he was found in a stream alright, but he was dead before he ever hit that. He actually had a weak heart and was on meds for it, but looks he stopped taking them and took other substances instead.

Basically his heart blew out and he just croaked it. That's not public knowledge though.'

'So he was maybe tortured, put under stress?'

They were nearly at New Malden now, making good time, as long as they didn't get pinged by a traffic cop.

'That's the problem mate, there was nothing. No sign of that on him at all. No other injuries.'

Katie stared at Moore with a puzzled expression.

'Anything else strange about it, Stevo?' he asked. 'I mean, it's all a bit odd but there's still nothing really to work with is there?'

There was another pause and Moore thought they'd lost the connection for a moment.

'This is the real guts of it mate, and like I say, it's on the total down low, yeah?'

'Of course mate.'

'Our guy over there was doing some work on it, and things just didn't feel right to him. He got control of the body and on pure gut instinct, did some hand swabs of young Mister Parker. Came back positive for traces of explosives.'

Moore and Katie stared at each other now, both thinking the same thing.

'Was that verified?' Moore asked.

'It was a hundy mate, don't you worry. It sent up all sorts of balloons around here, I can tell you.'

Moore pondered this bombshell for a few moments as he drove.

'Was that as far as it went?' he finally asked.

'Pretty much mate, it all came to a dead end in Indo. The body got sent back and got buried as well as the story. It got some media interest for a little while but the real facts never floated out-certainly not the explosives part. Can you imagine the shit storm that would cause?'

Moore could, and he knew why both a wealthy family and a government would want to keep it all quiet.

'Any links to any other similar cases that you know of?' he prodded.

There was another pause and he knew he'd hit paydirt.

'Officially no, mate.' A long pause, and Stevo dropped his voice. 'But if you were interested in that sort of thing, you'd probably want to look at the American girl Sinclair from a year or so ago. I did, and there are remarkable similarities.'

'Yeah I'm waiting to hear back from my friend here on that.'

Stevo chuckled. 'Bishop Michael? Good luck on that one mate. This is all to do with the Oldham girl, I take it?'

'It is,' Moore confirmed. He hung a left onto the A298 and overtook a battered Fiesta hatchback that was dawdling along. 'It all seems a bit familiar really.' On a whim, he asked, 'Ever hear of the White Lambs?'

More silence. 'No, not specifically, but that phrase popped up when we dug a bit on young Mister Parker. It was a password or something he used...a login maybe?'

Moore glanced at Katie. 'To a chatroom?'

'Could be mate, I'd have to have a look again.'

'Can you come back to me on it Stevo? I think it could be important.'

'No worries mate, I'll buzz you back later eh?'

They rang off and Moore turned to Katie. The Mondeo was still sitting on seventy as they closed in on Sutton.

'Any thoughts?'

She considered her response before speaking.

'Nothing good,' she said.

48

The history books showed that The Battle of Crete took place in 1941, resulting in huge loss of life for both the invading German forces and the Allied troops attempting to defend the island.

Left high and dry without the heavy weapons and equipment they needed, the Allies fought bravely against an invasion by air but were ultimately defeated. Between the 21st of May and the 1st of June the Allies withdrew from Crete, mostly from the small port town of Sfakia on the southwest coast.

Many troops did not make it. Over 21,000 died or were captured, and some remained behind, banding together either with other troops or with the Cretan Resistance to wage a guerrilla war against the Germans.

It was a resounding defeat for a vital foothold in the Mediterranean, followed by a vicious war of resistance where brutality was the norm and executions commonplace.

To mark the 75th anniversary, a series of formal occasions was being held. The main event was a commemoration ceremony on Saturday the 28th, to be held at the Sfakia International Hotel overlooking the bay where many of the Allied soldiers were extracted from.

Guided tours were bringing large groups of tourists, including many New Zealanders, Australians and British, as well as mainland Greeks. Both the NZ RSA and the Aussie RSL were sending parties of veterans and representatives, the handful of vets all now nearing 100 years of age. Formal groups of dignitaries were flying in, most of them only staying two or three days.

As Moore ran his eye over the list on his iPhone, Katie shifted in the seat beside him. She'd got the window but had fallen asleep as soon as the wheels left the tarmac. He wondered at the lack of stamina shown by the youth of today.

Mind you, he had to remind himself, she had shown plenty in the short time they'd had in London. She was an energetic and creative lover, making him feel young again, and he sensed a change in himself.

The funk he had slipped into prior to this mission was gone. His doubts about his own abilities had dissipated and he felt much more focussed, driven from within by the fire of old. Thoughts of Michelle were gone, leaving just a lingering bad taste and a nagging wonder about any potential fallout from that whole sorry episode. McGregor and her could both go to hell, he'd decided.

The drama with The Cutting Crew or whatever they called themselves still lurked in the background of his subconscious, and he knew it needed to be sorted with Wizz. First thing to do when he got back. For now it was put aside and he was on the job.

This was it; game on.

He looked again at Katie's face, peaceful and untroubled in sleep, a lock of dark hair falling across her cheek. She was young and beautiful and full of life.

He had no idea where it was going-whatever it was that they had-but for now he was just going with the flow.

He settled back and closed his eyes. Heraklion was still nearly three hours away, and he needed to sleep when he could.

. . .

JEDI KNOCKED on the door at 3pm.

Katie let him in and he put an aluminium briefcase on the table then took a moment to admire the suite they'd booked. It was the third floor of the Majestic Hotel, a classic Mediterranean establishment with a reasonable view over Chania towards the harbour only a couple of blocks away. The sun was pouring in through the open doors to the small balcony, and the ceiling fan circled lazily, moving the warm air around but doing nothing to drop the temperature.

'Good flight?' Ingoe asked, as Moore emerged from the bedroom, freshly changed.

'Can't complain,' Moore said, giving a wry smile, 'had to go Business Class though, sorry-apparently Economy was full.'

Jedi cocked an eyebrow but didn't bite. 'Lucky you got the worst room to make up for it then, eh?' He crossed to the open doors and shut them. 'The room's been swept but who knows who's outside. The Brits and Aussies are here, plus the Greeks obviously, the Germans and the Italians. It's a veritable smorgasbord of politicians and agencies here at the moment.'

Katie filled glasses from a pitcher of iced tea and they took seats on the twin sofas, Moore and Katie sitting together at right angles to Jedi.

'I read your email,' Jedi began, referring to the encrypted message Moore had sent him from the departure lounge at Gatwick. 'Interesting reading. Broken down individually, there's not a lot there, but collectively it certainly forms a picture we need to be looking at. I've briefed the rest of the contingent on the potential risk, and as a result things have changed. Vince and Nga were going to be a reserve team in case we needed them, but they're now on the CP team for the High Commissioner and the Minister.'

'Oldham himself?' Katie interrupted.

Jedi nodded. 'He has a couple of his own guys, Police Protection Services guys, but the High Commissioner doesn't. We were just going to be backing them up, but things have obviously changed. They are officially not armed, but it's the usual accepted rule that what the hosts don't see, they don't worry about.'

'So we're the new back-up team?' Moore guessed, and Jedi nodded again.

'Plus I need you two to be eyes and ears on the ground. I want you on deck for all the official events-I've got a schedule for you-and when you're not doing that you're out in the crowd being tourists, watching and listening. If anything goes down I want early warning and I want problems dealt with. Understood?'

'Got it,' Moore said, and Katie nodded.

Jedi tossed his head towards the case on the table. 'There's your kit there, anything else you need, let me know. The first event you'll need to be on deck for is a cocktail evening tonight, starting at seven. Briefing here at six, so you'll need to be ready.' He eyed Katie's shorts and T-shirt pointedly. 'Hopefully you've got appropriate evening wear.'

She pulled a face. 'Unless you want me in a cocktail dress, I'm all good.'

Moore couldn't suppress a snort, and Jedi gave him a critical look.

'You could tidy yourself up too, sunshine,' he rasped. 'A shave wouldn't go astray.'

As Moore's cheeks flushed Jedi stood and made for the door. 'I'm next door,' he called over his shoulder, 'see you at six.'

'Time check?' Moore asked as the door closed.

'Ten past three.'

'Right, we need to boogie.'

He got up and crossed to the aluminium case, popping the catches to reveal an array of kit set into foam lining.

There was a charging unit for the two hand held radios, earwigs and wires, covert Safariland hip holsters, belt pouches for the spare pistol magazines, and a pair of Sig Sauer P229 9mm semi autos.

While Katie got the radios on the charge, Moore checked the weapons. They had two spare mags each and there were two boxes of ammo-more than enough.

A good CP job resulted in no dramas and a smooth ride for the principal, and he was confident in the abilities of Vince and Nga to execute their roles perfectly. Despite that, he couldn't shake the nagging feeling of dread in his gut.

They loaded their weapons and Katie concealed hers in the bum bag she'd brought with her, securing it round her waist. Moore tucked his in the front of the waistband of his shorts, and they were good to go.

The hotel was situated in the Topanas district of Chania's Old Town, an area of narrow winding alleyways and historic buildings, many of which had been converted into hotels and eateries. It was busy tourist season and the cobbled streets and walkways were thick with foreigners, many laden with daypacks and clad in hiking gear.

An ideal cover for terrorists, Moore mused as he led the way, his bulk forcing a gap through the throngs.

Eleftherios Venizelos Square opened up ahead of them, the centre of the Old Town, and he skirted the crowds stopping for photos and browsing, and instead followed his nose down to the Venetian harbour.

The waterfront of Chania was what he had always considered to be classic Mediterranean with the promenade along its wide mouth, backed by stone and brick buildings with canopies over tables and chairs, the water just a few metres away, a full marina and a constant flow of tourists interspersed with locals.

It was the sort of place he imagined would be fantastic for a romantic getaway with a beautiful girl, and the thought brought a wry smile to his face. At least he was partway there.

The dry air was nearly still and his shirt was sticking to him already. He moved out of the flow of pedestrians and stopped outside a café, looking enquiringly at Katie. She nodded appreciatively and grabbed the only free table. A waiter was on them immediately, taking their order for two iced orange juices.

Moore felt himself start to relax as he sat and stared out at the blue waters of the harbour, the ancient lighthouse sitting out there at the tip of a walkway, the sun beating down. The stresses of the last few days were taking their toll and he was tired, but he couldn't switch off. His mind was constantly going, churning over the intel they had and figuring out what they were lacking, scanning the passing crowds for a familiar face or a suspicious movement, continually thinking, digesting, analysing. Despite the fatigue in his body he knew he was too keyed up to relax properly. Later, he told himself, you can relax later.

He glanced sideways at Katie, sipping her juice through a straw and watching the passers-by from behind dark glasses. Her toned arms were bare beneath her blue singlet, and her hair was down. She had bought a straw fedora with a colourful band from a street vendor near the hotel, and it was pulled down over her eyes.

Moore ran a hand through his hair and felt the joints in his neck click as he leaned back. He drained his glass and set it down on the table.

Katie took the hint, crunched some ice and stood. Moore tucked money under his glass and they headed along the promenade, skirting slower moving tourists but not moving with any great urgency.

'You ever been here before?' Katie asked suddenly, breaking the comfortable silence.

'No. Been to Greece, but not here. You?'

'No.' She smiled behind the glasses. 'It's on my "to do" list.'

'My granddad was here in the war,' Moore said. 'He and his brother were both at Maleme airfield. Granddad got wounded pretty badly, spent the rest of the war in a POW camp. His brother was killed.'

'So the Army runs in your blood then,' she said.

They turned into a side street and headed back towards the hotel.

'Yes and no.' Moore gave a crooked grin. 'It was for their generation, but not for my Dad. He was a pacifist, kinda justified it through Grandad's experience in the war. He protested against Vietnam, all that shit. Even did some jail time for burning a car at a protest.'

'Wow. Not what I would expect from your gene pool.'

'No. As you can imagine we're quite different. He's never been the biggest supporter of my career choices.'

'And a criminal to boot. Bad-ass.'

Moore grunted. 'Hardly. I think he spent about six months gardening at some low security clink. Came out and went back to teaching, buggered off and left Mum with the kids. Last seen shacked up with some hairy arm pitted greeny in New Plymouth.'

'And your brothers...sisters?' Katie prompted. It wasn't something they had discussed before so she didn't know what his family make up was.

'One of each. Sister's a nurse, married with kids. Brother's a DOC ranger, spends most of his time out in the bush so he doesn't have to talk to people.'

'Not big on conversation?'

Moore smiled. 'Not big on people. I got all the social skills in the family.'

'Gee,' she said dryly, 'that was lucky.'

They were walking up a narrow cobbled side street, approaching a small taverna in a stone building, when Katie made a pssst sound. Moore glanced at her.

'We're being followed,' she whispered.

He nodded briefly and smiled. 'I know. There's a guy up ahead in a blue shirt and shades, saw him earlier.'

'And a guy behind us too. White shirt and a moustache.'

'Uh-huh.'

'What do we do?'

They were almost level with the tavern now. There was a middle aged man sitting alone at a table, a newspaper spread on his lap. Smoke curled from a cigarette in the ashtray and he had a coffee at hand. He looked up with shrewd dark eyes as they came near. He was close to fifty and running to fat, with weathered features and a hefty moustache. He made eye contact with Moore and gave a crafty smile.

'I think we should ask this guy,' Moore said.

He stopped and looked down at the man. The man smiled. Moore looked back and waved to the guy in the white shirt who had been following them. 'It's okay,' he called, 'we found him. Thanks anyway.'

He pulled out a chair and sat. The guy in the white shirt stopped further down the street and got out his phone.

The man at the table looked to Katie, who stood awkwardly, unsure what exactly what was going on. He gestured to the spare chair.

'Please, sit,' he said in a thick accent. 'Miss Kathryn.'

She did as he asked and he surveyed them silently for a long moment before picking up his cigarette and taking a slow drag. He exhaled through his nostrils. Moore thought it made him look like a bad guy in some Steven Seagal B-movie, shortly before Steve and his ponytail kicked a dozen asses and whispered some cool lines.

'Welcome to Crete,' the man said. 'My name is Leon.'

'You obviously know who we are,' Moore said.

Leon nodded and stubbed out his cigarette. 'Yes. And what you are.'

Moore slid his sunglasses up onto his head and waited.

'I understand why you are here,' Leon said. He reached for his coffee and took a surprisingly delicate sip for such an indelicate-looking man.

'The High Commissioner always brings people with him,' Moore nodded. 'Can't be too careful these days, even in paradise.' He smiled engagingly.

Leon gave him the slightest frown, like a teacher with a slightly backwards child. 'You didn't listen,' he said. 'I said I understand why you are here, yes? It means I know why you are here, Mr Robert Moore.' His dark eyes studied Moore's face. 'Do we understand?'

Moore studied him back. Clearly the man was no fool. 'We do,' he said. 'You are...police?'

'No, no, no.' Leon tut-tutted and shook his head. 'Not police, no. We are...colleagues, you see?'

Moore nodded slowly. The Greek's National Intelligence Service was a very experienced and brutally efficient outfit, with access to the second-largest intelligence database in Europe. It wasn't surprising therefore that they had been rumbled.

Katie sat back and stayed quiet, letting Moore take the lead. 'We appreciate you touching base with us,' Moore said. 'I have heard many good things about your organisation.'

'And I yours.' Leon nodded graciously. 'We have many things in common I believe, one being maintaining the security of our own proud nations. These are troubled times, Mr Robert Moore, and we would all do well to tread carefully.' His dark eyes probed Moore's again, before turning to Katie and studying her for a long moment. He reached into his shirt pocket and produced a business card, which he slid across the table.

Katie picked it up. It simply had a cell phone number printed on it in plain black type.

'I sincerely hope you enjoy your short stay on our island. It has seen much unrest and trouble over time, and your countrymen's blood has unfortunately been spilled here helping us to defend our honour. I do hope there will be no more of this in the near future.'

Leon paused again. His meaning was clear. 'Should you have any questions or...problems, I would like you to call me before you do anything else. Yes?'

'I understand.' Moore gave a short nod. 'Thank you for taking the time.'

Leon nodded sagely, folded his hands over his portly stomach, and looked at them.

'A mule can be a stubborn beast,' he said carefully. 'They do not always want to drive the cart for the farmer, you see. We have found the old ways are usually the most effective. When the mule does not want to drive the cart, the farmer must dangle a carrot in front of its nose. This makes the mule move forward to get the carrot. It makes the mule behave nicely, you see.'

His dark eyes crinkled and the hefty moustache wriggled like a black caterpillar.

'But mules are not always smart,' he continued. 'So the farmer must also carry a stick. If the mule decides it does not want to do as it is told, well...' He shrugged expressively. 'That is what the stick is for, you see?'

Moore smiled and chuckled.

'Yes, I understand where you're coming from,' he said. 'I've always been a fan of carrots myself.'

Leon gave a low harrumph.

'Of that I am pleased.' He drained his coffee, slapped the table top and stood. 'It has been a pleasure,' he said. He shook hands with them both. 'Enjoy your stay. I look forward to not seeing you again.'

'Likewise.'

He stepped out and walked down towards the waterfront. The guy in the white shirt fell into step with him. The guy in the blue shirt, further up the slope, had disappeared.

Moore turned to Katie.

'Well,' he said, 'that's our welcoming committee.'

'He seemed nice,' she said with more than hint of sarcasm. 'Pretty hung up on livestock though.'

'You're fairly stubborn,' he observed. 'Maybe you're the mule?'

'Huh,' she snorted. 'I guess that makes you the horse's arse then?'

49

They reached the hotel with an hour to go. Katie stripped off and grabbed the first shower, while Moore took Jedi's hint and shaved. He dried his face and peered round the corner into the shower.

'Pervert,' Katie said, wiping water from her face and sweeping her hair back.

'I confess,' he agreed, tugging his pants down. 'You got me on that one, copper.'

He stepped into the shower with her and put his hands around her waist, pulling her to him. She leaned up and kissed him quickly before pushing back and taking the soap.

'No time for this,' she said, 'so behave yourself.'

She used the soap to build up a foamy lather in his chest hair, then turned him round and washed his back too.

'There. Done.' She put the soap back on the dish.

'What about the rest?'

She grinned impishly. 'I think you can manage that yourself. I'm getting out.'

'But you're still dirty.' He scratched at an imaginary mark on her shoulder. 'I'll help you.'

He took the soap and washed the "mark" away, then moved on to washing her chest. She didn't protest when he slipped his soapy hand across her breasts, dwelling on each nipple until it hardened beneath his palm. She pressed closer to him, and he turned her to the wall.

'Let me wash your back,' he said softly, rubbing the bar of soap over her shoulder blades, then down her back to her hips. She leaned forward and pushed back against him, feeling him rising against her buttocks.

Moore ditched the soap and shifted his feet for a better angle.

He hoped the hot water wouldn't run out.

INGOE HAD SNAGGED a double suite on the top floor of the Majestic, using it both for himself and as a briefing room.

When Moore and Katie arrived they found the Masoes and Ingoe with a pair of fit-looking guys in dark suits who had bodyguard written all over them. Another man stood with them, sipping a coffee and watching them as they entered.

He was average height and stocky, with greying hair and a goatee.

Moore ignored them all and motioned for Ingoe to follow him.He held the door open until Ingoe had joined him in the bedroom. Like anything that Ingoe touched the room was neat as a pin with everything in its place.

'We got rumbled in town,' he informed the Ops Officer.

Jedi's eyes twinkled with amusement, and he even cracked what may have been a smile. 'Fat guy called Leon?'

'That's him. Why am I not surprised you already knew?'

Jedi gave a modest shrug. 'I've met him before. That, and he knocked on my door about thirty seconds after I checked in. Did he give you the carrot and stick tale?'

'Katie found it highly amusing.'

'Huh. There's nothing amusing about that man, believe me. He's been with the NIS forever, and they're an outfit you tangle with at your peril. I figured he'd probably tap you two as well.'

'A heads up might've been good,' Moore said, feeling he'd been played.

'What was the point? It was going to happen anyway, and it wasn't like he'd haul you away in handcuffs. It was a good test for young Katie-she's used to being on the other side.'

Moore eyed him suspiciously. 'What, are you looking to recruit her?'

'Maybe.' Jedi's poker face came back, all signs of humour gone. 'Always looking, you know that. Good operators are a rare breed. She seems to be doing alright so far.'

Moore couldn't dispute that, and felt a stab of petty jealousy. It wasn't like he had any claim on the young detective, but it still irked him that plans were being made for her without any input from him. Jedi was watching him closely.

'So what exactly is going on with you two?' he enquired. 'Is it serious or situational?'

Moore felt his cheeks get hot. 'Does it matter?' he tried.

Ingoe's face got harder. 'Yes it matters, or I wouldn't be asking. It matters if you drop your guard because you're worried about your girlfriend, and it matters if you're not thinking straight because you're thinking about nailing her instead.' His hard eyes probed Moore's. 'So yeah, it fuckin' matters.'

Moore took a moment to get a grip on himself before replying. 'Honestly, I don't know. It could be something or not.'

It felt awkward talking about his feelings with another bloke. They were two battle-hardened SAS soldiers talking like lovesick teenagers. Moore wanted the ground to swallow him up and make the moment disappear forever.

'Rob, listen.' Jedi's tone was softer now. 'I know you've had a shit time of it and things are getting on top of you. This is your chance to prove yourself to yourself again. I know you're up to it. The Director knows you're up to it.' He paused, then jabbed Moore firmly in the chest with a finger. 'You need to believe in yourself, and get your mojo back mate. Don't let anything else cloud your focus on the job. Yeah?'

Moore nodded mutely. His cheeks were burning but Jedi's words struck a chord with him. He knew the other man was right. The drinking, Michelle, his angst over Danni, all the other stupid shit he'd been doing. He'd lost his groove, and he couldn't afford to.

He knew the drill; Jedi had spoken to him about it now, so that was it. No second chances. If he fucked this up he was gone. He may as well go and pack his bags. He shook his head, a thousand thoughts running through it. No way. No goddamn way. Not after all he'd fought for through the years. He wasn't going to be some nobody on a scrapheap, burned out and washed up and thrown aside for a younger, faster model. Fuck that.

He looked to Jedi, meeting his gaze.

'All good,' he said quietly.

Jedi nodded once, slapped him on the shoulder and opened the door. The talking was over.

They re-joined the others, and Moore noticed the man with the goatee studying him across the room while he sipped from a cup of tea.

Moore dropped his jacket on the back of a sofa, extending his hand to the man.

'Rob Moore,' he said.

The man's grip was firm.

'Mark Gutry,' he replied with a nod.

He had watchful green eyes behind wire rimmed glasses and wore a charcoal suit.

'Mark is from NAB,' Ingoe said, 'he's here for some liaison with our foreign friends.'

Moore nodded. The National Assessments Bureau was a very small intelligence agency which fell under the umbrella of the Department of the Prime Minister and Cabinet, mainly focussing on collating and analysing intelligence on other nations. He wondered if the man's presence was somehow linked to Paul Oldham's situation, or whether it truly was just a liaison visit. He decided there was no point in asking.

'Chris and Alex,' Ingoe continued, introducing the two Personal Protection Officers. 'They're with the Minister.'

There was another round of hand shaking before Ingoe began the briefing. Utilising his laptop he showed them the floor plan of the hotel they would be at, including vantage points, exits and planned escape routes if things went pear-shaped.

The lead PPO, Chris, ran through the planned movements for the dignitaries and Ingoe ended with an intel update. This consisted of the theories around Natalie's disappearance and the Parker kid's death, which was all news to both Vince and Nga and the two PPOs.

'Hence the need to boost the security,' Ingoe concluded. He looked around the assembled faces. 'I know it's unlikely to amount to anything but we're in the business of risk management. Any questions?'

There were none, so after a time check the two cops and the Masoes departed to collect their respective principals. Moore decided to give the NAB man a nudge and see what he could shake loose.

'So Mark,' he said, slipping his suit jacket on, 'what's the real reason you're here?'

Gutry shrugged nonchalantly. 'My role is liaision with the other agencies, so it's good to come to events like this where there's always a few of my peers floating about.'

'Uh-huh.' Moore looked and sounded unconvinced.

Gutry glanced at Ingoe who gave an almost imperceptible flick of his chin. Gutry put his hands in his pockets and considered his words carefully before continuing.

'It would be fair to say that the PM is also concerned about the situation with Mr Oldham and his daughter. I'm just keeping a bit of a watching brief.'

'So you have concerns over the Minister himself,' Moore pressed, 'or is it just the situation with Natalie?'

Gutry paused again before answering. He was obviously a man adept at information control.

'The concerns are not over the Minister himself, no,' he replied carefully.

'So what aren't you telling us?' Katie wanted to know.

Gutry took his hands out of his pockets and opened them expressively while he spoke.

'Look guys, I appreciate it's annoying when you think info's being withheld from you...'

'Which it is,' Katie cut in.

Gutry's cool green eyes flickered.

'You have to appreciate there are certain things that I'm not allowed to disclose to you, and you may not like it, but unfortunately that's the way it is.' He looked apologetic. 'If I could tell you, I would. It always makes sense to share as much info as we can to get the job done-we're all in the same game, after all.'

Ingoe stepped forward now, taking the lead back. 'Guys, you know as much as we can tell you, and pushing harder ain't gunna change that. Believe me, if there was something you needed to know, then you would know.' He looked between them. 'Okay? Right, we need to get cracking. We've still got a job to do.'

50

The cocktail evening was held in the ballroom of a plush hotel just outside Chania itself, an ancient stone building converted into a hotel.

It perched on the lip of a cliff overlooking the sea, with spectacular views. The waves crashed onto the rocks far below, foaming white in the evening light. The odd light bobbed at sea as fishing boats returned to harbour.

Various dignitaries and Government officials were in attendance, along with a select number of tour members with deep enough pockets.

The ballroom had been decorated with art, wall tapestries and candelabra, and tables covered in white linen held canapes and drinks. Red-coated wait staff circulated with trays and collected glasses.

Moore had to admit it was impressive, but the most impressive thing for him was the sight of the handful of elderly veterans being treated like royalty. There was no more than a dozen of them there, all around ninety or more, hunched and wrinkled but looking sharp in their dinner suits adorned with shiny medals.

He watched a couple of old boys laughing as they listened to a tale being retold by another vet, their eyes twinkling as they laughed like schoolboys. He recognised the service medals they wore, acknowledging their service in different theatres of war. One proudly wore a Military Medal on his now sunken chest.

'You pretty much get medals for turning up to work in the military,' he confided to Katie as they stood off to the side, trying to remain unobtrusive. 'Even a bloke who spends his whole career folding blankets in Waiouru or a chef in a field kitchen is going to get some gongs. But these guys are different-most of their shiny stuff is for actually serving in theatres of combat. There's one bloke over there with a Military Medal, which is for bravery.' He shook his head with admiration. 'These guys are the real deal, Katie.'

'My great grandfather served in the war,' she replied. 'He was in the RAF, got shot down over France and had to escape back to England. He never talked about it though.' Her face was sombre. 'Nana said he used to wake up shouting at night.'

Moore nodded silently, knowing exactly what she was saying. His own demons were not so distant.

He kept his eyes on the room, constantly scanning the faces, the hands, the body language. A threat could come from anywhere at any time, and there was really no way to truly prevent an attack if the attacker was smart and determined enough. A close protection team could eliminate the luck aspect and respond appropriately to any threat that presented itself, but the real trick was to pre-empt any action. He'd done these details many times with varying degrees of risk, but approached every task the same way-stay sharp, be professional, act fast.

CP details were inevitably boring, and therein lay the risk. Malaise and complacency were deadly.

He wondered again about Katie-how would she respond to a threat? She wasn't trained for this sort of role, but there was no denying she'd handled herself as well as any soldier in Iraq, and she had earned his respect in the process. So far, despite his early misgivings, she had proved to be an asset.

A face caught his eye and he nudged Katie's elbow.

'That's the High Commissioner,' he said quietly.

They watched him as he slid into a group of veterans, shaking hands and smiling politely as he spoke to them. Vince was a few metres away and Nga was off to the other side. Ingoe and Gutry were keeping a low profile, mingling amongst the crowd.

The High Commissioner had an easy manner about him and the veteran warriors were obviously comfortable with him. Another familiar face appeared beside him, moving himself into the same group. He was louder and bolshier than the High Commissioner, and one of the old boys stepped away and moved off to another group.

'Paul Oldham,' Katie murmured.

'That's Minister Oldham to you, Constable,' came a voice behind them.

They turned to see Tristan sidling up, resplendent in a black tuxedo with a white rose in his lapel.

Katie glanced to Moore then eyed the newcomer with disdain.

'That's Detective to you, whoever you are,' she returned evenly.

Tristan eyed her coolly, a superior sneer curling his lip.

'Nice attitude,' he said, 'are you always that ignorant and rude, or is it just to dignitaries?'

Moore saw her cheeks flush with anger and her jaw set. She was about to fire back when he moved in and touched her elbow gently.

'Katie, this is Tristan, assistant to the Minister,' he said smoothly. He gave Tristan a broad smile. 'Don't worry mate, she would never speak to the Minister like that, considering he's an actual dignitary.'

He held the younger man's arrogant stare, the point made.

'If you'll excuse us, we're on duty,' Moore continued, turning away. 'Unless there was something we needed to know?'

A nerve twitched in Tristan's cheek and he stalked away wordlessly.

'Twat,' Katie muttered.

'I couldn't agree more.'

Fortunately the evening was scheduled to finish at nine, and by about eight thirty the crowd had thinned out. Chris came on the net, advising that the Minister was to depart in four minutes and for the driver to bring his car round.

Moore and Katie floated towards the entrance, staying out of the way but ready in case of a drama. The local police were covering the exterior for them, and Chris came on the net again advising them that the party was moving to the doors.

There was no response and he tried again. Still nothing.

Moore hit the talk button taped to his thumb. 'Stand by,' he said. The tiny mic pinned beneath his tie picked it up clearly.

He moved quickly to the front doors and checked the exterior. The Minister's silver Opel waited at the doors with the engine running, the backup car behind it. The two uniformed cops supposed to be on duty there were off to the side, chatting and smoking. From the doors Moore could see that one held the radio the PPOs had loaned them.

Moore stalked over to them and whistled sharply as he approached. Both men looked round guiltily and tossed their smokes aside. Moore waggled his ear and pointed at the radio.

'Got your ears on?' he snapped.

The radio man flushed and checked the radio, turning it on with an audible click.

Moore suppressed a snarl and keyed his radio. 'Standby one.'

He turned to the two cops and angrily pointed them into position. The one without the radio, a fat guy with a bushy moustache, looked obstinately at Moore and said something in Greek. It clearly wasn't an invitation to dinner, and Moore shot him a glare.

'Really, sunshine?' Moore took a step forward. He was older than the cop but bigger and stronger, and clearly in no mood for a debate. 'Get moving before I kick your fuckin' arse.'

The message didn't need translating and they scurried off to their positions. Moore gave the all clear as he returned to Katie's side, silently fuming. Katie sensed his anger but stayed quiet,

They watched Oldham and his party-Tristan and a couple of other aides-finish up their pleasantries and head that way, Chris and Alex boxing them front and back.

He was pleased to note that the PPOs looked sharp and alert.

As the group moved past them, Oldham looked in their direction and seemed to break stride when he recognised Moore. There was a pregnant pause for the slightest of moments before Tristan ushered him on and the Minister disappeared out the door without a word.

Moore watched until the Minister was in the back seat of the Opel before he turned away.

Chris' voice came on the net through the earwig. 'Mike One mobile.'

Moore heard Nga acknowledge it and give a three minute warning to the High Commissioner's driver to bring their car round. He and Katie automatically moved, exiting the main doors and taking up positions on the flanks. This enabled them to have eyes outside before the principal emerged. He saw the pair of Greek police officers standing over where he had caught them, fresh cigarettes sparked up.

They were displaying no situational awareness, and he wondered at the sense of having used them for the outside watch during the Minister's departure. Whoever had decided that clearly had no tactical nous.

The fat one eyeballed Moore across the gap, made sure he had caught the foreigner's eye then turned and pointedly spat on the ground. He looked back with a sneer and blew smoke in Moore's direction.

Moore bristled but ignored him. He didn't have time for childish bravado.

'Moving to the doors,' Vince said over the net.

Moore subconsciously stood a little straighter and scanned the driveway and front apron. The maroon Toyota being used for the High Commissioner was in place by the doors, the security vehicle sitting back further.

The party emerged and moved towards the car, Vince getting the door. The High Commissioner and his wife climbed aboard and Nga took the front passenger's seat. As soon as the Toyota began to move the security car-a blue Skoda-slid forward and picked up Vince.

'Hotel One mobile,' Nga transmitted, and in seconds both sets of taillights disappeared down the drive.

The cop who had the radio ambled over and handed it to Moore without making eye contact before re-joining his fat mate. Moore and Katie headed back inside, finding Ingoe and Gutry making their farewells to the hosts. Ingoe gave them a nod and Katie headed outside again.

Being just the support crew, no driver had been supplied. Moore waited while the small talk and pleasantries wound down, nodding and smiling to some of the old warriors as they headed for the door.

He wondered if it would too late to get a snack by the time they arrived back at the hotel.

Suddenly the net opened and he heard a grunt in his ear, a muffled cough and some kind of rustle. Maybe Katie had inadvertently triggered her talk button. Another cough sounded followed by a groan and Moore moved fast towards the door.

He sidestepped a small group of guests as he ran towards the car park, hitting the talk button.

'Katie? Katie?'

He rounded the side of the hotel and spotted their car several metres away, the last official vehicle in their designated spot. It was a blue Toyota Corolla lift back-hardly the standard car for a protection job, but the Greeks seemed to like their small cars.

The lighting was dim round the side of the hotel, but Moore could see Katie on her hands and knees by the front of the car, her hair hanging down over her face as she moved feebly.

Moore sprinted to her, drawing his weapon as he ran and scanning for threats. He saw none but took a few extra seconds to circle the car before dashing back and skidding to a stop beside her. He took a knee and swept the area, his eyes and Sig working as one, checking again.

'What happened?' he asked, not looking at her.

'Ahh...shit...' She groaned and touched the back of her head gingerly. 'Someone...hit me.'

'Who was it?'

'Dunno...didn't see.'

He holstered his weapon and helped her to her feet. She leaned against the side of the car and let him check her over. Aside from a bang to the head which had produced a nasty lump and a small amount of blood, she appeared to be uninjured. She still had her weapon and the car keys; this was no robbery.

'Look at me.' Moore checked her eyes. Satisfied she hadn't been concussed, he helped her into the front passenger's seat then went and fetched Ingoe and Gutry.

He quietly filled Ingoe in on the attack as they walked back to the car, but left Gutry out of the loop for now. Despite being in the same game, he was from a different agency and Moore had never dealt with him before; therefore he was an unknown.

They took their places, Moore at the wheel with Katie beside him. Gutry raised an eyebrow at Katie's condition but said nothing. Moore put the Toyota in gear and moved out of the car park slowly, the headlights sweeping the Police Skoda near the main entrance. The two uniformed cops glanced at them as they went past and Moore caught a sneer on the fat guy's face.

He ignored him and rolled out to the road, nosing down the hill towards Chania and starting to move.

Katie was gingerly probing her head and grunted as the car hit a bump and she inadvertently jabbed her wound.

'Sorry,' Moore murmured, tapping the brakes.

The pedal was soft under his foot and he pressed harder, pushing it all the way to the floor. There was no resistance and the car continued to accelerate with gravity. They were already doing forty klicks.

'Oh shit...'

He dropped the auto transmission into second and felt the engine grab, the tach needle flicking up sharply as the engine tried to slow itself.

'Got no brakes,' Moore said sharply as he seized the hand brake and lifted it hard, keeping the button down with his thumb. 'Buckle up.'

The hand brake came straight up with no resistance and he realised it was gone too. He immediately hit the hazard lights and turned the wheel sharply, throwing the car into a zig-zag across the lanes to gain traction on the tyres. A hair pin turn was coming up fast and he zigged back onto the correct side of the road-all he needed now was an oncoming car.

The Toyota took the sharp turn at forty klicks and he began to zig-zag again as they entered a straight of a hundred metres or so. On the right was a safety barrier on the cliff side. The mountains loomed on the left, a steep bank dropping to the road with another safety barrier.

He needed dirt or grass to slow them down, but there was no other option. He continued to zig-zag, pumping the brake pedal as he did so in case he could build up pressure in the line, but it was like pushing on a sponge.

'Hope you got insurance, Jed,' Moore muttered, 'heads down!'

Katie covered her head and ducked as he zagged back her way. There was a bang and a shrill screech of metal as the front left wing connected with the safety barrier. He rode it hard, steering against the barrier and seeing pieces flying off the side of the car into the darkness, bright orange and yellow sparks cascading across the glass.

Moore jerked the car back to the right as the road turned that way, the speedo immediately picking up again from thirty. The tyres sang as he cut left sharply, the tail slipping a bit before he could recover-a slide now would be fatal.

He got the car back under control, slapped the gear stick down as low as it would go and aimed the nose towards the safety barrier on the left again, connecting at thirty five klicks with a horrendous screech. There was a jolt as the wheel clipped a post on the barrier and the car lurched to the right, headlights coming up fast behind them.

'Watch the back!' Moore shouted, hoping against hope it was not some drunk Greek meandering his way home after too much ouzo. Or worse still, their attackers coming in for the kill. In an incapacitated car and with one gun hand out of action, they were sitting ducks.

He swung back left, spotting the end of the barrier as the bank on the left dropped to an easier slope covered in brush. He rode up onto the slope with the left hand wheels, as far as he dared without risking a roll, feeling the long grass and smaller scrub grabbing at the chassis of the car and slowing it down. A larger shrub went down under the front of the car with a rustling crash.

The car behind them flew past on the right, the passenger gesturing angrily at them and the driver tooting loudly. The taillights disappeared around a bend and Moore followed, dropping back onto the asphalt again to take the curve. Rubber screamed as the Toyota slid across the road and careened off the right hand safety barrier. A hubcap rattled away and dropped off the edge into the darkness.

'Try to stay to the left Rob,' Ingoe said drily, 'there's a bloody great cliff down there.'

They got round the bend and Moore took it up onto the left hand bank again, swiping a sapling and scraping against a rock hidden by the undergrowth. The speed was bleeding off but momentum was still the enemy, dragging the car forward. There was still no response from the brakes so Moore left the pedal alone and focussed on the wheel, his hands in a strong 10-2 position. He brought the car back to the right again, throwing a fast zig-zag from shoulder to shoulder that tossed his passengers around but got good traction on the rubber and bled off ten k's an hour. He steered back into the left hand barrier, sparks showering over the windscreen and popping across his night vision like fireworks. The left headlight blew and the steering wheel was juddering in his hands, fighting against the resistance of the metal barrier. A right hand bend was fast approaching and headlights were coming with it. Moore flicked down the sun visor to protect his vision as best he could.

The other vehicle narrowly missed them as Moore slalomed in the width of his lane before crossing over to the right again and swinging it hard. He estimated they were probably half way down the hill now and they needed to stop before they hit Chania. An out of control car in a busy town centre would be disastrous. An out of control car full of foreign intelligence officers would be an international incident of epic proportions.

He hauled hard on the wheel, feeling the tail of the car lift and threaten to slide as he aimed for the grassy bank on the left. The front left wheel bumped up onto the grass just before the tail lost grip, and the car started to slide.

'Fuck!' shouted Katie as the landscape spun before them.

Moore steered into the skid, keeping his eyes on the grass bank and praying another car didn't suddenly appear on the scene.

The car flicked around in a full circle, the tyres screeching and pouring smoke so thick that Moore couldn't see even with one headlight still working.

He lost sight of the bank and fought the wheel, the steering juddering in his hands before the front right wheel thumped into the kerb and they were up onto the grass again, backwards now but moving slower.

He leaned into it, feeling the car slowing more, bumping over unseen objects he had no way of combating. There was a sudden crunch from the rear, a lurch and the back of the Toyota dropped.

The car came to an abrupt stop, the engine roaring and the front wheels spinning for grip. Moore grabbed at the key and killed the ignition.

Silence fell on the car and they sat for a moment, regathering themselves. The remaining headlight popped and died.

'I don't know about you guys,' Gutry piped up from the back seat, 'but we don't get this much at NAB.'

51

Both of them found it hard to unwind once they got back to their room.

Katie sat with an icepack on her head to reduce the swelling, a glass of water and strong painkillers ready at her elbow.

'I'm sure a decent drink would work better,' she grumbled, watching Moore pour himself a short bourbon over ice.

'Not with a head injury,' he said, recapping the bottle and picking up his glass. 'Keep that pack on your head for another four minutes.'

He took a swig and savoured the burn as it slid down his throat. They'd been over the night's events a dozen times and it never got any better.

An unseen, unidentified assailant cracked Katie over the back of the head as she was getting the car keys out, paused long enough to kick her in the guts and ran off. No attempt at robbery, no words said, not a damn hint of who they were. Then their brakes failed and they nearly all perished in a fiery crash down a mountainside.

Jedi had organised for the car to be towed and stored at the local Police headquarters, and Moore was going to look at it in the morning. There was no doubt in his mind though that it had been a deliberate act of murderous sabotage. It was clearly linked to the attack on

Katie, who had presumably disturbed the bad guy and spooked him into action. But why?

The question remained, hanging out there unanswered. Random? Highly unlikely. Linked to their mission at hand? Quite probable. Personal? Possible, but unlikely. Maybe the two cops Moore had rarked up, but they were obvious suspects and had a lot to lose if they were found out. They certainly had the opportunity though, the motive, and probably the knowledge.

The longer it tumbled round in his head, the more he kept coming back to the Minister's assistant, Tristan. Moore knew he had nothing to base his suspicions on aside from a strong dislike for the jumped up, objectionable little man, but he couldn't shake the feeling he was behind it. Something about him just gave Moore the creeps.

He took another drink and dug out his cell phone. He brought up a number and hit the call button. It took a few rings before Chris answered. He sounded sleepy.

'What's up?'

'When you guys left tonight, did you all go together?' Moore didn't apologise for waking him. His felt his heart pounding in his chest.

'Yeah, you saw us...what're you on about? Oh, hang on, umm...no.'

'No? What d'you mean no?'

'No, we didn't all leave together. We were going to, then one of them decided to stay and make his own way back to the hotel later.'

Moore put his glass down with a clunk. Katie stood now and walked over, the icepack in her hand.

'Let me guess,' Moore said, 'the Minister's assistant?'

'Yeah,' Chris replied. 'Tristan.'

'Thanks mate.' Moore disconnected and turned to Katie. 'I think we have a problem.'

THE OPEN PLAN office was mostly in darkness at nearly midnight, just a cone of light falling over a single desk as the lone intelligence officer worked late.

Sarah Loughlin lifted her mug and screwed up her face at the taste of the cold tea. Bugger it, it was better than nothing. She drained it and put the mug down, sitting back. The mug was bright red with white lettering-World's Best Mum.

Like hell, she thought bitterly. The world's best mum wouldn't be at work at this time of bloody night, would she?

She sighed and ran a hand through her hair. She felt like a sack of shite but was too wired to knock off just yet. There was a pair of night shift surveillance teams out there, trying their damndest to track down their target.

Melinda Ashford-Blaine had been missing for only a day and a half, and the police had barely raised an eyebrow so far. At Millbank it was a different story. Being the daughter of a well-connected Viscount ensured things got done that wouldn't normally get done, and in this case, it was just as well.

It had taken all of an hour to establish that Melinda-a twenty year old arts student-had been frequenting a particular café in High Wycombe, just up the road from her family's plush property outside Marlow. The Buckinghamshire countryside was hardly a hotbed of terrorist activity, but the working town of Wycombe was well on MI5's radar.

The café in question was run by a Pakistani family with known connections to various radicals, some of whom had been caught up in previous anti-terrorism operations. Not only had young Melinda begun frequenting the establishment, it seemed she had also hooked up with one of the sons and had spent at least one night at his flat, according to the text data one of the team had been analysing.

Melinda gushed enthusiastically to a girlfriend about how amazing Imran was, and how now that they had consummated their relationship-multiple times, no less-he had asked her to go away with him for a weekend. There was no way her parents would allow it, the ignorant bastards, even though everyone just knew Daddy was having it off with that slapper PA of his and Mummy was spaced on fucking Valium most of the time, so who the hell were they to question anything anyway?

The friend-another well-connected girl from old money-had promptly offered to cover for her and the plan was in motion. A reservation in a Cotswolds B&B had been booked and paid for on one of Melinda's credit cards, and a night full of promise awaited the star struck lovers.

Problem was, Melinda's cell phone was last polling on the way up the M40 heading north before suddenly dropping off the net. It was likely that she and Imran were heading to Birmingham where his family was known to have contacts.

Whether Melinda was consenting to that or not was a different story. Given a choice between a cosy B&B in Cirencester and a night in Birmingham, Sarah knew what she would have chosen. Sure, Birmingham had its own appeal, but it was just so, well, Brummy.

Enough alarm bells were ringing for the boss to authorise not only overtime but extra staff from other offices, and the last twenty four hours had been manic. Sarah didn't remember when she had last eaten anything other than a Mars bar or a peppermint from the stash in her drawer.

The only other person she'd seen in the last hour was Kevin, a night shift security guard doing his rounds. He'd stopped to chat but left quickly when he got the cold shoulder. Ever since she found out he got caught twanging his wanger over a girly mag at work a few months back, she'd found it impossible to talk to him. The fact he still had the guts to keep working there was incredible.

The bosses were aware of the intel from the Kiwis and Aussies and a smidgen of what the Americans had, and it all added up to a huge pile of trouble. Not only that, but the ears at GCHQ had picked up reference in the electronic chatter to a "spectacular."

In intelligence terms a spectacular was anything but, and generally meant a large number of innocent deaths in a high-profile attack. The 9/11 attacks were a classic, with the 7/7 bombings closer to home.

Sarah sighed and rubbed her temples. Her eyes hurt, her back ached and she needed to pee. Maybe she had a tumour.

A vibrating from her top drawer broke the hum of her computer. She opened the drawer and checked which phone it was-she had four. One personal, one for normal work, one for an agent she had been running-not needed for the next two years as the hopeless bastard got himself nicked in another stolen motor-and one for her contacts.

It was the contacts phone, with a number she didn't recognise. It began with 30, which she was pretty sure was the country code for Greece. She answered with a simple 'Hello?'

'Locky, we need to speak.'

Sarah felt her spirits lift at the sound of Rob's deep voice. It was like an oasis in a desert of eye strain and headaches.

'Yes, I'm fine thanks,' she replied with a smile in her voice. 'You obviously want something and of course I've got nothing better to do.'

She waited for a laugh that didn't come. Clearly the Kiwi had his serious pants on today. She checked her watch. Quarter past one, which made it just after eleven in Greece.

'I'm in Crete,' Moore told her. 'Things are happening fast but we've got some big gaps in our intel. I need some help.'

Sarah leaned forward and grabbed a pen. 'Go ahead, caller.'

THE BUZZ of his phone brought Pat back to consciousness, and he fumbled in the darkness for it.

Bringing it to his ear with his eyes still closed he cleared his throat and tried to sound compos mentis. 'Yeah?'

There was a crackle in the line before he heard a vaguely familiar voice. 'Pat, it's Rob Moore. Sorry to wake you.'

Pat sat up in his cot, rubbing his face. 'Oh hey Kiwi, how's tricks buddy?'

'Mate, I need some assistance.'

Pat swung his legs over the side of the cot and reached for the light. His watch told him it was midnight. Getting called at this time by a foreign officer was not unusual.

'First off buddy, how'd you get this number?'

There was a momentary pause before Moore replied.

'You know how it goes, Pat. The important thing is I've got you on the line, and there's something you will be very interested in.'

Pat stood, scratching his balls as he listened in silence for a full minute. At the end of the minute he licked his lips and hunted round for his pants. It was time to get to work.

'You're right,' he said, pulling his pants up one leg then hopping on the other foot as he struggled to dress himself. 'I'm interested.' He checked the screen of his phone. 'Gotcha number buddy, I'll call you shortly.'

He disconnected abruptly and jerked the pants up, slipped his feet into flip flops and headed for the door.

IT WAS an hour later before Moore's phone rang. He jerked upright in the chair and had the phone to his ear before his eyes opened.

He glanced over to where Katie was stretched out on the sofa, her dark hair fanning out over a cushion. She stirred as he spoke.

It was Locky. Moore listened intently for a minute, giving just the occasional uh-huh. When Locky ran out of breath he stood and walked to the window, looking out at the town lights in the velvet darkness.

'I see,' he said quietly.

Locky talked some more before he thanked her and disconnected. He turned and saw Katie sitting up, looking at him expectantly. She brushed her hair back from her face. He thought she looked pretty with her hair loose.

'Tristan's story isn't checking out,' he said. 'There is no record of him even existing before twenty two years ago, when he was about seventeen-if he's even using his real date of birth.'

'How the hell...' Katie trailed off, still processing the though.

Moore knew what she was getting at.

'Exactly,' he said. 'Apparently he came to New Zealand as a Serbian refugee from Bosnia. His parents were academics, and he was the only surviving child. His two sisters and his grandparents were killed in the war-some good old fashioned ethnic cleansing.' Moore stood and took a draught of water. It was still warm in the hotel room despite the hour. 'The village they lived in was accidentally hit by a NATO bomber. The family went to Aussie first then on to New Zealand a couple of years later. The real family name is Stefanovic, but the Dad changed it by deed poll to Stevens. Presumably to be more Westernised.'

Katie listened intently, and he could see she had her cop face on, all business now.

'They had no papers so got taken at face value like all refugees. Grew up there, went to school, and on to uni. Mum and Dad died in a house fire eighteen years ago, ruled an accident.'

'Really?' Katie arched her eyebrows. 'Not an arson with him bumping off the olds?'

'Officially ruled an accident. A clothes rack was left too close to a gas heater and the whole place went up. They were the only ones home that night and died in the fire.'

'Where was Tristan then?'

'At a meeting with some uni friends.' Moore's mouth hardened. 'A support group for Muslim converts.'

Katie's jaw dropped. 'Jesus.'

'All non-Arabs. Mostly white kids.'

'Let me guess,' Katie interrupted. 'They were known as the White Lambs?'

Moore nodded grimly in the darkness.

'How the hell was this not picked up on earlier? How did he get a job in a Minister's office?'

'Equal opportunities, Katie. That all sounds suspicious as hell to us, with what we know now, but he was obviously vetted and cleared.'

She shook her head in amazement. 'There was nothing criminal there, I guess,' she said, 'and you can't pre-judge someone on their political beliefs. I guess there are plenty of good Muslims around.'

'Exactly. The problem is the radicals, and I'm only presuming that the White Lambs group were exactly that.' He checked his watch. 'I need to wake up Jedi. This shit's going to blow up.'

52

The Cathedral of the Angels was an impressive, 16th century Catholic church in the heart of Chania.

During the war it had been a place of refuge for many, and was still a central place of worship. Topped by an impressive roof of spires with a tower bell which now only chimed for special occasions, with plenty of stained glass windows, the walls proudly bore bullet holes as battle scars of the town's history.

Moore and Katie approached the cathedral from the direction of their hotel, walking down a narrow cobbled street amongst the usual flow of tourists. The crowds had thinned out now with the heat of the day driving many to the beaches or inside for shade. The cathedral sat on a raised corner, dominating an intersection of busy streets.

The high wooden doors were open and a red carpet flowed from inside and down the stone steps like a river of blood.

Sharply dressed members of the Allied militaries milled around at the front, waiting for the start of proceedings. An elderly priest with a long grey beard stood at the top of the stairs, a prayer book in his folded hands as he chatted to an Australian soldier in a traditional lemon-squeezer hat.

Moore and Katie commenced a circuit of the building, moving

together with familiar ease as they started a block out from the cathedral and walked the surrounding streets in a full circle. Every parked car, every person, every window was checked. Nothing stood out immediately, but Moore expected that. Any terrorist worth their salt-and ISIS were experienced and very good at what they did-would not leave obvious signs.

What he hoped for, more than anything else, was for the day to go without a hitch. Hopefully the bad guys had changed their plans, hopefully they'd been scared off, hopefully the intel was bad. Hopefully.

A lot had happened in the last several hours, and finally the lines of communication had officially opened up between the various intelligence agencies. The Aussies had confirmed that Tristan had spent a year after uni working for the Parker family as a "manny"-Ingoe had had to ask exactly what the hell one of those was-looking after young Paul, before returning to Wellington and getting on board with the Oldham family.

A clear pattern was apparent, with the Parkers speaking in revered tones of the wonderful Tristan and how much their Paul had worshipped him. Worship was the right word, Moore had mused. They had no knowledge of their "manny's" religious beliefs and described him as a calm, peaceful sort, although they did recall him firing up once during a discussion over the War on Terror. They had put that down to his family experiences, and thought nothing more of it. There was no doubt he had heavily influenced young Paul, and they had stayed in touch after Tristan had moved on.

There was a gap in the intel as to how he was connected to the American girl, Leanne Sinclair, and the CIA were expressing doubts over whether there was a direct connection at all. It was clear that Tristan had recruited at least Paul Parker and Natalie Oldham to the cause, but whether he had a hand in the Sinclair matter was not known.

MI5's Sarah Lockwood had come back with a report that a Viscount's daughter had also gone missing in similar circumstances, but had been located at the Birmingham home of a Pakistani extremist. The cops had hit the place once she had put a push on, backed by the info on the other cases, and found her and her boyfriend packed and ready to go, with tickets for Karachi.

There was, as yet, no known link between them and Tristan.

But there was no doubting the issues with Tristan Stefanovic, who had disappeared from his hotel room overnight. Minister Oldham was aware that he had run but not of the full details-yet. For now the show had to go on, and hope for the best.

But there was no room for hope in a good plan, so they did their circuit. Moore had a heavy knot in his chest and his shoulders were tense. He had a bad feeling, and he knew that Katie felt it too. If he believed in such things he would call it a premonition maybe, but he had no time for airy fairy superstitions. What he did have was a keen sixth sense from years of soldiering, and right now it was dinging loudly in the back of his head.

They reached the end of the street and turned away from the cathedral, boxing round to start a new circuit a block wider.

'We'll do two blocks then come back in,' Moore said quietly, and Katie gave an "Uh-huh." She had been quiet all morning, pensive.

The nervous tension in each of them was feeding the other, and he forced himself to take a long slow breath, bringing his heart rate down. He rolled his shoulders under the lightweight cotton shirt and heard the crackle of gas bubbles popping in the joints.

They continued walking, trying to melt into the crowd without dawdling. It was fifteen minutes before their official party was due to arrive at the cathedral.

Moore transmitted an update to the CP team as they completed the second box and began to move back down a street that took them to the inner box.

'Once the party are in the cathedral we'll still hang outside,' Moore said.

Katie gave another "Uh-huh" and slowed as they approached a street vendor's stand. Bottles of water were stacked in the shade of the guy's umbrella and she gave Moore an enquiring look as she dug out her wallet. He gave a nod and stepped to the side, leaning against the wall of a building as he waited. The sun was hot and he was glad of his shades with the glare from the white bricks opposite. He watched Katie as she cracked the bottle and took a long draught. Despite the thump on the head last night she was doing well.

The bud in his ear gave a crackle and he heard Jedi's voice, giving everyone on the net a ten minute heads-up.

Moore glanced back to Katie, and as he turned something beyond her caught his eye. A vehicle turning into the street and slowing to a stop on the opposite side of the road, maybe forty metres away.

A plain white Toyota van, no sign writing, standard rims and nothing conspicuous about it at all. Just a plain old van, so unremarkable in fact that its very lack of any features made it noticeable. Moore noticed it, and in the next second he realised that somebody else had noticed it too.

A grey Citreon rolled past the intersection the van had just appeared from and he saw a flare of brake lights. Two seconds later a man appeared around the corner, shades on and one hand self-consciously touching his ear as he moved up the footpath towards the van.

Moore instantly recognised him as the guy in the white shirt who had accompanied Leon the previous day. Even at this distance he could sense the tension in the guy. Everything seemed to go into slow motion before him.

Moore's eyes flicked back to Katie, seeing her drain the bottle and let out a satisfied sigh as she turned towards him.

He heard the metallic scrape as the van's side door slid open and saw the vehicle move slightly as its weight shifted. He saw movement through the side window, somebody out now on the far side.

Katie lowered her bottle and looked at him, sensing something.

Leon's guy kept his head down as he moved towards the van, deliberately paying the vehicle no attention. Moore could see the guy was stuck now, committed to an action which took him right to what was presumably his target. Surely he was doing a walk past? This couldn't be a direct approach, could it? Nobody was that stupid; such an approach was a job for a fully equipped tactical unit, not a lone intelligence officer.

The person behind the van moved into view now and Moore saw a female figure, long blonde hair under a blue cap, emerge from the cover of the van and head away from it, towards Moore and Katie but on the opposite side of the cobbled street. She wore a flowing blue summery top over white leggings.

Natalie Oldham, Moore thought. Has to be.

His eyes flicked back to the van, seeing the driver now and realising the man was looking at him. Middle Eastern of some sort, short beard and a khaki shirt. The engine was still running. Leon's guy was barely ten metres from the van now.

Katie stopped still, the plastic bottle in her hands. Moore took a breath and discreetly moved a finger under the flaps of his loose green shirt. He pressed the talk button he had taped to his belt.

'Don't turn round,' he breathed into the mic under the lapel, 'eyes on me.'

She flicked her eyebrows to signify she understood.

The blonde girl was well clear of the van now and parallel to them.

Moore could no longer see Leon's man, hidden by the van. The driver's head snapped round and there was a shout, then gunfire split the thick air.

A loud shot, a shout, the roar of the van's engine revving, two more pistol shots then a long burst of submachine gun fire.

Moore pushed off the wall and yanked his shirt up, snatching the Sig from the holster there, Katie stepping and turning as she grabbed for the bum-bag at the front of her pants. The van lurched away from the kerb, seemingly towards them, a pistol fired again, the blonde girl began to run, the submachine gun ripped off another long burst, somebody screamed. Another engine behind them.

Tourists and locals stopped and stared.

Moore got the Sig up in both hands and bellowed, 'Everybody down! On the ground!'

The white Toyota van screeched towards them and he could see the driver's face twisted in a snarl, both hands on the wheel, eyes locked on them as he bore down. He had obviously clocked them and was presumably, mistakenly, lumping them in with Leon's man.

Moore stepped sideways, getting distance from the street vendor who had ducked for cover, his focus totally on the driver as he stared along the short barrel of the Sig at him. The pistol rocked in his hand as he triggered a shot, and another, the windscreen spider webbing but not breaking as both rounds ricocheted off into the sky.

His third shot went through and he saw a splash of red behind the crazed glass, and the fourth hit home, making the driver's body jerk.

He scrambled to the right now, needing space. The van's front wheels hit the kerb, bounced, then there was an almighty crunch as the van smashed into the wall where Moore had stood only moments before.

Moore could see the sliding door still open and somebody in the back, slumped on a seat, not moving. He stepped forward, pistol up, scanning the interior. The engine was screaming and steam was pouring out the front of it.

Another shot cracked out from the other side of the vehicle. A car skidded to a stop at the back of the van and he spun, seeing two men leap out with pistols. He brought his gun up but they had no time for him-their focus was on something beyond the van on the opposite side of the road.

The submachine gun chattered again and the furthest away man immediately went down in the road, dropping his gun. Glass exploded from the car beside him.

Moore raced forward, ducking behind the car-a grey Citreon. He jabbed his talk button.

'Contact, contact,' he said as calmly as he could, barely able to hear himself over the shouting, someone screaming, the ringing in his ears from the shots.

He crab walked to the rear of the car and snatched a look. He could see someone down on the opposite footpath, presumably Leon's man. Another guy crouched over him with a Skorpion machine pistol in his hands, pointing the stubby Russian weapon across the road.

Moore guessed he was focussing on Katie, wherever she happened to be. The other Greek intelligence officer from the Citreon was nowhere to be seen either.

The Skorpion rattled a burst and he heard glass smashing and the whine of ricochets-it was better than the slap of bullets punching into a body. Two more pistol shots and another burst of SMG fire. Moore raised himself up and sighted quickly and smoothly.

The guy started to come up as Moore fired and the first shot skimmed his elbow instead of lacing through his midsection. He yelped and partially turned.

Moore's second and third shots took him in the chest and knocked him back against the wall behind him. He jerked as someone else's rounds also struck him, then fell in a heap.

Moore couldn't see any other hostiles and the shooting suddenly stopped. His heard Katie's voice through the ringing in his ears.

'Rob? You okay?'

He pressed his talk button. 'Yep, are you?'

'I think so. Fuck!'

He looked up as a man loomed over him, a Glock aimed at Moore's face. He was bellowing something in Greek and his finger was on the trigger. Moore didn't speak Greek but the guy's directions were clear. He raised his left hand in the air and carefully lowered his Sig to the ground. Another car skidded to a stop and Moore glanced up, seeing a mane of blonde hair disappearing round a corner beyond the red Mercedes now blocking the road.

Suddenly Katie crashed into the guy with the gun in a full-tilt shoulder charge, sending him flying. She tumbled to the ground and rolled, the guy slammed onto the bonnet of the Merc and Moore leaped to his feet.

He was on the guy in a second, snatching at the Glock and ripping it free. Before the guy's feet even hit the ground again Moore had stripped the slide and magazine from the weapon and cast them aside.

Leon alighted from the passenger's seat, a younger man joining him from the driver's side. Katie hauled herself up and Moore recovered his Sig, jabbing a finger in the direction he'd last seen the blonde running.

'Suicide bomber!' he snapped. 'Come on!'

Leon barked something at his guys as the two Kiwis sprinted away.

They made the corner and belted around it, having a clear run now towards the cathedral two blocks away. Up ahead they could the girl still running, long blonde hair flowing from beneath the blue hat, her loose top flapping in her slipstream.

Sirens were wailing and Jedi was demanding an update over the net.

'Runner coming to you,' Moore panted into his mic, 'believe it's Natalie Oldham...probable suicide bomber...trying to catch her...one block away.'

'Natalie!' Katie shouted. 'Natalie, stop!'

The girl ahead of them faltered but kept moving.

'Natalie, stop! It's me!'

She slowed now, glanced back as she reached the last corner a hundred metres or so from the cathedral. She stopped.

Moore and Katie slowed up, half a block from her now. Even from here they could see her clearly.

Natalie Oldham stared back at them.

53

'Take the lead,' Moore hissed, 'I'll cover.'

He kept his Sig at the low ready and broke away to the side, letting Katie be the focus of the girl's attention. He kept Natalie in sight, flicking quick glances past her to check their surroundings. There were a few pedestrians in the street, most of them hanging back and watching the three newcomers, seeming to be aware that something was up. One guy on his own was strolling along with earbuds in, blissfully unaware of the drama unfolding just metres away as he approached Natalie from behind.

Moore waved a hand at him, hoping to get his attention, but the guy was focussed on the ground in front of him. Moore looked to Natalie instead. Her expression was a study in concentration, absolutely focussed, her eyes blank as she stared at Katie.

'Nat, it's me,' Katie called, still moving forward cautiously, her Sig down at her side. 'We need to talk. Everybody's worried about you.'

Natalie Oldham continued to stare at her, her eyes so hard and direct they seemed to have a living force of their own. She said nothing. Moore watched her hands. They hung at her sides, empty and still. He edged onto the right hand footpath.

The guy with the earbuds finally looked up, saw the girl standing in the middle of the road with two armed people facing her, and stopped. He was maybe ten metres away from Natalie now. He was in his mid-twenties, with thick curly hair struggling to escape from beneath a white cap. He looked from one to the other then took his phone from his pocket and held it up. He started to record the scene in front of him. Moore had an almost overwhelming urge to shoot him.

'Nat, talk to me,' Katie urged, still moving. 'I've been looking all over for you mate. What's going on?'

Natalie Oldham half opened her mouth, made as if to speak, then hesitated. She continued to stare at Katie for a long moment.

Moore edged forward, close to the wall now, feeling the strain on his muscles as he moved carefully. Any sudden moves right now would be counterproductive and probably fatal. Sweat was running down his back and his mouth was dry. The sirens he had heard only moments ago had gone silent.

Nobody else had entered the street since they had made contact with Natalie. The Sig was secure in his two handed grip, and he knew he had three rounds left in it. He cursed himself for not changing mags already.

The amateur videographer was still recording.

'Natalie,' Katie persisted, 'come on mate, talk to me.'

They were about twenty five metres apart now. Moore scanned Natalie again, more certain now that the flowy top concealed a suicide vest. How or why, he had no idea. One thing he was certain of though; she was no prisoner.

'Your dad asked me to find you,' Katie said, and finally Natalie's mask cracked-but it wasn't the reaction they had hoped for.

'Do not speak to me of him,' she spat. 'He is the infidel and I am the Azrael.'

Her chin lifted and she was looking down her nose at Katie, who paused mid stride and waited. The blonde girl's mask was back on, hard and inscrutable. The name Azrael took a moment to click in the back of Moore's memory, but when it did his stomach dropped. Azrael was another name for the Angel of Death referenced in the Quran, an archangel who was subordinate to the will of God.

Moore keyed his talk button. 'Katie, back off,' he breathed quietly. 'This isn't right.'

Katie stayed where she was, and he saw her flex her fingers on the grip of her Sig.

'We're on camera,' he breathed into his mic. 'Back off.'

The guy in the white cap was riveted by the scene playing out in front of him. Moore hoped he wasn't live streaming the incident-he had the distinct feeling this wasn't going to end well, and there was no way to hide his face.

Katie's head flickered slightly towards the guy but she didn't budge.

Natalie also hadn't budged; if anything, she looked more defiant than before. She stared at her old friend across the gap, her arms out to her sides now, the floaty top draping like wings. The sun behind her highlighted the blondeness of her hair and gave Moore a clear view through the light fabric of her top. He could clearly see a bulky vest underneath it.

'Katie,' he rasped, his throat dry, 'she's got a bomb vest on. Back up now.'

He scanned her for a trigger, but couldn't see one.

'It is time for the one true God's will to be done,' Natalie stated loudly. She raised her arms higher, almost shoulder height now. 'He is the one, he creates us in his image and he takes us back to paradise when our time is done.'

She cocked her head back and gazed skywards, closing her eyes. A smile crossed her face and for the first time since laying eyes on her in the flesh, Moore could see her real beauty. She looked childlike and peaceful, and he knew something had changed inside her.

It wasn't a good sign. He desperately scanned her again for any indication of a triggering device.

Natalie abruptly dropped her chin and opened her eyes, locking onto Katie before her.

'Allah giveth, and he taketh away,' she said. Her voice was tight and breathless. Moore saw her chest rapidly rising and falling. He readied himself. 'It is his way, and it is time.'

She suddenly dropped her arms and spun on her heel. Moore swung his Sig up smoothly, coming on line and starting to squeeze the trigger. But he could still see both the girl's hands as she began to run, and they were both empty.

'It is time,' Natalie shrieked as she gained speed towards the Cathedral of the Angels. 'Praise be to Allah! Praise be to Allah!'

In that split second Moore made his mind up. The device had to be on a timer. In seconds she would be at the cathedral.

He squeezed through the pull and felt the trigger trip. The Sig kicked in his grip and in the same instant Natalie stumbled forward and went to her knees, the bullet hitting her between the shoulder blades. He didn't hesitate with the second shot, drilling her straight in the back of the head. She pitched forward, her wings out to her sides.

'Stay back!' Moore bellowed at Katie, waving her away as he ran forward.

He reached the fallen girl, a large pool of blood rapidly spreading around her, and stood over her, yanking up the floaty top. Sure enough the black nylon vest beneath it was rigged with explosives.

He rolled her onto her back, desperately checking for the trigger. Secured to the front of the vest was a cheap cell phone with wires leading to the pockets of plastic explosive.

Without hesitation Moore snatched the phone and ripped it free from the vest, disconnecting it from the wires as he did so. This was not the time for finesse-if he fucked about now, innocent people would die.

He tossed the phone aside and ran a hand over the vest, checking for secondary triggers. This was obviously a device to be detonated by a third party, not the wearer, and he didn't trust the bastards not to have a back-up plan.

His fingers brushed across the lumps of Semtex secured in the pockets of the vest until they found something hard in a side pocket beneath the girl's right arm. In the background he heard a ringing sound. His eyes flicked to the discarded phone, seeing the screen flashing as the phone vibrated on the cobbles a few metres away.

Moore grabbed at the second phone and yanked it from the pouch, seeing it was switched on as he pulled it free. A pair of wires led from the rear of the phone back into the vest. He jerked it hard and the wires popped out as he stepped away. While the wires were still falling away the phone jumped in his hand and the screen lit up with an incoming call.

Moore instinctively hit the "Receive" button and put the phone to his ear. There was silence at the other end but he knew somebody was there. An unseen shot-caller.

A shadow dancer.

'Bad luck, Tristan,' he rasped. 'Your angel of death is dead.'

Deathly silence, but the line stayed open.

'And I'm coming for you next,' Moore said.

The line went dead. Moore dropped the phone back to his side and stared at the body at his feet. The 9mm hollow point had blown her brains out through her right eye and taken most of the nose with it. The left eye was an empty sightless blue and stared at the sky.

Moore looked up as Katie arrived beside him.

'I'm sorry,' he said quietly.

She nodded mutely, her face white and her eyes wide. She slowly holstered her weapon with a trembling hand.

54

Leon and his guys arrived within a couple of minutes of the shooting with the police hard on their heels.

Moore and Katie were quickly ushered off to a van with blacked out windows while cordons were thrown up and witnesses were corralled. As the van moved off Moore was pleased to see the guy in the white hat being grabbed by a cop and stripped of his phone. At least that was one less video to be uploaded to Facebook.

Leon joined them in the rear of the van with a phone clamped to his head and a dark look on his weathered face. He turned in his seat to eyeball the two New Zealanders in the back seat as the van moved off. Moore and Katie sat silently, waiting as the Greek spook talked non-stop in his own language. He disconnected but when Moore opened his mouth to speak he was silenced by a raised finger. Leon switched to English for the next ten minutes while he spoke to Ingoe.

Moore had seen the city slip away and realised they were heading for the airport. Not Heraklion, but Maleme, the scene of the battle in the war but rarely used now. He felt Katie trembling beside him and took her hand in his, giving it a supportive squeeze as the van rocked along a rural road. It was understandable; she was scared and well outside her comfort zone. The massive dump of adrenaline they had both received was quickly wearing off.

Finally Leon disconnected and put his phone away. His dark eyes met theirs.

'You heard all that,' he said without preamble. 'We have things covered here and you are to leave Greece immediately.'

Moore nodded. He felt Katie give another shudder.

'The Government of Greece appreciates your assistance today,' Leon continued, 'however you were never here. All traces of your presence in this country will be erased and you will be debriefed by your own people when you...regroup. You understand?'

'Completely,' Moore said.

Leon noted Katie's pinched face and silence, but said nothing. 'Today has been a very traumatic day for you,' he said, a hint of tenderness slipping into his voice now. 'Believe me, I know what it is like. I am an old dog who has seen many terrible things in my time.' He gave her a comforting smile. 'You will be okay.'

Katie nodded and pressed against Moore's side. He gave her hand another squeeze.

'But there will never be a public mention, or an official record, of the involvement of your service in today's events. The history books will record that Greek intelligence services terminated a very successful operation today to prevent a terrible terrorist atrocity. Are we clear on this?'

Moore gave a short nod. 'Crystal,' he said. Public recognition had never been a concern for him.

The van entered the grounds of the Maleme airfield and made its way to a hangar on the far side where a white Cessna Mustang 6-seater waited with its props turning.

As soon as the van pulled up Leon alighted and spoke to the pilot and co-pilot.

'Who the hell are these guys?' Katie whispered.

'Contractors probably,' Moore replied. 'Probably a legit outfit working on the side for the Government.'

Leon returned to the van and waved them out. He held his hand out and Moore passed him his pistol. Katie did likewise, then their phones and radios.

In return he handed them a folded wad of cash. Moore looked at the money-Egyptian pound notes.

'My people will take you to Alexandria,' Leon explained. 'That is where your Mr Ingoe has asked for you to go. The sooner you are off Greek soil the better, I think. From there...' he shrugged, 'your people will sort you out.'

'Thank you.' Moore shook his hand firmly. 'I'm sorry about your man.'

Leon gave a short nod. 'It is the business we do,' he said simply.

The pilot gestured from the open door and they took the hint. The two pilots were swarthy looking men in their forties with moustaches. Neither spoke to the two passengers.

As they settled into their seats the door lifted and they saw Leon's van disappear back towards the road. They had barely buckled up before the Cessna was taxiing down the runway, and a minute later they were airborne. Katie clutched his hand tightly and stared blankly at the wall.

Moore held her hand and closed his eyes, needing to clear his head. So much had happened so fast that it was hard to get a grip on.

For some reason he found his mind wander to Michelle McGregor and her jerk of a husband, Alan. He hadn't thought of them for days and wondered now how their lives had unravelled since he'd last seen them. God, what a mistake she had been. The thought of what he had done made him sick to the stomach-the lying, the cheating, the wrecking of another man's marriage for what-mindless sex? Moore took a breath and squeezed the bridge of his nose. He'd been a fool, just a lonely, self-centred middle-aged fool.

He thought too of his friends Vince and Ngawai, and mused on how busy they would be right now back in Chania. Whatever happened back there, he knew the VIPs were in good hands. They were good people, and he envied what they had-something he had never had.

Or if he had, way back when, he'd wrecked it for himself. He opened his eyes now and looked at Katie. She was still staring at the wall, tears running slowly down her flushed cheeks. She looked so vulnerable and he felt a wave of protective sympathy come over him.

He squeezed her hand and she crumpled into him, her body wracked with heartfelt sobs. Moore held her to him and stroked her hair, whispering soothingly in her ear as she cried her heart out.

They stayed that way a long time, and eventually the tears abated but still she let him cradle her, safe in his arms.

55

The contact who met them at the private airport outside Alexandria was a bearded man with a large gut threatening to burst free of his colourful Hawaiian shirt.

He drove a dusty grey twenty year old Nissan with fluffy black dice hanging from the rear view mirror like a pair of chimpanzee's balls.

He gave them a cheery hello in a Kiwi accent, held the door for Katie and cranked up Leonard Cohen on the car stereo as soon as they were moving. The two passengers sat silently in the back and watched the city streets slide by as the grey Nissan mingled with the traffic and faded into the background. It was near midday and the city was humming.

Moore guessed the fat man was probably a retired spook or some other kind of former Government employee, living here as an ex-pat and picking up jobs like this as and when needed in return for a healthy retainer. At the end of the day he didn't care-all he wanted right now was a hot shower and a cold beer.

The man parked outside a small hotel and left them in the car while he went in. He came back with a key and handed it to Moore, along with a bubble-padded postage pouch. Inside was a burn phone and another wad of cash-smaller than the one from Leon. This was the New Zealand Government, of course, and any expense was spared.

'My number's in the phone,' the fat man explained across the roof of the car as they got out. 'Call me if you need me.'

Katie stared at him. 'Thank you. What's your name?' she asked.

'I'm One,' he said with a smile, and with that he got back behind the wheel. The Nissan pulled away, leaving them on the footpath.

Katie turned to Moore, a quizzical look on her face. '"One",' she said.

'The man with no name,' he replied.

'You spooks are fucking weird,' she said.

Two minutes later they were checking out the basic surrounds of their studio room, decked out in seen-better-days and floral.

'Hardly palatial, is it?' Katie muttered. 'Reminds me of my Nana's.'

'Huh,' Moore grunted, 'it reminds me of my first flat.'

He made sure the door was secured and checked the windows. They were in the middle of the second floor, facing the roadside. No balcony, but a downpipe that was close enough if needs be.

He heard the toilet flush then the shower go on. He turned. Katie stood in the doorway of the tiny bathroom. He watched unashamedly as she stripped and dropped her dirty clothes to the floor. She glanced at him, checked the water temperature and looked back to him.

'Well don't just stand there,' she said.

Moore gave a mental shrug and quickly undressed. His clothes felt scratchy and sticky and it was good to get them off. He could smell the cordite on his skin, mixed with stale sweat.

He stepped into the shower cubicle and pulled the cheap plastic curtain across behind them. Katie pulled him close and put her hands on his chest. She rested her head on them and he wrapped her in his arms.

'Just let me be close to you,' she whispered.

He nodded to himself and kissed the top of her head, holding her softly to his broad chest as the water fell.

Later they dried each with the rough towels that had once been white and made their way to the double bed. The mattress was lumpy but it didn't matter. They made love with a tender passion, each yearning for something from the other, lost in their own vacuums as their worlds collided.

When it was over they lay quietly, holding each other close until sleep came calling.

Katie cried in her sleep, deep sobs wrenching through her core as her mind was terrorised by unseen monsters. Moore shushed her and kissed her forehead, pulling her closer and rocking her until the crying eased and she fell back to sleep again.

He eventually fell asleep himself, the deep slumber punctuated by flashes of light and visions of angels with wide feathered wings, the angels scowling at him with demonic eyes and serpentine tongues.

56

He woke with a start and stared at the ceiling.

It needed a repaint. Katie was sound asleep beside him, snoring gently. He watched her sleep, marvelling at her beauty and innocence.

Maybe not so innocent now, he thought. He wondered if she could ever come back from the events of the day. He knew tough soldiers who had cracked from less, and others who had gone through the fires of Hell with barely a flicker. Only time would tell.

He rolled off the bed and padded to the bathroom. The tap water was tepid but enough to wake him up. The clock on the burn phone told him it was nearly 4pm.

Moore pulled on his dirty clothes and pocketed the phone and cash. He had no idea when Ingoe would turn up, but his stomach was complaining and he felt parched.

He let himself out of the room and locked it behind him, making his way through the crappy hotel to the street. The sun was hot and the street was busy. Moore instinctively turned left and walked a few minutes until he found a mart and stepped into the cool interior.

Ten minutes later he re-entered the hotel lobby and crossed the worn red carpet to the stairs. The plastic shopping bag in his hand contained dried fruit, crackers, and bottles of water and iced tea. He emerged onto the second floor and as he took the first few steps into the corridor he saw the door at the far end softly closing.

The hairs on the back of his neck stood on end and he felt a chill run up his spine. He hurried to their room and inserted the key in the lock, putting the bag of groceries on the floor before throwing the door open and lunging in.

Nothing moved and the silence in the room was deafening. The window was still closed: the ceiling fan whirred slowly.

Katie was still in bed, curled on her side, her dark hair fanning onto the pillow beneath her head.

Moore paused, his senses screaming at him now. He ran his eyes across the room again, knowing something was wrong but unable to put his finger on it immediately.

He stepped to the bathroom and cleared it. Not a thing out of place. He turned again and his eyes fell to Katie. Her eyes were closed, a lock of hair falling across her face, one hand bunched into a fist near her chin.

Not moving.

Moore was at her side in a flash, his limbs feeling heavy as he dropped to his knees and touched her face. She was warm and soft. She wasn't breathing.

He leaned in closer to check, convinced that he had to be mistaken, knowing she would be fine and he was just imagining it.

Nothing.

'Oh Jesus, no,' he muttered, 'Katie? Katie, wake up sweetheart... please wake up. Oh Jesus Christ, please don't...no, Katie, please no.'

He yanked the covers back, preparing to drag her onto the floor and commence CPR, when his hand came up wet. He stared at it, the redness so distinct that he couldn't comprehend it. So much red. Red, sticky red everywhere, soaking the sheet beneath her. He couldn't see the origin and couldn't compute the brutality of it, but none of that mattered right now. The sheer volume alone told him that Katie was way beyond CPR.

He fell back to his knees and held her hand in his, pulling her to him and burying his face in her neck as his vision blurred and hot tears flowed freely down his cheeks.

Moore didn't hear the footsteps until they reached the door, accompanied by a tentative knock. He heard it, knew what it was, ignored it. It didn't matter.

Nothing mattered right now.

ARCHER STEPPED INTO THE ROOM.

'Rob,' he said, 'it's me, mate.'

No response. Moore stayed on his knees beside the bed, his head buried close to the still form of the girl. Archer wasn't even sure the man had heard him.

'Robbo,' he said louder, stepping into the room. 'Robbo, it's me. Look up at me, mate.'

Moore slowly lifted his head and stared at him from beneath a furrowed brow. His face was streaked with tears, crinkled into a painful grimace. The rawness of the pain was a palpable thing even across the room and Archer felt a kick in his chest.

'You poor bastard,' he said softly. He stepped in and shut the door behind him.

Moore continued to stare at him as he approached, his face a whirlpool of emotion. Fear. Exhaustion. Brutal agony and heart-breaking confusion.

Archer came round the end of the bed to him and lowered himself to a knee.

One glance at the girl told him all he needed to know. The sheet beneath her was saturated with blood. She was lying on her right side and an educated guess was that her carotid had been severed on that side, gravity assisting the artery to drain her life away. Nothing would have been immediately obvious from the door, nothing to stop Moore from coming into the room.

Archer's head snapped up as he heard the door open at the end of the corridor outside. Footsteps approaching, hushed voices.

Time to go.

'Rob, we need to move mate,' he said calmly, and reached out to take Moore's arm.

Moore jerked away, not comprehending.

'You've been set up here mate,' Archer said urgently. 'The cops're here and we need to go.' Still nothing. 'We need to move now.'

Archer pushed up and was at the door quickly, snibbing the lock and slipping the chain into place. He grabbed a chair and placed it across the door.

Moore slowly rose his feet, his chest heaving and a vein pounding in his neck. He looked at Archer as his old comrade came back to his side.

The footsteps stopped outside the door. There was a pause then a knock. Firm; a cop's knock.

Archer placed a hand on Moore's arm and locked eyes with him.

'We've gotta go, mate,' he hissed, 'out the back. Now. No time to fuck about.'

Moore nodded slowly as if he was just waking up.

Archer hustled him towards the bathroom, shutting the door behind them as the pounding on the front door increased. He opened the small window and peered out. The alley below them was lined with rubbish bins and skips, piles of shit everywhere. And a cop car, sitting there with the flashing lights going. Two cops stood by it, looking up.

One saw them and pointed, shouting something to his mate.

Archer pulled back and looked at Moore.

'Change of plan,' he said, 'we're going out the front. Hard and fast, right?'

Moore nodded, his wits coming back to him.

Archer darted back to the front door and ducked behind it just as it crashed open, the chain ripping free from the doorframe. The chair went flying. Two uniformed cops entered, both with heavy moustaches and thick waists. Both had pistols on their belts and moved with purpose.

They immediately saw Moore and began to shout. While their

focus was on Moore, Archer made his move. He slammed the door forward into one of them, knocking him sideways into the other side of the doorframe.

The front guy started to turn but was too slow to avoid a side kick to his knee. The guy shrieked and began to go down. Archer stepped out and grabbed the first guy, yanking him off balance and burying his knee in the cop's crotch. He too dropped, his eyes bugging in agony.

Archer stepped over him and checked the hallway. A terrified hotel manager was standing there, his hands up, quivering.

'Down!'

Archer pointed at the floor and the guy went down on his face, whimpering.

He turned back to see Moore removing a can of pepper spray from the belt of one of the cops, along with his handcuffs. The cops were quickly cuffed together and given a squirt of gas each in the face, enough to take them out of action for a while.

Moore ripped their radios away and stripped them each of their handguns while Archer stood guard at the door. He had come unarmed-the Egyptians didn't take kindly to armed foreigners.

He glanced back when Moore joined him, and accepted the pistol he was handed. It was a Smith and Wesson M&P .357SIG, the standard sidearm of the Egyptian National Police and a good weapon. He checked the load and safety.

'Let's go,' he said.

They walked past the cowering manager to the end door, took the stairs to the ground floor and into the lobby.

Another cop stood waiting, his head cocked to his radio as somebody babbled across the air.

He was younger and slighter than the other two, and looked nervous. Obviously the junior boy, relegated to guard the door while the big boys took the glory. He looked up as the two Kiwis approached him, uncertainty all over his face.

In two seconds they had him on the floor with a face full of gas and were moving to the front door. They moved together as smoothly as they had several years ago in the Group.

Archer took the lead, his stolen pistol tucked under his jacket as he exited the hotel and bleeped the locks on a plain red Hyundai Elantra parked near the entrance.

It was about the most common car in Egypt and he'd hired it for three days. He had a feeling the insurance had been a good investment.

57

Moore joined him and they moved off, seeing a hotel employee come running from the front door with a phone to his ear, looking after them.

'Hold on,' Archer muttered, and they both buckled up.

They got just past the side alley before a police car roared out, lights flashing and both occupants locking on them immediately.

Archer hit the picks and slapped it into reverse, slamming back hard into the front of the police car. A second later he raced off again, leaving the stunned cops behind as he threw a fast left at the first intersection, sirens ripping the air now nearby.

He hit the picks again and spun back the way they'd just come, tucking in behind another car as they crossed the intersection. Another police car skidded a left going the other way and they saw the car he'd rammed limping after it, steam rising from beneath the crumpled bonnet.

'Nice and calm,' Archer muttered to himself, checking his speed and taking a breath.

'What the fuck is going on?' Moore wondered aloud.

'Bad voodoo is what's going on mate,' Archer replied, taking a right then a left. 'You did good back in Crete, but it's not over yet.'

'Tristan?'

Archer looked at him. 'And some,' he said.

A siren sounded and the rear view mirror filled with flashing red and blues. A cop car was right on their tail and he could see another behind it. They were in a one-way street with shops on both sides. The traffic was moving steadily.

Archer indicated to pull over to the right and began to slow. The car behind followed them, and the second car pulled out, overtaking to cut them off.

Archer jerked the wheel hard left and accelerated into the passing cop car, crashing it sideways and pushing it into a parked van with a shower of sparks.

The cop car behind them immediately rammed them, throwing them both forward. Archer floored it and steered away from the crash, making space while he sought an escape option. Horns honked and people shouted.

The police car behind them was gaining and Archer spied a narrow alleyway to the right. He jerked on the handbrake, spun the wheel and gave it guts as he dropped the hand brake again. The Hyundai responded well, spinning sharply into the alley way and bolting forward. The cop car went past in a skid.

Archer gunned it down the alley, knocking rubbish bins and crap aside as he made for the far end, knowing they had only seconds to get away. He didn't know whether the Egyptian police had a helicopter, but either way they needed to ditch the Hyundai sharpish.

A rubbish bin bounced off the side of the alley, skittered up the windscreen and disappeared behind them.

Archer glanced at Moore beside him. His face had gone blank again. With the cops on their tail and a terrorist mastermind to take down, the last thing he needed right now was a passenger.

'Hey!' he said sharply.

Moore looked at him.

'Snap out of it,' Archer told him, hitting the brakes hard. 'We're the Division; this is what we do.'

Moore blinked, squeezed the bridge of his nose and nodded. He shook himself like a dog.

Archer's jaw tightened. He needed Moore to grip his shit, and fast.

Emerging onto a busier road he cut off a van and joined the flow, dropping back into a normal driving rhythm. He followed the road for a few hundred metres before spotting a car park outside a shopping centre. He ducked in and buried the car in the middle of the lot, disappearing into the melting pot.

Moore forced aside the horrific images in his head.

He needed to get back in the game before he got them both killed. Archer cut the engine and unbuckled his seatbelt.

Moore grabbed his arm, meeting his eye. 'Thanks pal,' he said quietly, 'and sorry.'

Archer gave a short nod. 'All good mate.'

'I've got my shit together,' Moore told him. 'Where're we going?'

Archer dug a cheap cell phone from his pocket and handed it over. He followed it with a wad of cash, mixed Egyptian pounds and American greenbacks-the universal currency of bribes.

'There's a text with an address on it,' he said. 'You'll be met there, and you'll be exfil'd. You won't know the contact meeting you, but they will ask you "what is blue." The answer is "skies." The second question is "says who," your reply is "Willie Nelson." Got it?'

'Blue Skies by Willie Nelson,' Moore said wryly, 'it's got Jedi written all over it.'

Archer grinned. 'Let's go. See you back in Blighty.'

With that he was gone, and Moore followed suit. The red Hyundai with the rear damage would be a hot target right now, and it was best he was nowhere near when it was found. He would have felt safer if they'd stayed together as well, but two Anglo men stood out from the crowd and they needed to disappear.

Moore had no prior experience in Egypt or with their Police or security services, but common sense told him that with at least three cops feeling the worse for wear there would be no welcoming arms if they were captured.

Most likely they'd be locked in a dank cell with no consular or legal support and would soon make friends with a heavy phone book, a rubber hose, or maybe even a waterboard.

He stuck his head down and strode away from the car, not worrying about where Archer was going, just focussing on getting some distance between himself and the car. He paused at a roadside stall selling crappy fabrics and clothes, and spent some cash to grab a thick cotton shirt in non-descript beige and a khaki shoulder bag.

He pocketed the change and ducked behind the stall to whip off his shirt and stuff it into the bag, pulling on the new purchase in a basic effort at disguise.

He threw a few turns as he made distance and stopped at another small shop to buy a floppy bush-style hat which added to his disguise. If anyone saw him leaving the Hyundai they may be able track him to the first stall and get an updated description. The second purchase would make it harder, and he threw another spanner in the works by stopping at another roadside stall to buy another shirt.

Ten minutes after leaving the car Moore had changed again and was feeling more comfortable. Confusion made it harder for him to be tracked, and every layer he added to that made it harder still.

He wondered how Archer was getting on. Archer was a good operator, but like Moore, he was in a foreign, hostile environment right now. He grabbed a bottle of water and a local map from a street vendor and downed the water while he walked. It tasted warm and stale but he didn't care-his body needed fluids right now. If he got the shits he could fix that later-that's what they made Imodium for.

Moore ditched the empty bottle and checked the phone. The text gave the RV location as a specific room number and a street address. He stopped to check the map, finding the address then checking the street signs around him to zero in on his own location.

The RV looked to be about five k's away. The chances of getting caught out on the street were reasonable, even in a big city, and that easily doubled when it was unfamiliar territory.

58

He walked to the nearest taxi rank and took the first cab, a dusty white Toyota that stank of cigarettes and armpits.

The driver looked at him in the rear view mirror, his eyes dark and unfriendly. He was a fat guy with a thick moustache. He could've been a brother of the cops from the hotel.

Moore had good enough Arabic to read the address to him and the fat guy grunted before starting the engine and pulling straight out into traffic to a loud honk from another driver. The cabbie didn't seem to care, just honked back and muttered something unintelligible. Moore wasn't familiar with Egyptian Arabic, but the curses were basically the same.

He took a few moments to catch his breath and try to plan his next move. No matter how hard he tried though, the gruesome images of Katie kept coming back. The images, the coppery smell of the blood, the taste of bile and tears as his body reacted. He shook his head but they stayed there, in his face and unshakeable.

'Fuck,' he muttered to himself, pressing his fists into his eyes, 'fuck, fuck, fuck.'

The cabbie eyeballed him in the mirror but said nothing. He

pulled up outside a block of grey-looking flats and looked at him again.

Moore thrust a couple of notes at him, more than enough to cover the ride, and got out. The cabbie peeled away and Moore realised why. The neighbourhood was run down and dirty. Mangy dogs loped about and discarded crap littered the streets.

Moore found the stairs on the side of the apartment block and took them to the second floor. It was a five storey block and looked like a throwback to Soviet Russia. The stairwell stank of piss.

The apartment he was looking for was the second one in from the stairs. He knocked at the door. The curtains were closed and the door was solid wood. He heard movement behind the door before it cracked open and a single eye peered out at him.

'What is blue?' The guy spoke in heavily-accented English.

'Skies,' Moore replied.

'Says who?'

'Willie fucking Nelson.'

There was a moment's pause.

'Who? You say who say it?' He sounded Eastern European, Georgian maybe.

Moore groaned, cursing himself for not just playing the game. He didn't like Georgians, either. 'Willie Nelson,' he repeated.

The guy paused, staring at him with the one eye before opening up. Moore stepped in and was immediately pushed face first against the wall as the door shut. He rolled with it as a hand stripped him of the Smith and cell phone, then the wad of cash. He was roughly spun around and a strong tattooed hand with several rings clamped onto his throat. A suppressed pistol was jammed against his left temple and hot breath filled his face.

The guy had been staring at him with one eye because that's all he had. The left eye socket was a patch of terrible scarring, lumpy and pink. He and the guy behind him wore black leather jackets and had shaved heads. Both were big guys, maybe 115kg each. Definitely Georgians.

The apartment was barely furnished. A manky yellow sofa, a bare table with two chairs, threadbare carpet. Stained creamy-brown curtains. Two light bulbs.

The second guy spoke in guttural English. 'Willie fucking Nelson get you killed, smart guy.'

Moore said nothing. It was enough for now just trying to breathe.

'You need exfil.'

Moore managed a slight nod, but even that was enough for One Eye to squeeze harder on his throat. Moore could feel the pressure building in his head and chest. If these guys were the welcoming committee, maybe he was safer on the street.

The second guy flipped through the wad of cash and tossed the captured Smith in his hand. 'Exfil cost money, hey? Not cheap.'

Moore saw how it was now. These guys were just local contractors, mercenaries paid on a job by job basis. He wondered if One had organised them. It seemed bloody good luck that the cops had turned up to their hotel room not long after One had delivered them there-and he was the only person who knew where they were.

Now he was being held at gunpoint by two thugs who were supposed to be working for the Service, but who seemed more intent on either robbing or killing him, or both. Easy to explain in a shit hole like this.

The second guy was eyeing him, sizing him up. He had a pistol in the front of his waistband and Moore's stolen Smith in his hand.

'So you pay, we play,' the second guy said with a grin.

One Eye chuckled. It sounded like an old Massey Ferg tractor trying to catch. He ground the muzzle of the suppressor into Moore's temple a bit harder. His finger was on the trigger. Moore registered subconsciously that it was a CZ75, a good weapon and a favourite of Eastern European hoods. The suppressor worried him-only one reason to use it. Shots attracted attention even in shitty neighbourhoods like this.

He tried to talk but only managed a croak. He played on that a second time, and the second guy took the hint.

'Let him talk,' he said.

One Eye eased off his grip but stayed in place. His good eye was scant inches from Moore's face. His breath stank of cheap cigarettes. Moore swallowed, trying to wet his throat.

'One sent you?' he rasped.

The second guy gave a barking laugh. 'One, yeah. Kiwi,' he said with a sneer.

'He wants you to exfil me? Where to?'

The second guy shrugged. He tucked the Smith into his jacket pocket and thumbed the cash again. 'Need more than just this. Exfil cost money, hey?'

Moore frowned indignantly. 'You're being paid,' he retorted, 'your boss works for my boss, so don't try and fuck me over, mate.'

One Eye grabbed him harder round the throat and shoved him back against the wall.

The second guy squared his shoulders and cocked his head. 'You don't talk like that at me,' he said coldly. 'You need us. We no need you, cunt.'

'Yeah.' One Eye's breath could strip paint. 'Cunt.'

Moore could feel his heart hammering in his chest and he felt cold panic growing deep inside him, blowing up like a balloon. The pressure on his lungs was intense and he began to hyperventilate. So this was how it was going to be. Years of putting his balls on the line for Queen and country, taking the hits, to be capped in a shitty apartment in a place he never even wanted to come to.

Maybe it was karma. God was kicking him in the bollocks for all the bad shit he'd done.

For being a shitty father to Danni, for screwing McGregor's wife, for ruining the lives of those he'd accepted without question were enemies of the state. For tangling with Jimmy the Blade and his scrote-bag mates, for dragging Wizz into it. For leaving Katie alone and letting her get killed in her bed. For dealing out death and destruction for most of his adult life.

He was falling apart inside, he could feel it. He was losing it. His body felt fucked and tired and achy. He was tired of running, tired of fighting. He was old now; it was a young man's game. Old bastards like him should be put out to pasture and let the young bucks take the reins.

Moore dragged a dry tongue across his parched lips. He could feel himself going down. Who Dares, Wins...whatever. Who Dares Too Long Gets His Arse Kicked, maybe.

His eyes flicked to his two captors.

The Georgians could see what was happening to him, and they were loving it. The fucking pricks. They were laughing at him. A pair of shit head thugs from an arsehole country that ripped itself apart and ate its young.

Moore felt a stab of anger, of resentment. The disrespectful fucks. Who did they think they were?

They weren't worthy of lacing the boots of the freshest SAS trooper. Moore had trained those guys, the freshest SAS troopers. They had worshipped him in his day. Jesus, even Craig fucking Archer had held him up on a goddamn pedestal. If Archer could see him now he'd be ashamed.

Moore felt the anger boil up inside. He wasn't going to let them all down. He wasn't going down like this. He fought back the panic. Panic was a killer, and he already had two of them to deal with right now-no point taking out his own legs as well. If he was going to survive this encounter he needed to be calm.

He thought of Katie. He pictured Danni's face. One dead and gone, nothing could change that. The other distanced from him physically and emotionally. He needed to fix that. He couldn't die here with these pricks.

The two Georgians had at least three handguns between them-one of which was against Moore's head with a finger on the trigger. They obviously knew what they were doing. Whether they were properly trained or not was another matter.

The international security circuit was full of guys like this. Some were ex-military, some just thugs making a buck. Moore pegged these two as the latter, which was both good and bad. Good because their skills wouldn't be as sharp, bad because amateurs were dangerous through stupidity.

'How much?' Moore said, keeping his eyes on the second guy.

He ignored One Eye, focussing on the leader instead. He wanted all the attention on him.

'How much more?' The second guy made a show of thinking, stroking his chin. 'Five thousand.'

Moore rolled his eyes and looked irritated. 'Five thousand what? Egyptian? Euro?'

The second guy sneered at him. 'US,' he said, rubbing his thumb and forefinger together for effect. 'Greenback, baby.'

Both men laughed and One Eye momentarily glanced at the leader while he cranked up the Massey Ferg.

Speed, aggression and surprise.

Moore's left hand shot up under One Eye's right wrist and shoved the CZ towards the ceiling. One Eye involuntarily fired, the noise still like a loud pop despite the suppressor, and a round went through the upper wall.

Caught by surprise, One Eye was off balance, his left hand still on Moore's throat. He tried to squeeze but Moore was already sliding down and left, getting under his gun hand and breaking the strangle hold.

The second guy grabbed at his own suppressed pistol but his target was blocked by his mate.

Moore got behind One Eye, slamming a double jab into the guy's kidney and smashing his knee into the side of One Eye's right leg. The leg buckled and he let out a throaty roar of pain.

Moore grabbed at the flailing arm that held the gun, keeping behind One Eye as he drove another jab into his kidney. He seized the gun hand, twisted down and back. The guy was strong but was distracted by the pain, and his pistol was beside his own head before he even realised.

The second guy saw what was happening, panicked, and fired. The round went dangerously close, punching through the wall beside Moore. His second shot skimmed One Eye's left shoulder and produced a scream.

One Eye was well off balance now, bent half backwards on a

damaged leg, his wrist trapped at an unnatural angle and his CZ75 pointing at his head.

Moore forced his own finger into the trigger guard and jerked back on it. No time for finesse.

One Eye managed to shriek before the hammer fell and the round blew his right eye back into his skull. Blood and brain sprayed everywhere, splattering the second guy who was moving in.

The second guy paused in shock, his mate's blood on his face.

Moore dropped the body, ripping the pistol free, and fired two shots into the second guy's chest. The guy rocked on his heels, a look of utter shock on his face. He dropped his gun and staggered backwards.

Moore stepped over the body of One Eye and lifted his foot, kicking the second guy backwards onto the manky sofa. Blood was flowing down the guy's shirtfront. Moore stood over him and took the Smith from the guy's pocket.

A quick pat down recovered the cell phone and cash. He also carried a switchblade and a set of brass knuckles, which Moore tossed aside. He pocketed the guy's phone.

'Who's paying you?' he said.

The Georgian's eyes were screwed shut with pain. The blood flow was steady and he was already pale. He groaned.

Moore grabbed an overstuffed gaudy orange cushion from the sofa beside the Georgian's hip. He showed it to the wounded man.

'I can stop the bleeding,' he said, 'and get you medical attention. Tell me who's paying you.'

'Fuck...' The guy cracked open an eye and tried weakly to reach for the cushion. 'Fuck...you...'

'Live.' Moore held up the cushion then the pistol. 'Or die. Your choice.'

The Georgian screwed his eyes shut again. Blood was trickling from his mouth now, a trail of red running over his chin and down his pulsating throat. His skin was pale and shiny.

'Kiwi...' he gasped. 'He...pay...'

'To kill me?'

The Georgian nodded weakly, barely strong enough to move his head. He coughed wetly and blood flecked his lips.

'Where is he?' Moore said. 'I need to talk to him.'

'No…I…' he hacked a wet cough again, 'I…don't…know…'

'He's in your phone?' Moore waved the guy's cell phone at him.

The Georgian managed a weak nod. 'Yes…only…him.'

'Thanks.'

Moore shoved the cushion against the guy's face, rammed the muzzle of the CZ into it and fired. The only sound was a muffled cough. The body twitched and slumped back.

He stood back, used his shirt tail to wipe the CZ clean of his prints, and placed it carefully in the right hand of One Eye. The guy was leaking fluids all over the floor and had shat himself.

Moore gagged and backed away, digging out the second guy's phone again. It was a cheap pre-pay, a standard burn phone. He opened up the contacts list and found one entry, aptly named Kiwi.

He checked the texts and found a series between Kiwi and the Georgian. All were from the last couple of hours.

Kiwi had contacted the Georgians and arranged for them to meet Moore at the apartment. He had identified Moore by name and given the security code details.

The Georgian had replied with a question. And what?

Kiwi's reply was simple and chilling. Kill him. I need photos.

The Georgian came back with How much?

Kiwi had replied 5k US.

The Georgian had sent a smiley face.

Moore opened a new text.

Problem. He have info. You need come.

He sent it and waited. One was obviously waiting by the phone. He replied within half a minute.

What info?

Moore made him wait a minute before replying.

Israel?

The next text bleeped up immediately.

10 mins.

Moore nodded to himself and pocketed the phone. He was reasonably confident that the altercation wouldn't have attracted any attention, unless the loose rounds from the two killers had punched right through into neighbouring apartments. He'd have to take his chances on that-getting his hands on One was the priority right now.

He wished Archer was there to help. He had the feeling everything was gaining momentum very fast and he was on a ride he couldn't get off.

He dragged the body of One Eye over to the sofa and heaved it up to slouch beside his dead mate.

He took the second guy's CZ and checked it. It had 14 rounds left. He upped the safety and shoved the pistol into his waistband.

Moore caught his breath, wiped his hands and checked the load in the stolen Smith. It had a full 15 round magazine and was in good condition. He tucked it into the back of his waistband and gave the apartment a quick search.

It was obviously just used as a safe house for things such as this, with no food or crockery at all, not even a fridge. The small bedroom had a foam mattress on the floor and a sheet with stains that Moore didn't want to contemplate.

The only piece of personal property was a nylon bum bag on the floor of the bedroom. Moore unzipped it, finding a couple of spare magazines for the Georgians' pistols, a pair of Polish passports, a basic digital camera, some cash and a set of keys.

He checked the passports. The photos matched the two Georgians. He checked the camera and found photos of the second Georgian naked with a young girl. The girl looked to be about fourteen and wasn't having a good time. Moore felt the bile rise in his gut. There were more photos of the two Georgians posing with guns, raising pints in a pub somewhere, and cuddling topless girls in another bar.

The next photo was of One Eye grinning and holding up a severed head by the hair. It took Moore a moment to realise the head belonged to the teenage girl the other guy had been violating a few frames back.

An image of Danni's smiling face burst into Moore's brain and he gagged. His gut heaved and he braced his hands on his knees. He fought to get control and lost. He vomited on the dirty floor and once he started the floodgates opened.

He emptied his guts and gradually the retching eased off. He sucked down some air and spat.

Getting a grip of himself, he flipped through to the next photo. It was another gruesome image, this time One Eye kneeling beside a woman's dead body on a patch of dirt, lifting the head up by the hair for a clearer image.

The body was in non-descript civvies and the throat was slit. Blood covered the front of the clothing and even at the angle, he could see the gaping slash in the throat.

It took Moore a second to register that he recognised the dead woman.

It was Evin, JJ's former assistant. He didn't know why she had been killed, or when or where, but he felt a small measure of satisfaction. The bitch had betrayed JJ, and now she was dead. Probably at the hands of her own treacherous comrades. Good job. At least they wouldn't waste any more resources looking for her.

Footsteps sounded on the walkway outside and the door knob started to turn. Moore straightened up and sucked down another breath, calming himself.

One was here. It was game time.

59

The door opened quickly and One was two steps inside before he realised anything was wrong.

He paused for a split second but it was too late. Moore reached from behind the door and grabbed him by the shirtfront, yanking him inside and down, kicking the door shut behind him.

One stumbled forward, one hand instinctively reaching for the hand gripping him while the other dived under his jacket for the weapon concealed there.

Moore's reaction was fast and brutal.

He slammed the heel of his hand into One's left ear as a distraction, released the shirtfront, and seized him by the left wrist instead. As One bent forward from the impact of the blow and the jerking on his arm, his right hand was trapped across his torso. He let out a squeal of pain and terror.

Moore wrenched his left wrist around on itself, straightened the elbow and drove One straight to the ground on his face. He locked the arm behind the other man's back and pushed his face harder into the floor.

He leaned down to hiss in One's ear. 'Don't fucking move.' He reached around and plucked a pistol from the guy's belt then pushed off him and stood up.

One rolled onto his side, blood seeping between the hands he clasped to his face, all thoughts of resistance long gone.

Moore used a boot to shove him onto his back and kept the CZ trained on him while he backed off to a safer distance. A scared and injured man was a dangerous beast.

'The welcoming committee wasn't so welcoming,' Moore growled. 'Who the fuck are these guys and what the fuck is going on?'

One shook his head gingerly and spat blood onto the floor.

'Contractors,' he said, sounding like he had a full blown cold. 'Used them before with no issues.' He looked warily up at Moore. 'What happened?'

'They jumped me as soon as I got here. Stuck a gun to my head and said they were going to kill me.' Moore shrugged as nonchalantly as he could manage. 'I told them I had some info, one of them got on his phone and I jumped the other one.' He pointed the gun towards the second guy. 'He came back in and luckily I got him too.' He gave his best aggrieved look. 'The bastards nearly killed me.'

One studied him, trying to suss whether he was being played or not. If he got it wrong, he was in the shit. Eventually self-preservation won out.

'I'm sorry mate,' he said thickly, before hocking a gob of bloodied mucus onto the floor. 'They tried to extort me, told me they'd only exfil you for an extra ten grand.' He shook his head bitterly. 'Thieving bastards, should never have trusted them. They totally played both of us. I came straight over, and here we are.'

He started to get up, but Moore waved the suppressed pistol at him.

'Not yet,' Moore said. 'How do I know I can trust you?'

'I'm your only friend here, mate,' One replied with an ingratiating smirk, holding up his hands. 'Your bosses trust me, and so should you.' He hiked his shoulders. 'We need to get moving and get you out of here.'

He started to rise again, and Moore let him get up. One shook himself off and straightened his jacket. He frowned at Moore.

'That was a bit rough, mate. I think you might have broken my nose.' He tenderly touched his face. 'Fuck that hurts.'

'What about your leg?' Moore asked.

One looked confused, and glanced at his legs. 'My legs are okay,' he said.

Moore fired a single round into the other man's left thigh, the bullet punching through and ending up in the sofa behind him.

One's mouth opened in horror and he clutched at his leg, toppling backwards. He landed on the sofa, sprawled across the two dead Georgians.

The pain hadn't registered yet but the shock was enough to make him scream. Moore jammed the cushion over his mouth and leaned in close.

'You scream and I'll do your fuckin' kneecaps,' he hissed, 'you need to start talking and do it now.' He gave the cushion a hard shove for emphasis. 'Fuck me about and I'll hurt you so bad you'll wish you were dead. Comprende?'

One gave the tiniest nod, his eyes watering with the effort of keeping his mouth shut.

Moore eased back and quickly checked the bullet wound. There was no external arterial spurting, and he was fairly confident of his bullet placement.

One clamped both hands onto the wound, his hands quickly becoming red as it leaked. Moore gave him a minute to get his breath back then took control again. Under his direction One secured his belt as a tourniquet and wadded his socks against the entry and exit wounds.

'Start talking,' Moore told him. He stood against the wall, the suppressed CZ at the ready. 'Name.'

One let out a slow breath. 'Calvin Jones,' he said. 'I'm fifty seven years old, from Christchurch.'

'Do our employers know your real name?'

'Of course.' Jones gave him a disdainful look. 'They're no fools, mate.'

'Clearly they haven't kept a close enough eye on you though,' Moore retorted. 'What was the point in killing me today?'

Jones was silent for a long moment, his brow furrowed.

Moore squeezed the trigger and a suppressed round punched into one of the Georgians with a wet splat. Jones jumped in fright.

'Don't think,' Moore snapped, 'just talk. I haven't got all day.'

Jones let out a breath again, his hands still pressing down on his leg wound. 'I was paid, what d'you think? You think I can fuckin' survive on what those pricks pay me?' He shook his head in disgust. 'It's not fuckin' easy mate, y'know?'

'My heart bleeds,' Moore said coldly. He cocked his head in curiosity. 'How much did you betray your country for, Mr Jones?'

Jones eyed him nastily. 'Don't judge me, Mr Moore,' he grated. 'You're no better than me. We're both just trying to survive in a world that doesn't give a shit about men like us.'

Moore gave a snort. 'Men like us? You know nothing about me, so don't pretend you do.'

It was Jones' turn to snort. He chortled briefly. 'I know all about you, mate, don't you worry about that. You and that tidy little piece of arse you were tapping.' His sneer grew bigger as Moore's face darkened. 'Shame about her, really. She was quite something, wasn't she?'

Moore felt his fist clench around the butt of the CZ, and it took all his willpower not to pump a round between the sneering bastard's eyes. He fought to keep his self-control.

'You're just a blunt instrument for your Government,' Jones continued. He licked his lips and sucked on his teeth. 'You think you're something special but you're not.' He shook his head again. 'They don't give a shit about you any more than they gave a shit about me.'

Jones caught the enquiring look on Moore's face.

'Oh yeah,' he confirmed, 'I was one of you in days gone by. Back in the early days, back before Division 5 ever existed. It was a different unit back then, but the game was the same.' A dark look crossed his sweaty face. 'Killing for The Man. You can smoke all the bad guys you want pal, but in the end it makes no fuckin' difference; they just keep coming. Used to be the Iraqis, the Georgians, Bosnians, Croats.' He jerked a thumb at the dead men beneath him. 'I probably killed their fathers. And who knows if they're really bad guys? Who has the goddamn right to make that judgement?'

Moore had had about enough of this guy's rambling, but he couldn't deny there was a ring of sincerity to it. He ignored it for now and waved the pistol at the other man.

'So far, so boring. Get to the point. Who paid you off?'

Jones raised a bloody hand to wipe at his brow before replying. 'I don't know,' he said. 'It was all anonymous, email and a bank transfer.'

'Caymans?' Moore inquired.

'Panama. Before you ask, thirty k.'

Moore raised an eyebrow.

'Yes, that's all you're worth. Sorry.' Jones' tone was sarcastic. 'Consider yourself lucky; I've have done it for much less.'

'And who were you to report back to afterwards? How do they know the job's done?'

'Email photos.' Jones' breathing was getting shorter and his face was betraying his pain. 'I need a doctor, man. You really fucked me up. I thought you'd be a better shot than that.'

'I am, but you're not worth it. Sorry.' Moore could do sarcasm with the best of them. He swallowed hard and licked his dry lips. 'What about Katie?' His throat was raspy. 'Who killed her?'

Jones let out a sigh. 'That was extra,' he replied.

'Who killed her?' Moore grated. 'You?' He gestured at the dead Georgians with his pistol. 'Or them?'

Jones sighed again. 'It was me,' he said resignedly. He looked up at Moore, pleading in his eyes now. 'Sorry mate.'

'Too late for sorry.' Moore raised the suppressed CZ and pumped a round straight into Jones' open mouth.

As Jones slumped back Moore gave him another two in the chest.

He stood still for a long minute, sucking down breaths and getting a grip on himself. Finally he wiped the CZ clean of fingerprints, placed it in the second Georgian's hand and wrapped the dead fingers around the butt. He dragged that Georgian off the sofa and positioned him on the floor.

He wiped the stolen Police Smith and Wesson clean of prints and put it in Jones' hand.

Straightening up, he recovered Jones' own weapon and checked it. It was an old Russian-made Makarov 9mm short. He shoved it back into Jones' pocket and picked up the Georgians' bum bag.

He filled it with all the cell phones and other bits he was taking then surveyed his work. With any luck there was enough confusion here to make it look like a scene of multiple murders, maybe a drug deal gone wrong.

It was time to get moving.

Just as he was about to open the door, there was a knock from the other side.

Moore jumped despite himself and his heart began to race again.

'It's Archer,' came a familiar voice.

Moore cracked the door open and saw Archer standing there alone. He let him in and quickly shut the door again.

Archer surveyed the carnage before him and raised an eyebrow. 'I see you figured it out then,' he said wryly.

'It didn't take much. Those two goons tried to rob me, then the other fool gave himself away.' Moore eyed him suspiciously. 'You knew?'

'Not specifically, no.' Archer pursed his lips. 'There was a suspicion though, and whoever killed Katie had to know where you were staying. It was either me or him.' He sniffed. 'I was pretty sure it wasn't me.'

'He admitted it was him.' Moore held the bum bag up. 'I've got their phones and stuff in here. There's some pretty sick shit on the camera.'

Archer took it from him.

'You need to move,' he said. 'I've booked you on a flight to Dubai leaving in...' he checked his G-Shock, 'seventy five minutes. Let's go.'

60

The taxi dropped Moore at the Borg El Arab airport just outside Alexandria in good time.

Archer had given a new package-clean NZ passport and driver license with a Visa card, a burn phone and some folding. After checking in at the Flydubai counter he spent some of the cash on an overnight bag and a few bits to throw in it, so he at least looked semi legit.

The flight was scheduled for 5:25pm, and he used his remaining time to wash up in the public toilets and brush his teeth. He had bought a bar of soap and a flannel in a pretty little gift pack, and used it to scrub the blood and sweat off his exposed skin. He took it into a cubicle and stripped to his briefs, using the wet flannel to wipe himself down while someone took a dump next door.

He felt shattered and knew he looked like a sack of shit, so anything he could do to improve himself was a plus. Despite having not eaten for some time he had no appetite.

Tossing the flannel and soap into a trash bin, Moore looked at himself in the mirror above the sink. He still looked beaten and hurt, but moderately better than he had a short time ago. He ditched his shirt and pulled on the clean shirt he'd bought, then finger combed his damp hair into place.

Sorted.

He checked himself again, and stared himself in the eye. They were eyes that had seen a lot. He had always believed that the eyes were the windows to the soul, and the only way to truly know a man's thoughts was to stare deep into his eyes.

Moore could see the machinations behind his own eyes, the churning inside his head that hadn't stopped since he'd been rumbled in the apartment.

He took a deep breath. The other punter flushed and came out to wash his hands, glancing at Moore as he did so. Moore ignored him, waiting until the man left the room.

He leaned forward on the vanity, staring into his eyes. The traitor Jones' words rang in his ears. The images of Katie's lifeless body hung heavy on his heart.

It was decision time for him, he knew, a critical time. Time for a call to be made.

Moore nodded at himself in the mirror.

'It's time,' he said softly.

ARCHER SAT nursing a bourbon in an airport bar with a view of the departure gates. All around was the usual hustle and bustle of the airport. Tearful farewells, joyful reunions, stressed and excited travellers.

He loved it, and fed off the energy of the place. He'd never been to Egypt before, but it was certainly a place to return to-maybe under a different identity.

Moore was short on time so should be heading through the gates at any moment. Once he did, Archer could relax properly, knowing he had completed his assignment. He intended to fill his belly in the food court, touch base with HQ and get his head down as soon as the wheels left the tarmac.

He felt sorry for his old brother in arms, stuck in the economy section of a budget airline for the best part of six hours. At least it got him out of the country, and he would be met in Dubai by a trusted contact who would escort him back to Auckland for debriefing.

Despite a fantastic effort in taking out the suicide bomber, Natalie Oldham, and thereby preventing a terrorist spectacular, Moore faced a shit storm when he got home. The hierarchy didn't like dead bodies turning up, especially pretty young women.

Not only that, but apparently MI5 had become aware of an incident involving a local gang and some kind of personal vendetta by Moore. They were doing their best to run interference with the cops-it sounded like he had a friend in the Service there-but he was still wanted for questioning over the incident.

Some Polish bloke was in a bad way in hospital, and one of the gangsters had died as a result of injuries he received shortly afterwards. Apparently he was a haemophiliac and had bled out from a gunshot wound to the arm. Nobody was directly pointing the finger at Moore, but his fancy Jag had been clocked on CCTV parked nearby and he was known to be a friend of the Polish gym owner-and one of the attending cops had ID'd him.

Archer drained the glass and put it down with a clunk. His old friend was in a real mess right now, and he wasn't sure how things would go when he got back to NZ. One thing was for certain, Moore wouldn't be walking away unscathed.

Archer stood and walked over to a pillar closer to the departure gates. He leaned against it and waited, hearing the last boarding call for Moore's flight. Still no sign.

He checked his watch and felt his anxiety-and suspicions-grow. He sent a quick text to Moore's burn phone, a simple question mark. He had the feeling there would be no reply.

There was still the chance that Moore would arrive at the last second, rushing up with his bag, acting the frazzled traveller. But it was unlikely. Not only would it draw unwanted attention to himself, but that just wasn't him. Moore didn't do either late or frazzled.

Archer gave it until 5:20, when he knew the plane would be

taxiing into position, ready for take-off, before dialling Moore's phone. It rang several times before the automated voice message began. Archer disconnected and pushed off the pillar. He had nearly an hour before he needed to board his Qatar Airways flight. No point in sending the balloon up just yet.

He conducted a methodical sweep of each floor, scanning everywhere for Moore.

He was nearly finished when his phone rang.

A FISHING TRAWLER was pulling into the docks, men ready at dockside to help unload the day's catch.

Seagulls swooped and soared above, vehicles moved about, men shouted. The sun shone. A busy working port. Lots of people and activity, a rough world with rough characters. The sorts of characters who didn't ask too many questions but who understand the basic economy of supply and demand.

Moore heard Archer pick up.

'Where the hell are you, mate? Did you forget the time?'

Moore smiled to himself. 'No mate, I didn't forget anything. But I did realise a few things.'

Archer was silent for a long moment. 'I saw those Moonies at the airport Robbo. Don't buy into their mumbo-jumbo mate, it doesn't suit you. Come to me and I'll get you a new flight.'

Moore shook his head, even though he knew his friend couldn't see him. 'No mate, I won't be coming to you, and I won't be on your flight. It's time for me to make my own way.'

'Come on mate...'

'Arch, I've made up my mind mate. I've had enough. I don't wanna end up like that prick Jones, some washed up old fuck. I just wanna be happy.' He watched the fishermen mooring up to the wharf, tying off thick ropes round the stanchions there. 'It's a tough gig, what we do. It's a demanding gig. I've done my time, and I've had enough.'

They were both silent for a minute. Moore pushed off the wire fence he was leaning on, and began making his way down the dock. The breeze ruffled his hair and felt cool on his skin.

'So that's it then,' Archer finally said. His tone was soft, non-judgemental. 'That's you done?'

'That's me done, son,' Moore confirmed.

'You sure this is the right thing for you? A life in the shadows won't be easy.' Archer paused, and Moore could hear him breathing down the line. 'You know they'll look for you.'

'They can try, but I'd suggest they don't.' Moore injected an edge into his voice. 'And don't you either, Arch.'

Archer grunted. 'I won't, don't worry.'

'Keep up the good fight, mate. I'd like to say I'll see you around, but if I do, then something's gone horribly wrong.'

Archer gave a chuckle down the line. 'I guess so. I'm sorry about Katie, mate.'

'So am I,' Moore replied softly. He felt a catch in his throat and squinted against the sun. 'So am I.'

They both went silent for a minute. Moore continued walking and reached the end of the dock.

'You know how to get hold of me if you need to,' Archer said. 'Just watch your back mate.'

Moore nodded again. 'I will. You too mate.' He smiled to himself. A pair of gulls fought over a scrap nearby, flapping their wings angrily. 'I won't be in touch.'

He disconnected and stood there for a long moment, the sun on his face, the breeze on his skin. The pair of fighting gulls parted ways and flew off. Moore pulled the battery off the phone, removed the SIM card and snapped it in two. He carried the pieces with him to a rubbish bin and dropped them in.

He dusted his hands off and turned towards the road. It was time to get moving.

He had things to do.

61

Four months later
Bab Al-Toub neighbourhood, Mosul, Iraq

Bobby had the butt of the Remington M2010 tucked in snugly to his shoulder, his right eye focussing down the Leupold scope.

He was flat on a sheet of cardboard, lying on top of a table a couple of metres back from an empty window, six floors up in an abandoned, shelled out apartment building.

His spotter in the next room over was a new guy, Aaron, who hailed from Minnesota. He'd only been on the team two months but had good skills and was keen to learn. They were a new team, but even new sniper teams in Delta were highly efficient. In the last month of deploying together they had claimed six scalps.

Eight hundred yards away was a café in the heart of Bab Al-Toub. The café was always busy and the neighbourhood was an Islamic State hotbed right now, despite constant operations in the city. Bobby hated those fuckers, and every time he dropped a target he counted it as an act of his own loving God. A Christian God.

He watched the activity at the café. It was unusually quiet this evening. Dusk was almost there and business was slow. Intel told them that meant the place was in use right this minute by the bad guys, probably for a meeting of some sort. It was run by a hard core ISIS supporter who was known to play host to senior leaders of the terrorist group.

He heard Aaron's voice over the net.

'Got a vehicle coming from the west. White Toyota, tooled up, two on the back.'

Bobby kept his focus on the café itself, the vehicle outside his field of vision at the moment. 'Roger that,' he replied.

'And a guy on a bicycle.'

Bobby frowned. 'Roger.' He stared down the lens at the front door of the café. It was green and had a large glass panel in the centre. 'What's with the bike?'

'Looks like an old guy. He's off it now.' A pause. 'The Toyota's pulling up now. Four heads.'

Bobby could see it now. Parking out the front, both doors opening and men alighting. Dish-dashes and AK47s all round. The two on the back stood, scanning the area, rifles at the ready.

The front door of the café opened and the owner appeared, a bearded guy in his forties, hard looking. He extended his hands to one of the new arrivals and they embraced.

'That's him.' Aaron's voice betrayed his excitement. 'The guy hugging the owner, in the grey robe with the red keffiyeh. That is our target, Zutan. Copy?'

'Copy that,' Bobby replied, 'confirming target Zutan is in the grey robe with the red headwear.'

Zutan was the codename given to the target of this operation. It was easier to use than his given name of Tristan Stevens.

Of all the fuckers Bobby hated, fuckers like Zutan were the worst. Converts to Islam, zealous terrorists fighting against their own countries. He knew this guy was a Kiwi, and today's operation had come about as a result of his unit's interactions a few months ago with the two Kiwi spooks.

After some action in Greece, according to Pat, it had been identified that Tristan Forbes, assistant to some politician, had in fact been the mastermind behind an assassination attempt. He had immediately disappeared and had only come back up on the radar a week or so ago. Operating in Mosul with hard core ISIS shitheels, and according to a source on the ground, walking about as if he owned the goddamn place. Well, as far as Bobby was concerned, that shit ended today.

He drew in his breath and curled his index finger around the trigger. In seconds a .300 Winchester Magnum round would send the traitorous sonofabitch to meet his maker.

As he took a bead on the middle of Zutan's upper back, right between his shoulder blades, something twinged at the back of his brain.

'The guy on the bike,' he said, 'where is he?'

'Wandered into a shop,' Aaron replied. 'Two doors up.'

'Where's the bike?' Bobby kept his focus on Zutan, who was lighting up a smoke. He watched him pass one to the café owner. He had a clear shot and started to exhale slowly.

'Leaning against the wall by the café.' Aaron sounded uncertain now, as it clicked in his head. 'Why would...'

There was a flash of flame from outside Bobby's limited field of vision and he saw the explosion blow the assembled terrorists off their feet. Zutan was knocked sideways by the blast, dropping from Bobby's view for a second. The two on the back of the Toyota were blasted clear by shrapnel and explosive waves. The two Delta operators couldn't hear the screams from their position, but the rolling sound of the detonation carried on the air.

'Fuck,' Aaron said over the net.

Bobby moved his scope back to the shop Aaron had referred to and saw a guy in a dirty dish-dash emerge, reaching under his robes as he approached the fallen terrorists.

The man produced a folding stock AK47 and pumped short

bursts into the nearest two men on the ground. He continued moving, putting a burst into the café owner as he tried to rise, dropping the guy back down in a spray of blood.

'Jesus Christ,' Bobby muttered, watching as the man methodically killed each of the men on the ground.

Another guy burst forth from the shattered café door, a pistol in his fist. The man turned and raked him from waist to throat, then sprayed a longer burst through the front door at somebody Bobby couldn't see inside the café.

'Who the fuck is that?' Aaron wondered aloud.

Bobby stayed glued to his scope, watching as the man reached the fallen figure of Zutan. The man stopped near him, raised the barrel of the AK then paused. Bobby saw Zutan struggling to rise to a knee. He could see blood on the terrorist's face, either from shrapnel or spray from one of his buddies.

There was a long pause and Bobby could tell the gunman was saying something. Zutan shook his head and raised a hand. The man lifted his keffiyeh away from his head. Bobby could see he was deeply tanned and bearded.

'Fuck me,' he muttered, 'it's the Kiwi.'

'Who?' Aaron wanted to know.

Bobby didn't reply. He watched as the Kiwi pumped a burst of rounds into Zutan's chest and knocked him flat, then stepped forward and finished him with a double tap to the head.

That done, he turned and scanned his surrounds.

Bobby saw movement behind him. A guy with an AK coming through the café door. Bobby's finger stroked the trigger and put a round through the guy's gut, dropping him instantly. He worked the bolt automatically to chamber a fresh round.

The Kiwi spun and put a burst into him too before dropping his magazine, slamming another into place and backing up to the wall. He looked left and right, spotted the two guys off the back of the Toyota getting to their feet in the road, and engaged them.

Bobby sighted on one and put a round through his neck.

'Nice shot,' Aaron commented.

The Kiwi dropped the second guy and began to run down the footpath. People were coming out of nearby buildings, tentatively at first then with more confidence as the sound of firing stopped. A group of ISIS shitheels in their black kit emerged from an apartment into the street, ripping off bursts into the air and shouting. People began to scatter again, providing good cover for the running Kiwi.

Bobby followed him until he reached the mouth of an alleyway and stopped. The Kiwi took a moment to regather himself, the AK back under his robes again. He scanned the horizon for a few seconds before his gaze settled on the building Bobby and Aaron were in. Bobby watched him through the scope.

The guy's head stopped moving and Bobby was sure he was looking right at him. The Kiwi lifted his right hand in a thumbs up.

Bobby nodded to himself, getting a full view of the guy's face. It was him alright.

'Five guys in black in the street,' Aaron reported coolly.

Bobby turned his attention back to the scene of devastation, sweeping across the bodies of the dead terrorists and the damaged Toyota, the blown-in front of the café headquarters, to the group of five ISIS terrorists in their black gear, waving AK47s in the air.

'Goose,' Bobby muttered over the net, borrowing a line from one of his all-time favourite movies, 'this is what I call a target-rich environment.'

He sighted on one of the men in black and eased out his breath, squeezing smoothly through the trigger pull. The guy dropped and Bobby worked the bolt.

He put aside thoughts of the Kiwi for now and got to work on the trigger.

62

Moore was sure he had pinged the sniper's position, whoever he was. He heard action back up the street, shouting and shooting, and turned to see the black-clad men emerging.

His job here was done. Time to go. He had a car stashed a few blocks away and a route mapped out in his head. It took him as far as Turkey, and from there, who knew?

He saw one of the ISIS shit-kickers suddenly drop, and guessed the sniper had also spotted them. The other men in black started firing wildly in all directions and making for cover. Another one stumbled and fell to the deck, his arms grabbing at the sky as he went down.

Rob Moore sucked down some air, getting his breathing under control, and spat in the dust.

He cast one last look around, making sure there was nobody close enough to pose an immediate threat.

Satisfied for now, he turned and ran down the alleyway, disappearing into the shadows.

END

The **Division** series continues with *The Berlin Conspiracy*, the fourth book in the series.

BONUS CHAPTERS

EARLY WARNING SERIES #1

MARTIAL LAW

Some would say I was paranoid, but they'd be wrong.

There's a difference between being paranoid and being smart.

To put it in real terms, if one President with a big red button and an ego problem butts heads with another with the same issues, it's probably a good time to start preparing for the worst. That's what I did, and every step of the way I prayed it would all be for nothing.

I wasn't the only one, but we were still the minority. Nobody wants their worst fears to be proved right, but I also didn't want to be one of the mindless sheeple that relied on someone else to pull their arse from the fire.

This was a country built by pioneers, tough resilient folk who travelled round the world to land on a handful of islands down near the bottom of the South Pacific. They battled adversity every step of the way, creating a national mindset of independence and humility. Shout your name from the rooftops? Expect to get cut down. Nobody round here likes a blowhard.

My name's Mark Dobson. I'm just the guy next door.

I don't care too much what people think of me, but of course there was another very good reason to keep my preparations quiet. If my predictions came true a lot of people would be caught short. Food and fuel would be the big issues. Lack of medicines. Unheated homes. Mental health issues would be exacerbated by the stress. Those that were desperate would steal to feed and clothe their families. The lowlifes would do that and more, whether they needed supplies or not. Violence would break out.

Those that were unprepared would fall victim to the predators. That wouldn't happen to my family, not on my watch.

No fucking way.

THE SERVICE SERIES #1

WARLOCK

Village of Magas
Drina Valley, North-Eastern Bosnia
June 1995

Death came at dawn.

The sun was creeping over the lip of the valley and the village was starting to come to life. It was a small settlement of simple houses, many already damaged by various attacks over the years and repaired as best they could be.

The main road into the village was rutted and narrow, potted with holes and horseshoe imprints.

The trucks of the short convoy crushed the ruts flat as they rolled down the road from the south, heavy diesel engines throbbing and gear boxes grinding as the drivers struggled to maintain momentum and stability at the same time.

The villagers heard the trucks coming and knew it was not good news. People started to come out of their houses, peering up the road to try and see who it was. Could it possibly be a UN visit? Probably not. Nobody cared enough about these poor peasants to send the UN to them.

A few people started to make haste, rousing their families and getting ready to run. But it was too late.

The first truck rounded the last bend and gunned it straight into the centre of the village, a small town square surrounded by a few basic shops and shuttered buildings. The head elder of the village had been awakened and shuffled out in his coat and hat, his pyjama legs flapping in the light morning breeze.

The first truck ground to a halt and the rear flap opened, discharging a dozen armed soldiers. They quickly spread out across one side of the village square, rifles at the ready and game faces on. They wore the standard Serbian Army uniforms with the shoulder patch of the Red Wolves, the feared elite paratroop unit.

The elder felt his gut go cold as he recognised the men before him, and he knew without a doubt what was about to happen.

More trucks rolled into the town square, a jeep in the middle of the convoy making directly for the elder. It pulled up beside him and the front passenger got out. He was a tall, barrel chested man in an impeccably smart uniform, and with a face like stone. His black eyes bore into those of the elder, who immediately recognised him.

Josef Durakovic, Major. Commanding Officer of the Red Wolves.

The elder felt his bladder loosen and warm urine trickled down his leg.

Durakovic walked slowly towards him as the soldiers kicked in the doors of the houses nearby, dragging the occupants out at gunpoint, women, children, men, old and young alike. Screaming, terrified.

They were bundled into a group in the centre of the square, soldiers surrounding them, rifles raised threateningly. The soldiers were calm and in control, waiting for orders.

Durkavoic halted a metre short of the elder, his eyes never leaving the face of the old man.

'You know who I am?' Durakavic asked softly.

The old man nodded slowly.

Durakovic nodded too.

'Then you know why I am here,' he stated.

The old man nodded again, slowly.

'I know,' he croaked through a mouth dry as tinder. 'You come to kill us.'

Durakovic' thin lips twitched into a smile, fleetingly then gone.

'Yes,' he agreed. 'All Muslim pigs like you. You had your chance to go. You didn't go.'

'We had no chance,' the old man croaked angrily, tears welling at his eyes. 'We are just peasants, we are nothing to you. We don't fight.'

Durakovic nodded again, not smiling now.

'That is correct,' he said. 'You are nothing to us.'

His right hand went to the holster on his hip, and undid the flap. As he started to draw out his pistol, the old man took a step forward and spat as hard as he could. The dry white spittle landed on Durakovic's tunic front and hung there.

'Serbian shit,' the old man snapped hoarsely, and Duracovic's pistol came up.

The single shot made the civilians jump, and the bullet blew a spray of blood and brain matter into the air behind the old man. The body dropped like a stone into a crumpled heap of stick-like limbs and thin tatty clothes.

A woman screamed and her scream echoed around the town square.

Durakovic turned to the sergeant standing nearby, and holstered his pistol.

'Kill them,' he said calmly.

The snarl of automatic fire was deafening as bullets ripped through the throng of people, and within seconds magazines were being rapidly changed as the eager soldiers tried not to be the last one to get a kill.

Silence fell again and the soldiers began to move between the bodies, single shots ringing out now as they administered kill shots to those still twitching.

Durakovic let his eyes wander across the buildings around them, seeing the odd flicker of movement as civilians who had been hiding made a break for freedom. He was happy to let them go; they would spread the word of what had happened here today, and his reputation would spread further.

He turned to his sergeant again and an unspoken warmth passed between the two men.

'Burn it,' Durakovic ordered.

MESSAGE FROM THE AUTHOR

Thanks for taking the time to read *The Shadow Dancers*. I hope you enjoyed this third book in the **Division** series. The fourth book in the series is *The Berlin Conspiracy* - A hijacked passenger plane above LA, an evil puppet master, and a personal agenda of revenge. Archer must stop him before innocent blood is lost, but who is he really up against, friend or foe?

I'd love it if you could please take the time to leave an online review of *The Shadow Dancers* with your favourite book retailer.

If you'd like to know about new releases and receive a free book, sign up to my **Hitlist** on Facebook -

https://www.facebook.com/writer-angus-mclean

Cheers,

Angus McLean

ACKNOWLEDGMENTS

The author would like to thank the advisers who have assisted with the writing of this book. They must remain anonymous for security reasons, but they (and only they) know who they are.

They are the true heroes who put their lives on the line to protect our freedoms. My sincerest gratitude goes out to them.

And once again, huge thanks to "Tori" who does my covers and provides great advice. You rock.

This is a work of fiction, and all errors are the responsibility of the author.

ABOUT THE AUTHOR

Angus McLean is a South Auckland Police officer.

His experience as a cop and a private investigator give his writing a touch of realism. He believes reading should be escapist entertainment and is inspired by the TV shows he watched as a youngster.

His real identity remains a secret.

www.writerangusmclean.com

www.ingramcontent.com/pod-product-compliance
Ingram Content Group UK Ltd.
Pitfield, Milton Keynes, MK11 3LW, UK
UKHW020425250726
13967UKWH00007B/2823

9 780473 560867